Popular Library is now publishing, in their entirety
in English for the first time,
all four volumes of the famous Vilhelm Moberg quartet:

THE EMIGRANTS   08561-4 $2.25

UNTO A GOOD LAND   08542-8 $1.95

THE SETTLERS   04290-7 $2.25

LAST LETTER HOME   04320-2 $1.95

VILHELM MOBERG
THE EMIGRANTS

POPULAR LIBRARY • NEW YORK

THE EMIGRANTS

THE EMIGRANTS
is translated from the Swedish Utvandrarna

Published by Popular Library, a unit of CBS Publications, the Consumer Publishing Division of CBS Inc., by arrangement with Simon & Schuster, Inc.

Copyright, 1951, by Vilhelm Moberg

ISBN: 0-445-08561-4

PRINTED IN THE UNITED STATES OF AMERICA

24 23 22 21 20 19 18 17 16

A NOTE ON THE
PRONUNCIATION OF THE
SWEDISH NAMES

å is pronounced like the *a* in *small* (cf. *Småland*, literally
   Small Land)
ä is pronounced like the *a* in *add*
ö is pronounced like the *ea* in *heard*
j is pronounced like *y*

By Way of Introduction

THE PEASANTS

This is the story of a group of people who in 1850 left their homes in Ljuder Parish, in the province of Småland, Sweden, and emigrated to North America.

They were the first of many to leave their village. They came from a land of small cottages and large families. They were people of the soil, and they came of a stock which for thousands of years had tilled the ground they were now leaving. Generation had followed generation, sons succeeded fathers at harrow and plow, and daughters took their mothers' place at spinning wheel and loom. Through ever-shifting fortunes the farm remained the home of the family, the giver of life's sustenance. Bread came from the rye field and meat from the cattle. Clothing and shoes were made in the home by itinerant tailors and cobblers, out of wool from the sheep, flax from the ground, skins from the animals. All necessary things were taken from the earth. The people were at the mercy of the Lord's weather, which brought fat years and lean years—but they depended on no other power under the sun. The farm was a world of its own, beholden to no one. The cottages nestled low and gray, timbered to last for centuries, and under the same roof of bark and sod the people lived their lives from birth to death. Weddings were held, christening and wake ale was drunk, life was lit and blown out within these same four walls of rough-hewn pine logs. Outside of life's great events, little happened other than the change of seasons. In the field the shoots were green in spring and the stubble yellow in autumn. Life was lived quietly while the farmer's allotted years rounded their cycle.

And so it was, down through the years, through the path of generations, down through centuries.

About the middle of the nineteenth century, however, the order of unchangeableness was shaken to its very foundations. Newly discovered powers came into use, wagons moved without horses, ships without sails, and distant parts of the globe were brought closer together. And to a new generation, able to read, came the printed word with tales of a land far away, a land which emerged from the mists of the saga and took on the clearing, tempting aspects of reality.

7

The new land had soil without tillers and called for tillers without soil. It opened invitingly for those who longed for a freedom denied them at home. The urge to emigrate stirred in the landless, in the debt-bound, the suppressed and the discontented. Others again saw no mirage of special privilege or wealth in the new land, but wanted to escape entanglements and dilemmas in the old country. They emigrated, not *to* something but *from* something. Many, and widely different, were the answers to the question: Why?

In every community there were some men and women who obeyed the call and undertook the uncertain move to another continent. The enterprising made the decision, the bold were the first to break away. The courageous were the first to undertake the forbidding voyage across the great ocean. The discontented, as well as the aggressive, not reconciling themselves to their lot at home, were emigrants from their home communities. Those who stayed—the tardy and the unimaginative—called the emigrants daredevils.

The first emigrants knew little of the country awaiting them, and they could not know that more than a million people would follow them from the homeland. They could not foresee that, a hundred years hence, one-fourth of their own people were to inhabit the new country; that their descendants were to cultivate a greater expanse of land than the whole arable part of Sweden at that time. They could not guess that a cultivated land greater than their whole country would be the result of this undertaking—a groping, daring undertaking, censured, ridiculed by the ones at home, begun under a cloud of uncertainty, with the appearance of foolhardiness.

Those men and women, whose story this is, have long ago quitted life. A few of their names can still be read on crumbling tombstones, erected thousands of miles from the place of their birth.

At home, their names are forgotten—their adventures will soon belong to the saga and the legend.

THE COUNTRY WHICH THEY LEFT

The Parish

Ljuder Parish in Konga County is about twelve miles long and three miles wide. The soil is black loam, interspersed with sandy mold. Only smaller bodies of water exist—two brooks and four lakes or tarns. Dense pine forests still remained a hundred years ago, and groves of deciduous trees and thickets spread over wide areas which now are used as pasture.

On January 1, 1846, Ljuder Parish had 1,925 inhabitants: 998 males, and 927 females. During the century after 1750, the population had increased almost threefold. The number of nonassessed persons—retired old people, cottagers, squatters, servants, parish dependents, and people without permanent homes—during the same time had increased five-fold.

How the People Earned Their Living

According to the assessment books Ljuder Parish originally consisted of 43 full homesteads which in 1750 were divided among 87 owners. Through further division of property at times of death, the number of independent farms had by 1846 increased to 254, two-thirds of which were one-eighth of an original homestead, or smaller. Only four farms now included more than one homestead: the freeholds of Kråkesjö and Gösamåla, Ljuder parsonage, and the sheriff's manse at Ålebäck.

The means of livelihood a hundred years ago were mainly agriculture and cattle raising and to a small degree handicraft. Included in agriculture was the distillation of brännvin; the price of grain was so low that the peasants must distill their produce in order to farm profitably. In the eighteen-forties the number of stills in the parish was around 350. About every sixth person had his own vessel for producing the drink. The size of the still was decided by law, according to the size of the farm; if a one-half homestead farm possessed a thirty-gallon still, then a one-quarter homesteader had only a fifteen-gallon one. The biggest still was at the freehold of Kråkesjö, and the next largest at the parsonage, which came as number two in homestead size. All distillers sold part of their product in order to earn their living. However, when Pastor Enok Brusander in 1833 became dean of the parish, he ordered that no brännvin be sold or served in the parsonage on Sundays, except to people of the household or workmen on the place. At a parish meeting in 1845 it was further decided that no brännvin should be sold during church services at a distance of less than six hundred yards from God's house. It was also stated that any parishioner who gave brännvin to a child who had not yet received Holy Communion must pay a fine of one riksdaler banko to the poor purse (in present-day currency, one krona and fifty öre, or approximately twenty-nine cents). The same meeting admonished parents not to let their children get into the habit of drinking "drop by drop." Only in those cases where the children showed "decided inclination for the drink" should they be allowed to "enjoy the drink in so great quantities that they might get sick and thereby lose their taste for brännvin."

Those Who Governed the Parish

The most important man in Ljuder during the eighteen-forties was the dean, Enok Brusander, who in his capacity as minister represented the Almighty, King in heaven and on earth. Next to him in power was the sheriff, Alexander Lönnegren in Ålebäck, who had his office from the Crown and represented worldly majesty, Oskar I, King of Sweden and Norway. The foremost man in the parish as to birth and riches was Lieutenant Sir Paul Rudeborg, owner of Kråkesjö freehold. He and his lady were the only people of noble birth and corresponding rights. Representing the parish on the county council was Per Persson in Åkerby, churchwarden and storekeeper, and next to Lieutenant Rudeborg the wealthiest man in the community.

These four men governed the parish, holding the spiritual and worldly offices in accordance with Romans 13, verses one to three: ". . . For there is no power but of God. . . ."

The Others Who Lived in the Parish

Besides the 254 peasants and cotters who owned and lived on assessed land, there were 39 persons listed as artisans and apprentices, 92 squatters, 11 enlisted soldiers, 6 innkeepers, 5 horse traders, 3 house-to-house peddlers. There were also 274 farm servants, 23 bedesmen and bedeswomen, 104 "ordinary poor," 18 sick and crippled, 11 deaf and dumb, 8 blind, 6 nearly blind, 13 almost lame, 4 lame, 5 near idiots, 3 idiots, 1 half idiot, 3 whores and 2 thieves. On the last page of the church book, under the heading "End of the Parish," were listed 27 persons who had moved away and never been further heard from.

The poor, "the ordinary poor," and other old and ill and incompetent people, were divided into three groups and cared for according to special regulations passed by the parish council. The first group included the old and crippled who were entirely incapacitated. They received first-class poor help, or "complete sustenance," which might amount to as much as three riksdaler in cash per year—about eighty-seven cents—plus four bushels of barley.

In the second group were those only partly disabled, who could to a certain degree earn a living for themselves and their children. They were helped with sums of cash ranging from twelve shillings to one riksdaler a year—from six to twenty-nine cents—and at the most two bushels of barley.

The third group included people who only temporarily needed help. They received alms from a special fund known as the Ljuder Parish Poor Purse, under the supervision of the parish council. This last group included also "profligate and lazy people who had themselves caused their poverty." They, according to the council's decision, "should be remembered with the smallest aid from the Poor Purse, thereby getting accustomed to sobriety and industry."

Destitute orphans were auctioned off by the parish council to "suitable homes at best bid." For these "parish boys" and "parish girls" the council sought to find foster homes where the children would receive "fatherly care and in good time instruction in honest habits and work."

Conditions were similar in other parishes in Sweden at that time.

The Spiritual Care of the Inhabitants

The people were fostered in the pure evangelical-Lutheran religion in accordance with the church law of 1686, and were protected from heretical and dangerous new ideas by the royal "Resolution and Order" of January 12, 1726, "this wholesome Resolution aiming at good order in the parish, and Christian unity in teaching."

In the church law the clergy were admonished to "see to it that the children learn to read so that they may with their own eyes see God's holy laws and commands." This instruction in reading, advisable only for salvation of the soul, was administered by schoolmaster or by parents. Each fall the minister held an examination in the tenets of the faith according to the Little Catechism of Luther. All unmarried parishioners at this time were probed concerning their reading ability, and were fined for failure to attend.

The parish in 1836 engaged its own schoolmaster, Rinaldo, an ex-enlisted cavalry soldier who, having lost an eye, had been permitted to leave the military service. The schoolmaster received a yearly fee of twelve bushels of rye, and one shilling (half a cent) per day for each child he taught. The parents gave him room and firewood besides. Rinaldo wandered from one end of the parish to the other, and held his school in the homes of the peasants, who each in turn allowed him the use of some spare room or attic for this purpose. The length of the term in each house was decided by the schoolmaster. He had been engaged to teach the children to read well enough to learn Luther's Little Catechism by heart. He ventured sometimes to include such wordly and useless subjects as arithmetic, writing, Swedish history, and geography. Most men and women could read fairly well; some could sign their names; few could write more than this, and very few of the women could write at all: no one knew what use a female could make of the art of writing.

Religious Sects

The so-called Åkian heresy had started in the neighboring parish of Elmeboda about 1780, and soon spread also to Ljuder. The adherents to the sect were called Åkians after the founder, Åke Svensson of Östergöhl, Elmeboda. They tried to copy the early Christian church and return to the ways of the apostles. The Åkians separated from the state church and recognized neither temporal nor spiritual powers in their community. All differences between people as to caste or property ownership were to them contrary to God's word, and so within their own sect they lived a completely communal life. None of them called a single object his own. They conducted their own services and held their own Holy Communion.

Some forty persons in Elmeboda and Ljuder Parishes had joined the new sect. Many of them belonged to Åke Svensson's family, which was scattered throughout both parishes. The home of the sect in Ljuder was Kärragärde, owned by Åke's brother-in-law Andreas Månsson.

The Åkians were soon called in for questioning by the bishopric of Växiö and were given strong warnings. But they were inflexible and met the dignitaries of the church with unpropitious words. The church pronounced its ban but the Åkians retained their convictions. They were then sued in civil court and were brought to Konga County Court in Ingelstad,* where the court admonished them to abide by the law and follow the regulations of the established church. Åke Svensson and his followers could not be persuaded to recant their heretical opinions; they refused to return to the fold of the only true church.

In order to maintain church peace and civil security the case was reviewed by the Göta Crown Court.† This court found the members of the sect "completely fallen into insanity, having lost the use of their sound minds," and held that, to maintain peace, and for the welfare of the dissenters, they should be confined in an asylum. Åke Svensson and seven other leaders of the sect "who had shown their insanity in many instances" were ordered transported to Danvik's asylum in Stockholm, "there to receive such attention as their condition warranted."

The eight sectarians who had fallen under the Crown Court's order were turned over to the sheriff. In 1786 they were taken to Danvik's asylum in Stockholm. Åke Svensson, Andreas Månsson, and two others died within two years, after having received "the attention their condition warranted." Åke was at the time of his death thirty-five years of age.

The other dissenters were gradually liberated and returned as cured to their respective homes, where the one-time asylum inmates lived tranquilly and harmoniously, and for many years it seemed as if the firebrand of Åkianism was for ever smothered. But in the eighteen-forties this dangerous heresy reappeared in Ljuder Parish. The circumstances, however, belong to the story.

V. M.

---

* Konga County Records for 1785.
† Göta Crown Court Proceedings, December 12, 1785.

PART ONE

Gates on the Road
to America

I

KING IN HIS STONE KINGDOM

1

Mjodahult is one of Ljuder's most ancient homesteads. Its name is mentioned in a court record two hundred years before the discovery of America.

The Nilsa family had tilled and lived on this farm as far back in history as paper is preserved, as far as the memory of generations can reach. The first known owner was Nils in Mjodahult after whom the family got its name. About Nils in Mjodahult it is further known that he had an unusually large and grotesque nose, which was said to have resembled a well-grown rutabaga. This nose was inherited by his descendants, and someone in each generation possessed it. It became a mark of the Nilsa family. Called the Nilsa-nose, it was believed to be endowed with the same magic powers as a birth cowl, and brought luck to its owner. Children born with the Nilsa-nose became the most fortunate and most successful members of the family, and, even though it was hardly a mark of beauty in a woman, it is not known to have been an obstacle in securing advantageous marriages.

The assessment book indicates that Nils' Mjodahult was still a full homestead in the eighteenth century. The farm was later split up several times, lastly in 1819 when two brothers, Olov Jakob's Son and Nils Jakob's Son, received equal shares. The records list four more brothers and three sisters. The new farms were by now only one-sixteenth of the original homestead. Nils, the younger brother, obtained the split-off piece: three arable acres on the outskirts, where he built his house among the straggling pines. The new farm is recorded as "one-sixteenth crown assessment Korpamoen under the mother homestead Mjodahult."

Nils Jakob's Son was short of build—only five feet—and he had not been endowed with the Nilsa-nose. He was nevertheless a capable man, strong-armed and persevering; his hands did not willingly rest if there was aught to do. Marta, his wife, was a strong and stately woman, a full head taller than her husband.

17

Korpamoen was at first hardly more than a cotter's place, but Nils developed his inheritance into a farm. The soil was sandy, strewn with stones. It looked as if it had rained stones from heaven here during all the six days of the creation. But Nils searched out every patch of soil that could be cultivated and attacked the stones with his iron bar and lever—the latter a long pole with a horseshoe nailed to the heavy end. His best tools, however, were his hands; with these he went after the stones deep in their holes, wrestled with them, turned them, finally rolled them away. And when Nils encountered a stone which he couldn't manage with his hands or his tools, he called for his wife. Marta was almost as strong as her husband; she hung on to the small end of the lever while Nils used the iron bar.

It was a silent struggle between Nils and the stone, a fight between an inert mass and the living muscles and sinews of a patient, persevering man.

This fight continued during all of Nils' farming years; each year he broke a new quarter of an acre, until at last there were more stone piles in Korpamoen than on any other farm in the parish. When Nils turned his field the plow circled stone piles; he used to say he became giddy from the ring-around-the-rosy dance in his fields.

Nils Jakob's Son was also handy with wood, and worked sometimes as a timberman in the neighborhood. He had built his own house. Even as a boy he had started to follow the woodmen and before he was grown he could join the corner timbers of a house, that most difficult task in carpentry. He was also a cabinetmaker and a smith. Throughout the winters he stood at his workbench and made all kinds of farming tools.

When he had moved to Korpamoen he had been forced to mortgage the farm, so that his brothers and sisters might receive their inheritance share in cash; the yearly interest on this loan required that he work as timberman and carpenter.

Of the marriage between Nils and Marta three children were born: two sons, Karl Oskar and Robert, and a daughter, Lydia. Twice Marta's pregnancy had ended in miscarriage; once on the same day she had been in the field helping her husband dig up a boulder.

Karl Johan, the new King of Sweden and Norway, had ascended the throne the year before Nils and Marta were married; their first-born son was named after him; the child's second name was for the new Crown Prince, Oskar. It was thought to be good luck to name one's children after people of high station—kings, princes, queens, princesses; even the poorest squatter could afford royal names for his offspring.

The first-born son, Karl Oskar, was also born with the lucky big nose of the Nilsa family.

Karl Oskar grew up strong of limb and body. Soon he helped his father at building and stone breaking. But early the boy showed a mind of his own; in work he would not do as his father told him, but rather followed his own way, though eating his parents' bread. No chastisement improved the stubborn child; Nils was many times angered over his son's independent ways.

One day when Karl Oskar was fourteen years old he was asked by his father to make slats for a new hayrick; they should be five feet long. Karl Oskar thought the hayrick would be too low with such short slats; he made them six feet, instead.

Nils measured the slats and said: "Do as I tell you, or go!"

Karl Oskar kept silent for a while, then haughtily answered: "I shall go."

The same day he hired himself as farmhand to a man in Idemo, where he was to remain seven years.

Taken at his word, Nils regretted it; his son had been a help to him. But he could not retract: a boy who had not yet received Holy Communion could not rule his father in his work. On the whole, however, all went well for Nils and Marta in Korpamoen for some twenty-five years.

Then, one day in the early spring of 1844, Nils Jakob's Son was alone in an outlying glade, breaking new land. Here he encountered a stone which caused him much trouble. It was smaller than many a one he had removed alone, but it lay deep in earth and was round as a globe so that neither bar nor lever got hold of it. Nils used all his tricks and soon the stone was halfway up. He now wedged it with the iron bar, intending to roll it away with his hands; but as he bent down to get a good hold for the final battle the earth slid away from under his foot and he fell on his face. In the fall he moved the iron bar that held the stone, which rolled back into its hole—over one of his thighs.

Nils lay where he fell. When he didn't come home for his

afternoon meal, Marta went out to look for him. She found
her husband in the hole next to the stone, and lifted him onto
her back and carried him home. Berta in Idemo, whose aid
was solicited for hurts and ailments, was sent for, and she told
him that the hipbone was broken and the joint injured.

Nils remained in bed for several months while Berta attended him with her herb concoctions and salves. The bone
healed and he could again stand on his feet, but some injury
was left in the joint and it remained incurable; he could not
move without crutches; from now on he could do chores with
his hands only, while seated.

Nils Jakob's Son was a cripple. His farmer's life was over.
For twenty-five years he had fought the stones, and in the last
battle the stones had won.

Korpamoen was no longer a cotter's place. The size of the
manure pile tells the size of the farm: it was not a mean
dunghill outside the stable barns at Korpamoen. The farm
now had seven arable acres; it could feed seven head of cattle
through summer and winter. Nils and Marta had more than
doubled the plot they first occupied twenty-five years before.
Now they must cede it.

The farm was too small to divide; a one-sixteenth could not
be split. And Nils did not wish to sell it to an outsider; one of
his children must reap the benefit of his many years of clearing. Karl Oskar was still in service in Idemo, and barely of
age. Robert, their second son, was only eleven, and the
daughter Lydia fourteen years old. Even the oldest son was
rather young to become his own master, but Nils offered
Korpamoen to him, nevertheless. The father by now had
more respect for the headstrong boy who had left home at
fourteen because he couldn't have his way about a few hayrick slats.

After seven years as a farmhand Karl Oskar was weary of
working for others, and would rather be master of the homestead; he was ready to buy.

"If you become a farmer, you'll need a wench," said Nils.

"I'll find one," said Karl Oskar, sure of himself.

"Braggart!"

A few days later, however, Karl Oskar announced that the
banns would be read for him the following Sunday. The parents were so much astonished they could not say a word: the
son had even arranged his marriage without their advice! In-

deed, the boy did have a will of his own. But they were also concerned; in the long run such a headstrong son would succeed only with difficulty.

2

On an autumn day a few years earlier Karl Oskar had brought a load of his master's firewood to Berta, the Idemo woman with healing knowledge. Berta offered him a dram in the kitchen, and there sat a young girl, unknown to him, spooling yarn. She had thick, light yellow hair, and a pair of mild eyes—green, blue, or perhaps both. Her face, with its soft, pink skin, pleased him, in spite of a few freckles on her nose. The girl sat quietly at the spooling wheel while Karl Oskar was in the kitchen, and none of them spoke. But when he was ready to leave he turned to her and said: "My name is Karl Oskar."

"Mine is Kristina," she answered.

Then she sat silent, and spooled as before. But she had given him her name, she who was to become his wife.

Kristina was a farmer's daughter from Duvemala, in Algutsboda Parish, and she was only seventeen when they first met. But her body was well developed, with the first marks of womanhood; her hips showed well-rounded curves and her maidenly breasts were cramped inside the blouse which she had long ago outgrown. In her mind, however, she was still a child. She loved to swing. A few weeks before she met Karl Oskar she had taken the ox-thong and set up a swing in the barn at Duvemala. During her play she had fallen out of the swing and broken her kneecap. The injury was poorly looked after, and gangrene set in. Her parents had then sent her to Berta in Idemo, who was known through many parishes for her healing ability, and Kristina was staying with the old woman while the gangrene mended.

Kristina still limped, and that was why she didn't rise from the spooling wheel while Karl Oskar was in the kitchen.

But he found excuses for calling on Berta to see the girl again, and next time he found her standing outside on the porch. He noticed then that she was a tall girl, as tall as he.

She was lithe and slender around the waist. Her eyes were bashful and tempting.

They met now and then while Kristina remained in Idemo. Her knee healed and she limped no more; no longer was she ashamed to walk about when Karl Oskar saw her.

The evening before she was to return home they met and sat outside Berta's cellar on an upturned potato basket. He said he liked her and asked if she liked him. She did. He then asked if she would marry him. She answered that she thought both of them too young, that at least he ought to be of age. He said he could write to the King and get permission to marry. Then she said they had no place to live, nor did she know how they could feed and clothe themselves. To this he had no answer, for it was true. He had nothing to promise her, therefore he kept still; a spoken word and a promise carried weight; one had to answer for it, it could never be taken back.

They had since met at the Klintakrogen fair three times, two springs and one autumn, and each time Karl Oskar had said that he still liked her and no one else was in his thoughts.

Karl Oskar was sure of what he wanted. As soon as he had been offered Korpamoen by his father, he went to Kristina's parents in Duvemala. They were much surprised by this visit from an unknown youth who asked leave to speak with their daughter alone.

Karl Oskar and Kristina stood under the gable of her home and talked to each other for twenty minutes.

Karl Oskar thought:

Their hour to get married had now arrived, he was of age, he was to take over his father's farmstead, they had house and home and means to earn food and clothing.

Kristina thought:

As they had met only a half-score times, they had hardly had opportunity to get to know each other. At nineteen she was still too young to become a farm wife; he must ask her parents if they wanted him for a son-in-law.

It turned out as Karl Oskar had thought it would. He was accepted into the family when her parents learned that his suit was earnest and that he owned a farm. He stayed in their house overnight and slept with his wife-to-be, fully dressed, in all honor. Six weeks later the wedding was held in Duvemala between Karl Oskar Nilsson and Kristina Johansdotter.

Karl Oskar said to his young wife: There was no person in the whole world he liked as well as her, because she never criticized him or pointed out his shortcomings as others did. He was sure he would be happy with her through his whole life.

3

King Oskar I ascended the throne of Sweden and Norway in 1844, and the same year Karl Oskar Nilsson (the old-fashioned spelling of Nils' Son was discarded by Karl Oskar, who had learned to write) took possession of "one-sixteenth of one homestead, Korpamoen." He still carried the names of the King and the Crown Prince, but now the order of the names was reversed: the new King's name was Oskar and the Crown Prince was Karl.

The price agreed upon for Korpamoen, with cattle and farming equipment, was seventeen hundred riksdaler. This sum (amounting to a little less than five hundred dollars in American money today) included the mortgage of eight hundred riksdaler. Nils and Marta also kept their "reserved rights" to the end of their days: living quarters in the spare room, winter and summer fodder for one cow and one sheep, three-quarters of an acre of arable land for their own sowing, with use of the owner's team, and twelve bushels of grain yearly, half rye and half barley. In the preserved deed it can still be read: "The reserved rights to begin July 1, 1844, this agreement entered into with sound mind and ripe consideration has taken place in Korpamoen, June nineteenth of this year, in the presence of witnesses." The deed bears the cross marks of Nils and Marta, who had never learned to write.

As was usual when parents ceded their farm with reserved rights, a division of inheritance was now undertaken. Each of the children received two hundred and ten riksdaler and twenty-four shillings. Robert and Lydia, not yet of age, let their shares remain as claims against their brother.

Karl Oskar had got what he wanted; and how was it with

him as a beginner? During his seven years in service he had saved one hundred and fifty riksdaler; with his wife he had received as dowry two hundred riksdaler; his inheritance was two hundred and ten riksdaler. But this money amounted to only one-quarter of the sales price. The other three-quarters remained as debt, debt which carried interest. He must pay fifty riksdaler a year in interest on the mortgage. And his greatest debt was the reserved rights to his parents. Indeed, the reserved rights were heavy for so small a farm—but they must be sufficient for the parents' maintenance. Karl Oskar's obligation to them was a debt on the farm which he must continue to pay as long as they lived; and Nils was only fifty-one years of age, Marta forty-eight. It was hardly a farm that Karl Oskar had taken over—it was debts to pay, with interest. But debt could be blotted out through work, and so he did not worry: he knew how to work.

Thus life continued in Korpamoen: Nils and Marta moved into the little spare room where they were to live out their years; Kristina arrived with her dowry chest and took Marta's place. It was a young farm wife who moved in. But with her own hands she had stitched the bridal cover which she now, the first evening, spread over the nuptial bed. It was the blue of cornflowers, and Marta had said it was nice; Kristina was proud.

Karl Oskar was pleased that his mother and wife could live in harmony; otherwise they might have caused each other great irritation. The contract stated that his mother had the right to cook in the kitchen and bake in the big bake oven; had they been unfriendly they could have been in each other's way in every corner.

But one day Kristina was discovered by her mother-in-law in the threshing barn, where she was playing in a swing which she had secretly hung from the rafters. Marta excused it and said nothing; Kristina was still a child in her ways, with a desire for play still in her body. It was peculiar, however, that Kristina would want to play with a swing since she had once fallen from one, injuring her knee. Besides, the wild play did not suit a married woman. Luckily no outsider saw her in the barn, hence no rumors spread in the neighborhood.

There was, however, something in regard to Kristina which Nils and Marta did not like: on her mother's side she was related to descendants of Ake Svensson, the founder of the

Akian sect. Her mother was Ake's niece. And her uncle, Danjel Andreasson, was owner of Karragarde, the meeting place for the Akians in Ljuder. Of course, more than fifty years had elapsed since the instigator of this heresy, the troublemaker from Ostergohl, had died in Danvik's asylum. As far as was generally known, nothing had survived in Karragarde of the horrible Akianist contagion. But the original ill feeling toward the founder had been so deeply rooted among a great many of the parishioners that it still survived —kinfolk of Ake Svensson did not brag about their relationship.

Nils and Marta said nothing to their daughter-in-law, but one day they did broach the question to Karl Oskar: "Do you know your wife is related to Ake of Ostergohl?"

"I'm aware of it—and I defy anyone to hold it against her."

There was nothing more to be said. Marta and Nils only hoped that Kristina's kinship with the Akian founder wasn't generally known in the village. In Korpamoen it was never mentioned again.

4

Early every weekday morning Nils emerged from the spare room, hobbling along on his crutches, slowly reaching his old workbench outside in the woodshed, where he remained through the day. He cut spokes for wagon wheels, he made rakes, and handles for axes and scythes. He could still use plane and chisel; his hands were in good health, and their dexterity remained. He taught Karl Oskar what he could of this handicraft.

During most of the summer days one could find Nils and his tools outside in the yard, where he sat in the shade of an old maple tree. From there he had a good view over the fields with all the piles of stone which his hands had gathered. His twenty-five farming years had indeed left marks; all the heaps of stone and all the stone fences which he had built remained in their places, and no doubt would long remain.

The invalid was not bitter. His belief was that all things happened according to God's preordination. It was his conviction that God in the beginning had decided that a stone in his field—on a certain day, at a certain hour—would roll back into its hole. He would miss his foothold and fall, the stone would break his hip joint, and he would ever after crawl about like a wing-broken magpie. It would be presumptuous of him to question the Creator. Nils Jakob's Son did not burden his brain with questions.

Now his son plowed and sowed the fields which he had cleared. He had fought the stones to the best of his ability; now his son reaped the benefit.

But Karl Oskar worried about debts and interest. If he only had a horse, then he could hire himself out and earn some money hauling timbers. But a one-sixteenth was too small to feed a horse, who chewed several barrels of oats during the winter; he needed three acres more to keep a horse. As it was he had to feed his parents and his wife and himself on seven acres, most of which was poor, sandy soil.

Soon he realized that he must clear more land.

He went out to inspect the unbroken ground belonging to Korpamoen. There were spruce woods and knolls, there were desolate sandy plains with juniper and pine roots, there were low swamplands with moss and cranberries, there were hillocks and tussock-filled meadows. The rest was strewn with stone. He carried an iron bar which he now and then stuck into the ground, and always he heard the same sound: stone. He went through pastures and meadows, through woodlands and moors, and everywhere the same sound: stone, stone, stone. It was a monotonous tune, a sad tune for a man who wanted to clear more acres.

Karl Oskar did not find a tenth of an acre within his boundaries left to clear; his father had done his work well; all arable ground was cultivated. What he now possessed to till and sow was all he would have. Until acres could be stretched and made broader than God created them, there would be no more arable land in Korpamoen.

And because the young farmer couldn't continue creation where God had left off, he must be satisfied with his seven acres, and all the stones wherever he looked: broken stones, stones in piles, stone fences, stone above ground, stone in the ground, stone, stone, stone. . . .

King Oskar had ascended the throne of the kingdoms of

Sweden and Norway; Karl Oskar Nilsson had become king in a stone kingdom.

5

His first year as a farmer—1845—was a good year. The crops were ample, he was able to pay the mortgage interest on time, and all was well. And in the spring Kristina had given birth to their first child, a daughter, christened Anna after Kristina's mother.

The second year also they had good crops in Korpamoen, but the harvesting was poor. The rye sprouted in the shocks, and bread baked from the flour was soggy. They sold a calf and half of the pig to help pay interest on the mortgage, and the twenty riksdaler he was short Karl Oskar borrowed from his crippled father: it was money the old one had earned through his handiwork. In the midst of the August harvest Kristina bore a son; he was named Johan after his mother's father in Duvemala.

The third year was filled with anxiety. When the meadow hay was cut in July such a heavy rain fell that the swaths were floating in water. When the flood had subsided some of the hay remained, fox-red, rotten and spoiled. It had a musty smell, no nourishment, and the animals refused to eat it. Karl Oskar and Kristina were forced to sell one cow. More bad luck followed: another cow had a stillborn calf, and a sheep went astray in the woods to become food for wild beasts. In the autumn it was discovered that potato rot had spread to their field—when picked, almost every second potato was spoiled; for one filled basket of good, an equally large one had to be discarded, hardly good enough for fodder for the animals. During the following winter more than one day went by without the potato pot over the fire. It was said the potato rot came from foreign countries, where it caused famine.

This year—1847—Karl Oskar went still deeper into debt. He had to borrow money for the whole amount of the mortgage interest. Nils had no more to lend him, and Karl Oskar did not wish to ask his father-in-law in Duvemala. Kristina thought he should try her uncle, Danjel Andreasson, in Karragarde, who was fairly well off. He was known as a quiet and kind man, although he was the nephew of the despised Akian founder—but it would be foolish to pay heed to happenings of fifty years ago. No sooner had Karl Oskar made the request than Danjel gave him fifty riksdaler for the mortgage interest.

The day before Christmas Eve, that year, Kristina gave birth to twins, a boy and a girl. The boy was sickly and was given emergency baptism by Dean Brusander; he died within a fortnight. The girl lived and was christened Marta, after Karl Oskar's mother. She would afterwards be known as Lill-Marta.

After three years in Korpamoen Karl Oskar had now one cow less in the byre and seventy riksdaler more debt than at the time of taking over. And yet during every day of the three years both he and Kristina had worked and drudged to their utmost ability. They had struggled to get ahead, yet it had gone backwards for them. They could not sway the Lord's weather, nor luck with the animals. Karl Oskar had thought they would be able to get along if they had health and strength to work; now they were aware that man in this world could not succeed through his work alone.

"It's written, 'In the sweat of thy brow shalt thou eat thy bread,' " said Nils.

"Aye—nor am I even sure to get bread through work and sweat," retorted Karl Oskar.

Karl Oskar, as well as his father, knew the story of the Fall from his Biblical history; the dean used to praise him for his quick answers at the yearly examinations.

Karl Oskar had got what he wanted, but it wasn't good for a person always to have his will. Most people thought he was a man with luck and of good fortune. He had two royal names, given him at baptism and formally recorded. He had the big Nilsa-nose—"Your nose is your greatest heritage," his father used to say. But what help now were the names of kings and princes? What help now was a nose that extended a little further into the world than another's? The day still seemed approaching when Sheriff Lonnegren might arrive at the farm and take something in pawn.

During his younger years Karl Oskar had often been teased by other boys about the big nose which distorted his face. He had always answered that it was the best nose he had. And he had believed his parents' stories about members of the family in generations gone by from whom his nose had been inherited—he had always believed it would bring him good fortune in life. Kristina did not think his nose was ugly; it would have been different in a woman, she thought, but menfolk it suited. She did not believe, however, that his big nose would have anything to do with his success in life. That would be a heathenish thought. Kristina sprang from a religious home, and she knew that God shifted people as He saw fit, according to His inscrutable and wise ways. Since they now suffered adversity in Korpamoen, this was only in accord with God's will.

6

So began the year 1848. Karl Oskar had bought an almanac from the schoolmaster, Rinaldo, for four shillings. He now read that the year was the five thousand eight hundred and fiftieth from the creation of the world. It was also the forty-eighth since "the High Birth of Oskar the First's Majesty and the fourth since Its Ascendance on the Throne." It was also the fourth of Karl Oskar's possession and farming of Korpamoen.

He read about the movements and appearance of the greater planets in the new year. He was familiar with the constellations whose signs were printed in the almanac for each day: the ram, with his great bowed horns, the scorpion, with its horrible claws, the lion, with his wide and beastly jaws, and the virgin, so narrow around the waist and holding a wreath of flowers. Weather and wind and perhaps also the destiny of man depended on the meeting of the wandering planets with these constellations.

Before the close of the old year people had already noticed alarming signs: wide parts of the Milky Way where the stars used to shine clear and brilliant were now nebulous and dark —the heavenly lights had disappeared. This could mean war and unrest, rebellion and dire times, sickness and pestilence. Intense cold and a "crow's winter" set in before Christmas; those who ventured out to the early service on Christmas morning came home with frozen ears. New Year's Day

opened with high winds; the steeple in Elmeboda blew down,
and also the great mountain ash at Akerby Junction, and this
the thickest tree along the whole church road. On the exposed
wastelands where the spruce were poorly rooted in the sandy
soil the wind mowed along like a sharpened scythe in
morning-dewed grass. And Noah's Ark, which had not been
seen since the dry year of 1817, appeared again in the heavens, with all its sinister majesty. The Ark was formed by
clouds stretching from east to west, thereby obstructing all
running waters and streams and preventing rainfall for the
coming year.

Throughout the winter and spring there were strange por-
tents in the weather. February was warm, while the spring
month of March was windy, dry, and cold. The winter rye
fared ill: wide gaping stretches appeared in otherwise green
fields after the winter snow had melted.

During the last week of April—the grass month—it seemed
as if at last spring had arrived. And early in the morning of
May Day Eve Karl Oskar pulled out the wooden harrow
from its shed, intending to begin the preparation of the fields
for the sowing. Then it started to snow; it snowed the whole
day; in the evening a foot of snow covered the ground. The
cattle recently had been let out to graze; they must now be
put in their stalls again. The April snow covered flowers and
grass which had only begun to grow. Again, the spring had
frozen away.

Karl Oskar pulled the harrow back into the shed. He sat silent at the food table this May Day Eve, and went to bed
with a heavy heart. As far back as men could remember it
had never boded so ill for the crops as during this peculiar
spring.

The young couple in Korpamoen lay together under the
cover, the one Kristina had stitched. It had now warmed
them at their rest during four years—more than a thousand
nights. Many of these nights Karl Oskar had lain awake,
thinking about the mortgage interest, and in many of these
nights Kristina had risen to quiet the children when they
awoke and cried. Four springs had stood green, four autumnal stubble fields had been turned since for the first time they
enjoyed the embrace of man and woman under the corn-
flower-blue bridal quilt.

That evening in the autumn, when they had sat together on the potato basket in Idemo, now seemed so long ago—it might have been an experience in another world. It belonged to their youth, and they spoke of their youth as something long gone by; they had been young before they were married, and that was once upon a time.

Karl Oskar had recently had his twenty-fifth birthday; Kristina would soon be twenty-three. Not so long ago she was a child herself; now she had brought four children into the world. Three lived and slept now in this room; she listened to their breathing, ever anxious.

Kristina thought at times about the happenings of her young life and the relation of events. If she hadn't fallen from the swing in the barn at home in Duvemala, and injured her knee, she would never have gone to Berta in Idemo to seek a cure for gangrene. Then she would never have met Karl Oskar and they would never have become a married couple. They would not have owned and farmed Korpamoen together, and she would not have had four children by him. Nor would they lie together here tonight under the bridal cover which she had made. She would not have Anna, Johan, and Lill-Marta, those three small beings sleeping so close to them.

Everything important in her life had happened because once she had made a swing from an ox-thong, at home with her parents, and had fallen from it. God surely had willed that she put up the swing; He it was who had directed all this for her.

And she still enjoyed swinging; a little while ago she had made a swing again in the threshing barn, when no one saw her. She knew that her mother-in-law thought it was ill done by a farm wife who had borne four children—thought she should think of other things.

Kristina had blown out the tallow candle when she went to bed. Through the window she could see the glittering snow which had fallen the last day of April and—as it seemed—might remain.

Karl Oskar lay quietly at her side, but she could hear that he was still awake. She asked: "Are you thinking about something?"

"Aye. About spring. It looks ill for the crops."

"It's true. It seems ugly."

Kristina's eyes wandered through the window; when she and her husband arose tomorrow morning the month of May would be here—yet it was snowlight outside.

She said: "We must believe God will let things grow—this year as all years."

"Believe! Yes—if faith were of help, we'd harvest a hundred barrels of rye this fall."

He had never before shown such anxiety; now he seemed dejected, disheartened. His low spirits were contagious; she too began to worry about the coming days.

He continued: Including his parents there were now seven people who must find their food on this small farmstead—a one-sixteenth. If the year were lean and the crops failed, he would not know what to do.

Kristina thought of the children, now sleeping their sweet sleep in this room. Those who had brought the children into the world were responsible for them and must see to it that their stomachs were satisfied and their bodies clothed. The children's welfare was much more important to Kristina than her own, and she knew Karl Oskar felt as she did.

Kristina folded her hands and said her usual evening prayer: "Turn Thy Grace to me and let me sweetly go to sleep this night. . . ." Before she said her Amen she added tonight a few sentences she remembered from "A Prayer for the Fruit of the Earth": "Give us favorable weather and protect the crops from all destruction. Bless us with corn and kernel. Through Jesum Christum, our Lord, Amen."

Karl Oskar seldom said his evening prayer any more; he usually was too tired after he went to bed. But as Kristina prayed and he listened, it might be for both of them. God must look kindly on a farmer in a stone country.

He turned over on his side to go to sleep, and Kristina felt for his hand, for she went to sleep sooner if she held it in her own.

They both lay quiet; Karl Oskar kept hold of his wife's hand. At her touch the desire of the body was awakened in him. He put his arm around her to pull her closer.

"No-oo, Karl Oskar, I do-on't know . . ." She struggled a little.

"What is it, Kristina?"

"I—I was thinking of the children."

"They are asleep, all three."

"I meant something else; I think of the food for the children."

"The food?"

She whispered close to his ear: "If we didn't—I thought— Then there wouldn't be any more."

There was a sense of shame in her voice. But now she had said it.

"If we didn't? For the rest of our whole lives? Is that what you mean?"

Kristina wondered herself what she meant. God created as many people as He desired; as many children as He decided were born. That she knew. But she knew this just as surely: if no man came near her, then she would bear no more children. It seemed as if in one way God decided, in another she herself could make the decision. The conflicting thoughts disturbed her.

Karl Oskar went on to say that he could not leave her alone when he had her next to him in bed during the night; no man who slept with his wife was built in such a way; at least not before he became so old that moss grew in his ears.

Kristina had no reply. No, she thought, they could not stay apart throughout life. She too had her desire, which she could not resist forever. But she would never fall so low as to let Karl Oskar know this.

He continued to seek her; he clasped her breasts, which swelled and hardened in his hands. Her own desire awakened. She opened up as a mollusk opens its shells; she gave in.

They were silent during their embrace, as they always were. In the moment of fulfillment she had entirely forgotten what she had said before.

About a month later Kristina knew that she was carrying her fifth child.

II

THE FARMHAND WHO
DROWNED IN THE MILL BROOK

1

Robert, Nils' and Marta's second son, was ten years younger than Karl Oskar. When he was little he had caused his parents a great deal of trouble by running away as soon as he was outside the house. He would disappear into the woodlands and they might spend hours looking for him among the junipers. They hung a cowbell round his neck so they could locate him, but even this did not always help, for they could not hear the tinkle when the child sat quietly. He did not change as he grew older: if he was not watched he would disappear into the woods and hide; if he was asked to do chores he might run away. And as the boy grew older they were ashamed to hang a bell on him as if he were an animal.

When his parents ceded Korpamoen, Robert was given employment during the summers as herdboy for Akerby *rote* (a *rote* is a parish district with common grazing rights, etc.). Thus there was one mouth less to be fed from the porridge bowl in the spare room. Robert received food from the farmers, and two daler a year in wages (fifty-eight cents). Every fall he received also a cheese and a pair of woolen stockings. He liked it well out in the wastelands, alone with the cattle. During the long summer days, while cows and sheep grazed lazily, he would lie on his back in some glade and stare into the heavens. He learned to whistle, and he sang without even thinking of it. Later, when his shepherd days were over, he realized why he had done these things: he had felt free.

For six weeks every year during three succeeding years he attended the school held by Rinaldo. Schooling came easily to him; the very first year he learned to read and write. Though Rinaldo had only one eye, he had seen more of this world than most of the parishioners with two. Once he had been as far away as Gothenburg, where he had seen the sea, and he told the children about his life's adventures. They enjoyed this

34

more than the Little Catechism and the Biblical history put together.

The day Robert finished school he received a book as a gift from the schoolmaster. It was a *History of Nature*. Rinaldo said that when school days were finished, children seldom touched a book; but if they never improved their reading ability, they would soon lose it. He gave this book to Robert so that he might continue reading when he finished school.

The *History of Nature* was Robert's first possession. But for more than a year it happened that he didn't open his book. During the winter he attended confirmation class at the dean's, and also helped his brother Karl Oskar fell oaks. The oak timbers would later be brought to Karlshamn to be used for shipbuilding. They cut pines, too, the tallest in the forest, for masts on ships. While Robert helped with tree felling and the sawing of timbers which were to travel on the sea, he followed the ships-to-be in thought. The harbor town of Karlshamn was fifty miles away, and the peasants bringing timbers there needed two days and a night for the round trip. Robert thought that he would like to ride with the timbermen to Karlshamn in order to see the sea with his own eyes.

Nils and Marta churned and sold some ten pounds of butter from their own cow in order to raise money for a Bible to give their son at his first Communion. The Bible he received was bound in leather and cost one riksdaler and thirty-two shillings—the same amount as the price of a newborn calf. But it was a Bible that would stand wear and tear; the Holy Writ must be bound in leather to last a lifetime.

Robert now owned two books, one worldly and one religious. Rinaldo had said that all people ought to read these books—from one they learned about the body and all earthly things, from the other about the soul and things spiritual. The *History of Nature* contained all Robert needed to know about this world; the Bible, about the world hereafter.

But Robert was still in this world, and he must now go out and earn his living. His father made all the decisions for his minor son. Nils had arranged for him to serve one year as farmhand in Nybacken, about a mile from Korpamoen. But Robert did not wish to serve. He argued with his parents that he did not like to have a master; couldn't he somehow avoid the service in Nybacken?

Nils and Marta were disturbed to hear their younger son

speak thus, and reprimanded him soundly: What kind of poor wretch was he, unwilling to work for food and clothing when hale and hearty? Would he like to become one of the tramps on the roads, or a beggar from the squatters' sheds in the wastelands? Or did he want to remain at home, a burden to his parents who lived but on reserved rights? And he soon fifteen! He ought to be ashamed of himself! His sister Lydia had been a maidservant for several years now. They were too many here in Korpamoen; Karl Oskar could not feed him, he could not afford a servant. Moreover, his father had hired him to Aron in Nybacken, and received the earnest money, according to the servant law—the contract could not be torn up and changed. Aron was to pay good wages: the first year Robert would receive thirty daler in money, one wadmal suit, and one pair of short-legged boots. He should be pleased, and he should also be thankful to his parents who had arranged this service for him.

So one May morning in 1848, at sunup, Robert Nilsson left his parental home to start his first service as farmhand. His mother had made a bundle of his belongings, tied in a woolen kerchief. She had gathered together his leather shoes, his wadmal pants, one Sunday shirt, and one pair of Sunday stockings. In one hand he carried the bundle, in the other three books, the Bible, the *History of Nature,* and the prayer-book which his mother had given him. The books were wrapped in paper so as not to become soiled.

It had rained during the night but now the sun shone down on the village road. A wet odor rose from the meadows on either side of the road where the rain had fallen on the fresh, new grass. The birches had just burst into leaf and shone green, and from the bushes came the twitter of birds at play. But the boy who wandered along the road with his two bundles felt no joy in the beauty of the spring morning around him. He was on his way to Nybacken, to begin the life of a farmhand, but he had never been asked if he wanted to become a hired hand in Nybacken. He dreaded the confinement of the service, he did not want to have a master. He was walking on the road to Nybacken but he did not wish to arrive. Now that he was grown older he was being pushed out from the home like a fledgling from the nest. He was the younger son, one of those without portion. And still, he did not envy his elder brother, who must poke between the stones, burdened with worries about the mortgage interest.

Robert stopped as he reached the bridge over the mill brook. What did it matter if he began his service half an hour earlier or later, at five o'clock or half-past? There would be ample time for work during the whole long year. He left the road and sat down at the edge of the brook. He took off his wooden shoes and his stockings and dangled his feet in the water. The brook rushed by, swollen with the spring rains. At last spring had come, and the water felt warm. It rippled around his feet, it whirled and bubbled between his toes, and he sat and watched it run away, passing by him, flowing under the bridge and hastening farther on. He saw the white bubbles of foam float on and disappear in the thicket of willows where the brook's bed made a curve. This water was free; the water in the brook was not hired in Nybacken; it needn't stay in the same place a whole year. It never remained in one place, it could travel anywhere. It could run all the way down to the sea, and then the way was open around the world, around the whole globe.

There would be no harm if he sat half an hour and watched the brook, a last half-hour before he became a hired hand.

In front of him in the creek bed there was a deep, black pool near a large stone. In this pool he had once drowned a cat, a gruesome memory. And there, beside the stone, a maid from Nybacken had drowned a few years ago. She had not drowned by will, she had slipped and fallen into the water as she stood on the stone and rinsed washing. The stone was so steep that she was unable to crawl up; her body was found in the pool. On the stone they had seen marks made by her fingernails: she had scratched and scraped with her nails, unable to get hold anywhere. Afterwards Robert had seen the marks and he could never forget them; the scratches told him of human terror at death.

A manservant could drown in that pool as well as a maid. When a hired hand sank into the water of the brook, no service contract would hold, and no earnest money which the servant had accepted on earth would have to be accounted for. A drowned farmhand had no master.

Robert considered this.

He unfolded the paper around his books. His mother had laid a little myrtle branch between the leaves of the prayer-book, and the book opened where the green branch lay: "A Servant's Prayer."

"O Lord Jesus Christe, God's Son. You humbled Yourself in a servant's shape. . . . Teach me to fear and love You in my daily work, and to be faithful, humble, and devoted to my temporal lords in all honesty. . . . What worldly good may fall to me I leave all to Your mild and fatherly pleasure. Teach me only to be godly at all times, and satisfied, and I will gain sufficiency. . . . Let me also find good and Christian masters who do not neglect or mistreat a poor servant, but keep me in love and patience. . . ."

Through the myrtle branch between the leaves his mother spoke to the young servant: Read this prayer! And Dean Brusander required at the yearly examinations that farm-hands and maids should "so act in their poor situation that they could say by heart 'A Servant's Prayer.' "

But now Robert had in mind to read a piece from his *History of Nature*. He had turned the corner of the page and he found the place immediately:

> "*About the Size of the Sea*:
> "Many might wonder why the Creator has left so little space on the earth as home for man and beasts. For almost three-quarters of the earth's surface is covered by water. But he who learns to understand why water takes so much space shall therein see another proof of the Creator's omnipotence and kindness.
> "These great bodies of water which surround the firm land on all sides, and which have salt water, are called Sea. . . ."

Robert looked up from his book. He thought of the sea which was three times bigger than the firm land on which he sat. No one owned the sea. But the land was divided in home-steads, in quarters, eighths, sixteenths, and the farmers owned them. The one who owned no land became a servant to a landowner.

He thought: On land there were many roads to follow. There were others besides the one which led to Nybacken. There was a parting of the ways close by, at the bridge over the mill brook: the right one led to Nybacken, the left one brought you to Abro mill—and if you continued on that road you would never reach Nybacken.

If you turned to the left you could disappear from the neighborhood. There were people who had disappeared from the parish; their names were still in the church book, written down under "End of the Parish." The dean called their names at the yearly examination, and inquired about them. Every year he called the name of the farmhand Fredrik Emanuel Thron from Kvarntorpet; not heard from since 1833. Someone always answered that no one in the village knew where he was. And the dean wrote about him in his book: Whereabouts unknown. This was repeated every year: Fredrik from Kvarntorpet was not heard from. For fifteen years—the whole span of Robert's life—the lost farmhand's whereabouts had been unknown. This was the only thing Robert knew about Fredrik Thron from Kvarntorpet, and because he knew naught else he wondered about the lost one's fate.

It had happened before that a farmhand had disappeared, had taken the wrong road.

When Robert was ready to pull on his stockings he missed one of his wooden shoes. It had fallen into the brook; now it floated on the water near the willow thicket, far out of reach. He stood there, startled that his wooden shoe could float. Now it caught on the branches of the willows where the brook turned. The water gushed and swirled round the shoe and Robert stood there and saw his own foot kick and splash; he saw himself lying there, drowning in the brook.

What he had just now vaguely thought of had begun to happen by itself. It only remained for him to complete it.

He stuffed his stockings into the remaining shoe and threw it into the brook. Then he took off his jacket and let it follow after and was pleased when he saw it float on the water. Then he picked up his two bundles and went up on the bridge. At the parting of the roads on the other side of the bridge he turned to the left; he took the road that did not lead to Nybacken, he took the wrong road.

Caught on a branch of the big willow at the bend of the brook there now could be seen a boy's little jacket. As the running water in the brook swung the branches back and forth, the arms of the jacket would wave to anyone passing the bridge, telling what had become of the hired hand on his way to Nybacken to begin his service: he had drowned in the mill brook, as the maid had done a few years earlier.

2

The ground under Robert's feet felt cold in the shadow of the wood: it was too early in the year to go barefooted. He had walked only a short distance when someone pulled up behind him. Robert prayed in his heart that it might be a timberman on his way to Karlshamn; then he would ask if he could ride with him. But it was only Jonas Petter of Hasteback, their nearest neighbor in Korpamoen, on his way to the mill with grain. He stopped. Yes, Robert could sit up on the sacks beside him and ride with him to Abro mill.

Robert crawled onto the wagon and sat down next to the farmer. Jonas Petter of Hasteback was a kind man: he did not ask where Robert was going; he said only that it was dangerous to walk barefooted so early in the spring. Robert answered that he walked easier without shoes and stockings. Apparently Jonas Petter had not noticed the jacket as he passed the bridge.

In the mill room at Abro there were already three farmers, waiting for their grind. They were unknown to Robert. He remained with them in the mill room, where it was nice and warm; a big fire burned in the stove, and the air smelled sweetly of flour and grain.

The peasants ate food which they had brought along and drank brannvin with it, and one of them gave Robert a slice of bread and a dram. He dunked the bread in the brannvin as children were wont to do, and he was a little conscious of this, now that he was almost grown.

The men had driven their grain wagons far alone, and now in company they were conversing loudly and noisily. Jonas Petter of Hasteback stretched himself full length on some empty sacks in front of the fire. He was a tall-grown man with fine black side whiskers.

Below the mill room the grindstones went their even pace and rumbled softly, like thunder at a distance; it was otherwise peaceful and quiet in here. Robert sat in front of the fire next to Jonas Petter. He was not going to work as a hired man, and his heart was light.

"We all remember old Axelina here at Abro," said Jonas Petter, "but does anyone remember how she got the mill and became the richest wench in the parish?"

The answers from the other peasants all were negative. No one had such a good memory as Jonas Petter; he knew all the old stories of the region, and now he must tell about Axelina, whom he remembered as the owner of the mill while he was still a youth.

She was an ingenious and clever woman, this Axelina. She came as a maid to Frans the Miller, who had owned the mill for many years and had had time to steal so much flour from the sacks that he had become as rich as ten trolls. At this time he was old and sickly, and Axelina made up her mind that she was to inherit from him. And now she went about it in the only way a woman can under such circumstances: she tried to inveigle him into carnal connections with her. In the evenings after he had gone to bed she would come into his room in her shift, and as often as she could she displayed her attractions. But Frans was played out, slow in the blood—no longer to be tempted.

One cold winter evening, however, as he returned from a Christmas party where he had drunk more brannvin than was good for him, he happened to fall into a snowdrift. When he did not turn up, Axelina took a lantern and went out to look for him. She found him frozen through and through. She helped him home, put him to bed, and gave him a pint of brannvin to revive his body warmth. Frans drank the brannvin but complained that he still felt cold. Then, said Axelina, she knew only one more remedy which could help him, and that one he probably wouldn't use. Frans was afraid he might contract a deadly sickness and he asked what kind of remedy she knew. Well, replied the maid, she must lie next to him and warm him with her own body. She had heard this was the best remedy against chills. Frans was a little startled, but he had drunk a lot of brannvin and said that if she believed she could help him in this way she might come and lie next to him. She would do it only to save his life, she insisted, and he must promise not to touch her. This he promised willingly— he had no such thoughts while shaking and shivering in his bed.

So Axelina lay down with her master, and she knew how to manage: it ended with the master and the maid being as close to each other as is possible. She used to say later that it took only half an hour until Frans the Miller lost the chills, and she could leave him.

Forty weeks after this happening Axelina bore a son who so much resembled Frans that no one needed to ask the father's name. Frans never forgave his maid who had taken advantage of him, and marriage between them was never talked of. But he was much attached to his boy, and when he died a few years later he left all he owned to the child, with a relative as guardian. Axelina did not get a penny.

However, the boy caught smallpox and died when he was four years old. Axelina then inherited from her son. She received the Abro mill and all Frans' other possessions, and became the richest woman in the parish: owner of more than forty thousand riksdaler. And she bragged later that she had earned it all in one half-hour, the half-hour when she lay in Frans the Miller's bed and warmed him after his exposure in the snow. Nor was it difficult work—she had lain quite still. No woman in the whole world, not even a queen or an empress, had earned so great an hourly pay as Axelina in her master's bed that evening.

Yes, said Jonas Petter, and sighed, women could earn easy money if they liked: only to lie quite still.

Robert stared at Jonas Petter; he always told such unkind stories about women. It was said that he did this because he himself was tormented by a wicked wife. The couple in Hasteback lived so ill together, and quarreled so loudly, that people could stand on the road outside the house and hear every word they said; horses had become frightened and bolted from the hubbub. It sometimes happened that Jonas Petter had to sleep in a stall in the byre because he could not sleep within the same four walls where his wife Brita-Stafva slept.

Robert stretched out on the floor before the fire and contemplated the cracked, sooty beams in the ceiling of the mill room. Again he thought of the farmhand who had chosen the left road instead of the right one.

Presently he asked Jonas Petter: "Do you remember Fredrik of Kvarntorpet who disappeared from home?"

"Fredrik Thron? Yes, I remember him, that cuckoo!"

He was a rascal, continued Jonas Petter. He was as lazy as a well-fed Christmas pig, and would rather steal than work. If anything was lost it was easy to know who had found it. Fredrik stole for pleasure rather than gain, but in either case it was unpleasant for the loser. And he was given to all kinds of pranks: he broke down gates, let the horses out of the church stables while people were in church, brought snakes into the church on Sundays. Every farmer in the parish was disgusted with the knave from Kvarntorpet.

The boy's father was a cotter under the manse, and he had persuaded the owner, Lieutenant Rudeborg, to hire his son as a farmhand and try to make a man of him. When Fredrik had been in Krakesjo for a week, he was asked by the lieutenant to fetch a pair of oxen bought at the Klintakrogen fair. They were fine animals, well-broken in, and a child could have driven them this short distance with a loose thong. But Fredrik, who was twenty, could not manage it; he arrived at the manse with another pair. The lieutenant had never seen these animals before; the ones he had bought had measured seventy-eight inches around the chest, and now his farmhand brought a pair of steers measuring hardly sixty-six. These animals were not worth half the price he had paid for the oxen at the fair. Lieutenant Rudeborg was in a red-hot rage at his new man.

On the way home from the fair Fredrik had done some trading of his own, and had exchanged the master's oxen for the smaller ones—with money in his own pocket, of course. But the damned fool swore up and down that these were the same beasts he had received: their color was identical, red with a white spot on the forehead. Fredrik was clever. These looked somewhat smaller, he admitted, but they had shrunk because they had been without fodder the whole day—that was all, they were indeed the same oxen.

Nevertheless, Lieutenant Rudeborg had witnesses who said the animals were not his, so Fredrik couldn't wriggle himself free that time. Rudeborg, however, felt sorry for the boy's parents. He didn't want to put his servant in jail, but he couldn't stand the sight of the fellow. He therefore suggested to his neighbors that they send Fredrik to North America; he would pay half the fare if they chipped in and paid the other half.

That country would suit Fredrik perfectly, said the lieutenant. America was a land for all rogues and misfits who could not live in law and order at home. Out there he could trade oxen with other villains to his heart's content. If he remained at home and they put him into prison, he would be on their hands again as soon as his sentence was over. But once in North America, they would be rid of him for time and eternity.

The farmers quite willingly contributed a couple of riksdaler each to free themselves from Thron's boy, who had been such a nuisance to them. So the money was collected, he was put on the coach at Klintakrogen, and Lieutenant Rudeborg even came down in person to see that his scoundrel servant started off to North America.

A few months passed by and all was well. No mischief was heard of and everyone said this was the wisest thing they had ever done—to send Fredrik to North America.

But one day the news spread that the American traveler was home in Kvarntorpet again.

He had never boarded the ship for North America. He had gone only as far as Gothenburg, and in Gothenburg he had remained the whole time. There he had stayed at an inn, and had drunk and caroused and lived like a lord as long as the money lasted. When it was spent he returned home, and now this debased youth looked honest people in the face as if expecting them to be happy to see him back again in good health. He had put on weight and he looked fine. On the money he had received from honest folk he had lived in idleness, gluttony, and debauchery. And the rogue said that if you wanted to live well you should not work. He was so shameless that he went around the village and thanked people for their contributions toward the journey, saying he had used them as well as he could, he had had much pleasure. And if they should have it in mind again, he would be most willing to undertake another American journey. He had always longed to get out and see the world, it was so useful and instructive for a person. And this parish was a dirty little hole not at all befitting decent, sensible people. He hoped that the contributions next time would be sufficient to take him a bit farther on his voyage to America.

By now people were so angry at the inveterate scamp from Kvarntorpet that they spit at him whenever they saw him. Evil was within him, and it "inclined him to evil, and disinclined him to good," as it is written. And Lieutenant Rude-borg, who had paid half his American fare and himself seen him board the Gothenburg coach, had no mercy on him this time: he reported him to the sheriff for theft of the oxen. However, when Lonnegren arrived at Kvarntorpet to fetch Fredrik, he had disappeared, and the authorities had not been able to lay hands on him since.

"That's fifteen years ago, now. No one here has seen Fredrik since that time. They say he took to the sea," Jonas Petter concluded.

Angry words were mumbled by the peasants as the farmer from Hasteback finished his tale. Probably, thought Robert, some of them had contributed toward Fredrik's American journey at the Gothenburg tavern.

A few words in Jonas Petter's story had especially impressed Robert and he pondered them: the lieutenant from Krakesjo had said that a land existed which fitted all those who misbehaved at home.

If one disappeared from one's service and from the neighborhood, one was written down under "End of the Parish." He could hear the dean call a name at the examination next autumn: Farmhand Robert Nilsson from Korpamoen. No one present knows where he is. And the dean writes: Whereabouts unknown. So it would be written next year, and the following. And ten years, fifteen years later the dean would still write in the church book about the farmhand Robert Nilsson: Whereabouts unknown. Not heard from since 1848. For all time it would appear about him in "End of the Parish": Whereabouts unknown.

It was thus written about those who were free.

How many miles might it be to North America? He dared not ask anyone present, they might begin to wonder about him. Perhaps he could learn from some book.

But America was the land for one who had taken the wrong road.

3

Robert became drowsy from the heat in the mill room and from the monotonous din of the millstones; he went to sleep on some empty sacks in a corner. It was late afternoon when he awoke. Jonas Petter and the other peasants were gone with their grind, and in their place two other farmers who had arrived were waiting for their flour and eating their provisions. They no doubt thought Robert was a farmhand who was waiting for his grind. And one of them noticed that he had no food and handed him a slice of bread and a piece of pork.

The same farmer told about a death which had occurred that very morning: a young farmhand on his way to service in Nybacken had drowned in the mill creek. It appeared he had fallen off the bridge. They had found his jacket, and Aron of Nybacken had dragged the pool, but his body had not yet been recovered. Strangely enough, a maid from Nybacken had drowned in the same pool a few years ago.

The farmer also knew that the drowned servant was son to Nils in Korpamoen. He was only recently confirmed. As a child he had been somewhat peculiar: he would run away from home, and his parents had been forced to hang a cowbell around his neck to locate him.

A young person's sudden death—a horrible occurrence, the farmer sighed. He added that fortunately the victim was old enough to have received the Lord's Holy Supper, so one might hope he was now with his Saviour in eternal bliss.

The last bite of bread stuck in Robert's windpipe; he coughed for a moment: the same man who had given him the bread believed he deserved a blissful heaven. He was a kind man, he must be thanked sometime.

Here at the mill Robert felt he might be recognized any moment; he must remain here no longer.

He knew in which direction he must go: he wanted to reach Karlshamn, the town by the sea; he must reach the sea.

He intended to ask if perchance anyone of the peasants came from the southern part of the parish; perhaps he could get a ride part of the way. But just as he opened his mouth to ask, the miller himself came into the room, covered from head to foot with white flour dust. He seemed to be looking for someone; he eyed Robert sharply.

"Are you Nils of Kopramoen's son?"

As he looked closer he added: "You're barefooted, and you haven't any jacket. You must be the one."

It was too late to ask for a ride.

"Your master is here. He heard about you from the other farmers."

Up the steps into the mill room came a big man with thick, fox-red hair covering his forehead. His cheeks were smooth and shone as if greased with pork fat, and he had small, piercing eyes. It was Aron of Nybacken.

Robert crawled backwards into his corner.

Aron smiled with a broad grin as he espied the lost farmhand.

"Well, well, if it isn't my boy, that little helper of mine!"

And he extended his hands toward Robert, a pair of hands covered with long, coarse, red hair. They were heavy and rough as gnarled birch clubs, they were the biggest hands Robert had ever seen. And they were fastened to a pair of powerful arms, the arms of Aron of Nybacken; they hung from the man who was his master.

Robert tried to pull himself into his shirt, into his trousers, he wanted to become small, so small that the master could not get hold of him, could not see him.

But Aron sounded very kind now, his voice was mild and soft as sweet cream: "Too bad you lost your way! My little boy, you didn't find Nybacken this morning—now I'll show you the way. Outside the coach awaits you."

And he stretched out his big hand and grabbed the boy by the shoulder.

"Pick up your bundles and come."

Robert walked out of the mill room followed by the farmer. He was hired according to law, he was bound to the man who had the biggest hands he had ever seen.

Outside the mill stood the horse and wagon from Nybacken, and here the master and the hired hand were alone. Aron got a good hold of Robert's ear, while his broad smile vanished: So-o, the little farmhand was of that sort of wool! So, he wanted to run away, did he! And he had tried to make people believe he had drowned! And had caused his master great trouble—the whole morning had been spent in dragging for the lost farmhand! Now, in the midst of the most pressing time of spring! So he was of that ugly breed that wanted to leave his service before he began it! Was it in this way that the little hired man honored his father and mother and revered and obeyed his masters? His poor parents had today mourned him as drowned and dead, tomorrow they would be ashamed of him as living. He was confirmed and grown, but he couldn't walk a mile from home without disappearing. He, Aron, would tell his parents they must still hang the cowbell on their boy before they let him leave home.

"You've earned a good thrashing, my little hired fellow. But I shall let you off with a small box on the ear."

And he gave his servant a box on the ear.

Robert was pushed backwards against the wagon wheel, and the world around him shook for half a minute, but he did not fall. The master's hand could no doubt have hit him much harder, Aron could have given him a real box on the ear. Robert could hear, and he understood: it was only a small box he had received.

And so the farmhand rode back with his master, the whole stretch of road he shouldn't have taken this morning, the whole road wrongly followed.

And when they arrived at the bridge over the mill brook, where in the morning he had taken the left road, the wagon now followed the right one.

So ended the day when Robert Nilsson tried to take his first steps on the road to America.

III

WHAT THE BEDBUGS IN A STABLE ROOM MUST LISTEN TO

1

The farmstead Nybacken had a master and mistress, plus an old mistress on reserved rights, three maids in the maids' room, and two farmhands in the stable room. Aron's hired men lived in the barn next to the horses' stalls. Their room had a deal table, a bench for each of them, two beds filled with straw, and a horse blanket each. In walls and beds lived bedbugs in great numbers, and they increased in undisturbed bliss, filling all holes and cracks.

Arvid, the elder farmhand, was grown, and sturdy and strong of limb, although a light, silky boy-beard still covered his chin. He had a reddish skin and old frostbites on his nose, which bled in cold weather. Aron called him his big hand; Robert was his little hand.

Arvid seemed slow of speech and shy with people, but the very first evening after they had gone to bed on their straw bundles in the stable room Robert began to ask his comrade in service about the master and mistress. What kind of place was Nybacken for a servant?

Before he went to sleep that night Robert had obtained from the elder boy a fair picture of their situation: Aron was hot-tempered, and if he became angry he might give his hands a box on the ear or a kick in the pants. Otherwise he was really a kind, decent soul who would harm no one. The mistress was less considerate: she hit the maids, and her husband as well, and Aron was afraid of her and dared not hit back. Both master and mistress were afraid of the wife's mother, the old mistress who lived in a "reserved room" in the attic. She was so old she should have been in her grave long ago, if the devil had attended to his business; but apparently he too was afraid of her.

The service was demanding because the master was lazy; the hired men had to do nearly all the chores. The food wasn't restricted in good years and they could eat as much bread as they wished. During lean years the farmhands and the maids must live on what they could get, here as everywhere else.

It was salt herring at every second meal—but in many places they had to eat herring every meal the year round, except Christmas Eve, and in many places the mistress herself cut the bread and portioned out the slices. So you couldn't complain about the fare in Nybacken. Of course, it might happen that the bread was mildewed, the herring rancid, the milk blue sour, and the cheese rat-eaten, so they could see the marks of the small teeth. But only once had they found rat-dirt in the flour porridge; Aron himself had picked out the small black pebbles. Arvid had served at other farms where the bread was nearly always mildewed, the herring always rancid, the milk always sour, and neither the mistress nor the master had bothered to pick out the rat-dirt from the porridge. So one need not belittle the fare at Nybacken, he said.

So much the "little hand" learned from the big one during the first evening. And every evening thereafter Robert tumbled into bed tired and exhausted, and slept like a gopher in his hole, unconscious even of the biting bedbugs, until morning came and Aron awakened him, shaking him by the shoulders: "My little hired man, hurry on up! It's four o'clock! My little hand, you know idleness is perdition! Don't lie there and be lazy. Hurry up to your work!"

Arvid was accustomed to the ways of the farm, and when he said that the service was hard he might as well have said it was hard to harness a horse or to carry a bucket of water.

Robert was the youngest on the farm, and all had chores for him to do: Aron, the mistress, the old mistress, the maids. All lorded it over him, sent him hither and yon, corrected him, hurried him, scolded him. Everyone on the farm was his master. Even the animals: the farm's four horses needed constant attention. He had to get up early in the morning to fill their managers with fodder, in the evening he must fill them again before going to bed. And the horses must be curried, they must have their stalls cleaned, hay must be brought down from the loft for them, oats fetched from the granary, fodder cut in the barn, and water carried from the well. Robert lived his farmhand's life in close quarters with horses, smelling horses, horse manure, horse sweat, leather and harness. Sundays and weekdays alike, the horses required attention.

The animals were bound in their stalls and the farmhands were bound to the animals. And the service year of a hired hand was three hundred and fifty-eight days, discounting his one free week a year.

During the very first week of his service at Nybacken Robert made the decision that he must escape from all his masters, human as well as animal.

2

The little hand who was bossed by all had good ears and quick eyes. He listened to and observed all that happened on the farm, and picked up its secrets. He heard all insinuations, he saw all winking eyes, as when there were hints and whispers about the white heifer which had been butchered at Nybacken last fall; a fine heifer—ready to calve—had gone to the slaughter bench because Aron dared not let her live. Why dared he not let her live?

Robert collected one word here, another there: *The white heifer was with calf without having been with a bull.* It was said to have happened that cows had borne calves with human heads and faces—horrible monsters, half beast, half man. That was why they had slaughtered the white heifer before her calving time was near.

Robert now wondered how the heifer had become pregnant without having been with a bull. It was answered, he had better ask Arvid. No one but Arvid knew, and he could surely give information.

So he learned gradually that the farm folk were directing a horrible accusation against his comrade in service.

Nothing was ever said in the open, everything was half said. All sentences ended in the middle, they were broken off as soon as they touched the accusation itself. The maids whispered and tittered; no one could speak aloud about such things. Robert asked, and he too made a half sentence: "Did they accuse Arvid of . . . ?" No—no one accused Arvid of anything; but anyone wanting to know more must go to him; he was the only person who knew the truth about the white heifer. They repeated only what the old mistress had said.

It had all originated with the old woman in the reserved room in the attic. One day last summer she had happened to see Arvid drive the white heifer into the cow barn. It was in the middle of the day, no other person was in the byre, no one had asked the hired man to drive in the heifer, and she could not understand why the animal should be taken into its stall at that hour. The old mistress had seen nothing more, nothing more than this: Arvid had driven the animal into the stable. She had not accused him of any forbidden or horrible deed with the heifer, she had merely said this to the maids: what he did with the white heifer in her stall, only he and God knew.

The old mistress had said no more than she could stand by.

From the time he was a little boy Robert had gone with his father when he brought cows to the bull, and when he was herdboy he had more than once seen a bull and cow mate. There was nothing unusual about that, he knew how animals acted and he could imagine how people acted. But he couldn't imagine people and animals together, not a man and a cow together—he did not believe his roommate guilty of the horrible deed.

Only God and Arvid knew how the white heifer had gotten with calf . . . it was the old mistress who had started the ugly rumor, and the maids had believed it. They treated Arvid as if he were leprous, they pulled away from him quickly if they happened to touch him, and they refused to be left alone with him. Furthermore, the rumor about the farmhand in Nybacken and the white heifer had begun to spread through the neighborhood, and other girls now shunned Arvid. For a while he had gone visiting with a maid on the neighboring farm; now he was unable to see her. No one wanted to have anything to do with a youth accused of so shameful a deed.

Robert could not make himself speak to his friend about the horrible accusation, but he knew Arvid was aware of its existence. Arvid had earlier been cheerful and sociable, lately he had become morbidly shy of people, and taciturn. One could easily understand why.

After having been in service for one month Robert asked leave to visit his parents in Korpamoen one Sunday, but was refused. The master had not yet sufficient confidence in his little hand to allow him away from the farm. Arvid said that perhaps Aron thought he would go home and complain about the service and belittle his master. And now Robert learned that his elder comrade had not been away from the premises in half a year, though his parents' home was only three miles distant. But Robert understood why he kept away from people: no one accused of connection with a heifer would wish to show himself more than necessary. It was a loathsome accusation if true, and still more loathsome if untrue.

Aron said that Robert would have no free days during the year because he had failed to report on time and had had to be fetched to service by the master. He also wondered why his little hand need run home to his mother: did he still nurse?

A hired man was no suckling; he could not leave the farmstead without permission of the master.

But the farmhands in Nybacken had some free moments in the stable room during Sunday afternoons in summer, when the horses were let out to graze and needed neither fodder, water, nor rubbing down. Then Robert brought forth his *History of Nature* and read aloud to his friend.

Arvid had attended school only two weeks, and had never

learned to read. He pretended he could; he would take the *History of Nature* and stare into the book with a thoughtful, studied expression as if reading. After a suitable time had elapsed he would turn the page slowly and seriously, as if he had deeply considered its contents. The same was repeated with the next page. But Robert had caught him once holding the book upside down.

Arvid did not "read" for very long, he complained it hurt his eyes; the words in the book were so small and crooked that they were hard to see; his eyes never had been strong; after reading for a while they began to smart as if he had been looking into a fire. He had had to stop school, he said, because his eyes were so poor.

And so he handed the *History of Nature* to Robert. "You read! Your eyes can stand it."

So the elder servant pretended that he could read, and the younger one pretended that he believed him.

And Robert read aloud from the *History of Nature*, about the air and the water, about the animals and the plants, about crocodiles and rattlesnakes, about silkworms and butterflies, sea lions and flying fish, spice trees and coffee bushes, about hot deserts and polar seas, about leaf lice and planets, about geysers and volcanoes. Arvid learned about all the amazing objects and phenomena which existed on the globe but which he had never seen. And when Robert closed the book, Arvid said what a pity he couldn't read as much as he wanted to, because of his poor eyes; his sight was good otherwise, but it was of little value when it came to words in a book.

Now, among all the foods in the world, Arvid liked rice porridge best. Rice porridge he could enjoy only once a year —at Yuletide. One Sunday Robert was reading about rice in the *History of Nature*. As he finished, Arvid said: "Read it again!"

Robert read:

"*About Rice.*

"Rice is a grain which is grown in unbelievable quantities in warm countries. The shelled seeds are shipped to us and are then called rice grains. From them is cooked with milk the white and delicious sweet porridge. The best rice comes from Carolina in North America. . . ."

Arvid listened with open mouth, dreaming his thoughts of sweet porridge. It was almost half a year to Christmas; between now and the plate of rice porridge were many hundred salt herrings which he must eat; Aron had lately been to Karlshamn and had brought home a barrel of herring, and they were expected to reach the bottom of it before the sweet white porridge would be cooked.

Robert went on with a new chapter:

"*About Sugar Cane*
"Nearly all sugar consumed in our country is made from sugar cane; this is a tall grass, eight to ten feet high, which grows in warm countries like the East Indies and America. . . ."

The elder farm boy scratched the back of his neck where there were a few fresh bites from last night's bedbugs. Then he looked out through the window, thoughtfully. A land existed where both rice and sugar grew, both the grain and the sweetening for the porridge. But he knew this was far away in the world, separated from his country by a great water. Neither he nor Robert had seen any greater bodies of water than the tarns here in the parish, and these were so small that a man could row around the shores in an hour. Arvid began to wonder about the sea which separated this country from America.

Suddenly, as if he had spoken too himself, he asked: "I wonder how broad the ocean might be?"

Robert looked up, startled. He could have answered the question, he could have told Arvid many things pertaining to the ocean. But he carried a secret which he guarded well; he must act wisely and carefully, he must not confide in anyone, not even his comrade in service.

Thus, on Sundays, Arvid and Robert sat there, looking out through the single window of their stable room. The small panes were spotted and unwashed, in the corners were cobwebs filled with dead flies, the whitewash on the sash had long ago disintegrated. A dirty, small, poor window let in the light to the hired men in Nybacken. But through this window they could see out into the world, they could look across the stable yard and see the farmland beyond, they could see the village road that passed by. And beyond their eyes' reach their thoughts struggled further, their thoughts ventured on roads never traveled, down to a sea never seen, and across the waters of the ocean.

One of them had made his decision, and he was the first in the parish to do so.

3

Arvid drew part of his pay in brannvin from the farm's still. One Saturday evening as the boys were sitting in their stable room after the day's toil Arvid brought out his keg, which had just been filled by Aron, and offered a drink to his friend. Robert had not yet learned to drink brannvin alone; he still dunked bread in it. In order to please Arvid he accepted a mug and drank it, and afterward he felt as if a juniper twig was stuck in his throat.

Aron had today mentioned that the yearly catechism examination would be held at Nybacken, and Arvid, who last year had been strongly reprimanded by the dean because he was unable to recite the Fourth Commandment, anticipated this day with apprehension.

"The dean asked who our masters were and I couldn't answer," he said.

"Our masters are all those who by God's ordinance are placed over us in the *home,* in the *state,* at *school,* and at the *place where we work*," Robert recited glibly.

"Oh, Jesus!" Arvid stared with admiration at his young friend, who gloated in his display of superior knowledge.

"God has given our parents and masters power over us so that they as God's servants may take fatherly care of us, and each in his station watch over our true welfare. Let every soul be subject unto the higher powers. For there is no power but of God: the powers that be are ordained by God. Wilt thou then not be afraid of the power? Do that which is good, and thou shalt have praise of the same."

"God Almighty!" exclaimed Arvid, and in his amazement he drank so much from his brannvin mug that he choked.

Robert could rattle off the old lessons indefinitely. He could also teach a little to his friend. "Do you know how many superiors and masters we have, Arvid? In the whole world, I mean."

"No-o."

Robert held up his right hand and counted on his fingers. For every lord and master he bent one finger. First was the King, then the Governor, below the King; the third was the Crown Sheriff, who came under the Governor. The fourth was Sheriff Lonnegren, and the fifth was the sheriff's hired man. The sixth was the dean, their spiritual authority, and the seventh their own master, Aron of Nybacken. The sheriff watched over them to see that they remained in their place of service, the dean watched over them at the yearly examinations, Aron watched over them to see that they worked and earned their pay. There were seven superiors and masters in all.

"Jesus Christ! What a lot of masters!"

"Now you can name them to the dean at the examination," said Robert.

"I'll try to remember." And Arvid began to count on his own fingers: "The King, the first master . . . What is his name?"

Robert explained: The King who by God's ordinance sat on the thrones of Sweden and Norway was named Oskar I, and through him all other authority derived.

He went through the list of masters with his comrade many times, and at last Arvid could name all those seven who according to God's ordinance had fatherly power over them.

After a time Robert tired of this holding school; he had drunk several mugs of brannvin and he felt drowsy; he undressed and crawled under the horse blanket. Arvid sat alone with the keg in front of him; he continued to drink; he had drunk more often of late. The stable lantern, swinging from a nail on the wall, spread a dim light over the room. From the other side of the wall could be heard the puffing of the horses and the sound of horseshoes against the stable floor. The hunters of the night—the bedbugs—emerged from their cracks and holes and hurried on their way to suck blood.

Robert went to sleep with the odor of brannvin in his nose.

Suddenly he was awakened by a noise. He had been asleep only a short time. The lantern on the wall was still lit, the door was open and banged in the gusty wind; the sound of it had awakened him. But Arvid was not in his bed, he had vanished.

Robert shook the keg on the table: it was empty. He was seized with anxiety for his friend.

Quickly he pulled on his trousers and hurried into the stable yard. Outside, in the clear moonlight, he could make out someone moving near the door of the woodshed. He went closer: it was Arvid, leaving the shed, staggering. He had an ax in his hand.

"What are you up to?"

Arvid weaved back and forth, his breath came quickly, his head was bare, his tousled hair blowing in all directions, and his mouth wide open. His upper lip was thick and swollen, his cheek bloody; he had fallen and hurt himself. In the moonlight his eyes were bloodshot and staring. From the woodshed he had fetched the heavy wedge ax.

"Are you going to split wood? In the middle of the night?"

"No . . . not wood . . . Something else."

"Are you walking in your sleep?"

"Someone . . . someone is going to die . . . now, tonight."

"Arvid!"

"The old mistress is going to die tonight."

"Arvid! Put back the ax!"

Arvid was drunk and apparently unconscious of his actions. His eyes were flaming, burning with rage. Robert shouted: "Drop the ax!"

"I'll kill the bitch!"

"You're crazy!"

"I'll split her snout, the old sow!"

"Arvid, please . . . please . . ."

"She's ruined my life. She must die!"

And Arvid staggered off toward the house.

Robert ran after. He grabbed his comrade by the arm, seizing the ax handle. "Arvid, please . . ."

"Let go the ax!"

"Listen to me. You'll ruin your whole life."

"It's ruined already."

"But listen, you don't know what you're doing!"

"Let go the ax, I say. Let go!"

The two farmhands fought over the ax. Robert was afraid

he might cut himself on the sharp edge; and Arvid was bigger and stronger and soon had the ax away from him. But Arvid's legs were unsteady from all the brannvin, and he slipped and fell on his back, dropping his weapon to the ground. Quickly Robert snatched it, unnoticed by Arvid, and threw it as far away as he was able; it fell among the gooseberry bushes near the barn. Arvid turned over and felt among the debris, searching for the ax. Robert tried to talk sense to him: "We're friends. I want to help you. Please, Arvid."

And soon the drunken man calmed down; he no longer searched for the ax, he only repeated, again and again: "I'm so unhappy . . . so unhappy . . ."

Robert was frightened by the rage which had come to the surface so suddenly in his good-natured comrade. He shivered in the cold wind, and from the fright he had experienced.

"I'm cold. Let's go to bed now."

And after a time he was able to persuade Arvid to go back into the stable room. The drunken man threw himself full length onto his bed; all his strength seemed to have left him; he lay there, limp and exhausted, and kept mumbling: "At times I feel like killing her . . . that devil's bitch in the attic."

Robert thought it best to leave his comrade alone until he grew more calm. And presently Arvid's stupor began to wear off and his head cleared. He sat up in his bed and his voice was normal as he asked: "Do you know what she accuses me of?"

"Ye-es."

"Hm . . . I thought so. It's the old bitch's evil invention— all of it! You know that, don't you?"

"I know that, Arvid."

The elder boy mumbled something incoherent, then said nothing for a time; apparently he was sleeping. But suddenly he sat up and continued, and now he seemed fully to have regained his senses. He had never done anything horrible or forbidden with the white heifer. If this were his deathbed and he were unable to say aught else, this he would say to the dean, to the sheriff, to the authorities—to all people on earth he would say this: he had never mixed with any animal. The old woman had said that only God and he knew what he had done with the white heifer in the barn. And God in His Heaven knew that he, Arvid, was innocent. But what joy did he get from this when people thought him guilty, when people believed he had done it?

Robert didn't know how to reply, except to say that he himself had never believed the accusation.

Moreover, said Arvid, the heifer had not been with calf, it was a lie, a lie which the hag in the attic had invented, long after the heifer had been butchered. The heifer would never have calved any monster with a human head if she had been spared.

"Why don't you sue the old woman in court?"

Yes, Arvid had thought of clearing himself that way, but he was afraid of the court; he didn't like to have to stand there, gaped at by all people; and the rumor might spread still worse if it were brought to the county court and the old woman found not guilty—after all, she had never accused him outright, she had only said that God and he alone knew what he had done.

Robert had seldom seen her outside the house, the little woman in the gray shawl and the black kerchief, a shriveled-up creature who didn't seem to have the strength to hurt a fly. Yet she had ruined Arvid's life, a terrible injustice had been done to him. Why couldn't God, Who was omnipotent, reveal the truth, so Arvid could be cleared?

"Do you know what they call me?" asked Arvid.

"No."

"Listen . . ."

Walking along the road the other day he had met some boys who mocked him. He had heard their words—something about the bull in Nybacken. They referred to *him*. People called him "The Bull of Nybacken."

They were silent again in the stable room. Robert felt sudden twitches in his eyes; he understood why his comrade had filled his brannvin keg so often of late.

Arvid resumed, and now his voice trembled. He was called the Bull. No wonder all women shunned him, no wonder the girls shied away from him. Who would want to be seen in the company of one called the Bull? And he would always be referred to by that name, although he had not harmed man or animal. He had tried to endure it, but the loathsome name would cling to him forever; he would be treated as fool and scoundrel, an outcast whom people would abhor. He could show himself nowhere in this countryside.

So Robert could understand why he went out and got the ax.

Arvid lay down again, but his body shook: he cried. He cried silently, his whole frame shaking. He lay so for some time.

By now Robert knew enough: Arvid could not bear being called the Bull of Nybacken; indeed, no one in his predicament could endure to remain in the neighborhood. Anyone suffering what Arvid did must move away.

And so Robert knew also what he must do: he must confide in his friend.

The next evening he disclosed his secret. The two farmhands sat as usual on their beds, ready to retire, alone in the stable room. Everyone on the farmstead slept. But Robert acted as if Sheriff Lonnegren had been standing outside the window listening to them. He moved over to Arvid's bed and sat down close to him; he spoke in whispers although no living being could hear him, except his friend and the bedbugs in their cracks and hiding places. And now he uncovered his criminal intentions: "I carry a heavy secret, Arvid. You're the only one I'll confide in. Can I rely on you?"

"If my head is chopped off for it I shall say nothing!"

They shook hands, and the younger one unburdened himself: he intended to escape from service. But this time he would not act as foolishly as he had done in the spring on entering service. He would wait till fall, when they carried oak timbers to Karlshamn. He could drive now, and he would no doubt have to join the timbermen, driving Aron's old mare. But once Aron had let him out of sight with the beast he would never see him again: the mare would return alone to Nybacken. By that time the driver would be far away. In Karlshamn he would board a ship which was to sail to North America—to the New World.

"Are you coming along, Arvid? You'll get rid of your name —the Bull."

Arvid found nothing to say; he just stared, such was his surprise; he could only look at his comrade, this fifteen-year-old boy so recklessly plotting to escape with his master's timber load—a daredevil planning to venture the ocean!

For Arvid knew nothing of what had transpired in Robert's mind since that day in spring when he had taken the wrong road at the bridge over the mill creek, on his way to service.

And Robert had discovered something which had helped him along on this road; he now took from its secret hiding place—under the straw of his bed—a little book in narrow, brown-specked covers and gold-stamped back: *Description of the United States of North America.*

Here was his secret help; through this book he had obtained all the information he needed.

When Robert worked on the dunghill with his manure fork, when he carried his scythe at harvest-time, when he stood in the hayrick or chopped straw in the barn, when he sat here in the room and looked out through the window—always his thoughts carried him across the sea. And little by little another land arose on the other shore. Like a flower which sprouts in black soil, puts forth buds and opens its crown, so that land grew in his imagination. By now he had crossed the ocean and become familiar with the land beyond: America.

There were two worlds—nature's world and the Bible's world, this world and the coming world. But *this* world was again divided into two parts: an old and a new. His home was in the Old World, in the world that was frail, worn-out, and full of years. Its people were worn-out, decrepit, old and weak and finished. In their ancient villages time stood still; in their old moss-grown cottages nothing happened which had not happened before; the children obeyed their parents and imitated them, and did the same thing again which their parents had done before them. The Old World could not go on for many years more; it would not be long before it tumbled and fell with all the decrepit people who lived there.

But far away, on the other side of the globe, there was a New World, recently discovered, recently settled. The New World was young and fresh, and full of splendor and riches beyond imagination. And those who had emigrated and settled there were young and swift and nimble people whose whole lives lay ahead of them. The New World was populated by the most daring and the most intelligent people from the Old World: by those who had left their lords and masters behind them. It was populated by all those who wanted to be free, who did not want to serve under masters. To the New World all those emigrated who at home were poor and oppressed, all those who were harrassed and suffering, the destitute and those full of sorrow, the hunted ones and those full of despair.

The one who was not satisfied with his lot in the Old World moved to the New World. America was the right land for Robert—and for Arvid!

4

When Rinaldo had held his school at Nybacken in the spring, Robert had asked him if he knew of some book with a truthful description of North America. The schoolmaster said he had recently seen such a book advertised in the newspaper *Barometern* for forty-eight shillings—one riksdaler—including postage. Rinaldo ordered the book for Robert, and advanced him the price until such time as the boy should receive his pay. The schoolmaster helped him willingly: Robert was his only pupil who read books of his own free will.

Robert had since—in his room during the summer nights— read the *Description of the United States of North America* three times over from cover to cover. It was written for simple uneducated folk who intended to emigrate to the New World. And it assured readers, even on the first page, that it was a true description: it said that to the innocent and the ignorant much of the contents might seem unbelievable, exaggerated, fabulous, but all was clear, clean, beautiful truth. Nothing was changed, added, or fabricated; all was set down in honesty.

Robert knew the most important chapters by heart, or almost by heart, and now Arvid could get all the information he wanted about the New World. The little farmhand related the facts, and the big one listened. There were in Sweden people of the ruling classes who spread lies about the United States of America. They said that the country was fit only for scamps. The lieutenant in Krakesjo had sent over Fredrik of Kvarntorpet, who was ill-liked in the parish (only Fredrik had turned back at Gothenburg). The lieutenant had maintained that mostly bandits, rascals, thieves, and other evil people lived in America. But this was a lie. The Americans were honest and upright in their doings and dealings, they were neat and clean in their homes and in their appearance, they were brave, generous, helpful, and moral. Of course, among them was an occasional evildoer. It was also a lie that America was so unbearably hot that only Indians, Negroes, and the heathen could endure the climate. People from the Old World could breathe the air, eat the food, and drink the water; no one suffocated or was poisoned. In the most healthy places the Indians lived to so ripe an age that they didn't die in the same way as people did here at home: they dried up and shrank in their old age, and became so light that they blew away and disappeared into the air. But what the masters kept secret was that the people of the New World were not divided into gentry and ordinary folk, as was the case in the kingdom of Sweden. In America no one had precedence over anyone else, for all were equals. Emperors and kings were forbidden; the Americans tolerated no masters; one need neither bow nor curtsy, because there was no one to bow or curtsy to. And no false pride existed among Americans; no one was looked down upon or snubbed because he had dirty or mean employment. All work was considered equally important; a farmer who owned a thousand acres of farmland worked himself all day with his hired men. When had anyone ever seen the lieutenant at Krakesjo go into the field with his men and spread manure? And he was the owner of barely a hundred and thirty acres! In America there was no servant law or earnest money, and hired men and maids could leave their service whenever they wanted without punishment. Nor need they slave as here from early to late: in North America no one worked longer than twelve hours a day.

The money was called dollars, and one dollar equaled two or three riksdaler—maybe more. A good farmhand could earn as much as a hundred and twenty-five dollars a year, and that was more than three hundred riksdaler. Arvid worked here in Nybacken for forty riksdaler a year and a suit of wadmal. If one counted the wadmal at ten riksdaler, one still earned more in one year in America than in six years at Aron's. And the food was seven times better. The Americans had good solid fare: all people ate pork and white bread every day, and Sundays they had double portions of pork to the bread. Salt herring was forbidden as food. The cattle in America were better fed than the servants in Sweden. The fare Aron in Nybacken gave to his servants would be rejected by the pigs in America, for they were very particular. A pig in the New World lived as well as a count in Sweden.

Robert related what he remembered from the book, the

words came pouring from his lips, and perhaps, in his enthusiasm, he added a little here and deducted a little there, but it evened out so that the truth about the United States of America did not suffer from it.

And he carried his comrade away so that Arvid trembled at the revelations. Now and then he put in his "No! No! God! God Almighty! The devil it is! Christ in hell!" and other expressions which he daily carried on his lips and which meant nothing in particular. Arvid had never read a description of heaven, since he could not read, and he had never heard the dean describe it from the pulpit, either, for the dean only spoke of happenings in hell; but if only half the contents of Robert's book were true, and the other half a lie, then the book must describe a heaven on earth.

But Arvid asked about other things, as for example the wild heathen, Indians who flayed people on the head with their knives and were unfriendly toward Christians. There was nothing in the book about Indians' scalping people, said Robert. Arvid then wondered if the wild animals in North America were dangerous. Were there any angry snakes there? He had always been afraid of crawling animals, never daring to kill a snake, and avoiding small quadrupeds. Robert admitted that in America great wild animals did live, and they could kill people, and were consequently a little annoying. The fiercest beast was the gray bear, who attacked all who tried to take his life. But if you lay down on the ground and pretended you were dead, the bear would leave you in peace. There were also lions and tigers and wolves there, but they had a natural fear of people and attacked only if wounded or frightened. There were poisonous rattlesnakes but they rattled and made a noise when they crawled in the woods and could be heard at great distances, so it was easy to run away from them. America had also some irritating small creatures, grasshoppers, blowflies, cankerworms on the fruit trees and others, but they were unable to kill people. The grasshoppers ate only crops, they were quite satisfied with this. No, no one need be afraid to live in America on account of wild animals.

No, Arvid wasn't afraid of them either, he had only asked for the fun of it. And now he knew how it was: when the bears came, one was to lie flat on the ground and pretend to be dead. And he had good hearing; no doubt he would hear when the snakes came rattling and have time to run away.

About those who were called Negroes and had black woolly hair, it said in the book that they were kept as slaves, and were bought and sold as if they were cattle. Robert did not think this was being fair to them. Otherwise they seemed to have it decent and comfortable enough, and he read for Arvid about them: "Many slaves have better living quarters, food, clothing, care, working conditions and old-age security than most of England's factory workers or the peasants in Europe. They have their own chickens and pigs, their own piece of land where they can cultivate whatever they wish and sell the yield for their own profit. A half-year may pass without abuse from their owner. It has therefore happened that liberated slaves—dissatisfied with their newfound liberty and its consequent responsibilities—have again sold themselves as slaves."

Arvid listened in amazement: the slaves had their own chickens and their own pigs? And their own piece of land? And better food and clothing than most peasants at home? Then the best one could do on arriving in America would be to sell oneself as a slave; it would be the wisest thing a farmhand could do. Here in Sweden he would never be able to acquire his own patch of land, or chickens or pigs.

Robert said it was forbidden in America for white-skinned people to sell themselves as slaves.

"Forbidden?" retorted Arvid. "But you said America was a free land, that all people could do as they pleased. You just said so."

"Yes, yes, but that kind of trade is forbidden anyway. For whites."

"But why should it be forbidden to sell oneself? When all have the right to do as they please?"

Robert was confused, he couldn't answer this. And Arvid thought that probably there was a difference between people in America, after all, if the whites did not have the same rights as the blacks to become slaves and have their own land with chickens and pigs.

He would have liked to read a few chapters in the book, Arvid would, if he had been able to, with his weak eyes; but he got such an eyesmart when he read; wouldn't his friend continue?

Robert turned the page to a new chapter, describing the life of the inmates of an asylum in the New World—an asylum in Pennsylvania: "In this house the weak-minded work in their clear moments with weaving, wood chopping, sewing, spinning, knitting, etc., to shorten the time and occupy their minds, besides which for the same reason there are available books, newspapers, chess games, musical instruments, like the flute and the pianoforte. . . ."

"For the crazy?" exclaimed Arvid.

"It says 'the weak-minded.' "

"They have newspapers? And play flutes?" For the first time Arvid voiced doubt.

"Well—look for yourself."

"God Almighty!"

But it was the truth, Robert's eyes were too good to make a mistake in his reading. And when everything was so fine and expensive for insane people in America, one could easily imagine how the sane lived.

Arvid agreed immediately to go with his comrade to the New World.

In the United States of America no one could have heard the ugly rumor which the old woman in Nybacken had spread about him. There no one knew of the horrible deed with the white heifer which he was accused of here at home. In America no one would call him the Bull behind his back; there the girls wouldn't shun him; there he could look all people freely in the eyes and be held in regard like other menfolk.

And on this the big servant shook hands with the little one: together they would cross the ocean.

5

The lantern in the stable room burned late into the night while Arvid and Robert planned their future emigration. And none but the bedbugs in the rotten walls shared their secret deliberations.

Robert had been clever when he figured on driving Aron's timber wagon to Karlshamn; thus the master would contribute, as it were, toward the fare for the journey to America. In the harbor town they would later come to agreement with some captain to sail them across the sea.

Arvid wondered: "How much is the fare across the ocean?"

Robert knew: The transportation from the port of embarkation in Sweden to New York in America, including provisions for the voyage, firewood, and fresh water, cost one hundred and fifty riksdaler* for a grown person. To this was added ten riksdaler entrance fee to America, and some other expenses, so that every emigrant needed about two hundred riksdaler. He himself had that sum—his inheritance—remaining with his brother in Korpamoen.

"Two hundred daler!" Arvid had risen, now he sat down again, so heavily that the bench creaked in every joint.

Two hundred riksdaler was five years' wages. And he had not one shilling saved. If he should save every penny, and didn't even allow himself a pinch of snuff during the whole time, he would have to remain here in Nybacken and serve for five years before he could save that much money.

He sat dejected and avoided looking at his friend; he had never dreamed that the transportation to North America would cost such an incredible sum of money. He must stay at least five service years more—during five more years he would be forced to remain here as the Bull of Nybacken.

A long silence ensued. The bedbugs thought their nightly victims had finally gone to sleep and emerged cautiously from their holes and corners.

Two hundred riksdaler! That boy there was lucky to have an inheritance to draw on. But Robert must go alone, even though a moment ago they had decided to keep company and had sealed it by a handshake.

"You mean you cannot raise the transportation?"

"No—I couldn't manage."

"Not in any way?" Robert was almost as disappointed as Arvid.

"No, there isn't any way out."

"There must be some way. Perhaps we can help each other."

And again they sat silent, and brooded and pondered.

Suddenly Arvid jumped up, his eyes gleaming. "I've got it! We may get across some other way!"

"What do you mean?"

Arvid grabbed hold of Robert's shoulder, intense, breathless. "The highway, of course—we hadn't thought of that!"

* 43.50 in today's currency.

Surely, there must be some road over firm land. They could walk *around* the ocean, and in this way reach America dryshod. They would have to take a roundabout way, it would take them longer, but in his case that would make no difference; he would rather walk the long road to America than remain here and be shunned like a villain. If he could arrive dryshod, on foot, he would willingly take a roundabout road; he had strong, sturdy legs and was a good walker, he needn't risk his life at sea. He was sure he could walk to America. It might take a few years, that couldn't be helped. He would not take too much with him that might be a burden to carry, he couldn't take his servant chest, he'd manage with a knapsack. He might take the keg too, he would need something to encourage him on the long journey if his legs alone must pay the transportation.

He couldn't believe anything else but that in some way they could walk around the ocean.

"It's impossible. No one can walk to America."

"It's impossible? There is no way?" Arvid's eyes were pleading for any little hope, the barest possibility, even if it meant the longest and most difficult road.

Robert answered definitely: No one could walk dryshod to a land which was surrounded on all sides by water. Arvid could see that on the map at schoolmaster Rinaoldo's. America lay there like a vast island in the world sea; they could not walk around that body of water.

"Under no circumstances?"

"Under no circumstances."

Arvid's face fell. Robert continued: In any case, that way was so long that if Arvid were to walk it he would not arrive until he was eighty, just in time to lie down in his grave. And he must take the village shoemaker with him to prepare him a new pair of boots a couple of times a year to replace the worn-out ones.

Arvid sat silent again, very long. Then he mumbled something between his teeth—four words: "That God-damned ocean!"

At last he crawled into bed, still cursing the ocean which separated the Old and the New Worlds. That evening he swore himself to sleep.

IV

KARL OSKAR AND KRISTINA

1

In this year—"the 5,850th since the creation of the world," according to the almanac—the early summer was the driest in thirty-one years.

During the month of June not a drop of rain fell. Dry, harsh winds from east and north blew constantly, but never the west wind, the wind of rain. The sun glared day after day from a cloudless sky. The grass in glades and meadows turned coarse and rough, rustling underfoot. The winter rye stopped growing at knee-height; grazing ended, and the cows went dry.

Haying commenced before June had passed; to leave the ready ripened grass standing would risk its strength. Hillocks and knolls turned brown-red—the color of animal blood, foretelling death under the knife for cattle, with fodder shortage ahead.

Karl Oskar and Kristina harvested the meager hay grown in their meadow. The straws were so short and spindly that the rake could hardly catch them; one could almost count the straws, Karl Oskar said.

He was angry and bitter as he raked; last year was a wet year and hay rotted in the swaths or washed away in the flood. This year it was drought, and the hay burned up. Which was the better for the farmer? Which one could satisfy him?

This year the only moisture in Karl Oskar's field was his own sweat. The Lord's weather was either too wet or too dry. Of what help was it, then, to bend one's back and toil and struggle? The Lord's weather ruined everything for him, all his labor was in vain.

"It's all the fault of the Lord's weather!"

Kristina stopped raking and looked at him gravely.

"Don't be impious, Karl Oskar."

"But—is this hay, or is it cats' hair? Is it worth our work?"

And Karl Oskar was gripped by sudden anger: he seized a

69

wisp of hay on his rake and threw it up into the air while he
shouted heavenwards: "As you have taken the rest of the hay
you might as well have this, too!"

Kristina let out a shriek, terror-stricken: Karl Oskar had
challenged the Lord in heaven and on earth. Her eyes followed the wisp of hay as if she expected it to reach the heavens. But the straws did not get high above the earth, they
were separated from each other by the wind and, scattering
over the meadow, they fell slowly to the ground. No one up
there in heaven would accept the hay.

"Karl Oskar. You have blasphemed."

Kristina stood there, her cheeks white, her hands clutching
the rake handle. Her husband had thrown their hay back to
Him above because he was not satisfied. What was he doing?
How dared he? Did he no longer fear his Creator? He must
know that God would not allow mockery. Frightened, she
looked toward the sky as if she expected that the presumptuous one would receive his punishment immediately.

"May God forgive you! May God forgive what you did!"

Karl Oskar did not answer. Silently he began to rake together a new swath. He had indeed learned God's
commandments, he knew the Lord endured no mockery,
and he felt a pang within him. He had lost his temper, the
gesture with the hay would have been better undone, those
words should not have been uttered.

The clear words of the Bible proclaimed that man on earth
should eat his bread in the sweat of his brow; he asked no
better than to be allowed to do this. But as he gave his sweat,
so would he like also to receive in return the bread. He did
not think it too much to ask that all might happen according
to God's own words.

In silence they continued to harvest their hay. But the
meadow hay barn which in good years was too small was this
year not half filled.

The drought continued.

Their well dried up and the people in Korpamoen carried
water from an old spring in the forest. Hungry and thirsty,
the cattle stood all day long at the stile, lowing plaintively.
The fields were scorched as if fire had passed over them. In
the beginning of August the birches turned yellow and began
to lose their leaves. The summer had never had time to bloom

and ripen before the autumn set in; this summer had died in its youth.

Karl Oskar had a stiff neck from looking for rain clouds. At times clouds did appear, dry clouds, empty smoke rings that passed across the heavens, visions of deceit, a cruel mockery. A few tiny scattered drops fell at times; they were like scorn.

The rye stood overripe, the grains ready to drop from the heads. At the cutting they must be careful not to lose some of the invaluable kernels. Karl Oskar and Kristina brought the quilted bedcover with them into the field, and spread it on the stubble before the swath of the scythe. They moved the quilt gradually, for the cut straws to fall on it and remain there while being tied into sheaves. Thus grains which might fall from the heads were collected on the quilt and saved. From the ground Kristina gleaned the broken heads, gathering them in her apron; when evening came they had collected in the cover a tenth of a bushel of the drop-rye, sufficient for a few loaves of bread. The rye field yielded only a third of its usual crop in this year of drought: what would one loaf of bread count when winter came?

Kristina tied the corners of the quilt into a sack and carried it home under her arm. Four years ago it had been her bridal spread, her cover during the first night with her mate, when she was transformed from maid to wife. Now the bridal cover was with them in their field and helped to garner their bread; it belonged closely to their lives.

Kristina thought: Four years ago, when this cover was new, Karl Oskar had more to say to me. Why is he nowadays so silent? She mused: Now he spoke mostly of work to be done; in the morning about what must be done that day, in the evening about tomorrow's work. And at least once a day either he or she said: Still no rain!

During this summer all people, it seemed, had become serious and sullen and short-tempered; the weather affected their minds. Talk was about the dire winter ahead, as though no one had a right to be joyous now because of the crop failure. Not even children dared show happiness: when a child laughed some older person at hand spoke harshly and silenced it. And all continued to speak of this: What would happen next winter?

Karl Oskar blamed everything on the drought. When he returned empty-handed from a day in the woods with gun and dog, this was because of the dried-up ground: the dog could get no scent of game. When he pulled nets and lines empty from the tarn, he blamed this on the drought: heat drove the fish into the depths. And three times he had brought a cow to the bull with no result: this too because of the drought. Such an opinion did not seem reasonable, as part of the blame might be laid on the bull. But Karl Oskar said that his neighbor, Jonas Petter of Hasteback, was also unable to get his cows with calf because of the heat.

One night toward the end of August Kristina was awakened by a great thunder. She was afraid of storms and she called her husband.

Karl Oskar sat up in bed and listened. It rumbled and thundered, and lightning flashed past the window. Shirt-clad only, he ran to stand on the porch, hands outstretched. An occasional fat raindrop fell; once it began there would be heavy showers. He could go back to bed and sleep again in the blissful knowledge that there would be rain.

He returned inside. Kristina was comforting the children, awake and frightened by the lightning and thunder.

Anna, the oldest child, was now in her fourth year and all were of the opinion that she had a mind far ahead of her years. She was wont to follow Karl Oskar in his work outside, close to him everywhere; if he drove or walked, the child was with him. He called her his big helper. Wise as an eight-year-old, he said.

The thunder boomed again, and Anna asked: "Will the lightning kill us tonight, Mother?"

"No! What nonsnsense! Who has given you such an idea?"

"Father. He said we are to die—all of us."

"Yes, yes, but not tonight."

"When will we die, Mother?"

"No one knows, no one except God. Go back to sleep now!"

And Kristina's eyes turned questioningly to Karl Oskar: What had he said to the child? He smiled and explained. When he had gone with Anna through the pastures recently they had found a dead baby rabbit, and then she had asked if they were to become like the rabbit, if they were all to die.

He had replied in the affirmative. He could not lie about such things to a child. But ever after the girl asked whomsoever she met when they were to die. The other day she had embarrassed her grandmother with the same question. He had had to assure his mother that the question was the child's own idea. She was a strange child, Anna.

Karl Oskar was very proud of this daughter, his big girl.

A clap of thunder sounded, louder than before, and the lightning pierced their eyes, sharp and blinding.

Kristina let out a shriek.

"Did it strike?"

"If so, it was near."

But the heavy rain was slow in coming; only an occasional few drops smote the windowpanes. Karl Oskar could not help the rain to fall, and he went back to bed. Before he was asleep the window was again brilliant, with a new light; but this time it was not lightning cutting through the dark and disappearing. This time the light remained, mobile and flickering.

The young farmer leapt up.

"There is a fire!"

"My dear God!"

"It's burning somewhere!"

As Karl Oskar reached the window he could see that the light came from the hay meadow.

"The meadow barn! The meadow barn has caught on fire!"

He ran outside, only half dressed, followed by his wife. By now Nils and Marta also had awakened in their room, and Kristina called to them to look after the children.

Karl Oskar ran to the well where two water buckets stood filled from the forest spring; he thrust one bucket at his wife and they rushed down the meadow with a pail each in their hands. The water splashed to and fro, and when they arrived at the burning hay barn hardly more than half of it was left. Nor did it matter; the fire by now had reached such proportions that a couple of buckets of water would be of no help. The whole barn was burning, flames leaping high from the dry shingled roof which went up like tinder. A fierce, voracious lightning-fire was burning, and it had found delicious fare: an old dry barn filled with the harvested hay.

The owners of the hay barn—the young farm couple—approached the fire as closely as they could for the heat. They stood there, water pails in their hands, and watched the fire; they just stood and watched, like a pair of surprised, amazed children listening to a cruel and horrible tale which—God be praised—could not be true.

People from neighboring farms had already seen the fire and come running. They too soon realized it would be hopeless to try to stop this fire. The conflagration had the barn within its scorching jaws—no one could hinder it from swallowing its prey.

Luckily, there was no wind. But the neighbors remained to see that the fire did not spread; what might not happen once it were loose in the drought-dry woods?

Already the rain was over; a few heavy drops had fallen, hardly enough to wet the stones on the ground.

Swiftly the meadow barn was burned, and hay and all became embers and sullen ashes. Karl Oskar and Kristina walked back to the farmhouse; there had been nothing for them to do, they had done nothing. On the way home they walked quite slowly, they did not run, nothing was urgent any more. In their hands they still carried their buckets, half full of water; without thinking, they carried the water home again.

At the meadow stile they met Nils on his way to the fire, hobbling on his crutches. He had managed half the way when his son and daughter-in-law told him to turn back. But he sat down on the stile to rest; for many years he had not walked so far from the house.

Watching the fire, Karl Oskar and Kristina had not exchanged a single word. They had only looked at each other a few times; perhaps they had been thinking the same thoughts.

Now on the way home Kristina said, "Do you remember the harvest this summer? When you threw the hay upwards?"

"Yes."

"It happened as you asked."

Karl Oskar kept silent; he could find no answer.

She continued: "It was the punishment. God allows no mockery."

Karl Oskar in Korpamoen walked back to his home carrying his bucket. He walked with bent head and looked at the ground. What Kristina had said was true. This time the Lord had answered his prayer—He had taken the rest of the hay.

2

The east wind blew and no rain fell. Those who could read in the book of the future predicted that rain would never fall again. Last time the Lord had wished to destroy mankind through flood, now He intended to do it through dought, and this time no Noah would be saved with wife and children to propagate a new race.

Karl Oskar sowed his winter rye on the fallow land, strewn with hard clods of earth—gray, lumpy, and unfertile as a field of crushed stone. Even below the topsoil the earth was scorched. It seemed futile planting here, he might as well sow in the ashes of his hearth. Last spring he had sown four bushels of barley in one field; now in autumn he harvested four bushels in return. What did he gain by all his work? Why should he plant seed corn in the earth when the earth did not multiply it? Nothing would germinate here before the rains came and loosed the hard crust of the field.

He entrusted the seed rye to his field without confidence; he had lost his confidence in the earth. Who could tell if it would bring him one single grain in return? It might have been wiser to grind the seed corn and make bread of it.

When God drove the first man from paradise He said: Cursed is the ground for thy sake; in sorrow shalt thou eat of it all the days of thy life. No words in the Bible were more true than these, for Karl Oskar. The Lord had also said to Adam that the earth would bring forth to him thorns and thistles. Hadn't he pulled up thistles in every field of this his stone kingdom until his back ached? The Bible's words were still in force, at least as far as the local fields were concerned.

It was rumored that rain had fallen in other places, in other parishes and counties. But here the earth was accursed.

Every evening Kristina read the "Prayer Against Persistent Drought" and sometimes he himself joined in. She was frightened by the lightning-fire which had burned down their meadow barn, and she believed the drought also was a chastisement from the Lord. Now she wished Karl Oskar would go to the dean and pray for absolution because he had blasphemed that time during the harvest; he must do it before they went to Holy Communion together again.

But he paid no heed to her admonition.

"Doesn't your conscience bother you?" she asked.

"Not because of that sin."

No. Karl Oskar would not turn to the dean: he had not committed murder, nor was he lying on his deathbed. What he had done in the field was done in sudden anger, which he had regretted, and God would by now have had time to forgive him such a small trespass and needn't plague man and beast with drought because of it. Nor was God so petty that He burned down the barn because of that small tuft of hay. One mustn't think the Highest One was an incendiary.

But Karl Oskar must know, retorted Kristina, that no one except the Omnipotent decided where lightning was to strike. And she continued urging: he ought to seek absolution before he prepared himself for his next Communion. No one except Dean Brusander could decide whether his sin was great or small. And they were on good terms with the dean, who commanded them both as frequent churchgoers.

But she could not persuade Karl Oskar to seek out the dean; he was so obstinate he would not unbend even for God. And as Kristina looked back over the years of their marriage, she wondered if she ever had managed to sway him. What he wanted to do, he did; what he didn't want to do was never done. His sister Lydia had said that her brother was difficult because of this stubbornness, but Kristina had never thought of him as being so before they married. Persistence was right for useful undertakings and good deeds. But Karl Oskar was equally stubborn in useless and foolish undertakings; large-nosed people were held to be stubborn.

"Your obstinacy is in your nose; that's why it is so large."

Until God gave him another nose he must use the old one, was Karl Oskar's answer. But he had noticed that it extended far enough to annoy some people.

Otherwise Kristina had no reason to complain of her husband. He seldom drank more brannvin than he could handle, and he could handle a great deal; she never had to drag a drink-fouled husband from Christmas parties, as did other wives. And there were married men who went to Ulrika of Vastergohl, the "Glad One," the most sought-after whore in Ljuder. To poor men she sold herself for twelve shillings or a quart of brannvin, but to homeowners her price was a whole riksdaler. In her youth Ulrika had been a beautiful woman, and she was not ugly yet. It was said that the churchwarden himself, Per Persson in Akerby, had frequented the whore in her better days. Karl Oskar would never degrade himself to such an extent that he would stir in other pots.

But Kristina worried because lately he had been so closed-up, and at last she asked him point-blank what was on his mind.

"Worries about living," he said. Where would food come from? And with more and more of them to feed.

Kristina was in her fifth month, soon they would be eight people in Korpamoen. The people increased, but not the land; the number of acres would never be more than seven.

Kristina did not like the reference to her pregnancy. "Leave the worries about the unborn to God."

"If I only could!"

"Do you think you are wiser than God?"

"No. But I don't think He would feed our children if we sat with our arms in our laps."

Her temper flared up and she exclaimed angrily: "Is God supposed to feed all children you make?"

"Kristina! What do you mean?"

"I mean you must not blame the Lord when you make your wife with child!"

He gazed at her. "But, my dearest—I have never denied my part in it."

She burst into tears. "You complain because we get to be more and more. Exactly as if it were my fault—because the lives come from me."

"I've never blamed you!"

"I don't want it! I've told you so! You mustn't think that!"

"I do not think anything."

"But now—when you walk about in silence, as if you accused me—what am I to believe?"

And she cried into her apron.

A pregnant woman was sensitive and easily hurt; he forgot it at times, and didn't watch his words.

He left her alone till she quieted, then he asked: How could she imagine that he disapproved of her? He kept to himself because he was depressed from worries, that was all. And how could she think that he reproached her for being pregnant again? He was not so unfair! She must realize how happy he was over the children she had borne him before. His children and his wife were his dearest possessions on earth. This he had shown her. She must have noticed, for example, how attached he was to Anna. And he would surely be as devoted to the new one as he was to the other three. But it was natural that he worried about food for the children in years of adversity and crop failure.

Kristina was drying her tears. "Do you mean that you like me as well as you used to?"

"You must know that I do!"

"Is it the truth you tell me, Karl Oskar?"

"Tell me the time I ever lied to you."

She could not. And he said they must remain friends, and stick together in adversity. For there was no other person in the world who would help them; they must help themselves.

Kristina realized she had acted foolishly; why she had behaved in such a way she didn't know; if you took exception, any word led to a quarrel. But she sensed that she did it from fear, fear of diminishing attention from him.

His assurances made her almost glad of their quarrel.

3

Karl Oskar went deeper into debt. This autumn also he went to Danjel Andreasson in Karragarde and asked to borrow fifty daler for the mortgage interest.

He wore a solemn expression when he returned. Kristina asked anxiously: "Did Uncle refuse you the money?"

"No. I got every penny I asked for."

"But why do you look so queer?"

"Something strange is going on in Karragarde."

"With Uncle Danjel?"

"Yes. Something has happened to him."

Karl Oskar had been startled today as he stepped over the threshold at Danjel Andreasson's. The house was full of paupers and loose people. Strangers sat at table with the house folk. There was Severius Pihl, a dishonorably discharged soldier, a notorious fighter and drunkard; the disabled maid, Sissa Svensdotter, the impoverished thief who now depended on the parish; but Karl Oskar had been most surprised to discover among these people Ulrika of Vastergohl, the old whore, as well as her illegitimate daughter. At first he thought that they must all, in their rounds of begging, have happened to reach the farm at the same time. But it came as a box on the ear when Danjel said that these people from now on would be living with him in Karragarde. Inga-Lena, his wife, confirmed it: they all lived there together.

Kristina burst out in loud laughter. "Are you telling April-fool jokes in October, Karl Oskar?"

"Do you think I lie?" he asked, a little hurt.

"You must have made up a story to see if you could fool me."

"It's the truth—all of it! Go to your uncle's house and see for yourself."

Now Kristina approached him and smelled his breath: had he perchance been drinking today, so that he didn't know what he was saying? Did he reek of brannvin?

"I've taken just two drinks the whole day."

"But you say Ulrika of Vasterghol, the whore, has moved in with my uncle?"

"He said so himself."

"And Aunt Inga-Lena, what was she doing?"

"They had been slaughtering, and she was boiling blood sausage for her guests."

"Did the Glad One eat, the old whore? Did my aunt boil sausage for her?"

"Yes. Go and ask yourself, if you don't believe me."

Now Kristina was truly concerned. What could all this mean? What had happened in Karragarde?

Karl Oskar continued: The strangest of all was the way Danjel acted when he handed over the fifty daler. When asked if they should count the interest as before, he had answered that he did not desire interest on the money. And when Karl Oskar asked for a delay in the interest on the old debt, Danjel had said that he would nevermore accept interest on loaned money. He said it twice, for clarity.

Now Kristina realized that something serious had happened to her uncle. Karl Oskar guessed that some mental disturbance must have affected him.

And not many days passed before rumors began to spread from Danjel Andreasson's farm. From house to house, from

village to village, the news was told: Ake Svensson's heresy,
supposed to be dead with himself more than fifty years ago,
had been revived by his sister's son in Karragarde.

V

AKE RETURNS FROM THE INSANE ASYLUM

1

Danjel Andreasson, at forty-four years of age, was the nearest surviving relative of the Akian founder. He was known as
a good-natured man, and until now his life had been quiet
and blameless. He had piously accepted the only right and
true faith, thus showing a sound religious concept. His home,
Karragarde, at one time sorely tainted by Akianism, had
many years ago been declared cleansed.

But one night in the fall of 1848 a strange happening took
place in Karragarde.

Before Danjel went to bed that night he was seized by an
undefinable anxiety, and to his wife Inga-Lena he expressed
apprehension about some approaching illness: at moments he
felt a queer dizziness. During the night he was awakened by
someone knocking heavily at the door and calling his name in
a loud voice. Thinking that maybe a fire had broken out, and
his help was needed, he hurried out of bed. When he opened
the door the room became illuminated by a brilliant light.
Two men stood outside. One of them was a youth dressed in
outmoded wadmal clothes and unknown to Danjel. But the
second man he recognized instantly from the altarpiece in the
church: it was the Saviour, Jesus Christ. Jesus carried a lantern in His hand, and it was this lantern that spread the
strangely clear illumination widely into the night. The
Saviour looked as Danjel had imagined Him. From His face
radiated such a strong light that Danjel could not look at it:
he had to drop his eyes.

The man in the wadmal coat at the side of the Saviour had
awakened Danjel, and now he called him again by name, say-

ing: "I am Ake Svensson, your mother's brother. I died young and came to my Saviour in heaven."

Danjel now saw that the man had the likeness of his uncle as described by old villagers. People were still alive who remembered Ake as he was before the sheriff fetched him to Danvik's asylum.

The Saviour studied Danjel with compassion, but remained silent.

Ake Svensson spoke again and said: "Your Saviour has awakened you this night that you may resume my work here on earth. The Spirit will tell you what you must do. Danjel, go out and complete my misssion! Your Saviour has called you!"

Twice, in a clear voice, Ake repeated this exhortation to his sister's son. Then the nocturnal visitors were gone, the light from Christ's lantern disappeared, and all was dark around Danjel.

He found himself on his knees at his threshold, praying, but quite calm. He had not been frightened by what he had seen and heard at his door, and kneeling there he was not conscious of anxiety. His breast was full of a peace which he had never before experienced.

He awakened his wife, Inga-Lena, and told her that the Saviour this night had visited his house in the company of Ake, his uncle who had died at Danvik's asylum. She thought he had had a dream. But he knew he had been awake the whole time. His ears had heard the knocks on the door when Ake called him by name, his eyes had seen the face of the Saviour. He could well describe the lantern which Christ had carried in His hand: it was in every detail identical with the one He carried in the picture above the church altar.

This was what had happened to Danjel Andreasson, and from that moment his life on earth changed.

Ake had spoken barely twenty words to Danjel, but he knew what he must do: the Spirit spoke in his heart. And after that night all his actions were dictated by the Spirit. Nevermore did he hesitate in his undertakings, nor worry about their outcome. Each time he felt in his heart that he was right. Christ had called him; he had become a follower of the Saviour, and from now on he would lead the same life here on earth as the apostles and the first Christians. He would preach Ake's teachings, which already were forgotten in the neighborhood. The Spirit guided him when he read the Bible, and moved his hand to those places which had commands for him: "Thy word is a lamp unto my feet, and a light upon my path." He had seen the light from Christ's lantern, he knew the path.

In that autumnal night when Danjel heard his name called, he was reborn into the world. Until he was forty-four years of age he had lived in the flesh; now began his life in the spirit.

And so he resumed the teachings of Ake. Every Sunday he gave Bible talks to his house folk—wife, children, and servants—and if some neighbor happened by, he was welcomed. He went to church every time it was Holy Communion, to enjoy the blessed sacrament. Even during his work he said his prayers—in the field, at plow or harrow, in the barn with the flail in his hand. He always bent his knees while praying. Sometimes he cried aloud during his prayers, which caused people near by to rush to him, thinking help was needed.

Danjel threw the farm's still on the scrap pile; not only did he discontinue the manufacture and sale of brannvin, he also stopped using alcoholic drinks, nor did he offer them in his home. He forbore swearing and the use of all profane language. Earlier he had sometimes been irritable and quickly angered—now his speech was always mild and gentle. Only about the clergy who had persecuted his uncle did he use hard words.

From now on Danjel considered all his possessions as gifts from God which, while they lasted, he must share with poorer brethren. He took into his house a few helpless creatures and gave them a permanent home in Karragarde, where they received both food and clothing. Two of them were the most notorious people in the parish, known for whoring, drunkenness, idleness, and general debauchery.

Danjel used no more bolts or locks in his house, but left all doors unlocked at night. Why would he need locks and latches when the Lord stood guard over his house? Could a weak lock, made by human hands, protect his abode better than the hand of the Omnipotent? Those who locked their doors did not trust in God; they committed the trespasses of doubt and disbelief, man's greatest sins.

To Danjel, as earlier to Ake, there were neither high nor low classes, neither exalted nor simple people—all were equal, equal as children in God's family. He discriminated only between those who continued to live in their old bodies and those who were reborn in Christ, between those who lived in the flesh and those who lived in the spirit.

After his rebirth he no longer shared his bed with his wife. Because Inga-Lena still lived in the flesh, they were no longer a true married couple. Those marriages where the mates lived in their old bodies were joined by the devil, and the same was true if only one of the couple was reborn. If Danjel now had sought his wife, he would have committed adultery. He therefore told her that they no longer could have marital relations.

They must also abstain because of future children. A clean offspring must be conceived without lust, therefore it must be conceived by sin-free, reborn parents. Danjel and Inga-Lena already had three children, born while they themselves still lived in the flesh, and he felt great anguish for the sake of these children. As they had not been conceived in a true marriage, they must be considered the result of adultery, he thought. But he prayed continually that his offspring might through God's grace be purified and accepted as clean.

Inga-Lena, the housewife of Karragarde, was in a difficult dilemma. She was devoted to her husband—next to God he was dearer to her than anyone. She lived only to serve him, and followed his will in everything: by nature she was irresolute, relying on him for decisions; he was the lord and master. After his conversion she still tried to please him but found it difficult to accept his new ideas, and the consequent changes in their lives. She would willingly share her loaf of bread with a hungry beggar who might come to the farm. But she was filled with sadness and anxiety when the number of house folk increased by four people whom her husband invited and whom the house must feed. And when she also must receive into her home Ulrika of Vastergohl, the most detested woman in the parish, she spoke to her husband with mild reproach. She wished to do naught against his will, nor say that he was wrong when he allowed Ulrika and her illegitimate daughter to live with them, but what would others think or say when he housed in their home the Glad One, the great whore herself? Danjel answered: We must obey God above man. Let that woman who is without sin come here and throw the first stone at Ulrika.

Inga-Lena was greatly disturbed, too, when her husband repeated the doings and actions of the Akians. Ake Svensson had aimed to establish a kingdom in which the Holy Ghost and not the King reigned, and where no one called anything his own, but all earthly possessions were common property. No wonder he had been sent to the insane asylum, where he had suffered a pitiful death after a few years—despite his being a young and hale person. (Though there were those who thought injustice had been done to him, who were convinced he had been tortured to death at Danvik.)

The fate of Åke had terrified all in the region, but no one was surprised; he who insisted that all were equal, and that they must hold their possessions in common and share them as brothers and sisters, such a one must come to an ill end; people were right in this.

Inga-Lena feared now that Danjel's path in his uncle's footsteps would lead to an equally horrible end. If you set yourself up against the ordinance of authority, you angered the clergy and came to no good.

But Danjel said that if you walked in Christ's bloody footsteps you were bound to cause anger and be persecuted by the church, the clergy, and worldly powers as well.

She began to worry about their belongings when her husband no longer locked the house. One night thieves went into the unlocked larder and stole pork and flour. Danjel said they kept a greater store of food than God allowed them, and that was why He had not prevented the theft. But Inga-Lena did not comprehend this. God Himself in His fifth commandment had forbidden theft. It was her responsibility that the food in the house should suffice for all; henceforth, unbeknownst to her husband, she locked the larder door in the evening.

But her conscience bothered her each time she disobeyed him. The Bible's words in Ephesians were clear and distinct: "For the husband is the head of the wife, even as Christ is the head of the church. . . . Therefore as the church is subject unto Christ, so let the wives be to their own husbands in every thing."

Inga-Lena, furthermore, had a feeling of being a defiled and unclean woman when her husband deserted the marital bed. She had disturbing and painful dreams during her lonely nights; she awakened, and called on God for advice and help. She confessed in her prayers that she was a woman of only poor understanding; her knowledge was insufficient to comprehend Ake's religion. She prayed God to enlighten her. Danjel prayed the same prayer.

And after a while the couple's prayers were heard: the Spirit came to Inga-Lena and she experienced her rebirth. She came to understand that she must obey her husband, not her own inadequate intelligence. Danjel was right in spiritual things, she had been wrong. And so their marriage became a true marriage. Danjel returned to the marital bed, and again knew his wife.

By now there was a small flock of Akians in Karragarde. The paupers who made their home on the farm, as well as a few of the neighbors, embraced the Akian teachings and saw in Danjel Andreasson a new Lord's apostle on earth.

But his wife Inga-Lena still committed, in secret every evening, the gross sin of doubt when she locked the farm's larder for the night.

2

The happenings in Karragarde were soon brought to the attention of Dean Brusander. It was said that people under pretext of devotion met at Danjel Andreasson's, where he preached the Akian faith—this heresy had again begun to spread its horrible poison in the parish.

Dean Brusander was a powerful clergyman who guarded the dignity and sanctity of his office well. Always he had maintained the purity of the evangelical-Lutheran church with unflagging zeal; never sparing himself, he watched over the flock God had entrusted to him, protecting it from heterodoxy. Now he sent promptly for the churchwarden, Per Persson of Akerby, who confirmed the story of the unlawful meetings in Karragarde. It was said throughout the parish that Ake Svensson had returned in the shape of his nephew. And Per Persson could affirm that Danjel used evil words about the dean, and called him a neglectful shepherd, because brannvin was distilled and sold in the parsonage.

Brusander was provoked that a parishioner should question his lawful right, shared by all the clergy who cultivated land. And on the King's estates too brannvin was distilled and sold, as well as on the Prince's manor at Backaskog. The farmer in Karragarde had therefore, through his criticism, committed a serious crime against the Crown. The sale and serving of brannvin in the parsonage was nowadays allowed only on weekdays; the drink was stimulating to laborers and servants after a day's toil. It was true that the well-known Dean Wieselgren in Vasterstad wanted to abolish brannvin altogether, and that in un-Christian hatred he persecuted his colleagues who only enjoyed their legal rights. Wieselgren in his blindness wanted to rob the peasants of their lawful trade; if they were not permitted to distill their grain to brannvin, the agriculture of the country would in a short time be ruined and the farmers impoverished. The price of grain would drop so low that the farmers would be bankrupt, which in turn would make the poor people more insolent; it would be difficult then to obtain servants and day laborers. Who would want to do day labor if a bushel of barley could be bought at six shillings?

Dean Brusander called Danjel Andreasson of Karragarde to appear at the parsonage, and in the presence of his assistant, Pastor Krusell, and the churchwardens of the parish, he questioned the farmer at length.

3

At this inquiry the assistant pastor made notes which were signed by the churchwardens as unbiased witnesses and deposited in the archives of the parish.

"Summoned homeowner Danjel Andreasson was first questioned briefly in religion by Dean Brusander; he showed satisfactory knowledge in the foundation and order of the salvation tenets. Questioned specifically, Danjel Andreasson admitted that at the present time several loose people maintained their residence in his house, to wit: court-martialed soldier Severius Pihl, disabled servant wench Sissa Svensdotter, unmarried female Ulrika of Vastergohl and her illegitimate daughter Elin. Ulrika being known since her youth for her lewd and immoral life, during which she had conceived four illegitimate children of whom three died in infancy. Danjel

Andreasson admitted that he fed and protected these people in his house.

"Questioned Dean Brusander: 'Is it true that in your house you conduct meetings with your housefolk and neighbors?'

"Answered Danjel Andreasson: 'It is true, Mr. Dean.'

"Asked Dean B.: 'What do you do at these meetings?'

"Answered Danjel A.: 'I explain the Bible word to my listeners.'

"Asked Dean B.: 'You admit then that you are practicing the office of the ministry?'

"Answered Danjel A.: 'I do what the ministers do not: I preach God's true word.'

"Asked Dean B.: 'Who has given you power to do this?'

"Answered Danjel A.: 'God's Spirit has given me that power in my heart.'

"Said Dean B.: 'You are seized by an evil spirit. No one is allowed to be minister unless called and ordained according to the church law. In the presence of these honest and trusted men I herewith command you, Danjel Andreasson, to forgo all ministering pretensions in the future!'

"Answered Danjel A.: 'You, Mr. Dean, have no power to forbid me this.'

"Said Dean B.: 'God has entrusted your soul to me. I am your spiritual authority. In all spiritual things you must obey me and no one else.'

"Answered Danjel A.: 'The Bible teaches that I must obey God before man. You are a man, Mr. Dean.'

"Said Dean B.: 'In Romans, Chapter 13, verse 2, the Bible says, "Whosoever therefore resisteth the power, resisteth the ordinance of God: and they that resist shall receive to themselves damnation." Do you not admit that my power is from God?'

"Answered Danjel A.: 'No, Mr. Dean.'

"Asked Dean B.: 'Do you refuse to obey law and order?'

"Answered Danjel A.: 'There is no law over the righteous.'

"Asked Dean B.: 'Are you obsessed by such religious vanity that you call yourself righteous?'

"Answered Danjel A.: 'I am possessed by God's Spirit. The guide for my conduct is the Bible and my conscience.'

"Asked Dean B.: 'Can you tell me: What is conscience?'

"Answered Danjel A.: 'He who is reborn will find out what conscience is. I hear that you are not reborn, Mr. Dean.'

"Said Dean B.: 'The devil, the soul-destroyer, is whispering his answers into your ears! Have you preached that no man has a right to keep possessions for himself alone?'

"Answered Danjel A.: 'Yes. You, Mr. Dean, should have preached the same, if you had preached God's true word.'

"Asked Dean B.: 'Do you accuse me of false teachings?'

"Answered Danjel A.: 'In Acts 4, verse 32, it is written of Christ's church: "And the multitude of them that believed were of one heart and of one soul: neither said any of them that ought of the things which he possessed was his own; but they had all things in common." You, Mr. Dean, have never preached Christianity for this parish.'

"Said Dean B.: 'You lean on some words in the Bible while you tear down others. You also have said that I am a negligent shepherd and lead my flock headlong to hell when they are drunk. Is it true you have said this at your unlawful meetings?'

"Answered Danjel A.: 'It is true, Mr. Dean.'

"Asked Dean B.: 'How can you defend this false testimony about your spiritual guide?'

"Answered Danjel A.: 'Is it not true, Mr. Dean, that you sell brannvin from the parsonage still?'

"Answered Dean B.: 'I use my possessions as I see fit. What right have you to deny me my income, to which I am lawfully entitled during my tenure of office?'

"Answered Danjel A.: 'People get drunk from your brannvin, Mr. Dean, and in their drunkenness they commit violence and adultery and other crimes against the Ten Commandments. Doesn't he who breaks God's command earn hell, Mr. Dean?'

"Said Dean B.: 'You are called in for questioning, not I.'

"Said Danjel A.: 'As long as I served the devil I received praise from you, Mr. Dean. Now when I serve God I am called in for questioning and receive blame and censure.'

"Said Dean B.: 'Your case is now clear, Danjel Andreasson. You have here admitted—in the presence of unbiased witnesses—that you have broken the law by practicing the ministry. You should now receive your punishment in civil court. But I wish your repentance, not your ruin. If you retract your heresy, and promise no longer to preach or to spread your false and ungodly doctrines, I will grant you grace and forgiveness for what you have done.'

"Answered Danjel A.: 'The grace belongs to God alone. Accordingly, you, Mr. Dean, have no grace to bestow on me, nor can I receive grace from you.'

"Said Dean B.: 'In the presence of these witnesses I have forbidden you to preach. If you still pursue your illegal activities you will be sued in civil court and be fined or sentenced to bread and water in prison. On a third offense you are liable to two years' exile.'

"Answered Danjel A.: 'Mr. Dean, you cannot exile me from the kingdom of God, not even for one moment.'

"In spite of strong admonishments from Dean Brusander, the interrogated Andreasson adhered to his heresy, and refused obstinately to retract any of his false doctrines. The dean consequently administered his first warning against the spreading of heretical doctrines tending to undermine church unity and threaten the order, welfare, and security of the country. The dean instructed the strayed one to remain at his calling and pursue lawful work. Andreasson was then allowed to leave."

4

This interrogation by Dean Brusander had extracted the truth from the very mouth of the questioned one himself.

Danjel Andreasson, a simple man of the rough peasantry, was blown up by self-righteousness and vanity, and in his heart was angry and malicious toward church and clergy. In his arguments he showed a certain cunning and shrewdness not uncommon among peasants. He harbored the most insane opinions concerning man's spiritual and temporal well-being. And his heresy was particularly dangerous because it attacked the bond of unity between authority and subjects; he incited disobedience of the holy church laws. And even foolish thoughts were easily accepted by an ignorant peasantry, as witnessed in the time of Ake Svensson. Danjel had as yet no proselytes besides a few loose and notorious persons; but well-thought-of people *might* be enticed into his false religious fold.

Brusander felt his high and holy duty: the only true religion must not be besmirched. No blemish must stain it. The evangelical-Lutheran religion—the faith of his fathers—must be preserved untarnished within his parish henceforth as hitherto. During the reign of the devout King Charles XI deviation from the pure religion had been punished by the gauntlet, and sometimes loss of life. Though to a later era this might seem severe, one must keep in mind that it concerned the Augsburg Confession and the purity of evangelical-Lutheran religion. At the present time Sweden had a milder monarch, her inhabitants lived in a tolerant and enlightened century, and milder means must be used against recalcitrant subjects. It would have boded ill for Danjel Andreasson in other times. The dean had thought to bring him to his senses through warnings and kind admonishments alone. He did not wish the poor man's ruin. He would pray God to enlighten his darkened senses. He wished to force the man to repentance, and free his parish from the abominable contagion of Akianism, without having to call in the secular authorities.

Dean Brusander duly warned his entrusted flock: three Sundays in succession he read from the pulpit the "wholesome ordinance" which prescribed fines, prison, or exile, for male or female, old or young, few or many, who gathered together in private houses under pretext of devotion. And all parishioners were warned about the farm Karragarde, which had once more become a forbidden meeting place.

After a short while it was again reported to the dean that Danjel Andreasson persisted in his unlawful Bible explanations. Brusander then resorted to the church ban: homeowner Danjel Andreasson of Karragärde and all his house folk were excluded from the Lord's Holy Communion and banished from the sacraments and fellowship of the church. It was the church's ban against the man who had returned from the insane asylum.

VI

"SUITABLE CHASTISEMENT"

1

The wagonloads of oak timbers began rolling toward Karlshamn in the autumn, but Aron of Nybacken himself went with his team. He said that he was so concerned about his little hand that he dared not let him out on long journeys. A door which had seemed open was shut in Robert's face. There were many closed gates on the road to America.

His master still had no confidence in him. And yet, ever since Robert began his service, he had been obedient and attentive and done all he had been asked to do. Only once during the whole summer had the master been impelled to discipline him: then, when he was told to fetch water for the horses, Aron had thought he didn't move fast enough or obey quickly enough, and he gave his little hand a kick in the groin. It could have been a harder kick; but as it was it hit his scrotum which swelled up and became sensitive. For a few days he walked slowly and with difficulty, and the maids poked fun at him and wondered what kind of sickness ailed the little man. But that was the only time Aron had been dissatisfied.

One morning about Michaelmas Robert was sent to clean a ditch in a field near the house. He loosed the stones with an iron bar and threw up the earth with a shovel; the ditch was deep, and when he bent down in his work his head was barely visible above the edge. After a few hours' work he felt hungry. Wouldn't it soon be time for breakfast? No call for food was heard, he became sweaty and thirsty, his back ached from the bending, the earth became heavier with each shovelful. The drudgery was heavy—interminable. He grew depressed, realizing he hadn't labored through half his service year; this period with Aron was endless. He saw all his future years as service years with farmers, and all were endless; everything in the world seemed to him wretched and endless. And he wondered if it were worth while to live, if he must remain a farmhand.

At last he put the shovel aside and lay down on his back in the bottom of the ditch, with his arms under his head, and watched the sailing clouds in the sky. During his herdboy days he used to lie like this, sometimes for half a day at a stretch; he enjoyed it now no less.

But in order to rest undisturbed by Aron it must look from the house as if he were still working.

Robert therefore took off his cap and hung it on the spade handle, which he held in such a position that the cap was visible above the ditch's edge; as he lay there he moved the spade a little now and then, back and forth, up and down, as one might imagine the head of a busy farmhand would move while he cleaned a ditch.

The notion scattered his depressing thoughts, he grew cheerful, almost gay: he could remain lying here, resting and enjoying himself, while from the farm his master kept an eye on his splendid little fellow, working in the ditch. Aron was satisfied and so was he. One could get a rest period now and then if one were clever.

Robert thoroughly enjoyed his rest. Above him was the expanse of the high heaven, stretched out like a blue sea of freedom over all the ditches on earth and over all farmhands who labored in them. He was so filled with joy that he began to whistle and sing.

This, however, he was soon to regret; a master would easily understand that all was not as it should be when one of his hands kept singing and whistling while he worked.

Suddenly the farmer from Nybacken appeared above him. "Are you playing dollhouse, my little fellow?"

Robert had not heard the master's approach. There he stood and looked down upon his servant, stretched out full length at the bottom of the ditch.

The boy jumped from the ditch in one leap, shovel in hand. He wanted to say that he had taken only five minutes' rest because breakfast was delayed. But he did not find time to say anything. Aron's jaws clenched, and he shook his fists in front of him. "So, you are loafing, you damned lazybones!"

And Robert encountered two gnarled clumps, the biggest hands he had ever seen on a human being. Terror-struck, he dropped the shovel and tried to escape; but he took only one step.

The master's right fist landed on his left ear. He bent like a jackknife from the blow and fell face down on a pile of dirt. His face was buried in the earth from the impact. The pain cut through his head, red stars sparkled before his eyes, the whole world around him whirled. He heard someone shriek; he did not recognize the voice—could it be his own?

He did not faint; the whole time his head was bursting with pain. He thought his skull was broken, split in two like a piece of wood under the chopping ax; he thought he couldn't live with his head in two pieces; he wanted to die to escape the pain. He had stopped shrieking and now he heard someone else shouting: the mistress stood on the stoop calling Aron to breakfast.

The master left, and the beaten farmhand rose slowly to a sitting position. His face dirt-covered, he tried to pick pieces of earth from his eyes. A sharp stone had scratched his nose; his mouth was full of dirt—he spat. He was still dizzy, the world around him still heaved, but the pain had abated a little.

Only once before had he received a box on the ear from the master—that day when he had entered the service. That time it was only a small box; today he had experienced a big box on the ear.

As soon as the pain from the blow had subsided, hunger returned. He stood up and attempted a few steps: the ground lay almost still under his feet; he followed his master home to breakfast.

Robert did not mention the box on the ear to anyone. He had been chastised, he was ashamed of it, it was nothing to talk about. He had been lazy in his work and punished for it. He had received what he had earned; there was nothing more to say. If a servant was lazy and disobedient, then his master had the right to discipline him. He knew this well, all others knew it, and if they hadn't known it, much less work would have been accomplished for the farmers. So it was according to the servant law which Dean Brusander reiterated at the yearly examinations: "If a servant is inclined to laziness" the master must correct this through "suitable chastisement." There was no other remedy.

Aron of Nybacken was his master, who according to God's ordinance had fatherly power over him. It was Aron's right and duty to administer suitable punishment; the little farm-hand had nothing to complain about. He was not wronged by anyone; he had been given the box on the ear according to God's ordinance.

He carried no hatred toward the master who had hit him. Once, when he was standing behind the barn, he had seen Aron beaten by his wife: she gave him a heavy blow across his neck with the byre besom; it was a big, rough besom, filled with cow dung, but Aron endured the blow without attempting to defend himself; he had looked frightened. Robert pitied his master rather than hated him.

When he went to bed that evening he could still hear a buzz in his ear from the hard blow; there was no sound around him, but there was a buzz in his ear. He lay there and listened to the humming sound and wondered what caused it. Outside in the yard as well as inside in the stable room complete silence reigned, but from inside his ear came a strange noise. He lay absolutely quiet and only listened within himself; he did not cause any sound; what could it be that buzzed and hummed so?

He let Arvid put his ear next to his own and listen. But Arvid couldn't hear anything, not a sound. It was inexplicable: Robert heard a sound which did not exist.

He awoke in the middle of the night. His left ear throbbed and ached intensely, and the noise inside had increased, and sounded by now like the roar of a storm. And his heartbeats were felt in his ear like the piercing of a pointed knife. He lay there on his bed and turned and twisted in agony. Something must have broken inside to cause the throbbing. He counted his heartbeats: the knife's edge cut and cut and cut in his ear; it felt like the sting in a fresh, open sensitive wound. The stings did not cease, the ache did not abate. He counted and waited and hoped, but it did not diminish. He was alone in the whole world with his pain and he did not know what to do about it. He began to moan; he didn't cry but he groaned quietly and at intervals. He folded his hands and prayed to God. He realized that the earache was in punishment for his laziness in the ditch, and he prayed for forgiveness. If God granted absolution He would also remove the earache. He had been a disloyal servant and he also remembered now that he had lately omitted reading "A Servant's Prayer." Tonight he recited it again in deep remorse: "Teach me to be faithful, humble, and devoted to my temporal lords. . . . Let me also find good and Christian masters who do not neglect or mistreat a poor servant, but keep me in love and patience. . . ."

After the prayer he lay in darkness and waited. But the ache did not leave him, it throbbed and throbbed and he felt the sting of the knife edge in his sensitive ear a hundred times each minute. God would not remove the ache, he fought his pain alone, and he was helpless and could do nothing to alleviate it. Deep inside his ear in a roaring storm his pain lived on.

He arose and lit the stable lantern. Arvid woke and wondered sleepily what had happened.

"I've a bad earache."

"The hell you have!"

"What shall I do?" Robert moaned pitifully.

The elder farmhand sat up in his bed and scratched his straggly hair. He cogitated.

The best remedy for earache was mother's milk, he said. But where would they get hold of a suckling woman who had some milk left in her breasts this time of night? The mistress had never even had a child; she was a dried-up woman. And the maids were virgins with unopened breasts.

But Arvid rose and brought forth his brannvin keg. "We'll try with brannvin on a wool wad."

He searched for a while in his servant chest and found some sheep's wool which he soaked in brannvin and put into his friend's aching ear.

"It will smart at first, but not for long."

The brannvin-soaked wool wad did smart so intensely that Robert almost pulled it out; he held his hands closed, cramp-like, so as not to shriek. And after a moment the throbbing pain abated, as Arvid had said it would. No enjoyment can be greater than diminishing pain. He understood now that God had sent Arvid to help him; luckily there had been some brannvin left in the keg. Soon he glided into sleep, but some pain remained, mingling with his dreams: his left ear was filled with stinging wasps, a whole swarm of them, and they crowded each other inside and stung, only stung. And his ear swelled up and became one big sensitive boil where all the wasps' stingers remained and hurt.

The pain in the ear was almost gone when Robert awakened the following morning, and within the next few days it disappeared altogether, but a thick, yellowish, malodorous fluid ran from his ear: it was the pain coming out. Something did remain inside, however: the strange sound which no one else could hear.

Yes, the buzzing and humming was still there; sometimes he heard it more loudly, sometimes lower, but he was always aware of it, inside the ear. It did not pain him, but he became tired and disheartened at hearing it follow him night and day. He put a bandage over his ear, he held his hand against it, he struck a piece of wool into it, but the sound remained; nothing could silence it.

One night as he lay there and listened to his own ear he realized what this strange sound meant which existed for him only: he was listening to the rumbling of a great water, it was the roar and din of the sea itself; it was the voice of the sea in his ear, calling him, and him alone: he was chosen. The ocean called him, urged him, and the hum in his ear became a word, a word which always followed him, through night and day, calling: Come!

Not yet could he come; all gates on the road still remained closed.

2

One Sunday morning Robert appeared unexpected at his parents' home in Korpamoen. He had not been to see them since he began his service, and Nils and Marta were pleased. Last spring when he threw his clothes into the brook and rode to the mill instead of going to Nybacken the boy had become the laughingstock of the neighborhood, but since they had not seen him the whole summer they would not mention that now. Marta thought he was thin and his cheekbones sharp, but when she asked him how he fared with Aron he gave no reply.

Robert stayed home the whole Sunday, and when, after

supper, he still remained in his chair, Nils wondered if he shouldn't go back to his place of service before bedtime. The boy answered he had come home without his master's permission; he would never again go back to Nybacken.

Nils and Marta exchanged perplexed blances. Nils said: "When one has received earnest money, one must stay to the end of the year."

Robert said that if they wished to send him back to Nybacken they must first bind him hand and foot and tie him onto a wagon like a beast on its way to slaughter.

The parents did not know what to do; the son remained on his chair and said nothing more.

The mother called Karl Oskar: his brother refused to return to service of his own will.

"Did you leave Aron without permission?" asked Karl Oskar.

Robert removed his jacket and showed his bare back. Broad red streaks extended from one side to the other; the skin was broken and it had been bleeding.

Marta let out a cry: "You've been flogged, poor child!"

"Who has beaten you?" asked his brother.

Robert told the story. Yesterday he was bringing home a wagonload of rutabagas and had to pass a narrow gate; there was a curve in the road just before he reached the gate, the mare was hard to hold and didn't obey the rein quickly enough, he wagon hit the gatepost and broke its shaft; he couldn't help it, he had held the reins as firmly as he could. But Aron had grabbed a fence stake and hit him many times across his back. The stake had protruding knots which tore into his flesh. His back had ached the whole night, and in the morning he had left for home without letting anyone know. Not long ago, too, Aron had given him so hard a box on his ear that it still rang and buzzed. He would never again return to Nybacken.

Karl Oskar inspected the red streaks on his brother's back. "You needn't return. No one in our family need accept flogging. We are as good as Aron."

"Do you think Aron will release him without trouble?" wondered the mother.

"He can do as he pleases. The boy does not go back."

But Nils was worried. If Robert left service without permission, Aron would have the right to send the sheriff after him, and according to the servant law Robert would then lose half his pay and must defray Aron's expenses. Wouldn't it be better to settle amicably?

"I'll go and speak to him," Karl Oskar said firmly. But it didn't sound as if he were thinking of reconciliation.

Robert regretted he had not returned home earlier and confided in his elder brother. Marta brought out some pork bile and covered her son's wounds with it.

His brother's bloody back was an insult to Karl Oskar and to the whole Nilsa family. Since the father was lame and broken-down, and not able to defend his younger son, it thus became his duty.

Karl Oskar picked up his cap and went straight to Nybacken. At a distance he caught sight of Aron, who stood at the cattle well and hauled up water. Karl Oskar approached the farm cautiously, looking around as he crossed the barnyard. No one was in sight. It seemed he might have luck on this visit.

Aron did not notice Karl Oskar until the visitor stood next to him; he was so surprised that he almost dropped the well bucket which he was just removing from the hook. As he looked the unexpected caller in the face he began to retreat around the well curb, at the same time looking about as if in search of help.

"Are you coming to take your brother's place? Then I'll have a real hand!" He attempted a weak smile, timidly.

Karl Oskar went up close to the farmer of Nybacken. Aron could not move, his back was already against the wall around the well; he acted as if he intended to call for help.

"You've beaten my brother. You bastard! Do you realize he's only fifteen?"

"He got a little chastisement, he was lazy and careless."

"Drawing blood is not a little chastisement. You'd better get yourself another hand to flog. You'll get none from my family."

"Your brother had better be here tomorrow morning! Otherwise the sheriff will get him."

"Come and get him yourself! You'll get a welcome in Korpamoen!"

Aron's face grew whiter.

Karl Oskar took another half step, forcing his antagonist still closer to the well curb. He looked quickly about: no one was in sight. Aron became panicky, dropped the pail, and was just going to call for help when Karl Oskar grabbed him by the neck, choking the words in his throat.

Karl Oskar pushed him slowly backward until he was extended across the well opening; Aron was a living lid over the well, he lay there kicking and struggling, terror-stricken. With Karl Oskar's viselike grip at his throat he was unable to produce any sound but puffs and grunts. He did not know if Karl Oskar intended to choke him to death, or drown him, or both, but he was convinced he was going to die.

And Karl Oskar let him think so for a few minutes.

He pressed the farmer's throat a suitably long time before relaxing his grip. Aron collapsed like an empty sack against the well wall. Karl Oskar warned him that it would be enough for this time. They would undoubtedly meet soon again; it happened sometimes while they hauled timber during the winter. They had met more than once in out-of-the-way places— they might meet again, far from people. They would then continue their conversation. For he was most anxious to meet alone anyone who laid hands on a member of his family. And any bastard who attacked a fifteen-year-old was easy to handle.

Then Karl Oskar turned about and went home to Korpamoen. Robert met him at the gate.

"You'll have no more trouble from Aron, that much I can promise."

Robert had never been intimate with Karl Oskar, who was ten years older. If anything, he had been a little afraid of his big brother. For the first time today they felt really close. Shyness prevented Robert from telling his brother what he wished to, but someday he would show Karl Oskar that he thought more of him than of any other person in the world.

3

Robert remained in Korpamoen; but as he was a deserter, no one knew whether he would be left in peace at home. Karl Oskar advised him to be prepared to hide in the woods when visitors came.

A few days went by and nothing happened. Karl Oskar had suggested that Aron come to Korpamoen and get Robert, but he didn't show up and Karl Oskar did not expect him; as he scanned the road now and then he feared other callers. And one evening before dusk as he was standing near the gate the bitch began barking. Karl Oskar looked down the village road: an open carriage was approaching the farm. Two men were sitting in the wagon, and one of them wore a cap with broad yellow bands which glittered at a distance.

Robert was at the sawhorse next to the woodpile and Karl Oskar ran to warn him. But as soon as the dog started barking his brother had thrown away the saw; he now saw Robert disappear into the wood lot near the byre.

The carriage stopped at the gate, and Karl Oskar went to meet his callers.

"Good day, Karl Oskar Nilsson."

The long, wide uniform coat hampered Sheriff Lonnegren in his movements; he almost tripped as he stepped down from the carriage. He told his man to tie the horse to the gatepost.

Lonnegren was an unusually tall man. At fairs his head could be seen above all others. He was as strong as he was tall. When he had to stop a fight, he often grabbed one combatant and used him as a weapon against the other. When he corrected some wrongdoer he invariably said: You scoundrel! This was his word of greeting in the community when he executed his office. If he spoke to a more hardened person he would say: You big scoundrel! And when he dealt with thieves and criminals: You damned scoundrel! Lonnegren was severe in his office, but folk were agreed that he was not a bad man.

"I'm looking for your brother, the farmhand Robert Nilsson," he said.

"He's not in this house," answered Karl Oskar.

"Where is he?"

"I don't know where he is at the moment."

Sheriff Lonnegren gave the farmer of Korpamoen a piercing look. Karl Oskar looked back equally firmly.

The sheriff ordered his man to look around the farm and see if he could find the deserter.

He continued: "Aron of Nybacken has asked the assistance of authorities in bringing your brother back to his service. I presume you know he left last Sunday morning?"

"He left because the farmer flogged him."

Lonnegren nodded: Aron had said that he had corrected his hand with suitable chastisement, as was the right of masters, according to paragraph 5 of the servant law. But this chastisement was intended to improve the servant: the boy ought to have accepted it in mild submission. It did not give him the right to desert.

"My brother has shown me his bloody back."

The sheriff gave Karl Oskar another searching look.

"You've met, then? Has he been here?"

"Yes, but he isn't here any longer."

"Is he close by?"

"I don't know how close he might be."

Karl Oskar tried to evade the truth without lying.

The sheriff stroked his chin in deep thought. From his coat pocket he pulled a large stamped paper which he now unfolded. According to paragraph 52 of the servant law, and Chapter 16, paragraph 7, of the land code, a master had the right to enforce the return of a deserted servant. In the name of the law he now asked Karl Oskar to divulge his brother's whereabouts.

"I am not responsible for my brother."

"The boy has once before tried to get away. It's a second offense."

The sheriff's man returned: the escaped one could not be found outside the house.

The sheriff's patience was coming to an end. "You are harboring the deserter, you scoundrel! Turn him over!"

Karl Oskar answered: According to the law he did not consider himself duty-bound to help the authorities apprehend his own brother. In any case, he would first like to see the paper concerning such duty.

The sheriff did not answer; this big-nosed peasant was not born on the porch, he knew his rights. And if it were up to him alone, the boy might well go. It was a most unpleasant task to hunt poor farmhands who evaded the servant law. But law was law and duty was duty; it was his business to see to it that the servant law was followed.

Karl Oskar watched the sheriff's face and became bolder. If the sheriff himself had a brother who had escaped from his master because of flogging, would he then report his brother for apprehension?

The sheriff shouted in answer: "If you cannot tell the truth, you might at least shut up, you scoundrel!"

But he looked up toward the sky for a moment, and Karl Oskar thought: What people said about him was true; if he hadn't been sheriff he might have been almost a good man.

Lonnegren turned his back on Karl Oskar and called his man to accompany him; they went into the house. The sheriff and his servant searched the main room, they went into the kitchen where Kristina stood with the frightened children hanging on to her skirts. They looked into the reserved room where Nils and Marta sat silent and immovable on their chairs, and felt the shame of the search; no sheriff had ever before been to this house. They went up the stepladder into the attic, where they felt in a pile of old clothes; the dust rose from the rags and the sheriff came down angry and coughing. They had looked through the house, and the search continued now through the barns. Lonnegren remained in the yard while his helper went through a heap of unwashed wool in the byre, ascended the hay loft and kicked here and there in the hay, went down into the cellar, through the wagon cover, the woodshed, and the outhouse.

The authorities had to leave, their errand unsuccessful. Karl Oskar escorted the sheriff to his carriage. When Loonegren was seated he said: "I'll get the rascal if he remains in this district. Do you hear me, Karl Oskar Nilsson? I'll catch up with your brother if he remains *in my district!*"

The young farmer in Korpamoen looked thoughtfully after the sheriff's departing carriage: he had got the implication; he understood.

4

Karl Oskar stayed up late that evening and waited for his brother. Toward midnight Robert knocked on the window and was admitted. He had been over in a neighbor's field, and had hidden in Jonas Petter's meadow barn the whole evening. The night frosts had set in, and he shivered and shook. There was still some fire on the hearth and Karl Oskar put on a pot and warmed milk for his brother.

The sheriff's statement, he said, must be interpreted to

mean that Robert need not worry about being returned to Nybacken if he stayed outside the sheriff's district. He could therefore not remain at home any longer. Kristina had suggested that he stay for some time with her parents in Duvemala. The parish of Algutsboda was outside Lonnegren's district. He could safely remain there until some other opening turned up; Kristina's parents needed a hand, they were both considerate and would treat him well, not on account of the relationship only. Few of the farmers hereabouts treated their help as badly as Aron in Nybacken.

Robert said he was glad to obey his brother and sister-in-law: early in the morning he would set out for Duvemala.

Still feeling cold after the many hours in Jonas Petter's windy barn, he moved closer to the hearth; across from him sat Karl Oskar and stirred the embers with the fire tongs. The brothers had seldom been together at home; Karl Oskar had been away in service while Robert grew up; they had been strangely foreign to each other until last Sunday, when Robert came home with his wounded back.

Robert was thinking: He had been a lazy and negligent farmhand; perhaps it was his inborn sinful nature which inclined him to idleness and disobedience. He had, according to the ordinances of God and man, received chastisement, and he was now a deserter, hunted by the sheriff. But he was no longer afraid of anything in this world because he had a big, protective brother. He need keep no secrets from this brother. Now as he sat here alone with him in the night was the right moment. Now it must out, now it must be said, what he ought to have said long ago, what he regretted not having said last spring.

He could hear the echo of Aron's hard box in his ear, that eternal hum, the sound of that water which covered three-quarters of the globe's surface, the great sea's message to him, the ocean's command: Come!

It was dark in the room, only a small section near the fireplace was lighted by the flickering embers. Now it must be said, now when they sat here together, as intimate brothers.

Robert did not look up as he began: "You've been good to me, Karl Oskar. I want to ask something of you."

"Yes? If I can give it to you."

"I would like to get my inheritance from the farm. I intend to go to North America."

He had managed it, he had spoken, it was done. He inhaled deeply, then he waited.

A few minutes passed and Karl Oskar had not yet answered. He had heard big words from his brother, he had heard the fifteen-year-old speak as a grown man, he had heard him say boldly, challengingly, like a man: I intend to move to North America. But he did not answer.

Several more minutes elapsed and still nothing was said between the brothers. The elder kept silent, the younger one waited for him to speak. The grandfather's clock in the corner creaked and snapped, the dying embers crackled on the hearth. And in Robert's ear was heard the humming, roaring sound of the great water, challenging him to come and sail upon it.

Rays from the fire lit up Karl Oskar's face. The younger brother sat close to the hearth and stared into the glowing ashes; he dared not look at his brother just now.

What could he expect? He knew in advance what he was going to hear. Through his one healthy ear he would hear his brother speak of childish ideas, notions of a fifteen-year-old. What possesses you, Robert? You know very well, my little brother, that you cannot handle your inheritance before you are of age, before you are twenty-one. And you think a boy like you can travel to the other end of the world? Much is still lacking in your head; you must stay at home and eat many loaves of bread before you can leave the country. You must ripen in your notions, my little brother. Your big brother knows more about the world than you. Listen now to what he has to say, this your elder, wiser brother.

But the surprising thing was that Robert couldn't hear his brother say anything at all. Karl Oskar sat with the fire tongs in his hands, his elbows on his knees, and poked in the embers and kept silent. Robert dared not even look toward his face. Had his tongue become paralyzed from shock when he heard his brother say: I intend to go to North America?

Robert began again: "You were startled, Karl Oskar . . . ?"

"Ye-es."

"I understand."

"Never before in all my life have I been so startled!"

Now Karl Oskar raised his head and looked at his brother

with a broad smile. "Because—I could never in the world have guessed that you had the same thoughts as I!"

"You too—Karl Oskar?"

"Yes. Those ideas have been my own lately. But I haven't mentioned a word to anyone except Kristina."

What was this that Robert's healthy ear heard tonight? Weren't Karl Oskar's words a hearing-illusion, like the storm of the sea in the other ear?

Had two brothers ever before so surprised each other as Karl Oskar and Robert did this night, sitting together round the dying embers of the fire? When before had two brothers so promptly agreed in a great, life-important decision, as these two now did—before the embers on the hearth had even blackened?

Karl Oskar said: Robert need not move alone; he would have the company of his brother and sister-in-law and their children, he would have the company of all who were young on the farm.

The hum in Robert's ear was intense and persistent tonight, louder than usual. Now he could answer "Yes!" to the message and the challenge in his sick ear: I come!

He had opened his first gate on the road to America.

VII

ABOUT A WHEAT FIELD AND A BOWL OF BARLEY PORRIDGE

1

The first ships have already crossed the ocean, bearing emigrants away from the land.

There is a stir in peasant communities which have been the home of unchangeableness itself for thousands of years. To the earth folk, seeing their plots diminish while their offspring increase, tidings have come of a vast land on another continent where fertile soil was to be had almost for the taking by all who wished to come and till it. Into old gray cottages in tranquil hamlets where food is scarce for folk living according to inherited customs and traditions, a new restlessness is creeping over the threshold. Rumors are spread, news is shared, information is carried from neighbor to neighbor, through vales and valleys, through parishes and counties. These germs of unrest are like seeds scattered by the wind: one takes root somewhere deep in a man's soul and begins its growth unknown to others; the sowing has been done in secret, thus the sprouting surprises neighbors and friends.

At first the movement is slow and groping. The only evidence of this new land is supplied by pictures and rumors. None in the home communities had seen or explored it. And the unknown ocean is forbidding. All that is unknown is uncertain—the home community is familiar and safe. Argument is rife, for and against; some hesitate, some dare; the daring stand against the hesitating, men against women, youth against age. The cautious and the suspicious always have their objections: *For sure,* we know nothing. . . .

Only the bold and enterprising have sufficient courage: they are the instruments which stir up the tranquil hamlets and shake the order of unchangeableness.

These separate from the multitude and fill a few small ships —a trickle here and there starts the running stream which in due time swells to a mighty river.

2

Karl Oskar Nilsson had seen a picture. He had called one day on the churchwarden, Per Persson in Akerby, and had borrowed a newspaper; there he had seen the picture.

That same day, after he came home, he plowed his rye stubble. He drove an ox and a cow; he had been forced to sell one ox, so now he hitched the cow under the yoke; the two beasts made a poor and uneven team. From time immemorial farmers had driven oxen—he felt ashamed to drive a cow along the roads, it was in some way degrading. And he felt sorry for his cow, who had to pull the plow as well as to give milk. The pull cow was with calf also, he could see the calf stir in her. She walked heavily in the furrow, her udder already so swollen she moved her hind legs with difficulty. The team dragged at a snail's pace across the field because of the poor cow. Karl Oskar had not the heart to prod an animal who had to carry a calf as well as drag a plow.

God was hard on the people, and the people were hard on the animals. He suffered because he must use the poor cow, but he couldn't pull the plow himself, and he must plow the field lest his children be without bread next year. His children, too, were innocent beings. But according to God's world order, which he had never been able to understand despite much thought, the innocent must suffer with the guilty. Drought and crop failure hit the righteous and the unrighteous alike.

Suddenly the plow hit an earth-bound stone which threw it from the furrow. Karl Oskar looked closer and saw that part of the plow remained in the ground: the wooden plowshare was broken, split in two.

He unhitched the team and went home. He knew enough about carpentry to make a new plowshare, but he did not go to the workbench. Instead, he went inside the house and sat down. It was the middle of the day and Kristina was surprised: was he already back from the field? He answered that he had broken the plow; it was a damned earth-bound stone; all the fields round here were damned.

He wouldn't curse and carry on so because of some such small mishap, she thought; it wasn't like him. And, she added in her thoughts, neither was it like him to sit here inside in the middle of the day, and neglect his work.

Karl Oskar looked out through the window at the unplowed rye stubble; his brow wrinkled in discouragement. After a time he picked up the paper he had brought from the churchwarden's. It was borrowed property, and he wiped his fingers on his trousers before he touched it; he handled the sheet carefully, as if it had been a valuable deed. Then his eyes fell on the picture: "A Wheat Field in North America."

It was a field at harvest-time, and the crop was still standing in shocks. An even field was visible, an endless field without borders or fences. The wheat field had no end at the horizon, it stretched beyond the place where sky met the earth. Not a single stone or heap of stones, no hillock or knoll was visible on this whole wide field of wheat stubble. It lay even and smooth as the floor boards of his own cottage. And in this field shock stood by shock so close they almost touched each other, so close a rick could hardly pass between them. The strong sheaves rose from the shocks, spreading out their long, swollen, full-developed heads of wheat, like golden crowns. A powerful, strong-grown seed was shocked on this field. Every head of wheat was like a mighty blossom, every straw like a sapling, every sheaf like a shrub.

From a clear sky the sun shone down on this multitude of golden grain. The sun shown down on a fertile field, a field to which had been given grain and kernel. The shocks were as innumerable as the billows on the sea; here surged a sea of golden grain, a tremendous granary of endless dimensions. It was the fruit of the earth that he saw here, an unmeasurable quantity of bread for man: "A Wheat Field in North America."

A story could be invented, people's word could be inaccurate, a description could be imaginary. But a picture could not be false, a picture could not lie. It could only show things as they were. What he saw must be somewhere before it could be pictured; what his eyes beheld was not illusion: this field of wheat existed. This ground without stones and hillocks was somewhere in the world. These potent sheaves, these golden heads of wheat, had grown; no one could step forward and deny it. Everything he saw in this picture, all this splendor to a farmer's eye, it existed, it *was* somewhere—in another world, in the New World.

Karl Oskar Nilsson, owner of seven stony acres in stone-country Korpamoen, sat quietly for long, his eyes lingering upon the picture. His mind's eye reveled in this grandeur. He held up the paper reverently before him, as if he were sitting on a church bench of a Sunday, following the hymn with the psalmbook in his hand.

It was in the Old World that God once had cursed the soil because of man; in the New World the ground still was blessed.

3

A few words were printed under the picture: "It has been said that work-willing farmers have great prospects of future success in the United States."

It happened the day when Karl Oskar plowed his rye stubble and broke the plowshare. That was the beginning; then it went on through many days and—as he lay awake—through the nights.

He wasn't actually slow when it came to making up his mind; but this was the greatest decision of his life, and more than one day was needed for it; it must be made with "common sense and ripe consideration," as is stated in bills of sale and other important documents. He needed a few weeks to think it over.

So far he had shown the picture of the North American wheat field only to Kristina, and she had looked at it casually. She could not know that her husband carried that picture in his mind wherever he went.

Through the long autumn evenings they sat in front of the fire, busy with their indoor activities. Karl Oskar whittled ax handles and wooden teeth for the rakes, and Kristina carded wool and spun flax. At last, one evening after the children had gone to sleep and it was quiet in the room, he began to talk. In advance he had thought over what he should say, and in his mind he had fought all the obstacles and excuses his wife might make.

As for himself, he had decided on the move and now he would like to hear what she thought of it.

She asked first: "Are you making fun of me?"

What was she to think? Here he sat and suddenly announced that he intended to sell his farm, and all he owned. Then with his whole family—a wife and three children and a fourth not yet born—he would move away; not to another village or parish, nor to another place in this country, or to any country on this continent. But to a new continent! He might just as well have stretched it a little further, it would have made no difference to her had he announced that he intended to move them all to the moon; he must be jesting with her.

But as he continued to talk, she realized he spoke in earnest. This new idea was exactly like Karl Oskar, like no one else. He never let well enough alone, he was not satisfied with what others considered sufficient. He was never satisfied with anything in this world; he reached for the impossible, the little-known. He had told her once before he would sell Korpamoen; then he wanted to be a timberman. Another time it had been a horse trader, and again, enlistment as a soldier. And when he decided to move, of course nothing less than North America would do—the other end of the world! If he had been satisfied with less he would not have been Karl Oskar.

But now Kristina must answer with innermost sincerity and let him know what she felt in her heart. So they talked, and exchanged their opinions, evening after evening, while the crackling fire alone interrupted their conversation and at times was even louder than they.

Why did Karl Oskar want to move?

For four years now they had lived in Korpamoen, and today they were several hundred riksdaler poorer than when they started. Four years they had spilled the strength of their youth here, to no purpose. If they remained they would have to continue struggling and slaving until they could move neither hand nor foot, until they finally sat there, worn out, worked out, limp and broken. No one would then thank them for having ruined themselves for no earthly good. They could mirror themselves in his father, who sat crippled in his room. In this place they had nothing more to look forward to than the reserved room; it would be ready for them one day, when they were able-bodied no more, and from then on they would sit there, like his father and mother now, and reproach themselves all through their old age; health and strength would be gone, but from all the work through all the years they would have naught to show but the reserved room with its meager bread.

However much they struggled and toiled, they could never improve their situation here in Korpamoen.

He didn't know much about conditions in the United States, but he did know that once there he would be given, for next to nothing, fertile, stone-free soil which was now only waiting for the plowshare. Things which he had no money to purchase here could be obtained for very little in North America. They were both of them strong and healthy and accustomed to hard work, and that was all that they need bring along: their ability to work; it was all America asked of them. Perhaps they must face as much drudgery as here, but they would do it in another spirit, with another hope, another joy. Because the great difference between the two countries was this: *In America they could improve their lot through their own work.*

He for his part was weary of the struggle which led no-where. Nonetheless he could continue his work with a happy heart if he believed he could improve the situation for himself and his. People liked to fight for a goal, at least while still young, as they both were. What else was there to live for? But one day their children would be grown and shifting for themselves, and what sort of future awaited them here? One child would inherit the farm, but what about the others? They would have to work as hired farmhands or become squatters. No third choice existed. There were already so many hired hands that they competed in offering their services to farmers; there were too many cottagers already, soon every opening in the forest would have its rotten, rickety shack with the black earth for floor. The people in these huts seldom had meat with their bread—and many days no bread. Karl Oskar and Kristina did not want their children to become hired farm-hands or crofters; but they could do nothing better for them unless they took them from this impoverished place. If they felt responsibility for their children, they must move away.

On one point all information from North America agreed: the people had in every way more liberty in that country. The four classes were long ago abolished there, they had no king who sat on a throne and drew a high salary. The people themselves elected a President who could be thrown from office if they didn't like him. They had no high officials who annoyed the people, no sheriff who came and took the farm-ers' belongings. And at the community meeting everyone spoke as freely as his neighbor, for all had equal rights.

If he now sold his farm with everything on it, chattels and kine included, Karl Oskar would have enough money to pay the transportation for all of them with some small part left over for the settling in the new country.

He had long turned it over in his mind, thought about it, weighed arguments for and against, but this conviction re-mained with him: a farm couple still in their youth, hale and hearty, could undertake nothing wiser than to emigrate to the United States of America.

Why Kristina wanted to remain at home:

Karl Oskar had drawn a beautiful and sanguine picture. If Kristina could believe it all as he painted it for her, she would not for one moment hesitate to follow him.

But she was afraid it might turn out to be a wild-goose chase. Her husband believed all he heard and saw about America. But who could guarantee its truth? What did they have to rely on? Who had promised them tillable soil in the United States? Those who ruled over there had not written him a letter or given him a promise. He had no deed to a piece of land that would await them on arrival. One taking such a journey needed written words and agreements before starting.

They had never met a single person who had been to North America; they knew of no one who had set foot in that country, no one who could tell them what the land was like. If a reliable human being who had seen the country with his own eyes had advised emigration, that would be different. In the printed words of newspapers and books she had no confidence.

If moving to North America was so advisable for young farm folk, then there must be some who had already done so. But they knew no such folk. He could not mention the name of a single farmer—young or old—who had emigrated with wife and children; the wisdom of such a move existed only in his head.

He had also forgotten to mention the fact that they must sail on a fragile ship across the ocean; he had said nothing about the dangerous voyage. How often had they heard about ships wrecked and sunk? No one knew if they would ever reach America alive. Even if exposing themselves to all these dangers were advisable, had they the right to venture the lives of their children on a voyage which wasn't necessary, which they weren't forced to undertake? The children were too young to consult, and perhaps they would rather remain at home, even as squatters, than be pulled down into the depth of the ocean; perhaps it were better to earn one's bread as a farmhand, and live, than to be a corpse on the bottom of the sea, eaten by whales and other sea-faring monsters.

Karl Oskar wanted to emigrate because he felt responsibility for his children; Kristina wanted to remain at home for the same reason.

And what did he know about the children's lot in the foreign country? Had someone there written him that Anna would become a lady, or that Johan would be a gentleman of leisure?

He hadn't mentioned, either, that they must separate from their parents, brothers and sisters, relatives and friends—in short, all those they knew. Had he realized they would come to places where every human being they met was a stranger? They might have to live in communities where people were ill-natured and cruel; they were to live in a land where they would be unable to speak one word of the language, unable to ask a single soul for a drink of water if they needed it; where they might have to die without their tongues being able to cry for help. In such a land they would wander about like changelings, alien and lost. Had he never thought that their life might be lonely and bleak?

If she moved so far away she might never be able to return home; she might never see her nearest and dearest again; ever meet parents, brothers and sisters. At once she would lose them all, and even though they lived they would be dead to her; they would be alive and yet dead.

True enough, things had gone backwards for them and they had had bad luck. But it might soon change, they might have a good year, they might have good fortune. At least they had the necessary food each day, and even though—as it looked for the moment—they might have to starve a bit this winter, they would most likely eat so much the better next year. They weren't dressed in silk and satin, of course, but at least they were able to cover their bodies and keep their children warm. Surely they would gain their sufficiency at home in future as they had in the past, as other people did.

All wise and thoughtful men whose advice he might seek would answer him as she had.

Kristina wanted to remain at home.

4

Through many autumnal evenings, while busy with their respective handiwork before the fire, the husband and wife in Korpamoen exchanged their divergent views on this decision which would determine their future. Karl Oskar held out the prospect of new advantages and possibilities through emigration; Kristina saw only drawbacks. When she came to the end of her objections, she always had this argument to fall back on: "If only someone we know had emigrated before. But none in these parts has ever gone."

His answer was always the same: "Let us be the first; someone must be first, in everything."

"And you're willing to shoulder the responsibility?"

"Yes. Someone must be responsible, in all undertakings."

She knew her husband by now: he had never relinquished what once he had decided upon, and hitherto he had always had his will, defying her and his parents. But this time he must fall in with her; this time she would not give in; this time he must change his mind.

She spoke to Nils and Marta: they must help her to dissuade Karl Oskar from this dangerous project.

But the parents only felt sorry for their foolhardy son and could give his wife no assistance. Nils said: Ever since Karl Oskar was able to button up his trousers alone in the outhouse, he had never asked advice or help from his parents. He would persist even more stubbornly if his father and mother tried to influence him.

Kristina began to realize that this time more than ever Karl Oskar knew what he wanted. And so did she.

5

After the drought and crop failure came winter now, and famine. The summer had been short, had died in its youth; the winter would last so much longer with its starvation.

The sheriff's carriage was seen more often on the roads. His errands concerned the poorest farms, and the carriage remained long at the gates: The sheriff's horses were seldom in their stalls this winter: they were tied to gateposts, waiting for their master, who had much to do inside the houses; the horses were covered by blankets but still cold: they had to wait so long.

> "Hurry up and hide your mittens!
> The sheriff comes to take each pittance."

Even before the snow had set in, little children could be seen along the roads, pale, with sunken cheeks, their running noses blue. Once arrived at a farm, they didn't go to the main entrance; they went to the refuse pile near the kitchen door, where they remained awhile, scratching in the debris, searching. Then they went inside the house but stayed close to the door. The boys bowed, the girls would curtsy. With their forefingers they would try to dry their noses; then they would stand there, in the corner near the door, silent, timid.

They had no errand. They had already brought their message to anyone who looked closely: the mute testimony of hunger.

Parents sent their children begging, ashamed to be seen themselves. To the small ones, begging was no shame. For wretched, starving children begging was a natural occupation, the only one they were able to perform, their only help.

Perhaps some time might elapse before anyone in the house paid notice to the unknown children, huddling in their corner at the door. Perhaps the house folk sat at table; then the children waited until all had eaten, inhaling the smell of food, the savory odor of boiled potatoes, beef soup, fried pork. They stood there watching, their eyes growing big, their nostrils extended. The longer the meal lasted, the bigger grew their nostrils, and sometimes it happened, when they had stood there a long time, smelling the food, that one of them might faint and fall to the floor.

At length they would be spoken to, then they would ask if they might pick up the herring heads and beef bones which they had seen outside on the refuse pile. The bones could be crushed to get the marrow which their mother would boil to soup. And if there was something for the refuse pile in the house, might they have it? It could be used at home. Father and Mother had taught them what to say.

The parents had told them not to ask too much. They must beg for such as the people in the house had no use for themselves; they must not boldly ask for bread. For he who asked least often obtained most. But if they sometimes happened to receive a slice of bread, they would gulp it immediately; Father and Mother must never know.

The children trudged along, sucking their salt herring heads, dragging their bundles of clean-gnawed bones. They went to the next farm, searched the next refuse pile; no one snubbed them when they came inside and asked for herring heads which they saw glittering outside.

The small children were famine's pure witnesses. No one had the heart to hurl at them the word which adults feared: Shame!

Each one was supposed to beg in the parish where he lived. But those who felt ashamed would rather go to distant parishes, would rather beg from unknown people. The hunger tore and dug in stomach and bowels, but the humiliation of begging dug itself into the crevices of the soul.

Even older persons walked along the roads, big, full-grown men who carried on their backs brooms, brushes, baskets, or wooden vessels which they offered for sale. They pursued an honest calling, no one could accuse them of begging, but if they were told in some house that no trade would take place, they still remained sitting. They kept their errand secret under the burden on their backs but after sitting for a while it would escape: Give me a piece of bread! I'm too weak to go farther. It smarted deep in the soul of many a wanderer before those words escaped. Therefore the pale children were sent upon the roads.

6

Kristina baked famine bread; when the rye flour did not suffice she added chaff, beechnuts, heather seed, and dried berries of the mountain ash. She also tried to grind acorns and mix them in the dough, but such bread caused constipation and the bowels would not move for many days. She boiled an edible porridge from hazelnut kernels, and used it instead of the clear rye porridge which they had to do without this winter. No real nourishment was found, though, in famine food: sprouts, seeds, nuts, and other products from the wastelands did fill the stomach but gave no lasting satisfaction. One left the table because the meal was over, not because one was satisfied. And however much they stretched and added, all the bins and foodboxes would be empty long before the next crop was ripe.

In the middle of the winter the time was up for Kristina,

and she bore a son. They were now eight people in Korpamoen.

Owing to the meager fare this winter the mother had not sufficient milk for the newborn; her breasts were dry long before he was satisfied, and a suckling could not stand the bitter milk from their starved cows. This was a bad winter for a new arrival into the world. Kristina must now choose the most nourishing pieces for herself, in order to give milk to the little one. But the other children needed food too; she noticed that Anna, the eldest, had fallen off and grown very thin. Kristina felt as if she stole food from three of her children to give to the fourth.

The newborn was to be given the name Anders Harald, and was to be called Harald. But whom should they ask to carry him at the baptism? When Kristina wished as godparents her relatives in Karragarde, Danjel and Inga-Lena, this caused great consternation in Nils and Marta: Danjel was preaching the heresy of Ake Svensson, and the dean had excluded him from the Lord's Supper because of his unlawful Bible explanations. This impious man was not to carry their grandchild to his baptism.

Karragarde had once more a bad reputation. Kristina did not understand how her uncle could take loose, bad people into his home, but she had known Danjel since she was a little girl, and he had always been good to her. Nor had he done harm to any other person; she knew of no man more kind than he. So she thought that the dean had done him a great injustice: only the greatest sinners were excluded from the Lord's Supper table. Ulrika of Vastergohl had long been forbidden the body and blood of Christ, and it was only right that one who for gain lay on her back with any man should be forbidden to kneel with honest people at the altar. But Uncle Danjel had neither whored nor murdered, neither defrauded nor stolen. In Ljunder Parish there were many much greater sinners who enjoyed the holy sacraments. He was mistaken in spiritual things, but he did not deserve to be pointed out and avoided as a robber and evildoer. Kristina wanted to show all people that she considered her uncle an honest man —and therefore she wished to invite him to be godfather to her newborn son.

Marta asked: Was she prepared to leave her innocent child

to be carried to baptism by a man possessed of the Evil Spirit? Was she willing to hand over her own offspring to the devil?

Danjel had said that he no longer accepted interest on money which he lent, and from this Karl Oskar deduced his wits were failing; the peasant of Karragarde had been stricken by a disturbance of his senses when he embraced Ake's teachings. But no one should be punished because of illness, even though it were illness of the mind. The dean therefore had no right to exclude Danjel from gatherings of Christian people, and give a bad name to his home, for anyone who passed through the gate of his farm, now, was almost considered eternally lost. It was foolish of Danjel to gather whores and drunkards into his house, but God would hardly punish him because he fed and protected paupers.

Karl Oskar agreed with Kristina; they would show the dean what they thought of Danjel, and invite him to godfather their little one. Karl Oskar himself bore the invitation to Karragarde.

He returned home disappointed; Danjel had said he was excluded from christenings as well as communion; he could be neither godfather nor witness to a baptism in the church; he was forbidden to carry their child to its christening.

Kristina was downcast, but Karl Oskar was angry at the dean who prevented them from choosing godparents for their own child. He felt a strong desire to go and tell the dean that he interfered too much. But Brusander was his pastor, and for the sake of one's salvation one should not be on bad terms with one's spiritual guide. This much, though, he was sure of: in North America, no minister had power to prevent any person from carrying a child to Christian baptism.

Instead, they now asked their neighbors in Hasteback, Jonas Petter and his wife Brita-Stafva, to be godparents for little Harald. No one else was invited to the christening ale, except Karl Oskar's sister Lydia, who served as maid in Krakesjo.

Nor was there much from which to prepare a feast this winter. Kristina cooked the christening porridge from some barley grains which she had hidden away in a small sack for this very day, and she had also a little butter and sugar to put into the porringer. Her three children stood around her as she poured out the pot. It was a long time since the little ones had seen such food in the house, food with such odor. Kristina poured the porridge into a large earthen bowl, not to be touched until the godparents returned from church with the newly christened one; she put the bowl in the cellar to cool off.

Karl Oskar and Kristina attended to the chores in the byre while Jonas Petter and Brita-Stafva were at church. The children were alone inside.

When the parents came in again they missed Anna. They started to look for her, inside and outside the house, but they were unable to find her. Nils and Marta did not know where she had gone; she was four years old, and able to go alone to the neighbors, but she never left the farm without permission.

Karl Oskar was greatly disturbed; what could have happened to the child? She was as dear to him as his own eyes, his constant comrade at work, keeping him company everywhere. Only today he had promised to take her to the shoemaker and have her feet measured for a pair of shoes; her old ones were entirely worn out. This she could not have forgotten; so much the stranger that she had disappeared shortly before they were to leave.

They looked in vain for the child in the wood lot, and the father was about to go to the neighbors to inquire when Kristina came running and said that Anna was in the cellar; she had passed by, had heard a faint crying, and had opened the door.

Anna lay stretched out on the floor of the cellar. She cried as if with pain. Next to her on the floor stood the earthen bowl which Kristina had put there a few hours earlier to cool off; at that time it was filled to the brim with barley porridge, now only a third was left.

The little girl was carried inside the house and put to bed. Tearfully, she asked her parents' forgiveness for what she had done. She had been unable to forget the bowl of porridge which she had seen and smelled in the kitchen; she was so hungry for the porridge. She had seen her mother put it away in the cellar; she could not resist her desire to steal down there and look at it. At first she had only wished to smell it, then she had wanted to taste it a little—so little that no one would notice. She found a spoon and began to eat. And once she had started eating, she was unable to stop. Never had she tasted anything so delicious; the more she ate, the more she wanted; each spoonful tasted better—she could not stop until most of the porridge was gone. Then she became afraid, she dared not go back into the house, she dared not show herself after her disobedience. She remained in the cellar, and after a while she was seized by fierce pain in her stomach.

Anna had eaten herself sick on the barley porridge; it was too strong a fare for her after the famine food of the winter. Her stomach swelled up like a drum, firm and expanded. She let out piercing shrieks as the pain increased.

Berta of Idemo was sent for. She was accustomed to relieve stomachache with the heat from woolen clothes, and now she laid a thick bandage of warmed woolen stockings around the waist of the child. She also wished to administer mare's milk for internal relief, and Lydia ran to Krakesjo, where a mare had recently foaled; she returned with a quart of milk from the mare and Anna was made to drink this.

But nothing eased the suffering of the child. Berta said the barley grains had swelled in the bowels of the little girl to twice their original size, thus causing something to burst. She could not take responsibility for healing such damage.

Anna cried loudly and asked someone to help as the pain grew agonizing. Again and again she asked her parents' forgiveness for having disobeyed: she had known that no one should touch the porridge before evening when the guests returned.

During the night she became delirious at intervals. Berta said that if she didn't improve before morning, God might fetch the child home; she wanted to prepare the parents to the best of her ability.

Anna heard her words and said she did not wish God to fetch her home; she wanted to remain here. She was wise for her years, she used to ask many strange questions which the grownups couldn't answer. As her suffering increased she called her father to help her; she wanted to get up and go with him to the cobbler for the measurements of the shoes she had been promised. Her cries could be heard out into the byre, where the cows answered with their bellowing, thinking someone was on his way to feed them.

Early in the morning the child died in her agony.

Anyone who spoke to Karl Oskar during the next few days got no answer. Nor did a second or third attempt help much.

At length, he might answer with a question, showing that he had heard nothing at all.

Nils asked if he should go out and make a coffin for Anna. This time Karl Oskar heard, and answered at once: The coffin for his dead child he wished to make himself; nothing else could be thought of.

He went out to the work shed where he kept a pile of well-sawed spruce boards; there was more than enough lumber for a coffin. Nor would many boards be required for a coffin to enclose Anna's little shrunken body. The father began to examine the pile, he wanted to choose straight, fine, knot-free boards, clear and without bark. But he discarded every one his hands touched; all were either crooked or warped, or outside boards, or knotty. He picked up one plank after another, inspected it, and threw it aside; it was impossible to find a single one in the pile that he could use, that would make a coffin good enough for Anna.

After a while he tired of searching for good boards and remained sitting on the chopping block, doing nothing. He sat there and listened to the child who had only lately spoken to him: "It hurts to die, Father. I don't want God to fetch me if it is so painful; I want to stay home. Couldn't I stay home, even though I ate the porridge? I'll never again taste anything without permission—please, let me stay home! You're so big and strong, Father, can't you protect me so God won't take me? Oh, Father, if you only knew how it hurts! Why doesn't anyone help me? I am so little. Would you like to die, Father? Do you want God to come and get you?"

As long as the father could still hear calls for help from his dead child, the living ones around him would receive no answer; he did not hear them.

In the evening Nils asked his son how he was getting along with the coffin. Karl Oskar answered he was still choosing boards.

The following day, also, no sounds of hammer and plane were heard from the woodshed. Karl Oskar's only explanation was that he was looking for boards.

On the third day, when it still remained silent in the shed, Nils hobbled out on his crutches and sat down at the workbench. He then made the coffin for the dead one while Karl Oskar looked on.

When the work was finished the son said: "It's not good enough."

Now, Nils in his life had made more than one hundred coffins, and all who had ordered them had been satisfied—not one had ever been discarded. For the first time he had completed work that was not accepted, that was discarded by his own son: he had used one board with a big ugly knot, another was cut crookedly, and here a nail stuck out. Was Anna, his little girl, to rest on sharp nails? Karl Oskar found many faults with the coffin his father had made; he took an ax and smashed it to pieces.

Nils was hurt, his eldest son once and for all was an impossible person; nothing suited him. Now Karl Oskar must make the coffin himself. At last he found some straight, knot-free boards, which he accepted; he carried them to the workbench, where he remained through the night; in the morning the coffin was ready.

It was a father's labor, done during a lonely night of sorrow, in the dim light from the lantern out in the woodshed. Those who saw the coffin perhaps didn't understand. Perhaps, indeed, there was no difference between this coffin and the broken, discarded one. But this one was made by a father's careful hands, it was nailed together by fingers which still were reaching out for something lost.

God gave to two parents a child to love and care for, and when they had had time to grow attached to the little one, deeply, then He took her back. Had they committed some sin to deserve this? What evil had Karl Oskar done that he must make this coffin?

During the same week, christening and grave ale were held in Korpamoen. Karl Oskar carried his child's coffin in his arms to the grave, where the dean filled his shovel with earth and said that Anna would now be like the earth on that shovel, and would not live again until awakened on the last day.

The child had eaten of the barley porridge.

Of the wretched barley which grew last summer they had garnered only a few bushels, and of this a small portion had been ground to grits. From the last grits Kristina had cooked porridge for the christening. But when the barley field stood green, no one had said to the child: If you eat of this you shall surely die!

Anna had died because the earth here was cursed. It must be so; this field where the deadly barley had grown must be stricken by the Lord's word to Adam.

Karl Oskar beheld the pale beggar children wandering about, searching for sustenance in the refuse piles, and he thought: My child found good food, her bowels burst from sugared and buttered barley porridge. Yet she too was a pawn to hunger.

For many weeks after the funeral Kristina was crushed; most of what she did she did wrongly, and other chores stayed undone. A thousand times she reproached herself, asking: Why didn't I hide the bowl of christening porridge where no one could find it? Why didn't I let the children taste it before putting it away? If I had done this, Anna would be alive.

A long time elapsed, and the parents had not mentioned the name of their dead child. They never spoke of the little girl they had lost; their sorrow would have become doubly heavy if it had been brought out into clear daylight, and its power acknowledged. Now they tried to push it away, not let it penetrate beyond thought. As long as words didn't help, why use them? Exchanged between two mourning people, they were only a dissonant sound, disturbing the bitter consolation of silence.

A month had passed since Anna's funeral when Kristina one evening said to Karl Oskar: After what had happened, she had now changed her mind; she was not averse to their emigration to North America. Before, she had thought she would be lacking in responsibility if she endangered her children's lives on the ocean. Now she had learned that God could take her little ones even on dry land, in spite of her great care. She had come to believe that her children would be equally safe on the stormy sea, if she entrusted them to the Highest. Moreover, she would never feel the same in this place again. And so—if he thought it would be best for them and their children to emigrate, she would comply. They could know nothing of what was in store for them in so doing, but she wanted to take part in the emigration, she wished to go away with Karl Oskar.

The couple agreed: they would look for passage in the spring of next year.

So the decision had been reached, a decision which determined the course of life for both of them, which determined the fate of their children, the result of which would stretch through time to come to unborn generations—the decision which was to determine the birthplace of their grandchildren, and their grandchildren's children.

VIII

WITH GOD'S HELP AND THROUGH THE ASSISTANCE OF THE AUTHORITIES

1

One day in February the churchwarden, Per Persson, came to Dean Brusander with grave tidings: behind locked doors in Karragarde Danjel Andreasson gathered his house folk and neighbors to nightly meetings and administered the Lord's Holy Supper.

At first the dean would not believe his warden: the news was too shocking. But Per Persson had the word of eyewitnesses; some young people happening by the other night had peeked in through the windows in Karragarde, and had seen people gathered inside around a Communion table. After hearing of this, he himself last night had gone to the farm and looked through the window to ascertain the truth. He had seen some ten people sitting around a table, while Danjel conducted confession and Communion among them; no person with eyesight could remain in doubt as to what was taking place. By reliable people in the neighborhood he had also been informed that Danjel, through one of the timber drivers, had sent to Karlshamn for several gallons of Communion wine.

Dean Brusander sat for a long while with bent head after hearing the warden's report.

He had tried to bring Danjel Andreasson back into the church through peaceful and gentle means. He had warned, and thought he had enlightened him with kind admonitions. He had sought with mild measures to correct his false opinions of God and spiritual freedom. He had avoided commotion in the parish, and had treated the poor man with caution and consideration. Only when Andreasson had inoculated simple, spineless people with his poison, and had continued to gather them to meetings in his house, had Dean Brusander excluded him from the Lord's altar. But through all his kindness, patience, and tolerance with the strayed one, he had apprently only given freer scope for the Evil Spriit: the miserable people in Karragarde were now led so far by the devil that they confessed and held Communion among themselves.

The sacred sacraments, Christ's body and blood, the church's most holy jewel and exclusive prerogative, these sacraments were desecrated by an ignorant peasant, they were soiled by the hands of a coarse and criminal person. Andreasson was inflated with spiritual vanity; he had commenced with Bible explanations and thereby encroached upon the ministry, later his presumption had gone so far that in his house he organized his own congregation and held his own church.

Thus Danjel Andreasson in Karragarde set himself above temporal and spiritual ordinances. If God still hesitated and did not defend His holy and catholic church, then secular authorities must enter in, must discipline the strayed ones, rebuke the leader and agitator.

Per Persson said: What now took place in Karragarde would stir and upset parish people profoundly.

Deeply grieved, Brusander looked at his warden. "I fear the same. We must immediately avert these excesses."

He now wished to ask the advice of Per Persson, his most trusted churchwarden. Brusander had been unlucky in his choice of wardens: one used to steal into the sacristy during weekdays and drink from the Communion wine, so that one Sunday when Brusander had announced a Communion he had been forced to call it off; another had appeared drunk in church and placed the numbers of the hymns upside down; a third had, on the holy Christmas morning, repaired to a corner of the organ loft and there let his water, in the presence of several women. But always the dean had had full confidence in Per Persson. Because he consumed only a fifth of brannvin per day he was, in sobriety, a worthy example for other parishioners. It was true that ugly rumors had circulated concerning his moral life, but these were, fortunately, unverified. When he had been accused of causing the pregnancy of a fifteen-year-old girl boarding in his house, as a parish pauper, the dean had questioned him privately, and Per Persson had repudiated the false accusation, saying it was spread by the malicious and jealous. And it was a fact that the warden's great success in worldly affairs had made him the object of much jealousy in the parish.

"Speak freely, Per Persson! What means shall we use against these Akians?"

The warden answered: Old parishioners remembered how much trouble Ake Svensson had caused in his day. This time they must prevent the dissenters from disturbing the parish tranquillity. There were already hot-tempered persons who wished forcibly to chastise Danjel and his followers: a few sturdy men intended to go one evening to Karragarde and with suitable weapons drive out the devil. This Per Persson had heard; but he thought it would be ill-advised and cause an unhealthy stir in the parish.

The dean agreed; he could easily understand the noble zeal which called for forcible discipline against the Akians; if a few good men were to go to Andreasson's house on such an errand, then this in itself would be commendable, proving an ardent devotion to the purity of evangelical teachings. But he must disapprove; they could use legal means only against the sectarians.

The churchwarden wished also to report that there were people who spoke well of Danjel and lauded his generosity toward the poor and homeless. As yet they weren't many, but their numbers might increase, and it would menace community peace and order if two parties were to arise, one for and one against the Akians.

"May God prevent such a calamity!" exclaimed the dean with emphasis.

The peasant of Karragarde showed an exaggerated and harmful zeal for things in themselves good, thereby misleading credulous people. No tempter was more dangerous than he who twisted the tools of deceptive goodness into the service of transgression. Brusander realized that he ought to have used stronger means against Danjel Andreasson's activities from the very beginning.

"The ministry must call on the secular authorities for help," advised the warden. "This malpractice of dissenters cannot be handled in any other way."

The dean nodded eagerly. He, also, could see no other way. And a conviction began to take shape within him: an overpowering certitude that God's patience with the heretics in Karragarde was now drained to the last drop.

He asked the churchwarden to keep him posted when the Akians next prepared to gather round their unlawful Communion table in Karragarde. This Per Persson promised before he left; a couple of boys would help him and watch near Danjel's to keep him informed.

Dean Brusander had been working on his next Sunday's sermon when the warden arrived, and his thoughts returned to his work when he was again alone. It was the first Sunday after Septuagesima, and the Bible text was the story in St. Matthew, Chapter 8—of Christ driving the devil from two possessed men into a herd of swine which charged down a steepness into the sea, to perish in its waters. Now, with the churchwarden's news fresh in his mind, he realized how profound this text was, a text that called for explanation and application. And to those listeners familiar with the appalling happenings in Karragarde, little explanation was necessary: "And when He was come to the other side into the country of the Gergesenes, there met him two possessed with devils, coming out of the tombs, exceeding fierce, so that no man might pass by that way. . . ." In like manner today, any man within this parish, on any road or at any moment, might meet a man in plain peasant dress who was possessed by the devil and tempted with the Evil One's words and promises. Never before during his time in office had he so felt the urgency of his message as he did about next Sunday's sermon.

Dean Brusander looked out through the window; snow had fallen the whole day, it was still snowing, and drifts were beginning to form on the road outside the parsonage. With an expression of concern his eyes followed the wafting flakes: perhaps the heavy snowfall might keep distant parishioners from church on Sunday, and they would miss a sermon of the utmost importance to their spiritual welfare.

Brusander was the son of a peasant who had fed and brought up eighteen children in a little cottage with two windows. He thus sprang from the peasantry which made up his congregation. He was the eighteenth child, and his mother had died at his birth. Even in early childhood he felt a strong call to the ministry; he had studied under great hardship, with no financial aid from his poor father, who was barely able to provide him with food during his school years in Vaxio. But the peasantry in these parts were flesh of his flesh and bone of his bone; he felt for these people as for his own children, and embraced them in fatherly love and devotion. He grieved over their vices and errors, their ignorance and drunkenness, their violence and whoring. But most of the parishioners were peace-loving, pious and devout, and hitherto subservient to their spiritual teachers and others who had fatherly power over them. *Hitherto*—he stopped short at that word; in these latter days, he had observed a dangerous sign of change.

At this time a great unrest was visiting all nations. The people were revolting, using force against their legal authorities, and many heretical teachings were spread and believed. The old and approved order was being thrown aside, the customs of forebears disregarded. The evil had its roots in disobedience to God's Fourth Commandment, in the disintegration of the bonds between children and parents, between servants and masters, subjects and authority. Those holy bonds which, according to God's ordinance, kept society united, and preserved order and security, had been attacked by gnawing, corroding evil.

Even in Ljuder Parish there had been signs of contempt for authority, and disobedience toward masters. Maids and farmhands left their employers in the middle of the service year, and had to be returned to their duty by the sheriff. In a few cases the authorities had been so lenient that the escaped servants were not returned to their service but had been allowed to go their way. Such happenings were spots of shame on a Christian church; such examples were dangerous. If the servant law were not obeyed by servants, society might sink into lawlessness, wildest disorder might ensue. Regard for laws and ordinances in force was based on the Fourth Commandment, tranquillity and security depended on that very commandment. God's world order rested primarily on adherence to His Ten Commandments, and the servant law—being part of God's world order—could not be set aside without setting aside the whole order; it was the covenant between masters and servants.

It became more and more apparent that literacy was, in the main, harmful to the common man who couldn't use it wisely. As knowledge of reading spread, so also spread heresy, dissension, and insubordination. Simple folk made wrong use of their reading knowledge. Here the authorities ought to keep stricter supervision and inspection; if you gave to the people a new knowledge—useful in itself—then you must also see to it that this knowledge was not abused. This was the holy duty of the authorities; the people must feel the guiding paternal hand. And the first duty of a spiritual teacher was to impress upon the common man the enduring order, created after God's will and not to be changed without His permission.

But the fundamental cornerstone of the community's existence was unity in religion. One God, one church, one congregation which strove to be one soul—only when humanity reached this perfection would the kingdom of God be established on earth, for eternity.

The Akians broke religious unity and tried to overthrow God's church. And who was the Enemy insinuating himself with fair words and promises—to cause strife and dissension among them? Hotheaded but righteous men in the parish wanted forcibly to throw out the devil from Karragarde. It was a method of simple folk, but their intent was Christian. God had been patient, and had waited, but now the time had come to defend the sanctity of the ministry and the purity of religion.

And the dean lost himself in new thoughts while preparing his sermon. He had much to say to his congregation next Sunday, deriving from Matthew 8:28.

He had also something to attend to today, something which could not wait. He sent for his servant and told him to pull out the sleigh and harness the fastest parsonage horse—he wished to drive to Sheriff Lonnegren in Aleback on an urgent matter.

Dean Brusander remained genial throughout. He was convinced he could take care of the Akian heresy—with God's help and through the assistance of the secular authorities.

2

In the middle of the big room in Danjel Andreasson's house stood a long table which Inga-Lena had put in order this evening. She had pulled out the extra leaves, she had polished two tall brass candlesticks until they shone, she had lit the candles and placed one candlestick on each end of the table. She had brought forth the tallest candles which they had made at Christmas. She had covered the large table with a newly woven cloth of whole linen, which she was using now for the first time; it was washed and ironed and white as the snow without. From her linen chest she brought forth her finest and most precious possessions, for tonight they expected the most important visitor a human being could receive in his house. Tonight their old table was the Lord's table, their tallow candles were God's altar candles, and Inga-Lena's new linen cloth was God's altar cloth: the Lord Jesus Christ would be their guest tonight.

In the center of the table, between the candlesticks, she had placed the earthen jug with wine, sweet wine from Karlshamn, and the cake plate with newly baked rye cookies; Inga-Lena had made the Communion breads in the shape of a cross.

The gathering around the Lord's altar in Karragarde was to take place one hour before midnight. The people from the neighboring farms, two married couples, had just arrived. They were stamping off the snow in the entrance hall, where they were met by Danjel, who bade them step inside and join the brethren in Christ's body. Those already congregated consisted of the house folk and the lodgers. No more visitors were expected, and Danjel locked the door and bolted it. The only time he allowed locked doors in his house was when the Lord Himself made a call. From the storm and snow outside the neighbors stepped into the pleasant, intimate stillness which reigned in Danjel's house. He asked his guests to find their places at the table. With his *psalmodikon*—a musical instrument with one string, resembling a violin—he himself took the seat at the upper end.

Danjel Andreasson was shorter than average, narrow-shouldered, and slenderly built. His face was covered by a light-brown, unkempt beard, and his thick, round-cut hair fell down to the collar of his jacket. The little peasant was gentle in manner, slow in movement, thoughtful and mild in speech. Under a broad protruding forehead his brown eyes had a look of peace in them. His lips parted often, as if about to smile.

At the table's long side, to the right of the master, sat the house folk: dishonorably discharged soldier Severius Pihl, a tall man with a disfigured face, sunken and devastated by smallpox and brannvin; invalided servant maid Sissa Svensdotter, lame in her right arm and crippled in her left foot; and unmarried Ulrika of Vastergohl and her daughter Elin. This daughter was the only one surviving of the four children of unknown fathers whom Ulrika had borne. Elin was barely fifteen years of age and would tonight receive Holy Communion for the first time. Because of her immoral life, Ulrika of Vastergohl herself had for many years been denied the holy sacraments by the church. It seemed remarkable to all that her life in adultery had not left noticeable signs of curruption, but her face retained the innocent features of a pure maiden, showing hardly a wrinkle; her well-shaped body, with its full bosom, was still supple and well preserved. Elin resembled her mother when young. She was a delicate maiden with a fair face.

At the opposite side of the table, to the left of Danjel, sat the people from neighboring farms, two men and two women. Inga-Lena had her place at the lower end of the table. There were ten guests in all at the devotional supper about to begin.

Danjel asked his wife to close the kitchen door, then he knelt beside his chair and prayed a silent prayer. All sat immobile, still and waiting. Outside, the snowstorm increased, and some loose boards at the corner of the house slapped as the gusts of wind pulled and shook them.

Danjel arose and said that Jesus had now arrived.

"We'll meet our Saviour with the hymn about Gethsemane: 'The Sacrifice Is Near. Bleed, My Heart!' "

The farmer of Karragarde picked up his psalmodikon; he tuned the instrument and began to hum the hymn while he listened to the howling snowstorm outside as if he were trying to imitate the sound of the blizzard in the tune of the psalm. Then he drew the wooden bow across the strings, he played and sang:

"Wake, O Christian, while thy Saviour
Bids thee share His cup of woe!
Leave the haunts of sin forever—
He alone can peace bestow.
'Watch and pray,' He pleadeth ever,
'Darkness seeks thy overthrow.'"

All joined in the singing, each according to his ability, and the hymn rose strong and powerful under the low ceiling with its cracked and sooty beams. The Akians sang while the wind whirled round the cottage and filtered through cracks in walls and windows, causing the candle flames to flicker in the draft. The tallow candles lit up only part of the room, a small circle around the table, leaving the rest in semidarkness.

The people gathered here tonight had come to tarry with their Saviour, not to deny Him, like Peter, not to betray Him, like Judas. All those sitting here around Danjel's table, waiting for him to give them the bread and wine, had experienced redemption through *their own faith*, the faith that Christ had suffered and died on the cross for their sins. In embracing this belief they felt that the body of Christ had taken possession of their own bodies, that they had sloughed off their old, sinful ones. Thus they were reborn, untainted, righteous, cleansed of all sins. The Lord's new apostle, sitting here at table with them, had said to them: "Your sins are tied up in the linen napkin which was about Christ's head when He was buried, and which He left in His grave." And they all believed this.

Tonight again Christ bade them eat His body and drink His blood. This was the covenant between the Saviour and the saved, which must be resealed. It was simple for everyone to understand. Christ's body was inside their bodies, while theirs were inside His, as His own words in Danjel's Bible on the table verified: "He that eateth My flesh, and drinketh My blood, dwelleth in Me, and I in him."

They were sundered from the church, no longer received at its altar ring. But the Lord was omnipresent and they could find Him everywhere, in all places under the roof of the heavens. Jesus had allowed Himself to be born in a stable, He could place His Communion table wherever He pleased, be it a byre, a woodshed, or a barn. He was with them wherever they sought Him, the Lord's table stood wherever He was present.

And tonight He was with them again; they were sitting around His altar table. The ceiling of sooty beams above their heads was the vaulted ceiling of the Lord's shining temple. This was a holy place.

> "The hours pass, keep praying, sinners,
>   Follow Christ in happy mood."

The hymn rang out to its close. Danjel moved his Bible close to the tallow candle, so that its light fell on the leaves, and he began to read in a clear and even voice the sacred words of the institution of the Lord's Supper: "Our Lord Jesus Christ, in the night when He was betrayed, took the bread, gave thanks and brake it and gave unto His disciples, and said: 'This is My body, which is given for you' . . ."

The males had precedence in receiving the sacrament. With slow movements Danjel took from the plate a rye biscuit, broke it, and held a small piece to the mouth of soldier Pihl. "Jesus Christ, Whose body you receive, keep you in eternal life."

The old soldier sat with his hands folded and his eyes closed. He bent forward while his lips received the crust of the rye cookie from the peasant's hand. Severius Pihl was toothless; slowly his gums ground the bread to pieces. From the earthen jug Danjel now poured wine into a tin mug, and when the old man had swallowed his bread, Danjel held the mug to his mouth. The soldier drank the wine eagerly in one swallow, then gave thanks to the Saviour in a deep sigh.

> "Jesus Christ, Whose blood you receive . . ."

The other Communion guests had folded their hands and, deeply aware of Christ's presence, made not a single motion. A gust of wind shook the loose boards, which squeaked and banged. The candle flames flickered in a sudden draft from the window, the shadows moved quickly back and forth over the white tablecloth. The blizzard raged without, but the people locked in here were in a peaceful room, sanctified to the God Who had redeemed them, Who had gathered all their sins in His bloody napkin cloth.

Danjel Andreasson had administered bread and wine to the men; he continued with the women, and was about to give the bread to Ulrika of Vastergohl when a new sound from outside was heard above the storm: a man spoke with a coarse voice. The little peasant's hand, holding Christ's body, stopped in mid-air as for a moment he listened. Then he went on with the Communion as if nothing had been heard. He gave Ulrika a piece of the broken bread, and was about to hand her the wine when he was interrupted by another noise: someone knocked, then banged on the outside door.

All turned their heads and listened. Danjel put down the mug with Christ's blood on the table. The blows on the door came in even intervals. But Danjel said nothing and his expression did not change.

Apprehension came over the others; they began to whisper. Inga-Lena said: "Please, Danjel, do not open!"

His neighbors looked at Danjel, fear in their eyes, but he reassured them: they need not be afraid, they must remain fearless, sitting quietly on their chairs. The Lord Jesus was with them in this room tonight, no one need fear harm. Whosoever stood outside and tried to break in had no power against the will of the Almighty. This they must know.

The master of Karragarde went with sure steps out into the entrance hall. Before touching the door lock he asked gently: "Who is disturbing the stillness of our house this night?"

"Sheriff Lonnegren! Open!"

"Whom do you search for at this late hour, Mr. Sheriff?"

"You, Danjel Andreasson! I order you in the name of the law, open your door!"

Other voices were heard, several men were on the porch.

"I do not obey the laws of man."

"My official duty compels me to break down the door if you don't open!"

"Then I must help you, Mr. Sheriff. I cannot allow you to commit a great outrage and increase your sins against God."

Danjel opened the door. He saw horses and sleighs outside in the yard, but the horses had no bells, the visitors had driven without sleighbells so as not to announce their arrival.

Sheriff Lonnegren stepped inside, followed by Dean Brusander. After them came the assistant pastor, Krusell, and the churchwarden, Per Persson of Akerby, and lastly the village bailiff, and Sheriff Lonnegren's hired man. Danjel followed the callers inside; six men entered the room where Danjel's little flock waited in trepidation—three from the spiritual authorities and three from the temporal. Dean Brusander and Pastor Krusell were dressed in the official garb of the clergy. Both ministers were pale and serious, and their black garments inspired awe.

Sheriff Lonnegren removed his uniform cap but was still unable to stand erect under the low ceiling of the peasant cottage; he hit his forehead against a beam and half exploded in an oath before he remembered the clerical company. He turned to the owner of the farm. "What are these people doing here in the middle of the night?"

"We are gathered in a devotional repast," answered Danjel calmly.

The sheriff looked sharply at the neighbors. "I recognize people who do not belong to your house, Danjel Andreasson. It seems to me an unlawful meeting is taking place here."

The two neighboring wives whispered anxiously to their husbands as the sheriff requested their names and place of residence. Danjel again called on his guests to remain calm and unafraid.

Ulrika of Vastergohl did not seem alarmed, rather angry. She glared with disgust at the peacebreakers.

The dean still remained silent while he studied the parishioners gathered around the old table: Pihl, the old soldier, reveler and gambler, often reproved but never improving until at last dishonorable discharge ended his crown service; Sissa Svensdotter, a poor creature, crippled, lame, and committed twice for thievery; and Ulrika of Vastergohl, repulsive harlot to whom the devil had given a fair body to entice men for whoring, and who had been mainly responsible for adultery within the parish. Indeed, the new Akian master had gathered the dregs of the community around him.

Brusander caught sight of the wine jug on the table, he looked at the cake plate with cookies in the form of crosses, and his face paled still more. He drew in his breath deeply, his voice vibrated with indignation, rising to despair: "Your poor confused creatures! You defile the holy sacrament!"

"We enjoy the dear sacraments," answered Danjel, humble yet inflexible.

"Which you have denied us, Mr. Dean!" injected Soldier Pihl.

"Because we no longer crawl under the priest cape!" added Ulrika.

Without paying attention to these remarks the dean turned to Sheriff Lonnegren, pointing at the table. "What more is needed? Danjel Andreasson administers the holy sacrament to these people! We have caught him in the act in his own house. We are all your witnesses to this offense."

The sheriff regarded Danjel's Communion table with a thoughtful and somewhat annoyed expression: he had set out tonight on this business most unwillingly, at Brusander's request. People gathering for devotion within four walls did not distress him as they did the dean. He liked to leave people alone as long as they were quiet within doors, didn't disturb the peace in public places, and didn't harm their fellow men. These here did not harm other people, they were poor, wretched creatures, in rags, with defects and ugliness, poor devils, but no nuisance here. And when others were allowed to gather in peace for gambling and drinking, why shouldn't these poor drones in religion be left undisturbed, as long as they in their turn left others undisturbed? The sheriff had advised the dean to attempt a reconciliation between the dissenters and the church.

However, the reconciliation had not taken place; and their meeting *was* forbidden by law. Law was law, and duty was duty, and it behooved a crown sheriff to do his official duty in this place.

Lonnegren spoke to Danjel sternly: "Do you admit that you hold meetings and administer the holy sacrament?"

"Yes, Mr. Sheriff."

"Have you tonight administered the sacrament to these people?"

"Not to all of them as yet. I was interrupted by you, Mr. Sheriff."

"But you must know that no one is allowed to hold Communion without being ordained?"

"That I do not know."

"But the dean here has told you so."

"I do not obey the dean, but Holy Writ. The Bible says nowhere that our Lord Jesus was ordained."

"Don't get yourself into an argument with this hair-splitter," advised the dean. "These things are too deep for the simple and ignorant."

"You hear what your pastor says!" said Lonnegren. "Aren't you going to obey him, you scoun—scou—" The sheriff's usual term of address froze on his lips this time. He met the calm, fearless look of the little peasant, and swallowed the other half of the word. There was something strange in that man's unchangeable meekness and unswerving politeness. In some way, through his gentleness and calm, he was beyond reach. It seemed to the sheriff that he couldn't touch Danjel with his reprimands.

Lonnegren continued: "It has been proved that you have broken the law pertaining to the sacraments, Danjel Andreasson."

"There is no law over those who live in Christ."

"There, you hear for yourself!" interrupted Brusander. "He sets himself above the authorities and public ordinances."

Danjel could only make matters worse through his fearless answers, and Lonnegren did not wish him to worsen his case. He might have a tedious investigation on his hands if this meeting came under the sedition paragraph; he wanted to finish the business as quickly as possible.

"I'll call you in for questioning, Danjel," he said. "After that you will be sued in civil court, as well as all others gathered here."

Danjel listened unmoved to the sheriff. Of late he had felt the time of persecution nearing.

Lonnegren ordered the bailiff to take down the names of all present at the meeting. The neighbors, on hearing that their names would be taken, immediately rose from the table, slowly easing themselves in the general direction of the door.

The dean held a whispered consultation with his assistant, then he stepped forward and demanded attention. "I have once forbidden you, Danjel Andreasson, to meddle in anything pertaining to the ministry. You persist in your excesses and it is therefore necessary now to treat you according to the letter of the law. The same holds true for the others who have broken the sacramental law here tonight.

"But I beg you to think of your eternal salvation. Each one of you who regrets his transgressions, and recalls them, will be again received by me into the fold of the church. I cannot be responsible to my God unless I do all I can to save you from eternal fire."

He now had tears in his eyes.

Ulrika of Vastergohl threw looks of hatred toward the spiritual guide of the parish. "We have our Redeemer here among us. We don't have to hang on to the coat tails of a priest. To hell with you!" She spat.

"You blaspheme, woman!" Pastor Krusell exclaimed excitedly.

"This is our temple. Get out of the light, priests! You darken this room. You stand there black and evil like the devil himself!"

"This woman reviles the ministry!" said Pastor Krusell to the dean.

Dean Brusander turned to Ulrika of Vastergohl, in all his dignity. "I see that you have not mended your ways." He looked at the wine mug in front of her, and repugnance and loathing crept into his voice: "You harlot, how dare you take Christ's blood into your foul mouth!"

"I do as I damn well please, you God-damned priest!"

Brusander recoiled. He took a step backward and sucked in his breath; he mustn't lose his head.

The churchwarden, Per Persson, stepped forward to help the parish pastor. He shouted to Ulrika: "How dare you insult the dean!"

"Watch out! I might insult the warden, too!"

"Before you speak to our clergy you should wash out your mouth!"

"How? With parsonage brannvin or priest piss?"

"Shut up, you old whore!"

"Whore? Did you call me a whore?"

Ulrika jumped up so abruptly her chair overturned with a great clatter. Her whole body shook, her eyes flashed with rage, and she screamed at the warden: "A whore? To you, Per Persson? *You* call *me* a whore, you old son of a bitch?"

"What are you talking about, woman?"

"A whore to you, Warden? What was it you used to say in the old days, when you came with a daler in one hand and your cock in the other?"

"Shut up! Insane creature!" roared Per Persson with the full strength of his lungs.

"What was it you said then? When you wanted me to lie on my back for you—for just a little while? Then you came crawling, then you asked, and begged, and fawned! Then I was good enough for you! Then the whore was good enough!"

By now words stuck in the throat of the churchwarden, and he could no longer answer Ulrika. But she drew breath to gather new strength.

Complete silence ensued after this exchange of words. The soldier Pihl and Sissa Svensdotter looked at the dean in malicious joy. The dean and assistant pastor looked at each other in bewilderment, and the sheriff stood open-mouthed and looked from the Akerby warden to the fuming woman.

Danjel remained quiet and stared at the floor, waiting for the foul weather to pass.

Someone began to weep—it was Ulrika's daughter; Inga-Lena moved her chair closer and comforted Elin.

Ulrika's shrill voice was heard again: "That whoring son of a bitch Per Persson is not denied the sacrament in church. Why? Because he is a good friend of the God-damned priests —those black devils who darken the light for us! Those lazy potbellies who live in their fat flesh!"

The dean and his assistant were still silent and irresolute, shocked by Ulrika's explosion. Per Persson shook his fisted hands as though he would grab her throat.

Sheriff Lonnegren did not interfere in the exchange of words between Ulrika and the churchwarden; experience gained from many hard years in office had taught him not to argue with whores; it led nowhere. And he felt no sympathy for Per Persson, whose lust for power made him difficult. He did not begrudge the warden this humiliation. And he experienced a great relief as he stood here and recalled a happening of many years ago, in his youth. One evening while drunk and reckless he had been on his way to Ulrika's cottage—on the same errand as Per Persson and many other men; the devil must have guided his steps. But Ulrika had not been at home; she had accompanied some caller a bit on his way, and he had had to return without having effected his purpose. An act of providence had averted his undertaking and sent the woman away at the right moment. Now he could bless this act of providence, he could thank God he didn't have to suffer disgrace from the mouth of the harlot here this evening.

The dean felt Ulrika had spoken the truth about his warden. He knew already that she had misled many honest and upright men, and with her body enticed them into her nest of sin, but this was not the right time or place to divulge the truth and lay bare Per Persson's debaucheries, his much-to-be-regretted youthful dissipations. Here the truth was not used in its right place; it became a raw insult to a trusted and well-thought-of man. But nothing could excuse or forgive the rude words (to say the least) which the sinful woman had used.

Brusander went over to the sheriff. "You must put a stop to this painful and shameful scene." By the strength of his office Lonnegren must disperse the gathering and send those present on their way.

The sheriff did not ask for anything better than to conclude his unpleasant mission here tonight. Danjel Andreasson had admitted his offense, the names of his accessories were inscribed, and he had nothing more to do in this house.

"In the name of the law I now order this meeting to disperse. Each go quietly to his own house!"

The bailiff said the neighbors had already left after giving their names and places of residence. Those remaining here belonged to the farm. In the words of the law the meeting was already dispersed.

But before Brusander left he had something to say still to the master of the house: "I strictly forbid you to continue Communions at this table."

"You cannot forbid the Lord Jesus my house, Mr. Dean," said Danjel.

"Who has told you that the Lord is here?"

"He has shown Himself to me in my heart."

"You think all your whims are inspirations from God. I assure you they are from the devil!"

The warden Per Persson interrupted, still red-faced from anger: "We'll throw out the Karragarde devil, we'll get rid of him when you, Danjel, are in prison on bread and water!"

Danjel had spoken to Ulrika in a fatherly way, silencing her. His words had power over her. But now the fiery woman could contain herself no longer. "Get out, you God-damned priests!"

And Soldier Pihl added in a rasping voice: "Leave the

house of the righteous and repair yourselves to the sinners' den!"

Pastor Krusell had a more easily disturbed temper than the dean, and he now exclaimed: "This is enough! Are we to accept such insults?"

It looked as if a new row were to ensue. Danjel admonished his people to keep quiet. To make sure, he reached for the psalmodikon and began singing a hymn:

> "Let me live in peace and stillness
>   Giving to no soul offense;
> Pain or pleasure, health or illness
>   Take I from Thy providence.
> Never wounding, ever healing,
> Thus a Christly life revealing."

And all the Akians joined in:

> "Here my cross with patience bearing,
>   I will go where Jesus leads,
> All enduring, all forbearing . . ."

Danjel and his flock continued the hymn, verse after verse, as if no outsider were present in the room. Dean Brusander several times attempted unsuccessfully to make himself heard above the singing. He said to his assistant, for these hardened people nothing could be done. Lonnegren had performed his duty and was ready to leave with his men, who, he thought, might as well have stayed at home; vaguely it seemed to him that Danjel in his unshakable belief was in some way beyond the reach of the secular authorities.

All the intruders had left before the psalm was ended.

Danjel went outside on the porch: both the dean's and the sheriff's sleighs were gone. He locked his door for the second time this night; then he went back to his place at the upper end of the table. With sadness he gazed on the four empty chairs at the Communion table, lately vacated by his neighbors. Fear of worldly authority had been too much for them; they had not been steadfast in their faith; they had deserted their Lord and Master. As Peter once denied Jesus to the servant of the High Priest, in like manner Danjel's neighbors had denied him to Sheriff Lonnegren.

Danjel Andreasson comforted the devoted followers who still remained with him: the time of persecution was upon them; they should thank the Lord Jesus that they were chosen, thank Him for the joy of suffering for His sake.

So the farmer of Karragärde once more reached for the tin mug which served as chalice, and which had remained in front of Ulrika of Västergöhl; he held it to her mouth: "Jesus Christ, Whose blood you drink . . ."

Christ was still there, they felt His presence, and this was a holy place.

3

At Konga County spring court, 1849, homeowner Danjel Andreasson of Karragärde was fined two hundred daler in silver for transgressing the sacrament law and the ordinance pertaining to unlawful meetings. Those who had received the Holy Communion in his house were fined one hundred daler silver each. As most of the offenders were without funds and unable to pay, the fines were changed to prison sentences and each one served twenty-eight days on bread and water.

Six of the condemned—former soldier Pihl, maid Sissa Svensdotter, and four neighbors—returned to the fold of the church after serving their sentences. They expressed to Dean Brusander their deep repentance over their errors. Since they again confessed the only true and right religion, they were admitted to Communion with the rest of the congregation.

Only Ulrika of Västergöhl and her daughter remained in Karragärde to follow the teachings of their master. Through the sentence of the county court Danjel's little flock had been scattered. No new followers came to him. The danger of Akianism in the parish was averted—with God's help, and through the assistance of the secular authorities.

IX

THE AMERICA CHEST

1

A whole year passed during which Karl Oskar and Kristina made preparations for their emigration, feeling as if they were already on the move. There was so much to do and to think about they could not sink too deeply into sorrow over their dead child.

Karl Oskar let it be announced from the church pulpit that his farm was for sale. News soon spread through the parish that the farmer of Korpamoen intended to move away from the country, intended to emigrate to North America, taking with him wife, children, and his only brother. There was much talk in the village about this strange projected undertaking. Whence had he got the amazing notion? Serious-minded older peasants shook their heads and came up to Karl Oskar on the church green on Sundays. To one who was younger they could speak as father to son, and they wished now—with the best of intentions—to dissuade him; how could he relinquish his farm, the parental home whose deed he had, and reach out for land in faraway North America, a country which neither he nor anyone else had seen? Wasn't it like trying to catch the will-o'-the-wisp on a misty morning? The project seemed rash to them; he would enter into a dangerous game in which he might win a little, but lose all; this they must tell him as older and more experienced farmers. It was not that he was forced to give up his farm. The sheriff had been to many farms this last year but he had not yet come to take anything in pawn from Korpamoen. Many were harder pressed on their farms than he, yet they remained at home.

Karl Oskar answered proudly that he acted according to his own good judgment, and after much thought. He understood well enough that a peasant who had tilled his farm some fifty years might think himself ten times wiser and more experienced than he, who had worked Korpamoen only five years. But did anyone gain in wisdom from living on the same

143

place and tramping in the same furrows all his life? If a man's wisdom increased because he remained all his life on the patch where he was born, then the oldest farmers in the parish should by now possess more wisdom than King Solomon himself. But the fact was that most of them were squareheads.

Karl Oskar was considered arrogant and proud when he rejected his neighbors' kind advice. His emigration was taken as a reproach, an insult even, to the parish as a whole and to each individual: the community and the people here were not good enough for him. The old story of the Nilsa-nose was remembered; Karl Oskar's big nose protruded so far that he was unable to turn about in the parish. The whole of Sweden was not large enough to house his nose—he must travel to a bigger country, far away in the world, in order to be comfortable. And some wit started a saying which spread through the village: when Karl Oskar came to North America, his face too would be long.

Perhaps he thought himself such a bigwig that he could look down on his home community? Others surmised something wrong in his head; he was seized by a delusion of grandeur. Such ideas didn't suit a one-sixteenth homestead peasant.

Karl Oskar knew that people poked fun at him and spoke ill behind his back. But he didn't bother to get angry; after all, he tried to please himself, not others. If you spent your time worrying about what other people thought and said, you wouldn't get much done in your life. Outside his home everyone was against his proposed undertaking; even within his home, only his wife was for him; but she was the only one he needed on his side. His parents were against him, though they kept silent. Their reserved rights would now have to be met by an outsider, and this was not to their liking.

Once only did Nils quietly reproach his son: "You take many along with you."

"There will be six of us."

"You take many more. Your descendants are more numerous than you know."

Karl Oskar did not answer. He felt the grief he caused in taking the family from their own country to a foreign land.

"You have not asked the opinion of children and grandchildren," continued the father.

"I must be the one to assume responsibility. I do think of my children."

Nils sat on his chair, his fingers twisting the well-worn crutch handles; he answered softly: "I too think of my children."

He had but two sons.

Karl Oskar understood his father, who now asked himself of what use it had been for him to clear the ground here in Korpamoen, when this ground was now no longer good enough for his own son. Those twenty-five years of fighting the stones must now seem to him a futile strife, as it did not benefit either of his sons.

His mother thought Karl Oskar showed a sinful ingratitude by discounting his gain here at home. He had done nothing wrong, he was not driven by the whip to flee the country. But neither she nor Nils wasted much time in persuasion—they knew Karl Oskar. They turned to the Almighty in prayers that He might change their son's mind and make him give up the American journey.

Time passed—a summer sped by, and an autumn, and winter came again. But their prayers brought no apparent sign of change in Karl Oskar. Nils and Marta concluded at length that God had some secret purpose in their son's and daughter-in-law's emigration to the United States of North America.

2

Robert returned home for his "free week" after a year's service with Kristina's parents in Duvemala, where he had been treated well and given no chastisement. No one thought the sheriff would look for him any further and he remained in the parental home; Karl Oskar would need his brother's help this last year on the farm.

With Robert the United States also moved into the peasant cottage. From his "description book" he knew everything about the new land. Long ago he had landed on the other side of the ocean and made himself at home on distant shores. On the map which he had made up in his mind were marked the lakes, rivers, plains, and mountains of North America, all roads, on land and on water. He insisted he would not get lost in the New World once he arrived there, and now he must help his brother and sister-in-law to find their way. Karl Oskar, too, had begun to read in his brother's book, and every day he obtained new information from Robert.

In America the kine fed on a grass that stood belly-high.

In America wild horses and oxen existed by the thousands, the fields were overrun with them and one could easily catch a hundred in a day.

In America it would have been impossible for David to kill Goliath; if he had searched forever he would have been unable to find a stone for his sling.

In America one could say "thou" to the President himself, and one need never remove one's cap for him, if one didn't wish to.

In America any capable and honest man could step directly from the manure wagon to the presidential throne.

In America there was only one class, the people's class, and only one nobility—the nobility of honest work.

In America there were no taxes and no examinations in the catechism.

In America you need not pay the minister's salary if you did not like his sermons.

All sounded too good to be true, and during the long winter evenings Robert read to his brother and sister-in-law about the strange roads of iron which existed throughout the United States:

"In America one travels a great deal with the help of steam and steam wagons, but for this are required roads which are built in a peculiar way and which are called iron roads or railroads. Such a road must be almost even and practically level. On the road are placed crossbars of wood and to these are tied strong iron rails which serve to guide the wagons. The wagon wheels have on their inside a rim all the way around which forces them to follow the rail on the road.

"On such roads one travels with great speed, twelve to eighteen miles an hour, nay, even faster. Several big wagons are tied together and pulled by a steam wagon, or that wagon on which the steam engine is placed. At the end of each wagon is a small bridge which enables the traveler to pass from one wagon to another during the journey, should he desire to speak to an acquaintance. Every wagon has a comfort room which makes it unnecessary to leave the wagon even on a long journey.

"These railroads, where with the help of steam one can enjoy a comfortable and inspiring journey, have now in America a length of 8,000 miles. . . ."

Kristina said: "It will be fun to ride with no beast pulling the wagon!"

She enjoyed riding in all kinds of vehicles, and in spite of her years she most of all, still, enjoyed swinging on a rope. Only a few days ago Karl Oskar had surprised her in the threshing barn, where she had again fastened the ox-thong to the beams and sat riding the swing.

There was now something she wondered about: "How can they steer the wagons when the railroad is snowed under in wintertime?"

"I don't know," said Robert, "perhaps they stable the wagons during the winter."

The book also said that no steam wagons were in use on Sundays. The drivers were at church, of course; and maybe the steam also needed rest to gather strength.

"I wonder about those iron rails," said Karl Oskar. "They lie without guards in the wilderness, night and day. Isn't the iron stolen?"

Robert told him with a superior smile, there was such an abundance of iron in America that no one cared to steal as much as the filings of a saw. And it was the same with gold and silver. Why should people steal and go to jail when they had more than they needed of everything? In America it was so easy to earn one's living in an honest way that no one was tempted to dishonesty. A thief was immediately strung up, often before he even had time to confess his crime. Therefore all thieves in that country were now exterminated. The gentry here at home lied in saying that North America was full of robbers and murderers and wickedness, when in truth it was populated by the most honest and upright people in the whole world.

"They must have an occasional scoundrel there, too," Karl Oskar said.

Robert admitted that this might be so but insisted that evil people were exterminated much more quickly than here at home.

Karl Oskar wished to settle in that part of the country where soil was the most fertile. Robert had read that the best regions for farmers were around the upper end of the great river Mississippi and its tributaries. This neighborhood was fertile, healthy, and rich in forests and beautiful mountains, in valleys and spring waters. The grass thereabouts was so abundant that in two days a man could cut and harvest sufficient winter fodder for a cow, and in three days enough for a horse. One farmer who had cultivated land on the Mississippi shores had in five years earned a bushel of gold.

Kristina did not wish to live in a place where there were crocodiles. Recently she had read in a paper a horrible tale about a settler family in America who had happened to spend a night in a cave where crocodiles were nesting. Early in the morning the man went out to hunt, and when he returned his wife and three children had been eaten by the crocodiles. The old crocodile had just swallowed the wife: only the head of the poor woman was still visible in the mouth of the beast, who had choked and lay there dead; the ground was drenched in human blood. Kristina could not forget the poor mother watching the crocodile feast on her small children while she was waiting her turn. But of course the woman had taken revenge by choking the beast with her own head.

Robert had never read about man-eating crocodiles in America; the piece in the paper must have been a lie; some duke or count must have had it printed to discourage simple folk from emigration.

Arvid, whom Robert had met again, had also been afraid of wild beasts in America. He had had to leave his service in Nybacken; Aron did not wish to keep a servant called the Bull. The old mistress was dead and Arvid was sure she came back to him in the stable room, accusing him of having tried to kill her—which indeed was true—so he had moved without regret. But he had asked at many farms before he found work; he was known everywhere as the Bull from Nybacken. At last he was hired by Danjel in Karragarde, who was unable to find another hand this winter. All servants were afraid of the place now that the devil had moved in there. People had actually seen the Evil One hanging to the back of Danjel's wagon as he drove along the roads; sometimes he even occupied the seat next to the driver, laughing and pleased. The devil was now the real master on that farm.

Arvid was saving every penny of his wages for his transportation to America. For a whole month he had bought no brannvin. Long before his confirmation he had learned to chew snuff (although children weren't supposed to use it before they had participated in the Lord's Supper); he would save three daler a year if he stopped, and this would help him a bit on the road to America. He realized he must give up some things in the Old World to make possible his move to the New; so he had thrown his snuffbox on the dunghill.

But giving up the box was difficult for Arvid. It had been good company for him, he had carried it in his pocket and enjoyed its contents. It had been a loyal companion in work and loneliness. The snuffbox had been his only friend after Robert moved. And now he had thrown it away—into the depths of the dunghill. He felt his pain keenly when others brought forth their boxes and used them without offering him a pinch: then he had to turn away to escape the sight of the refreshing mixture.

He admitted to Robert that after three weeks of suffering he had bought a new snuffbox. And again he bought half a gallon of brannvin each Saturday night. For at last he had clearly understood that a person had no right to treat his God-given body according to his own will; he had no right to torture and plague it and deny it all its pleasures; one could not treat one's body like a dog, denying it even the comfort of snuff.

Would Arvid ever follow him on the road to America? Robert did not believe so; apparently, in one year and a half, he had not saved a single daler; in his whole life he would be unable to save two hundred daler.

But in Korpamoen everything was now being put in order. One day the Nilsa family's old clothes chest—of solid oak painted black—was pulled forward from its place in a cobweb-infested corner of the attic, and carried down into the kitchen for inspection and dusting. No one knew how old this chest was—the hands which made it were mixed with the earth of the churchyard many hundreds of years ago. It had passed from father to son through numerous generations. More than one young bridegroom had entrusted his finery to it after the wedding feast, more than once had the farm's women fetched winding sheets from it when there was a corpse in the house to shroud. Under the lid of the chest valuable things had been secreted; this lid had been lifted by the shaking hands of old women, and by young, strong, maiden fingers. It had been approached mostly at life's great happenings: baptisms, weddings, and funerals. This enduring piece of furniture had through centuries followed the family, and at last been pushed away into a dark attic corner where it had long remained undisturbed. Now it was pulled out into the daylight once more; it was the roomiest and strongest packing case they could find—five feet long and three feet high, wrought with strong iron bands three fingers wide.

In its old age the Nilsa family clothes chest must go out into the world and travel.

It was tested in its joints, and the still-sound oak boards passed the inspection. It was scrubbed clean inside, and old rust scraped from hinges and escutcheons. After timeless obscurity the heavy, clumsy thing was unexpectedly honored again. From its exile in attic darkness it was now honored with the foremost place in the house. The chest had been half forgotten, years had passed without its lid being lifted; now it became the family's most treasured piece of furniture, the only one to accompany them on the journey.

The four oak walls of this chest were for thousands of miles to enclose and protect their essentials; to these planks would be entrusted most of their belongings. Again the old adage, "Old is reliable and best," was proved. And the ancient clothes chest which was about to pass into an altogether new and eventful epoch of its history was even given a new name in its old age. Through its new name it was set apart from all its equals and from all other belongings. It was called the "America chest," the first so named in this whole region.

3

One night Karl Oskar was awakened by a noise from without. Kristina also woke up and asked: "What can it be?"

He listened. "Someone at the door."

Now they both heard knocking.

"Who can it be at this time of night?"

"I'll go and see."

Karl Oskar pulled on his trousers and lit a stick of pitch wood to light his way in the entrance hall. Robert too had awakened, and came from the kitchen where he slept. He asked in trepidation if it mightn't be the sheriff . . . ? Rumor had it that Aron of Nybacken was still urging the sheriff to catch his runaway farmhand.

"I'll warn you before I open," assured the brother.

But there was no fierce, threatening sheriff to answer his question when Karl Oskar inquired as to who was knocking; it was a kind and friendly voice—Danjel of Karragarde stood on the stoop.

"God give you peace on your house, Karl Oskar."

Robert felt relieved; but he was curious.

Karl Oskar, surprised at this late visit, let his wife's relative into the house. In the light of his firestick he looked at the grandfather's clock in the corner: it showed half-past twelve. Something serious must have happened.

Kristina was both pleased and alarmed; she hurried out of bed and put on her skirt and night jacket; she took her uncle's hand and curtsied. Karl Oskar pulled up a chair for him and he sat down. His errand must be urgent, and they waited for him to communicate it at once, but he acted as if there were no hurry. As usual, he was slow and calm in his movements.

Kristina remembered that Inga-Lena only lately had given birth to a child, and had been seriously ill at the time.

"Is something wrong at home? With my aunt perhaps?"

"No. All is well with wife and child."

Inga-Lena had borne him a daughter since the couple's marriage had again become a true marriage.

Their curiosity increased. Why did Danjel disturb them at this late hour if nothing serious had happened?

"Has something . . . ?"

"I have a message for you, Karl Oskar."

"A message?"

"Yes."

"From whom?"

"From God."

"From God?"

Karl Oskar and Kristina exchanged quick glances.

"The Lord awakened me tonight and said: 'Go at once to

Karl Oskar in Korpamoen, the husband of your sister's beloved daughter.' "

Karl Oskar looked closer at Danjel but could see no sign of
agitation or trouble in his face; his eyes were not bloodshot
like a madman's.

"Now you must listen, Karl Oskar. I come with an order
from God."

Robert crept into the room and sat in a corner near the
hearth, listening to the strange message brought by the peasant of Karragarde.

Danjel continued, and it seemed as if he took his words directly from the Bible.

"Last night the Lord said unto me, Danjel Andreasson, as
He once said unto Abraham: 'Get thee out of thy country,
and from thy kindred, and from thy father's house, unto a
land that I will show thee!'

"The Spirit exhorted me to look up Genesis, Chapter
Twelve, verse one, and obey the words written therein. I
arose from my bed and lit a candle and read. Then I asked:
'How shall this come about?' Tonight the Spirit gave me the
answer: 'Go to Karl Oskar in Korpamoen. He will show you
and help you.' "

Had Danjel entirely lost his mind? Karl Oskar and Kristina
wondered. His actions were calm and his eyes peaceful and
mild. His words were strange, but not confused, and gradually
it all fitted together and took on meaning; soon they could
guess his errand.

The dean had reconciled many of the Akians with the
church again but had been unable to bring Danjel back to the
right religion. At the fall session of the county court last year
he had been cited for a second offense, and again fined for
preaching his heresy. But disregarding the court's judgments
at two hearings, he had continued fearlessly to hold Bible
meetings and administer the holy sacrament in his home.
Again this spring he had been summoned to appear in court
for the third offense, and people were sure that this time
Danjel would be exiled.

Kristina clapped her hands in delight. "Uncle, are you
coming with us to America?"

Danjel rose and went up to his niece, laying both hands
upon her shoulders, as if in blessing. "I live in a time of persecution in the land of my fathers. I am prevented from con-

fessing my God. But the Lord shall open for me a new land."

"You mean America, Uncle?"

"Yes. God has so ordered it: we shall move there together. And none shall have fear; He is with us. I bring my God with me."

Kristina forgot that a moment ago she had feared their tardy visitor was mad. Now he was just her dear Uncle Danjel, whom she knew well. When she was a little girl and he had visited her home he had always had lumps of sugar in his pockets for her; he was still so kind to her, twice he had helped them with the mortgage interest. Without his aid they might not now be in possession of the farm. No one could make her believe her uncle was an evil, dangerous man who should be exiled. His peculiar ideas in religion should be left undisturbed—he hurt no one but himself with them.

It gave her a feeling of security to know that Danjel would accompany them on the long journey to America, a journey which secretly still worried her. She felt almost as though her own father were to go with them.

Now she must prepare coffee for her uncle, from the few ounces left of the pound she had bought for Christmas. She stirred up the fire on the hearth, washed out the old coffee grounds from the kettle, and placed it on the tripod over the fire.

Karl Oskar was not as well pleased as his wife at the prospect of Danjel and his Akians' company; their religious peculiarities would cause inconveniences and trouble, he thought. And when Kristina learned that Danjel was to take along Ulrika of Vastergohl and her daughter—now his only followers outside the family—she too lost some of her enthusiasm. She could not believe that the old whore had become a new person, and decent people ought to be spared the companionship of Ulrika's ilk. She hoped to dissuade her uncle from paying that creature's passage.

Danjel had fulfilled his errand: Karl Oskar would—according to God's command—help him find a passage to the land the Lord would open to His exiled apostle.

Whether God ordered it or not, Karl Oskar was anxious to help Danjel find his way. Besides, he was indebted to him for help with the loan, and was prepared to assist him in return.

Harald, the year-old baby, awakened and began to cry. Kristina had to sit down and take him in her arms to quiet him; Karl Oskar tended the coffee while he talked with Danjel about the crossing to North America.

Spring was the most favorable time to emigrate: partly because the winter storms were over and it was less cold at sea, partly because they would arrive at their place of settlement early enough in summer to till and sow; they must have a fall harvest to meet winter needs. They ought to start their voyage in early April. Karl Oskar and Robert had already written to a firm in Karlshamn and been promised passage on a ship called the *Charlotta*. A down payment of one hundred daler for the transportation of six people had been required, and he had sent them this sum. Their ship was a merchant vessel sailing with cargo and emigrants. They were to embark in Karlshamn about the second week in April. They would sail to the town of New York in North America, without docking at any harbor on the way—it was best to sail direct. The *Charlotta* was said to be a good strong ship, commanded by an honest, upright captain who did not cheat his passengers.

Robert would write for Danjel and obtain contract for his passage, too, if the ship had space for more.

"How many of you will there be from Karragarde?"

Danjel thought a moment. "Nine—including children and house folk."

"Is your hired hand to be shipped too?"

"Arvid? Yes, I've promised him."

"Well, he might be of help to you, in America."

Robert listened and smiled to himself; he had anticipated Danjel's errand, had not been so much surprised by it as Karl Oskar. Yesterday he had met Arvid, who, in exchange for promises of secrecy, had related his master's offer; he had shed tears of joy.

As the patriarch Abraham when he was seventy-five years old departed with all his household out of Haran to the land of Canaan, so now the homeowner Danjel Andreasson at the age of forty-five was to depart with all his house folk from Sweden to North America. Robert knew his Biblical history: the patriarch Abraham had no children because his wife Sarah was as barren as the mistress of Nybacken, and he took along many souls whom he fed in his house, the same as Danjel. Abraham was afraid of being killed in the foreign land because of his beautiful wife; therefore he passed her off as his sister. He was a coward; Danjel would never behave like that. Of course, Inga-Lena was not a fair woman; it was hardly to be supposed that some American would murder Danjel in order to marry his widow.

In some ways God's order concerning the emigration remained foggy; He could hardly have referred to the United States when He spoke of the land in the Bible verse, because Columbus had not yet discovered America in the days of Abraham. Danjel must have misunderstood, but there would be no use in correcting him, thought Robert. Danjel had heard that Karl Oskar was to emigrate, and he wanted to emigrate with him as long as he was to be exiled anyway. Now he believed the idea was God's command. But no doubt he was honest in his false belief.

"I'll write about passage tomorrow," Robert promised him.

As they talked further he was amazed to learn how little Danjel knew about America; the farmer from Karragarde was only familiar with the word "America," he knew only that it was the name of another continent, he had not heard of the United States, did not even know where the continent was situated. He knew nothing of its people, government, climate, agriculture, or means of livelihood. Danjel needed enlightenment, and as they sat around the table and drank their coffee Robert tried to share with him his own knowledge of the country where they would settle.

The United States was located southwest of Sweden. To reach it one must sail across a sea that was about four thousand miles wide. With good wind and a speedy ship one might cross in five weeks. But unfortunately the wind on the ocean was mostly westerly, blowing straight against the ship, thus requiring eight or nine weeks for the crossing. At times contrary winds might be so persistent that three months would pass before reaching America.

Danjel listened patiently and with a benevolent smile to the seventeen-year-old boy; the lad sat like a schoolmaster and taught a pupil of ripe age. The peasant stroked his beard, brushing away the crumbs that clung there, and said with conviction: They need not fear contrary winds for the crossing; the All-High ordering him to depart would see to it that they were not delayed by the weather. No winds except favorable ones would blow in their sails; their ship would require only a month of sailing to North America. The Almighty would surely shorten their voyage as much as He could.

Karl Oskar remembered that the Konga spring court convened toward the end of April; Danjel would be out of the country when the sentence of exile was pronounced.

The farmer of Karragärde had paid huge sums of money in fines for his Bible meetings, and Karl Oskar could not help saying: "It's none of my business, Danjel, but why don't you stop holding meetings when they are unlawful?"

Danjel looked up in surprise. "Stop holding them? I?"

"Well . . . yes. No one else can do it."

"But you must know that I myself do not live any more?"

"What do you mean?"

"Hm . . . I thought you knew."

"No. I don't understand a bit any more."

"I don't live in myself any longer—Christ lives in me."

"But you do the Bible explaining?"

"No-o." Danjel smiled kindly and said in his meek way: "I myself do nothing more here in the flesh. Because I do not exist now as before. Christ has taken my place; He does all through me, and is responsible for me. He holds Bible explanations through my mouth. I need not be afraid of anything; what do I care about worldly courts and judges? They cannot hurt me; nothing can hurt me here in the flesh where I no longer live."

Again Karl Oskar and Kristina were confused, wondering how it was with Danjel's mind. Kristina poured some more coffee for him; for a moment there was silence around the table.

Danjel turned to Karl Oskar. "Where do you intend to spend eternity?"

That was a peculiar question, nor did Karl Oskar bother to answer it. He thought Danjel spoke clearly enough of worldly doings, but when he dealt with spiritual things he turned queer; there was no object in arguing with him.

The peasant of Karragärde continued: All of them sitting here around the table tonight, all their sin-bodies, that is, had died on the cross with Christ. He himself had carried his dead and rotten body for many years, until one night two years ago, when it fell off like a dirty rag, and Christ moved in in its place. His dear relatives should understand that the Saviour would not move into them as long as they carried their sin-bodies, their old rotten remains. They must understand that Christ would not dwell in them before they were reborn, before they had laid off their sour old bodies. Who would wish to live in a house that stank of cadavers, of corpses?

No one answered this amazing speech. Danjel rose abruptly from the table, saying he now would leave.

Robert had wished to teach him something about the New World; as an emigrant he needed knowledge of the United States. But Danjel said before he left that, about those things in America which were useful for him to know, the Lord would no doubt enlighten him before he set out on his voyage.

Karl Oskar reflected, as he returned to bed, that he was now no longer alone in his strongly criticized venture. There were now two homeowners. And Danjel was giving up a farm many times larger and better than Korpamoen. That thought was comforting.

Of course, he must admit, he must sadly admit, that he considered his companion a little unbalanced.

4

And so it happened in those days that another old chest, in another attic, on another farm, was dragged forth, inspected, dusted, scrubbed, and put in order—another America chest, the second.

Only a month before their scheduled departure Jonas Petter of Hasteback came to Korpamoen one evening to warn Robert: his neighbor had met Sheriff Lonnegren, who asked whether the hired hand had come home. Aron of Nybacken insisted that his servant be returned; the boy might try escaping to America when his brother left.

This message did not surprise Karl Oskar, who knew that Aron harbored an intense hatred toward him. For a few minutes once he had inflicted the greatest fear possible on Aron; now his hatred sought revenge on Robert: the farmer of Nybacken would try to prevent the boy's emigration.

Karl Oskar said it would be safest for Robert to keep out of the sheriff's reach during the remaining weeks.

Tears came into Robert's eyes. He had been afraid to appear in public since he returned home; together with other deserters in the parish recently he had been rebuked from the pulpit. The dean had preached a sermon about "unfaithful servants" who deserted their masters and set themselves up against God's ordinances; he had said that disobedient farmhands were spots of shame on a Christian community. Robert had felt so much disgraced that he never went out in public, and spoke to no one except Arvid, who also was disgraced although in another way.

Now he said that rather than return to Nybacken he would go to the mill brook, and this time it wouldn't be his jacket and shoes only. Perhaps that really was the fate awaiting him: a farmhand drowned in the mill brook.

Jonas Petter spoke comfortingly: Lonnegren didn't wish to harm any poor devil; he was sure to look for Robert in his home only. The sheriff never bothered more than was necessary about deserters. Robert should come with him to Hasteback. There he would be safe till it was time to leave. "And I promise to hide you if the sheriff comes," the neighbor assured Robert.

Karl Oskar advised his brother to accept the offer: "Dry your tears and go with Jonas Petter!"

Robert felt ashamed of having cried, grown-up as he was, but his heart ached at this thought: "Suppose . . . suppose I couldn't get away."

He obeyed his brother and departed with the obliging neighbor.

Jonas Petter sat down to supper in the kitchen at Hasteback, and asked Robert to join him. He took out the brannvin jug and poured two equally tall drinks for them: the boy was a man now. And Robert was eager to take a drink, perhaps two or three, for brannvin seemed to silence the humming sound in his left ear, which still bothered him. He had lost his hearing almost entirely in that ear, yet he heard a sound which no one else could hear. Perhaps it would never leave him, perhaps this echo from Aron's box would hum as long as he lived.

Brita-Stafva, the farm wife, came in from the byre carrying her wooden milk pails. She was a knotty woman, with hard, manly features. Dark shadows of an unmistakable beard covered her lips, and there was also a tuft of hair on the tip of her chin. A woman with a beard aroused fear in some way. Jonas Petter had a bushy, black beard, yet Robert did not fear him. But those thin hairs on the wife's chin made him uncomfortable; they were outside the norm. All children were afraid of Brita-Stafva.

She put down her pails and eyed the boy sullenly. But the look she then turned on her husband was hardly sullen: it was more—evil, full of hatred. Jonas Petter never tried to hide the fact that he and his wife lived on bad terms.

The men at the table drank their brannvin. Brita-Stafva said sharply, looking at Robert: "The sheriff's carriage just passed."

"Oh yes, my boy, he went to Korpamoen. Now you see, lad, we were lucky not to meet him!"

Robert lost interest in the food but he drank the brannvin. The roar in his ear was violent tonight, almost frightening him.

"Eat, lad. Don't be afraid," Jonas Petter encouraged him. "I've a safe hiding place if the sheriff comes here and asks for you."

Brita-Stafva was busy straining the evening milk; when she heard that the sheriff's passing might concern Robert, she became curious and looked questioningly at him. He felt ill at ease under her gaze, he could not help looking at the beard-tuft on her chin.

Jonas Petter poured himself more drinks; his eyes were taking on a blank look.

"Lonnegren is a decent sheriff," he said. "Sharp in his words but he's a hell of a nice fellow. I've known him since he was a boy—he's the son of the 'Stump of Orranas.'"

"I've heard about that farmer," said Robert, mostly to say something. "Why was he called the Stump?"

"How did he get the nickname? I'll tell you, my boy!"

Jonas Petter glanced in the direction of his wife, busy with the milk pans; he was by now quite lively from all the brannvin.

"It's an amazing story. It's a story of a woman who sharpened a knife."

At these last words a rattle from the milk strainer was heard. The farm wife had made a quick movement. It was almost dark where she stood in the hearth corner, but Robert noticed that her head jerked at her husband's words.

He also had noticed that the couple had exchanged no words.

Jonas Petter knew of all unusual happenings which had taken place in Konga County within the last hundred years; he was about to tell Robert how it came to be that Sheriff Lonnegren's father was called the Stump.

A Story About a Wife Who Sharpened a Knife

The farmer of Orranas was christened Isak, Jonas Petter began. He was known far and wide because he was crazy about women, and often led astray by them. He couldn't keep his hands off a woman who was shaped well enough to be used by a man. It didn't matter what her face was like, whether she was spotted and marred by smallpox, harelipped, warp-mouthed, or with any other defect; Isak would try to seduce her. He was married and in his own conjugal bed he had a plump, good-looking wife to play with. But this didn't diminish his desire to visit other marital beds; neither married nor unmarried women were safe from him. He had a strange power over women, perhaps from the devil, perhaps from somewhere else. His visits to married women often had got him into trouble with offended husbands; once his arm was broken and another time his nose smashed in. But still he persisted, he still had the same power even after his nose was flattened.

His wife was exceedingly jealous of other women, and many times she threatened to leave him; but each time he promised and swore he would mend his ways and stick to his own bed. She tried to find a cure for his sinful lust through many concoctions which she mixed and gave to him—juices from roots, bitter herb porridges to cool his blood. But no matter what he ate or drank, strong as ever the whoring desire still possessed him.

There was, however, one successful cure for him, a cruel and horrible cure, and his wife finally administered it.

One day she told their hired man that she wanted a cutting knife sharpened: she needed it to cut old rags. He believed her, of course, and sharpened the knife as she herself pulled the grindstone.

In bed that evening Isak as usual sought his wife; he attended to her as often as she could wish, and never neglected her for other women. And it seemed now as ever that she was willing; he had no suspicions, poor man. He did not know that his wife had sharpened a knife and hidden it under the mattress.

As the husband now was ready she took out her knife and cut off his implement, root and branch.

Isak fainted and bled in streams. His wife had in advance sent for a blood stancher, who arrived at the house immediately after the occurrence. He now did what he could for the injured one, and the wife, also in advance, had made concoctions from *skvattram* and bloodroot, which herbs were used to stop bleeding from injuries. Together they stanched the wound of her husband before he became conscious.

The wife then nursed Isak with much love and care till his recovery.

Nor was it known that the couple became unfriendly toward each other because of her action; they lived together until their dying days.

But Isak of Orranas was never the same man after his operation; he grew slack and dull in his mind, and showed no interest in what he was doing. He neglected his farm more and more. After a few years he sold Orranas, which consisted of half a homestead, and set himself down on reserved rights.

Ever after he kept his hands and other limbs away from women. Indifferent as a gelded steer, he had no more interest in them. From now on he lived a harmonious and pious life with his wife, to whom he was greatly devoted in his old days.

The limb which the wife had cut from her husband she dried and put away. She wanted to keep it as a souvenir. She only brought it out once in a while, when visitors came, or at some celebration or other when relatives and friends were gathered. While Isak listened in silence, she would tell how she went about it that time when she cured her husband of his sinful lust. She would also take out the Bible and refer to that place where it says a man must cut off that limb that is an offense to him in order to save his soul from eternal suffering; she had done for her husband what ought to be done, because all must agree that the limb she had relieved him of had been a great offense.

It was rumored, however, that Isak of Orranas still had a

small part left, and this led to his nickname, the Stump, concluded Jonas Petter.

5

In the silence ensuing after the story's end Robert heard his
ear roar more clearly. The wife had by now finished straining
the milk, and was removing the dishes from the table. Her
mouth was closed in a narrow line. She had looked at her
husband a few times while he was telling the story, but remained mute. Robert had not yet heard them speak to each
other this evening.

Jonas Petter many times before had told him tales of
women's evil deeds, and Robert could guess why the farmer
spoke so. But this, as far as Robert knew, was the first time
his own wife had been listening.

It was a cruel fate that had overtaken Isak of Orranas, and
Robert thought he must be careful before he lay down with a
woman—he must always feel under the mattress to be on the
safe side.

"The son who became sheriff was born many years before
this," added Jonas Petter, as if this explanation were necessary.

In hearing the sheriff mentioned, Robert's fears returned:
the sheriff was on the roads, looking for him. Wouldn't it be
wise to run away and hide in the woods? His ear kept on
throbbing, the brannvin could not silence that sound tonight.

Suddenly he rose: he could hear wagon wheels on the road;
it must be the sheriff on his way back. Brita-Stafva, too,
heard the sound of the carriage and went out on the stoop.

Jonas Petter said: "Sit down, lad! Don't be afraid!"

Robert did sit down but he was afraid. A desperate fear
filled his breast; it felt too small, it was overfull, he could not
ease the pressure. It didn't help to exhale, it was still full, it
was strained and squeezed.

And a storm raged in his injured ear: Here, my little hand,
here is a big box! This one you'll remember!

If . . . if he were left behind? If he weren't allowed to go
with Karl Oskar? Then the gates on the America road would
never open for him.

The wagon noise from without was heard more distinctly,

it came from light wheels, rolling speedily; it was a light carriage. It could be no one else but the returning sheriff.

The wife had gone outside and did not return. She had hard eyes and a beard on her chin. And she looked queerly at him. Why did she slip out as soon as she heard the carriage? What was she doing outside?

Robert moistened his dry lips with the tip of his tongue: "Jonas Petter . . . She went out. . . . She won't say anything?"

"Brita-Stafva?"

"Yes."

Robert was convinced the farm wife would betray him if in doing so she could vex her husband.

"She won't hail him?" the youth whispered; he was short of breath.

"She should dare!"

Jonas Petter's voice rose. He bent forward across the table toward the boy whom he had promised to protect against the sheriff. "If she dares, *then I'll sharpen the knife tonight!*"

Robert stared at him, forgetting his own fear at the words of the peasant. What did he mean? Sharpen the knife? What knife?

"Sharpen the knife . . . ?"

"Yes. *Otherwise I'd thought of doing it tomorrow.*"

What did Jonas Petter intend to do? He had lived in deep discord with his wife for many years—did he intend to harm her now? Would he cut her up? What kind of knife did he want to sharpen? He was getting drunk—it could be heard and seen.

The sound of the carriage had died down, and Brita-Stafva came inside.

She said it was the churchwarden, Per Persson of Akerby, driving by. He had been in Korpamoen to speak to Karl Oskar about the impending auction of the farm chattels.

At last Robert's chest felt free, he could breathe easier. He poured himself another drink.

As yet this evening he had not heard the couple of Hasteback speak to each other. Brita-Stafva now opened her tight lips, but only to eat of the potato porridge she had prepared for herself. Jonas Petter's eyes were brannvin-bleary, he repeated in a mumble, again and again: *A man, too, could sharpen a knife.*

There was really no meaning to what he said: it was always the menfolk who sharpened tools, knives and such. So Robert could not understand what the farmer sitting there meant with his insinuating remarks. He could not know what was to take place the following day between the husband and wife of Hasteback. There were to be no witnesses to these happenings—it was after Robert had gone out.

Story of a Man Who Sharpened a Knife

When they had finished their breakfast the following morning the farmer rose slowly from the table and turned to his wife, who was washing the dishes near the fire. He wanted to do some sharpening; she was to go with him and crank the grindstone; no one else was available at that moment; Robert was already in the fields.

Brita-Stafva did not answer. To answer would have been to use unnecessary words between them. After their latest great quarrel, three days of silence had passed. Today was the morning of the fourth day.

The wife dried her hands on her apron and followed her husband outside.

The grindstone stood under the large mountain ash near the barn gable. It was cool there in the shadow of the tree during hot summer days; now—in early spring—the wind howled around the corner of the house. Brita-Stafva wiped a drop from her nose-tip, while she leaned against the grindstone bench, waiting for her husband who had gone to the well.

Jonas Petter returned and poured well water into the grindstone trough. His wife took hold of the crank handle to begin.

But where was the ax? Brita-Stafva looked around; she had thought they were to sharpen an ax. A scythe wasn't used this time of year, and she knew of nothing else that needed sharpening. She almost asked: Have you forgotten the ax? But she remembered in time, she must not use unnecessary words. She would show her husband that she could keep silent as long as —nay, longer than—he.

Jonas Petter was not going to sharpen his ax today; he took out a knife.

His wife pulled on the handle, the grindstone turned, and the water in the trough rippled smoothly as water in a gutter. The crutch was dry, ungreased, and squeaked and whined; the peasant splashed a handful of water from the trough in its direction; the crutch, satisfied, was silent.

The wife gazed at the knife in her husband's hand. It was a sticking knife, used in cattle slaughter. Jonas Petter had had it for years, and many pigs, sheep, and calves had given up their lives to it. It was a good knife; she had borrowed it herself at times when she needed a sharp cutting tool. Jonas Petter used to say that it was sharp-edged as a razor when newly honed.

But no slaughter was impending on the farm. They had no animal to kill. Not before October would they have slaughter again, and this was only March. If one is going to use a sticking knife in October, one doesn't sharpen it in March. So much was sure and true.

Brita-Stafva was apprehensive; indeed, she had reason to be. And fear crept over her as she recalled the words her husband had repeated last night after telling the story of the Stump of Orranas. Why was he sharpening this slaughter knife today?

Jonas Petter stood bent over the grindstone, his countenance dark, his lips tightly pressed together. He looked sharply in front of him, eyes focusing stubbornly on the knife edge. He was sharpening his knife and it seemed that nothing in the world existed for him except his current occupation: the sharpening of this knife.

He turned the knife and sharpened the other side of the edge, moving it back and forth across the stone, from handle to point. But his eyes did not leave the edge. His face wore an expression of determination; there was determination in his immobile position, in his bent back, in his tightly closed lips. Every part of him radiated determination. He acted like a man who had made a decision which nothing could persuade him to change in the smallest detail.

And his wife at the grindstone handle asked herself: What was he going to do with the sticking knife?

She turned the crank. The stone was not heavy. It had been large and heavy once, when it came to the farm, but after all the scythes, axes, and knives whose edges had been sharpened against it, it was now no bigger than a Christmas cheese. A child could crank it. And when the wife let out a sigh, this was not because of the heavy stone or the hard work; it was caused by something entirely different: her husband's preoccupation.

During their marriage she had always been quick to correct him when he made mistakes. If his actions lacked common sense, or were willfully wrong, she used to tell him so; this was a wifely duty. But now he accepted her corrections no longer. She continued to point out to him all his foolish and unreasonable actions, great or small. But no more did he listen to her. He called it criticism and scolding, and he didn't like being blamed and censured. Yet he persisted in such behavior that she was forced to show him right from wrong. Then he grew angry. At the least word from her he grew angry. She, in her turn, both upset and sad, told him the truth: he was an evil husband who cared not what she thought or felt.

Owing to his difficult nature quarrels between them occurred at shorter and shorter intervals, increased in bitterness, and began to last longer. After each quarrel the words between them seemed to dry up entirely; they went about in silence, without a syllable's crossing their lips for days at a stretch. Even the time of silence was extended, sometimes into weeks.

How she had worried lately over his unreasonable behavior! No one knew what the devil might put into a person's head and make him do.

It was some time ago—after an intense and long-drawn-out quarrel—that he had said: Rather than let you torture me to death, rather than be nagged to death, I'll do it myself, I'll kill myself with a knife! *I would rather cut myself to death!*

And what a look he had in his eyes that time, Jonas Petter! Since then she had been in constant anxiety. What mightn't the devil tempt a weak human being to do? Since then she had hidden away all cutting tools—all but this slaughter knife, which she had not found. But this was not sufficient to reassure her; he might get hold of a thong, or a strap, and go to the nearest tree or beam; he might jump into the well. There was always something handy if you wished to take your own life, always One ready to help you, always and everywhere.

For a while she had tried to keep back words that might irritate him. She would correct him only about small chores and such, not worth mentioning. Nonetheless, he still became upset and angry. What could she do with so difficult a husband?

And what was he planning now, with this knife? He wanted

it so sharp, it seemed he would never get it sharp enough! Never before had he needed so fine an edge, not even at cattle slaughter. What was she to think of all this sharpening?

Jonas Petter stretched his back for a moment, took the knife in his left hand and felt the edge with his right thumb, testing the bite. Brita-Stafva stopped cranking and the stone rested.

Still he was not satisfied with the edge on his knife; she must crank some more. Again the stone turned, the water in the trough purled and swirled. And he kept on sharpening the knife, morose, relentless, mute.

Perspiration was breaking out at the back of Brita-Stafva's neck, drops ran down her spine. It was not caused by the weight of the grindstone, but by the questions she asked herself. A knife could be well sharpened in five minutes; he had kept on for fifteen. What did it mean? It didn't make sense. He would never be satisfied with the edge—he seemed to want a razor edge today. *Was he sharpening the knife for his own neck? If not, for what?*

The peasant kept on sharpening, now and then testing the bite against his thumb, carefully, deliberately, then putting the knife back to the stone.

And the wife cranked on. This was not sane. What was it he had said last night?—A man, too, can sharpen a knife. And the way his eyes had looked of late, showing whites under the pupils; he no longer had the eyes of a sane person. It was plain he contemplated some madness.

She could ask: Why do you sharpen the sticking knife? No slaughter is imminent. But she had hardly spoken to him for three days, wanting to show him that she could hold her tongue. Moreover, she would receive no clear information, perhaps he might say something like: A sharp knife is always needed in a house.

Peace, also, was needed in the house; but that they would never have, except in the dull silences between their squabbles.

Now she had cranked the grindstone almost half an hour. No sane man acted thus, sharpening the same knife hours on end. She couldn't stand it any longer, her forehead was wet with perspiration, her body limp, her legs shook, unable to hold her up.

And when her husband tried the knife edge against his

thumb for the tenth or eleventh time, she burst out: "Won't you ever get it sharp? Are we to stand here the whole day? Are we to keep on for eternity? Get someone else to crank!"

She let go the handle and went over and collapsed like an old empty sack on a stone near the barn.

Jonas Petter did not look in her direction; it was as if he hadn't heard her. He felt with his thumb along the edge of the knife, slowly, unhurried. Then he dried the knife against his trouser leg, mumbling to himself: "I believe it'll do now."

He picked up the empty water pail in one hand and the newly sharpened knife in the other and went toward the house.

The wife followed his steps with vigilant eyes; when she saw him enter the kitchen she rose to follow. She didn't run, but she hurried. Did he intend to commit the crime inside the house? Perhaps he had gone up in the attic to be alone. There was no one in the house now, the people were at their work, the boy from Korpamoen with them; she and her husband were alone. And alone she could not get the knife away from him, she did not have sufficient strength. Should she run to a neighbor for help?

Brita-Stafva went after her husband into the kitchen. He was not there. He must have gone up into the attic; she thought she heard steps up here. Looking about, she seemed to remember something; she stretched herself on tiptoe and looked on the shelf above the fireplace: there lay the newly sharpened knife, glistening; her husband had put it back in its usual place. She let out a long, long sigh of deep relief.

Grabbing the sticking knife, she hid it under her apron and went out. She walked to the wagon shed and found her way into the darkest corner. There she stuck the sharp knife behind a beam against the roof. She pushed it so far in that no one could even see the handle. A more secret hiding place she could not find on the whole farm, she thought, as she climbed down again.

Meanwhile Jonas Petter had returned from the attic where he had walked about for no particular reason. On entering the kitchen he too went over to the shelf above the fireplace and looked. He nodded in confirmation, and satisfaction radiated from his eyes: exactly as he had hoped. The knife was gone; the threat had worked; he was safe from her now. It had gone so far that he had been forced to sharpen a knife for half an hour in order to get her where he wanted her.

He was pleased now; he knew that he would get the rest and peace he needed in the home during the time that was left—during the three remaining weeks before he was to break free from his wife, before he left her forever. He needed peace and quiet during this time of preparation. To gain this had surely been worth half an hour at the grindstone.

6

Robert remained at Hasteback for three weeks, and no sheriff came to search for him.

One evening Jonas Petter called him aside and said: "We'll keep company to America, you and I. I sail on the same ship as the others."

In secrecy, one more America chest was readied in this region—the third.

X

A PEASANT BOWS FOR THE LAST TIME

1

This was the dawn of a great era in the lives of the old clothes chests throughout the peasant communities. After centuries of neglect in dark loft corners they were now being scrubbed and polished and prepared for their voyage across the great sea. These chests were to be in the vanguard of history's greatest migration. To them would be entrusted the emigrants' most cherished belongings.

What must be brought along, what must be left behind? What was obtainable in the new land, and what was unobtainable? No one could advise, no one had traveled ahead to ascertain. It was not a move where wagon after wagon could be loaded; one small cartload must take care of all. Only the least bulky and most indispensable things were chosen.

In the bottom of the Korpamoen America chest were placed the heaviest items—iron and steel, all the timberman's and the carpenter's tools: adz, hatchet, chisel, drawknife, plane, hammer, horseshoer's tongs, auger, sticking knife, skinning knife, rule and yardstick. Also the hunter's gear: gun, powder horn, and the skin pouch for small shot. Karl Oskar took apart his muzzle-loader to facilitate its packing. There was said to be as much game in America as there was shortage of guns. A gun was said to cost fifty daler. Robert thought of all the streams and waters abounding in fish, and he packed trolling gear for pike, and hooks, angling twine, wire for fish snares. Nils brought out an old bleeding iron which might be of use to his sons; he advised the emigrants to bleed themselves often; the most reliable cure for all ills was to let one's blood.

Kristina packed her wool cards, her knitting needles, sheep shears, and her swingle, a betrothal gift from Karl Oskar, who had painted red flowers on it. A great deal she left because it would take up too much ship space, things she knew she would need later. She could not take her loom or her flax brake, her spinning-wheel or her yarn winder, her spooling wheel or her flax comb. She had been accustomed to working with all these implements; they were intimate and familiar to her hands; she knew that she would miss them in the foreign land.

Marta had helped her weave a piece of wadmal from which the village tailor had sewn them fine, warm clothing for the journey. And she packed warm woolen garments for both big and little, underwear and outer wear, working clothes and Sunday best. Woolen garments were scarce in America, she had heard somewhere, as they had not yet had time over there to make as many looms as they needed. She must take along woolen and linen yarns, and needles and thread of all kinds, so that they could patch and mend their clothing and stockings, for it would surely be a long time before they would again have new things on their bodies; the old must last. Between the clothes Kristina placed camphor and lavender to prevent mildew and bad odors; no one knew how long these things must remain in the chest.

Their bridal quilt they must take, and all bedclothes, sheets, mattresses, and bolsters were packed in two great four-bushel sacks which were then sewn up at both ends with heavy twine. All small gear to be used on the crossing was packed in the knapsack: drinking vessels, eating tools, mugs, wooden plates, spoons, knives, and forks. Kristina must also prepare a food basket for six people. The ship was to provide their food on the voyage, but no one knew if they could eat the ship's fare, and they had a long way to travel before they embarked, and after landing, too. The basket must contain dried, smoked, and salted foods which would keep well and not spoil on the ocean. A roomy willow basket with a wooden lid would serve as their food chest, and into this Kristina packed eight rye-meal loaves and twenty of barley, a wooden tub of strongly salted butter, two quarts of honey, one cheese, half a dozen smoked sausages, a quarter of smoked lamb, a piece of salt pork, and some twenty salted herrings. This filled the basket to the top. They must also find space for a pound of coffee, a pound of sugar, a bag of dried apples, a few small bags of salt, pepper, stick cinnamon, wormwood seed, and cumin.

They must keep clean and tidy during the voyage: they must not forget the pot of soft soap, and the phosphor salve for lice. Kristina had bought two excellent fine-tooth combs of brass to keep the children's heads free of vermin.

But even more important were the medicinal needs of the emigrants: camphor, and the tiny bottles of medicine containing Hoffman's Heart-Aiding Drops, The Prince's Drops, The Four Kinds of Drops. As a cure against seasickness Karl Oskar prepared half a gallon of wormwood-seed brannvin; a drink of this every morning at sea on empty stomachs would keep bodies in working order; wormwood-seed brannvin was also good for ship's fever, and protected the body against cholera and other contagious ship maladies.

Berta of Idemo called to warn Kristina about the seasickness; married women were badly attacked by it, worse than men or unmarried women, for unknown reasons. Perhaps the bodily juices in a woman changed when she entered into holy matrimony, so that afterward she became sensitive to the sea. Berta's father had been to sea and he had taught her the way seamen cared for their health and cured their ills. She had sewn camphor into a small skin pouch which she gave to

Kristina; this she must hang around her stomach while on board ship; it would ease seasickness. This was not a mortal disease, yet it was one of the most painful God had sent as punishment to man. Kristina must also eat a few spoonfuls of oat porridge every day, and take along a quart of vinegar to mix in the drinking water to freshen it up before drinking, because often water turned stale and poisonous on long voyages.

Kristina had confidence in Berta of Idemo, who in her youth had cured her gangrene-infected knee, and she listened to all the good advice: she must use pepper brannvin for diarrhea; indeed, she must guard well against diarrhea and constipation. She must keep a vigilant eye on her stool, to see that it had the right firmness—there was nothing more important for seafarers than to keep the stool firm; this the old seamen knew. And Berta had heard that people after landing in North America often suffered from intense diarrhea; even the intestines would run out, if they were not looked after. People became so wasted that they could hardly stand or walk; nothing helped except a drink of brannvin into which had been mixed a pinch of ground pepper.

The earth in America was said to crawl and creep with poisonous vipers and insects, and this might not be healthy for children running barefooted. Kristina was to put dry camphor into the wounds of snake bites. In all other fresh wounds warm urine, of course, was the best ointment; it cleaned and healed and had for thousands of years been their forebears' washing water for wounds. And if someone had an injury which didn't seem to heal, but might turn into gangrene, then Kristina must scrape the wound twice daily with a clean, sharp cutting knife—this perhaps she remembered? Broken arms and legs must be put into splints as soon as possible, and the firmer she got the splint the sooner the break would heal.

A question stole into Kristina's heart long before Berta had finished giving advice about injuries, accidents, diseases, and sicknesses which the emigrants might encounter on land or sea—the old, anxious question: Was it absolutely necessary that they carry out this dangerous foreign venture? *Must* they walk into all these dangers?

2

Karl Oskar sold Korpamoen to a farmer from Linneryd. His asking price had to be cut down; after all, the one emigrating was forced to sell, while the prospective buyer was certainly not forced to buy. Karl Oskar had to be satisfied with one hundred and fifty daler less than he himself had paid. On the other hand, his cattle—which were sold at auction—brought good prices because there was a great shortage of animals after the enforced slaughter during the famine year. But the auctioneer, Per Persson, the churchwarden, kept a quarter of all proceeds as he was to advance the money. Those were hard terms, but Karl Oskar could not stay home half a year to collect from all the bidders.

After the auction of the farmstead belongings the house seemed almost empty to Karl Oskar and Kristina. All objects sold were carried off except the beds, which they were to use until the day of departure so as not to have to sleep on the floor.

The emigrating farmer could now take stock of his position. One thousand two hundred daler remained from the sale of the farm and from the auction, after deduction of the mortgage and other debts. Their passage to America would cost six hundred and seventy-five daler for the whole family, three adults and three children. Karl Oskar would arrive in the New World with about five hundred daler. Then they must pay the entrance fee to America, and the transportation to their place of settling—an unknown way of unknown distance. Karl Oskar hoped to obtain land practically free of charge, but not much remained for the purchase of farm implements and cattle. Nils and Marta were dismayed when they heard how much the passage cost: almost half the amount necessary to buy a farm—their son threw half a farm into the sea!

Karl Oskar asked Kristina to find some safe hiding place for their five hundred daler; their only remaining security must not be lost or stolen during the long journey. She sewed the money into a sheepskin bag which he could fasten to a belt and carry next to his body.

Any person of good character was permitted to leave the country nowadays without having to petition the King. You could even leave without the extract from the parish register. So had Fredrik of Kvarntorpet done, and others who were listed under "End of the Parish." Robert, having escaped from service, dared not go near the dean to ask for his papers. But Karl Oskar did not wish to leave as if he had done wrong. He wanted to separate openly from his parish. He went to Dean Brusander and asked for his papers, as he and his household intended to emigrate to North America.

The dean looked quizzically at this first parishioner to come on such an errand.

"I've heard about your intentions. Why do you wish to emigrate, Karl Oskar Nilsson?"

"I have debts and hardships and cannot improve my situation here at home."

"It has pleased God to send us a year of famine. But a devout Christian does not complain in time of tribulation. You know your catechism, Karl Oskar Nilsson, that I remember. You must therefore know that trials and tribulations are sent for your soul's betterment?"

Karl Oskar stood there, three steps from the high-backed, leather-covered chair where his spiritual adviser sat before a desk. He held his old cap in his hands but did not answer; how could he argue on tenets of faith with the dean, who was schooled to understand and explain?

"You are known as a capable, industrious farmer. Can't you find sustenance in your home community?"

"It doesn't seem so, Mr. Dean."

"But you have adequate sustenance for your household. A person ought to be satisfied with adequate sustenance!"

Karl Oskar twisted his worn skin cap. He could mention Anna, his child, whom he had lost because of hunger. But he knew the dean would answer that this was a trial sent for his betterment. He could not argue with his pastor in spiritual matters.

"You'll make an unfortunate example for my other parishioners, Karl Oskar Nilsson."

And the dean rose from his chair and walked across the floor.

He had heard nothing but good about the people from Korpamoen; they were related to Danjel in Karragarde, but they had not been tainted by his heresy. Karl Oskar and his wife were among the most trusted, most devout people in the parish. Ill-willed persons would say that conditions in the parish must be beggarly when this industrious, diligent couple were unable to earn their living at home, and were forced to emigrate to another continent.

"The demented farmer of Karragärde has forfeited his right to live in this kingdom," continued Brusander. "He still goes free, thanks to our enlightened times. But I wish to keep an honest man like you in my parish."

The dean laid his hand on Karl Oskar's broad peasant shoulder. "Have you thoroughly thought over the adventure you throw yourself into, with wife and children? Do you know the truth about this land that tempts you?"

Brusander did not give the farmer time to answer; he himself began to explain conditions in the New World. North America had been from the very beginning populated by rebels and troublemakers who had tried to overthrow legal order in their own lands. From the time of its discovery America had been settled primarily by disloyal and refractory individuals, insubordinate to authority at home, people who had broken laws and wanted to escape just punishment. It had been overrun early by dissenters, sunderers of religion, exiled from home when spreading heresies. So it had been through many hundreds of years, so it was today. Those who incited others against spiritual and temporal authorities in their homelands in Europe escaped to the United States. To the United States fled murderers from the block, thieves from jail, swindlers from their victims, dishonest people from their debts, seducers from seduced and pregnant women, all those who feared something in their homeland, all those who did not like the order of a sound and pious community. In North America they had nothing to fear, they were safe there, all those rebels and criminals from the Old World.

Among the emigrants there were also, of course, honest people who had not broken the laws of their own country. But what drove these into adventure? Nothing but the desire for worldly gain, for enjoyment of the flesh, for vain and transient things. It was the evil desire in their minds that drove them away; they were too lazy to earn a living through honest work; they wanted to gain riches without work; the emigrants wished for quick riches so they might afterwards live in gluttony, drunkenness, idleness, and adultery. The greatest part of them were arrogant, foolhardy, reckless people who spoke ill of their fatherland, who spit at the mother who had borne them.

It was true that the soil was fertile in North America, so the inhabitants could find their living easily. But a Christian must also consider the spiritual situation of the American people. In that country there were still wild, red-skinned tribes who lived almost like animals; and even among the white-skinned people there were many who were unfamiliar with the true God and the pure evangelical teachings. True Christians ought not to be haughty toward them, ought rather to feel sorry for them; but all people living in Swedish communities should thank God that He had let them be born in a land where true Christianity was taught. It might be true that Swedes had to work a little harder for their food than Americans, nay, at times even eat their bread in the sweat of their brow. But their forebears in Sweden had for long ages had to eat bread from the bark of trees, and endure hunger, yet they had done great things, much greater things than the Swedes of today. Bark bread gave spiritual strength to men. They also found strength in their contentment, and in their obedience to God and authority.

Great confusion and chaos existed in the United States. Dissenters and preachers of unsound doctrines went about on the loose, allowed to do what they wanted. The authorities stupidly let them alone. There were no less than eighty-seven false religious sects. The Americans were building a new tower of Babel to reach into the heavens. But the Lord soon would destroy and crush this confused land called the United States. For a sound, enduring order could be built only on unity in religion, on the only true and right teaching—the holy tenets of the Augsburg Confession.

The Lord God was a strong avenger. Within fifty years those United States would exist no more; within fifty years they would be obliterated from the face of the earth, like the empires of Rome and Babylon.

"Within fifty years! Remember my words! Remember my words!"

The dean stopped short; he had intended to say only a few words, and now he had preached a whole little sermon, to a congregation of one parishioner. But he must tell Karl Oskar

Nilsson that America was a land for false prophets such as Danjel Andreasson, for adventurers and rouges such as Fredrik Thron—not a place of settlement for an honest, able farmer like himself.

And he pleaded: "Karl Oskar Nilsson! Remain in your home community and earn your living decently, as before!"

During the dean's speech Karl Oskar had stood quietly, twisting the cap in his hand, in right turns; now he started twisting it in the other direction, toward the left, while his eyes wandered along the walls of the big room in the parsonage, where hung many portraits of Brusander's predecessors in office. Perhaps a dozen deans and vicars and curates looked down on him from the four walls, some kindly admonishing, others urging more strongly, but all definitely dissuading—all agreeing in their successor's appeal: "Stay at home and earn your living honorably!"

"Aren't you misled? Aren't you seeing illusions and mirages?" the dean went on.

Karl Oskar stopped twisting his cap—then he began again, this time to the right. It was like an examination in the catechism, and, when he left home, he had not been prepared for an examination in order to obtain his papers. He could have answered these questions; but some of the awe for his confirmation teacher remained within him; he knew the dean did not like to be contradicted, and whatever he said the dean would twist so that he, Brusander, would be in the right.

The dean's brow wrinkled: a peasant leaving his farm to emigrate to North America—a new sign of that spiritual decay which had set in among the country people, tearing asunder holy ties. The outermost cause of this evil was disobedience of the Fourth Commandment; as a result of this primary disobedience, even the last tie might be broken, the tie holding people to the beloved fatherland.

"Your venture might be the ruination of you and yours; therefore I advise against it. And you must be aware I speak only for your good."

"I think you mean well, Mr. Dean."

Karl Oskar had always felt that his pastor was sincere in the fatherly care of his parishioners' spiritual and temporal needs, even though at times he assumed too great authority.

The dean went on: Because the emigrants were driven by selfishness and lust of the flesh—man's base, carnal desires—

emigration to the United States was contrary to God's commandments and the true evangelical Lutheran church. Emigrants from Sweden had already been made aware of this in a frightful way. A group of people from the northern provinces—from Helsingland and Dalecarlia—had been led astray by an apostle of the devil, an instrument of falsehood, a peasant named Erik Janson, and in their blindness had emigrated to North America. On their journey they were stricken by cholera, that scourge from God. Hundreds of the poor people had died before they reached their destination. The Lord God was a powerful avenger, and cholera His instrument. The horrible punishment had calmed restlessness at home in the last year, quenched desire to emigrate.

After the experience of these sectarians one could comprehend God's opinion of emigration.

"Answer me honestly, Karl Oskar: Is it not the desire for high living that drives you to emigrate?"

Karl Oskar was still twisting his cap with both hands as before. He did not contemplate the voyage to North America in order to abandon himself to those vices enumerated in the catechism: debauchery, gluttony, adultery, and others, which tended to shorten one's life. He had not had high living in mind, of that he was sure.

"No. It isn't because of that. Do not think so, Mr. Dean. It isn't because I desire high living."

"I believe your word," said the dean. "But you are seized by the spirit of dissatisfaction. Otherwise you would remain in the land of your fathers. And have you thought of your parents, whom you abandon? And your father a cripple!"

"Their reserved rights go with the property, as usual. The old ones will manage."

"But if all young people and those fit for work should emigrate, and leave the old and decrepit behind, who would then take care of the helpless?"

Karl Oskar kept silent, twisting his cap with fumbling, clumsy fingers. If only he were quick-witted; whatever he might say, the dean would surely put him in the wrong. And it seemed to him that he must tell his pastor it was time to stop his dissuasion. If the bishop himself were to come to the dean's aid, he, Karl Oskar, still would not change his mind; nay, not even if the King tried to persuade him. Moreover, it was too late.

He now said, somewhat tartly: "I've already sold out. I'm free and without obligations. Perhaps I could have my errand attended to . . . ?"

Dean Brusander sat down and leaned his head against the high back of his chair. He set his lips, and his mouth took on a sterner look.

This peasant from Korpamoen seemed on the surface tractable and decent; but apparently he had a bullish nature. Through all the dean's kindness and repeated advice he had not been able to move Karl Oskar one iota. Occasionally he had answered a few words, but for the most part he had persisted in a silence that was deaf to God's words and his pastor's admonitions. No human power could remove the man's emigration notions. And now he sounded almost importunate, as he referred to his errand. It might well be that he lacked respect for the office of the ministry. Perhaps after all he was a horse of a different color.

At any rate, the dean had done his duty as teacher and pastor. And he was pretty sure this farmer would be alone in his America ideas. This desire for emigration among the peasantry, which had broken out here and there throughout the kingdom, would probably die down as quickly as it had flared up. Twenty years from now there would be no one in the land with a mind to emigrate.

"You shall have your papers!"

A silence ensued. Only the quill's scratching against the paper was heard from the desk. Karl Oskar took a step backward, as if wishing to leave the dean undisturbed with his writing.

Dean Brusander turned and handed the farmer the extract from the parish register.

"Once I gave you Christian baptism. Once I prepared you for the Lord's Supper. I've baptized your children. Now I pray God to bless you and yours during your voyage to a faraway land. May you never regret your bold decision!"

Karl Oskar bowed. "Thank you, Mr. Dean."

Brusander extended his hand. "May you be within God's protection! Such was the blessing of our forebears at times of parting."

"Thank you most kindly, Mr. Dean."

And Karl Oskar bowed once more, this time perhaps

deeper than he had ever bowed to the dean before. After all, it was the last time he would bow to his parish pastor.

Dean Brusander wrote a few words in the parish register, words which he never before had written about any one of his parishioners: he noted that homeowner Karl Oskar Nilsson of Korpamoen, on the twenty-eighth of March, 1850, had requested extracts from the records for himself and his household for emigration to N. America.

And the remaining blank pages in the parish register were in time to be filled with the repeated notation: "Moved to N. America." Through years and decades they were to be filled, page after page, with the names of Karl Oskar Nilsson's followers.

XI

ONE EMIGRANT PAYS NO FARE

1

In the newspaper *Barometern,* to which some of the farmers in the village subscribed, there appeared early in spring a news item about a lost emigrant ship: "Owing to absence of communications of any kind, one is now forced to admit the sad foundering and total loss of the small schooner *Betty Catharina,* built in 1835, measuring 80 lasts, on voyage from Soderhamn to New York. The schooner had taken on a load of pig iron in Soderhamn. On board the vessel were 70 emigrants who had left their fatherland to see a precarious living in a foreign country. The *Betty Catharina* sailed through the straits of Ore Sund on April the 15th of last year but since that date her owner, the firm P. C. Rettig et Cie., has had no word from her. Since now almost a year has passed without the slightest information as to the ship's whereabouts, notice of the deaths of the crew—nine men—has been published in their respective home communities. The ship's Master was Captain Anders Otto Ronning. The emigrants came from different parishes in Helsingland; among them were 25 women and 20 children."

This copy of the paper was widely read in the village, and

no wonder, in those days; it was even lent to families who did not subscribe. Berta of Idemo brought it to Korpamoen, and Kristina read about the ship whose sailing time was supposed to be about five weeks yet after fifty weeks had not reached her destination. The *Betty Catharina*'s passengers had not arrived in a new land; they had emigrated to the bottom of the ocean.

A stab of pain went through Kristina's heart as she tucked in her three little ones that evening—". . . among them were 25 women and 20 children." All her earlier anxiety returned and pressed upon her. The children were left in her care by God—wasn't she an irresponsible mother to take her helpless little ones out in a fragile ship to cross the forbidding ocean? She did not fear for her own life; but had she the right to endanger her children? If they went down with the ship, then it was she who drowned them, and God would ask accounting for them on the Day of Judgment: How did you look after your children? What did you do with them? Who forced you out on the ocean? Weren't you warned of the danger?

Wasn't the notice of the lost ship a last warning from God, arriving as it did on the eve of their departure?

Karl Oskar said that most people on land died in their beds, yet people went to bed every evening. Only fools were frightened by stories of wrecks. Robert wasn't afraid either. He wasn't old enough, he didn't have his mature senses as yet. As if it were a pleasure to him, he now read a horrible piece to Kristina from his *History of Nature,* about "The Billows of the Sea."

"Because water is a liquid which can be stirred up, so it is also moved by wind and storm. This causes billows which are great or small depending on the wind's intensity and the size and depths of the sea. In heavy storms on the great seas the billows rise above each other to a height of thirty or forty feet; then they fall down with unbelievable power and crush all in their way. When such a huge billow falls over a ship it may break away large pieces of the vessel, splinter yard-thick masts, yea, even fill the whole ship with water, making it sink immediately."

"Think of it, Kristina!" exclaimed Robert excitedly. "Waves three times as high as this house!"

"Are you trying to make me feel better about the voyage?" And she couldn't help smiling at the boy. He didn't care what might happen as long as he became free and got out into the world. But he had only his own life to account for.

Kristina did not wish to approach Karl Oskar with her worries. She had once agreed that all should be as he decided, and she couldn't take back her words. He had once and for all assumed responsibility for their emigration. She liked to lean on him and have confidence in him. He was headstrong and stubborn, but she liked a husband who could order and decide for her at times; what woman would be satisfied with a weakling, a shillyshallying husband? All the men in the Nilsa family, born with the big nose, were said to have been like Karl Oskar; unafraid, perhaps even a little refractory, not to be swayed, never yielding. Of all the men she knew, Karl Oskar was the one who most definitely knew what he wanted, and because of this she liked him.

Kristina had not felt well lately; she was weak and had lost her appetite. At first she thought this might be caused by her worrying about the America journey. But when—on getting out of bed one morning—she had to run outside behind the gable and throw up, she knew how things stood with her. She had had this ailment before, four times. It always followed the same course: her monthly bleeding was delayed beyond its time, then came weakness, loss of appetite, worry and mental depression; and at last the vomiting, as a final confirmation. Everything fitted in, there was no longer any doubt, she was pregnant again.

She had feared a new pregnancy. She still gave the breast to the little one and intended to continue to suckle him— Berta of Idemo had said that women would not become pregnant while still suckling a baby. Berta herself had suckled each of her children three years, and within a month after stopping each time she had become pregnant again. It had never failed. Occasionally there might be a wife in the neighborhood who suckled her children until they started school; when the children had to eat from food baskets they must stop suckling and eat the food of grownups. Rarely did it happen that a mother went with her child to school in order to feed it from her breast in between lessons; children who didn't stop suckling at school age were usually dull-witted; they hung on to their mother's apron-strings, always hungry, always pulling up a chair for her to sit on.

Berta's advice had not helped Kristina, but, indeed, the old woman had been careful to add: if she should become pregnant while still suckling her baby, then that might be the fault of Karl Oskar. Some men had seeds so vital that no prevention ever helped.

A few times during the past year Kristina had been seized by an evil temptation. She had wanted to pray to God that He would not make her pregnant any more. This thought had come over her for the first time when she laid Anna in the coffin after only four years on earth; she did not wish to bear children who were to die. But she had been able to withstand the temptation, she had not prayed this sinful prayer. How very sinful it would have been she realized now, when a new life was being created within her.

She must resign herself to the decision of the Highest One. As yet she had said nothing to Karl Oskar.

2

One thought constantly hammered within Kristina's head during the evening before their departure: Do not forget anything. Up to the last moment she kept finding indispensable objects, things which must be taken along but which she had not thought of earlier. She had forgotten tapers, and pitch splinters—they would no doubt need light sometimes while traveling. The children would want playthings on the ship—for Johan she took a clay cuckoo, and Lill-Marta must have her rag doll—neither one was bulky. The baby Harald, who during the last days had taken his first stumbling steps across the floor, and who handled toys only in a destructive way, could be without anything. She was annoyed with herself when she came across the tripod copper kettle, a wedding gift from her parents; why hadn't she thought of it before!

Now the only space she could find for the kettle was among the bedclothes in one of the sacks that had not yet been sewn up. As she put her hand into the sack to make room for the kettle she got hold of a pair of children's shoes, ragged and worn out. They were Anna's shoes! It was her first pair of shoes—and her last.

Kristina stood, deeply moved, with the tiny shoes in her hand. None of the other children could use them, they were too far gone, they barely held together in the seams; she remembered she had thrown them away. Karl Oskar must have picked them up and put them in the sack that was to go with them to America.

As soon as the girl had learned to walk she had followed her father, in these shoes she had often walked with him, in them she had gone long distances at his side. And as Kristina now found them in the sack they conveyed something new to her about her husband.

For a moment she fought back her tears; carefully she put the shoes back into the sack.

Then she pushed down the coffee kettle, which made the sack look out of form: it stood there on the floor like a hunchback.

The America chest was locked and tied with the thickest ropes they could find; it had already been carried out into the entrance hall in readiness. On its front Karl Oskar had printed in red chalk the owner's name and destination—there it stood in flaming red letters: *Homeowner Karl Oskar Nilsson, N. America.* Now the chest would not be lost or mixed up with another.

The Bible, the hymnbook, and the almanac were still on the table; these were the books to be taken along; their place was in the knapsack, they were to be used on the journey.

Karl Oskar came in. He had been to the village to fetch the new high boots which the shoemaker had made for him and which had not been ready until the last moment. No one knew what kind of slipshod footgear they were using in America, and to be on the safe side he had ordered a pair of high boots, to be made of oak-bark-tanned ox leather, the best to be had. The uppers came all the way up to his knees, they could be used in all weathers and on all types of roads. On the boggy roads in the wilds of America one had better be well shod if one wished to get through.

He pulled on the new boots and took a few steps across the floor so Kristina could admire and praise them. They were polished shining black and reinforced at the heels with irons, like small horseshoes. In these boots he could step on shore in America without having to feel ashamed. These boots he could show to the Americans with pride.

But the irresponsible cobbler had almost not finished them in time.

Kristina was brushing his Sunday-best clothes, which he was to put on tomorrow morning. She had put the children to bed and they were already asleep, newly washed and newly combed, in new clean night clothes. Johan and Lill-Marta knew that they were to get out and ride on a wagon tomorrow, that they were to go on a long journey, but the mother felt a sting in her heart as she reflected that otherwise they knew nothing. They had no idea of the long road they were to travel with their parents; it would be long before they were to sleep again in the peace of a home's protection.

Now, this evening, she ought to speak to Karl Oskar; before they began their journey he must know that still another life was on the way.

"I had better tell you. I am that way again."

He looked at her, confounded. Before he had time to ask questions she assured him she was not fooled by false signs: they were to have a little one again, he could rely on it.

"Hmm."

Karl Oskar looked around at the bare, empty walls of the home they were to leave forever tomorrow. At last they were ready, at last all the long, tiresome preparations were over, and when finally this evening he had fetched his boots, which he had worried about, he had felt satisfied with practically everything. Then he was given this piece of news, for which he was unprepared.

A sentence escaped him: "It could not be more ill-timed or awkward."

"What are you saying?"

"I mean, it is ill-timed just now."

She flared up. Her voice rose: "I cannot be pregnant to suit you!"

"Now, dear, don't take it so . . ."

"What exactly do you mean, then? Is it only I? Is it only *my* fault that I get to be with child?"

"I haven't said that."

"You have said it's ill-timed. Can you deny that? But is it not your fault also? Have you not had part in it, perhaps? Even more than I? Is it not you who have put me in this condition? Isn't it you also who come ill-timed?"

"Kristina! What has come over you? Father and Mother in there can hear you!"

But his wife's flare-up convinced him of her pregnancy

more than anything else; at those times she was always short-tempered and irritable and caught fire at every little word that could be interpreted as an insult.

"Must you take it so hard?"

Her eyes were flaming, her cheeks had turned red. "It sounds as if you accuse me! As if I alone were responsible! I'm to blame less than you! You should feel it yourself! If you for one day, for one hour, had to feel so ill as I . . ."

She threw herself face down over the kitchen table, her arms folded in front of her, and burst out crying.

Karl Oskar stood there helpless. He couldn't understand his wife's acting thus. He almost flared up himself. But he must keep his head, for he had no indisposition to excuse him. Kristina, besides, must be worn out with all the preparations for the journey.

He put his hand on her shoulder, patting her clumsily: he had used ill-advised words, which she had interpreted wrongly. He regretted them, but he had meant no harm. He had not tried to shun his responsibility in the pregnancy. How could she think anything as foolish as that? He had not accused her of anything. He had only meant that it was bad luck she happened to be pregnant just now, when they were starting out on their journey—which in this way would be harder for her. And perhaps they would barely have arrived in their new home when she would have to go to bed in childbirth; that also wasn't so good.

"You're afraid I'll be trouble," she sobbed.

"I've never said that. But I'm afraid it will be harder on you when we have one more."

It was during the first months of her pregnancy that she always felt indisposed and irritated. This difficult time, during which it was impossible to please her, would now fall during the actual crossing. But he would have acted more wisely if he had never voiced his apprehensions.

He took hold of her hand, which was limp and without response. But he kept it in his own and continued.

Things had to be as they were; no one could change them. And as long as they had nothing to accuse each other of, they might as well forget their quarrel. Now, when they were to travel so far away and build their home anew, they must stick together. Otherwise they would never succeed. They would ruin things for themselves if they quarreled and lived at odds with each other. They would hurt only themselves and their children if they pulled in different directions; they would ruin their good natures and their joy in work, now when they more than ever needed to be hardy and fearless. Shouldn't they, this last evening at home, agree to be friends and peaceful at all times? She wanted to be his friend, as before, didn't she?

"Of course I want to, but . . ."

She sobbed dryly and was seized with hiccoughs after crying.

"Why but? As long as you want to."

"Karl Oskar . . . You understand . . . I don't feel well."

"I know it."

"You must speak kindly to me."

"I won't speak unkindly to you, Kristina."

"Will you promise?"

Kristina was becoming more calm; she realized that she too had been unjust. She had lost her temper. But he had used such irritating words: "It could not be more ill-timed." Those words had escaped him and he must have meant something by them. Didn't he mean that she would ruin the journey for him through her pregnancy? It had sounded as if she had done all she could in order to be with child again. When, on the contrary, it always was he who was ready in bed! Perhaps she had misunderstood him; however, it was difficult to forget such ugly words.

But she remembered also how kind he mostly was toward her. Like that first time she was with child: her complexion had changed, her face had been covered with ugly brown spots. She used to be shocked when she looked in the mirror, she had looked like an old woman although she had been barely nineteen. She had felt she must run away and hide from people, particularly from Karl Oskar. She had never dreamt that wedded life would distort her. She had complained to her mother, who only laughed and said her brown complexion would soon disappear. The one to comfort her had been Karl Oskar, who had said that the brown spots were becoming to her. He was happy over them! She had the spots because she was to bear a child, she was to bear a child because she had been with him, and she had been with him because she loved him. The ugly brown complexion was to Karl

Oskar a proof of her love for him. How could he be anything but happy over it?

She would never forget the time he said this. And now she was again expecting the brown spots which would ruin her skin. She knew that she otherwise had a fairly nice face, perhaps even handsome, with evenly rounded, fair cheeks. But her face remained pretty such short times—only in between pregnancies.

Kristina's hand grasped her husband's fingers more firmly. "Karl Oskar, we must be friends . . . for all times!"

"We agree, then."

"Yes. It's true, as you say; we must hold together. Nothing else will help us."

And she rose hastily and busied herself; how could she have time to sit here and shed tears an evening like this when she had a hundred chores to do, chores which could not be delayed till tomorrow—not one of them. Now she must hurry as if it were butter to be raked from a fire; the buttons must go on Johan's new jacket, Lill-Marta's newly washed nightshirt must be mended and ironed, and her own nightshirt, and Karl Oskar's shirt for tomorrow, and then—then—She was a foolish woman, causing trouble this last evening.

Karl Oskar was soon adjusted to the thought that in seven or eight months his family would increase.

He said this was really good luck for them because now the captain would be cheated out of the passage for one person; their fourth child would accompany them without a penny's expense! What mightn't one day become of this emigrant who already was so clever that he managed to get a free passage to America?

Then Kristina burst out in joyful laughter. Shortly before she had wept; now she attended laughingly to the last chores for the journey to the land where she and Karl Oskar were to build their second home.

THE FIRST EMIGRANTS

from Ljuder Parish, who left their homes April 4, 1850

KARL OSKAR NILSSON, homeowner, 27 years.
KRISTINA JOHANSDOTTER, his wife, 25 years.

Their children:

JOHAN, 4 years.

MÄRTA, 3 years.

HARALD, 1 year.

ROBERT NILSSON, farmhand, 17 years.

DANJEL ANDREASSON, homeowner, 46 years.

INGA-LENA, his wife, 40 years.

Their children:

SVEN, 14 years.

OLOF, 11 years.

FINA, 7 years.

EVA, 5 months.

ARVID PETTERSON, their servant, 25 years.

UNMARRIED ULRIKA OF VÄSTERGÖHL, status unknown, 37 years.

ELIN, her daughter, 16 years.

JONAS PETTER ALBREKTSSON, homeowner, 48 years.

WHY THEY EMIGRATED

KARL OSKAR NILSSON: I seek a land where through my work I can help myself and mine.

KRISTINA: I go with my husband, but I do so with hesitation and half in regret.

ROBERT NILSSON: I do not like masters.

DANJEL ANDREASSON: I wish to freely confess the God of the twelve apostles in the land He shall show me.

INGA-LENA: "Whither thou goest, I will go; where thou diest will I die, and there will I be buried."

ARVID: I want to get away from the "Bull of Nybacken."

ULRIKA OF VÄSTERGÖHL: Sweden—this hellhole!

ELIN: My mother has told me . . .

JONAS PETTER OF HÄSTEBÄCK: I can no longer endure cohabitation with my wife Brita-Stafva; from now on let happen to me what may.

XII

ALL GATES OPEN ON THE
ROAD TO AMERICA

1

They set out on a Thursday, and the day was well chosen. The heathen god with the hammer—Thor—had been a mighty god in whom their forebears had put their trust, and still far into Christian times his weekday was considered an auspicious day for the beginning of a new venture. Besides, there was a new moon, a good omen for the emigrants.

Nearly a thousand years had passed since people of this region had gathered into groups to sail the sea toward the west. At that time women and children had remained at home. But then as now the departing men had taken edged tools on their journey; the foregathers had armed themselves with weapons, this time the weapons were implements of peace, packed in the bottoms of the chests—broadaxes, augers, hammers, planes. This time the people traveled on a different errand.

Karl Oskar had hired a team of horses and a flat-wagon from the churchwarden in Akerby, and the team and its driver arrived shortly before sunup. He, Robert, and the driver loaded the wagon; the America chest was so heavy that the three of them had to use their combined strength to get it onto the wagon.

The leave-taking from the relatives took little time. Lydia had a day off to say farewell to her brothers. Karl Oskar called his sister aside and begged her to look after their parents, particularly later as they grew older and couldn't manage for themselves: he would pay her for this. Marta took each of her grandchildren into her arms and said: "May God protect and keep you, you helpless little creature!" The sons shook hands with their parents, a bit awkwardly, perhaps shamefacedly, almost like little boys who had been disobedient but were embarrassed to ask forgiveness. Neither one of them had ever said that he intended to return. Now Karl Oskar remarked, with an attempt at a smile, that when he had earned enough money in America he would come home and buy the manor at Krakesjo, and for his sister Lydia he would buy back Korpamoen. All knew he was joking, but no one smiled. Nils and Marta felt they were seeing their sons for the last time this bleak April morning.

Kristina had already said goodby to her parents, a few days earlier in Duvemala. She had not cried while there, but returning home she had been unable to hold back the tears any longer as she thought of her mother's parting words: "Remember, my dear daughter, I wish to meet you with God."

All that they owned in this world was now on the wagon. The load was high and wide, with the two large sacks on top; yet Karl Oskar thought there was room for more—it still didn't reach the sky!

Nils and Marta stood on the stoop.

"Drive carefully through the gate," said Nils to the boy who drove. Those were the last words his departing sons heard him utter. And the admonition was pertinent: the gate was narrow for such a broad wagon, the steering shaft caught one of the posts, and the team with the load could barely make it through the gate.

"Everything is narrow, here at home!" said Robert.

Karl Oskar was sitting next to the driver with Johan on his knee. Kristina sat behind with the smaller children, who in spite of the early hour were fully awake, looking about them with their clear eyes. Robert sat on the horses' hay sack on top of the load.

As they reached the village road Karl Oskar turned a last time and looked toward the house: his father and mother were still on the porch, watching the departing ones—his father gnarled and stooped and hanging on his crutches, his mother close by her husband's side, tall, her back straight. Here on the wagon sat the young ones, departing—there stood the old ones, left behind.

Karl Oskar could not see either of his parents make the slightest movement. As they stood there on the stoop, looking after the wagon, they seemed to him as still and immobile as dead, earth-bound things, as a pair of high stones in the field or a couple of tree trunks in the forest, deeply rooted in the ground. It was as if they had assumed that position once and for all, and intended to hold it forever. And as he saw them in the half-mist, this early morning, so they were forever to return to his mind: Father and Mother, standing quietly together on the stoop, looking after a cart driving through the gate and onto the road and after a minute disappearing among the junipers at the bend. In that place and in that position his parents would always remain in his mind. After many years he would still see them standing there, close together, looking out on the road, immobile objects, two human sculptures in stone.

Kristina did not mention to Karl Oskar that she had happened to hear a remark by Nils as the wagon was ready to depart: "I must go outside and behold my sons' funeral procession."

2

The spring was late this year; the ground lay frozen still. There had been a freeze during the night, and the April morning was chilly; the sky was overcast and it was not yet full daylight. The load was heavy but the wheels rolled lightly on the frozen road.

From his high seat on the hay sack Robert could see the horses' manes waving below him like young birches in the wind. Their strong-muscled necks rose and sank at regular intervals, their hairy flanks moved in soft billows, and the sharp horseshoes cut sparks from the stones in the road. Anticipation without measure filled his breast: this was no ordinary mill-wagon, this was not a slow timber load, nor was it a depressing Sunday church carriage. At last he was riding the chariot of adventure.

He would reach the sea tomorrow.

They passed Nybacken, and as the wagon gained speed downhill on the other side of the farm, Robert began to whistle. He could not hold back any longer, and his brother and sister-in-law said nothing about it.

He whistled a piece again as they passed the parsonage: he wondered if it could be considered sacrilegious. He had not asked for his papers, and he could hear the dean call his name at all the yearly examinations: Farmhand Robert Nilsson, not heard from since 1850. And the dean would write: Whereabouts unknown. After ten or twenty years it would still be written about him: Whereabouts unknown.

Every time they came to a gate on the road Robert jumped down to open it. Before they reached Akerby Junction he had opened five. He counted them carefully, he was to be gate-boy, he must count all the gates on the road to America.

The road also went through pasturelands, where the gates had been removed for the winter; but Robert still counted the openings as gates on the America road—if their emigration had been delayed a month, these gates too would have been closed.

Lill-Marta and Harald had gone to sleep in their mother's arms, rocked to sleep by the movement of the wagon. Johan played driver, holding on to one rein and shouting at the horses. Karl Oskar and Kristina sat silent and serious, their eyes tarrying on well-known places: this is the brook with the swimming hole, we are passing it for the last time; in this meadow we will never see the lilies of the valley in spring again. We want to remember what these places are like, we are anxious to remember them—they were once part of our youth. . . .

The emigrants had agreed to meet at Akerby Junction, and the other wagons awaited them there. Danjel of Karragarde had hired a team from Krakesjo. He too had a heavy load—his wife, his four children, and Ulrika of Vastergohl. Jonas Petter of Hasteback drove his own single-horse wagon and was accompanied by his hired man, who was to drive the horse back from Karlshamn. Two of the people from Karra-garde, unable to find room on Danjel's wagon, rode with Jonas Petter—the farmhand Arvid, and Ulrika's daughter Elin.

The wagon from Korpamoen had, besides its load, four full-grown persons, and Jonas Petter thought it should be made lighter; Robert therefore moved over to him and found a seat between the driver and Elin. Behind him, next to Jonas Petter's hired man, sat Arvid, who now welcomed Robert with a broad grin; the two farmhands from Nybacken were journeying together to the New World after all. Otherwise things weren't going as they had planned during their nightly combats with the bedbugs in Aron's stable room: they didn't sneak away in secrecy on a load of timber, nor were they alone on their journey.

There were nineteen of them at the meeting at Akerby Junction this morning. Three drivers were to return from Karlshamn. The emigrants were sixteen, none grownups and seven children. Together they made a suitably large family, said Jonas Petter as he counted them. But who was to be head of the family?

All looked at Karl Oskar. He said he could hardly be head of them all, he was the youngest of the three farmers.

"You are the oldest one, Jonas Petter."

"But you were the first one to decide on this journey, Karl Oskar. I was the last one."

The loaded wagons started moving again, toward the province of Blekinge. Jonas Petter drove first, he knew the roads, and Robert continued to jump off and open gates. They drove a wagon length apart and mostly at a slow trot, or letting the horses walk to save their strength, as it was fifty long miles to Karlshamn. On steep downgrades they kept still farther apart, to give the horses more room.

As Kristina eyed the three wagons she thought of her father-in-law's words about his departing sons; it was true, their company looked like a funeral cortege. A small one. But there had been no more than three carriages when Anna was buried.

Now she would rather forget what Nils had said in the bitter moment of leave-taking—he had not thought anyone would hear him. Somewhere, some place, a grave awaited every mortal, somewhere there was a patch of earth which one day would open for one's body. So it might be said that every moment man was on his way to that place; all people's journeys were one long funeral procession.

Some one, or perhaps several, of this company might return home again—no one knew. Kristina supposed that most of them—though not Karl Oskar—nourished in secret the hope of returning. Of course, they wished to come back rich and well-to-do, not poor, impoverished wretches. Yet it was most likely that none in their group would ever travel this road again.

Robert was now opening gates which he had never before seen. They had left the roads he was familiar with, they were in strange country. They passed farm after farm, and he asked Jonas Petter the name of this place, and that. They passed a church with a much higher steeple than the one at home. They met completely unknown people who greeted them sharply and morosely and who stood for long moments looking after the three wagons—with open mouths, impolitely. But they were something to look at: three flat-wagons full of people and loaded high with chests, boxes, sacks, baskets, and bundles. One might indeed wonder what kind of travelers these were.

"They must think we are gypsies," said Jonas Petter. "These loads look like gypsy carts."

But they themselves did not resemble gypsies, thought Robert. Nearly all the grownups of the company, women as well as men, were tall with blond hair and light complexions. Gypsies were short and dark. And all of this company were well dressed, washed and clean; gypsies were ragged and dirty. And they traveled their way quietly and peacefully and soberly, while gypsies lived ill, shouted, and were drunk and evil-natured. It irritated Robert that they might be mistaken for such rabble. He wanted to call to all staring people whom they met: We are not gypsies! We are honest, decent people! We're emigrants! We're going to a country where there are no bad people, where we never will meet any rabble! Don't stand there and stare at us—go home and harness your horses and come with us to the sea, to the ship waiting for us!

But after a while he thought that if he told the people they met about about the members of his own group, then perhaps the strangers wouldn't join them. Those sitting here on the wagons were not too well thought of at home. How about Arvid, sitting there behind him? He was so much looked down on that no one except Danjel was willing to hire him. And how about Danjel himself? Nearly all at home were pleased and grateful that he left the parish. The dean was most happy; the sheriff, too, was pleased. And Ulrika of Vastergohl? All decent women thanked God that she was leaving the district. And, not to forget himself. Sheriff Lonnegren no doubt was thankful that he had left the village for ever, he had caused him so much trouble; the sheriff hated to chase "servant-scoundrels." No, outside of his parents, and his sister Lydia, no one at home would miss him.

And perhaps no one missed the others in the group either. At some time in the future, maybe fifty years hence, they might hold a celebration at home in memory of the day when they got rid of the rabble that was taken for gypsies on their America road.

— **3** —

Robert cast glances at the girl sitting next to him on the driver's seat. He had never seen Ulrika's daughter at close hand before. Elin was little and spindly, but her small-girl limbs had begun to fill out; she would soon be a woman. She had long hair falling to her shoulders, and it had a sheen of golden ripe barley. Her big eyes were dark blue, and gleamed like sloeberries. She was pleasant to look at. What a pity that her mother was the Glad One, the foremost whore in the parish.

Jonas Petter was broad through the hips, and the three of them were crowded in the driver's seat. It was lucky that Elin was so slender, said Robert, otherwise he would have been forced to walk beside the wagon. After he had said this he noticed that the girl kept moving away from him, but each time the wheels hit a stone in the road her body was moved closer to his and he could feel her thigh against his own, soft and tender as the supple flesh of a calf or a lamb. Never before had Robert had a girl so close to his body.

Elin kept silent; she was shy and bashful. Perhaps she was afraid of Jonas Petter, perhaps of Arvid sitting close behind her; perhaps she had heard of the Bull of Nybacken. She was only sixteen and her mind wasn't as yet developed, but she must have sense enough not to be afraid of *him*.

Robert tried again: "No one would ever take *you* for a gypsy."

The girl didn't answer this time either, and Jonas Petter nudged Robert in the side to silence him. After a while the driver stopped, and the men went off to let their water. As they stood together on the road's edge Jonas Petter explained the prod in the ribs: no one knew for sure who Elin's father was, perhaps not even the mother herself. But rumors had it that a gypsy was just what he was.

Robert felt embarrassed and had nothing more to say.

Elin wore a dark dress which had belonged to Inga-Lena, and which was too large for her. On her knees she held a basket. Her narrow blue-veined hands held tightly on to its handle, as if she were afraid someone might try to snatch it from her. It was a small basket for so long a journey, thought Robert, too small for emigration to the New World. It was only a berry basket, large enough for picking blueberries or wild strawberries—not much to go out into the world with. But probably the poor girl didn't need a larger packing box; all she owned must be contained in that little basket.

Elin belonged to the Akians; Ulrika had permitted Danjel to confirm her. The mother had been in prison on bread and water for participating in the illegal Communion in Karragarde, but Elin was under age and had therefore escaped punishment.

Suppose her father was a gypsy? The girl couldn't help who he was, she had not shown the way to her mother's bed; and she couldn't help who her mother was, either. Robert felt sorry for her, and thought he would be kind to her. They were to journey in close company for some time, perhaps several months. They couldn't sit together and not speak to each other, like this, the whole way to America. They must talk, she too must talk. He had no experience with girls, he had hardly shaken hands with a girl before. What ought he to say to make her answer?

They drove by a fine gray manor house on top of a knoll, and Jonas Petter pointed with the whip, saying that this was Galtakullen. Lotta Andersdotter had lived there, she who had become infamous through a horrible deed done to her first husband.

Robert thought probably the farmer would tell one of his stories again, and his supposition proved to be correct.

Yes, continued Jonas Petter, it was said that the farmer of Galtakullen could never satisfy his wife in bed, she was that kind of woman whom no man could please however much he worked and tried. Now she wanted to exchange her husband for the enlisted man of the village, a strong, bed-worthy man. And the soldier was tempted by the promise that he was to be farmer of Galtakullen. One night when her husband was sleeping soundly Lotta Andersdotter got out of bed and went to the toolbox for a hammer and a five-inch spike. With the hammer she drove the spike full length into the skull of her sleeping husband. He never awakened—unless it were in heaven or hell. Some blood splurted out of the hole in his head, but the murderess dried it off and left the nailhead well covered by her husband's hair.

Then she announced that her husband had died from a stroke; as people knew, he had been somewhat ailing lately. A grand funeral was held. The widow wanted to show that she mourned her husband deeply, and she cried profusely and bitterly at the graveside. No one suspected her of a crime.

As soon as her widow year was up she married the soldier. He in his turn died, after ten years of wedded life, from somewhat more natural causes than the first husband: people said from overwork in bed. The housewife of Galtakullen remained the same craving woman; she was about to take a third husband, but he became frightened of her, and changed his mind before it was too late. He is supposed to have said that the widow of Galtakullen was almost as much man as woman, that she had the organs of both sexes—though no one could be sure of this.

After two marriages she sat, a widow, on her farm for the rest of her life.

Then thirty years after her first husband's sudden death the gravedigger was one day opening a new grave in the churchyard. While digging he got hold of a skull on his spade. He usually paid no attention to a skull, big or small, any more than a potato picker looks at his potatoes; for human skulls grow in a churchyard as profusely as tubers in a field. But this skull was different: a long rusty-red spike hung rattling inside it. The gravedigger carried his find to the dean, and pointed out to him where he had found the skull. The dean looked up his records and made sure of who had once been buried in that place. Then he tied the skull up in a piece of black cloth, took it under his arm, and went directly to Galtakullen. The widow was at home and he handed her the parcel, saying: Here comes your first husband to visit you; he wishes to speak about the nail in his head. Later you can come to me and speak about your wretched soul.

With this the dean went home. The following day the widow Lotta Andersdotter went to the parsonage and confessed her crime, and in the evening that same day she hanged herself in the milk cellar of her farm.

"Right in there, in that gray house up there," concluded Jonas Petter.

Everyone looked toward the farm. Jonas Petter knew of all

the crimes and evil deeds perpetrated by wives against their husbands in Konga County during the last hundred years, but Robert thought he shouldn't tell them in the presence of a girl. Elin had looked straight ahead and acted as if she had heard nothing. Perhaps Jonas Petter had thought that the daughter of the Glad One was hardened.

Robert could see her eyes under the kerchief she had drawn forward over her brow, but she always looked away if he tried to meet her gaze. She did not appear sociable. So he turned his back to her and began speaking to Arvid behind him. He intended to buy a book in Karlshamn to learn the American language, he said; he would no doubt have time for study while crossing the ocean.

This was said for Elin's benefit, and for the first time the eyes under the kerchief turned to the youth beside her.

He met her gaze. "You can borrow the book—if you wish."

"I don't need it," she answered.

"You mean you speak English?"

"Not yet. Not before we land in America."

"Do you think you can speak fluently as soon as we land?"

"Yes, of course."

"Really?"

"I don't need to learn the language because I'll know it when we arrive," repeated the girl with assurance.

"Who has told you that?"

"Uncle Danjel."

And her eyes now looked into his, clear and trusting: Danjel had told them that all who were reborn in Christ would be able to speak the English tongue fluently as soon as they stepped on shore in America.

Robert was stupefied; he could hear and see that she believed this promise to the very letter.

Elin continued: Danjel had told them not to worry about the foreign language, for at their landing all believers would be filled with the Holy Ghost as once had happened to the apostles on the first Whitsuntide. Thus they would be able to understand and speak freely the language used in that land.

"*You* must learn the language, you yourself, of course," she added, "because you don't live in the spirit. But we who are reborn need not learn it."

"Can that be true?"

"Do you think Uncle Daniel would tell a lie?" She sounded hurt. "Or do you think I lie?"

"No, no! Indeed not—but . . ."

He didn't like to contradict Elin now that she had begun to talk; he wanted to agree with everything she said. But faced with Danjel's promise, he was unable to hide his doubts completely.

"I've never heard that story about the Holy Ghost," he excused himself. "That's why I was a little surprised."

"Have you never read the Acts?" she asked, a little puzzled.

"Yes. Yes, of course I have."

"You can read about Whitsuntide in the second chapter, if you don't believe Danjel. But he has never lied to us."

"I understand now. You won't need a book to learn English."

"That's so."

"Well—I didn't know. That's why I was confused a moment ago."

Arvid too had listened in amazement. He had not been received among Danjel's followers, but the master had high hopes that his servant would "awaken" one day. What Arvid now heard about the great advantage of the Akians, with the American language, made him thoughtful.

They were driving up a steep hill and the men stepped down to spare the horse. Arvid asked Robert: What were they to think of the girl's statement? Was the new language to come running from the mouths of the Akians as soon as they landed?

"I won't believe it until I hear it myself," said Robert flatly. "The girl seems cocksure."

What she said might be true, admitted Robert. It was written in the Bible that the Holy Ghost once filled the apostles so they could speak new languages. But it said nothing about their speaking English on that first Whitsuntide—the language was not yet invented in the days of the apostles, that much he was sure of. So no one knew if the Holy Ghost could teach people to speak English.

The air was colder; the north wind had begun to blow. It felt like a steel brush on their faces. The old frostbites on Arvid's nose, developed when he was hauling timber during severe winters, took on a red color, cracking a little and bleeding. On the horses the sweat foamed, remaining as white crust on their necks. Sparse, hard snowflakes fell and lay on the road like scattered rice. The emigrants sat silently on the wagons, hour after hour, mile after mile, a chill creeping into their bodies.

They had passed the border of a new province, Blekinge, once part of another kingdom—Denmark. There was still hatred between the inhabitants dwelling along the border, said Jonas Petter. When the Smalanders came driving their loads they were often attacked by Blekinge men, who were evil-tempered and used knives; they were another type of people. And their women, it was said, were hotter under their shifts than women farther north.

The emigrants now drove through wild, uninhabited regions. They rode through a forest of high pines where everything seemed deserted and dead. This was known as the snake forest, said Jonas Petter, for the stone-covered ground was filled with poisonous snakes—more poisonous here than the vipers in the north. Here it was that the Blekinge men used to lie hidden when the Smalanders came with their wagonloads, and here the two peoples often had fought bitterly. If one looked carefully on the stones along the roadside one might still see spots of blood from the old fights; the ground here was in a way sanctified.

Jonas Petter himself had once participated in a fight in the snake forest; a swarm of Blekinge men had surrounded him, buzzing and hissing like wasps on a hot summer day, cutting and hitting at any part of his body they could reach. When he returned home after that journey his body was cut up, open as a sieve. For many months he could keep no fluids in him because they ran out through the holes which the Blekinge men had cut through his body. It was half a year before he could drink brannvin again.

Robert's eyes shifted from side to side in the semidark underbrush of the forest, looking for men armed with knives, ready to waylay the travelers. But Jonas Petter assured him that it was much more peaceful on the Blekinge road nowadays, and they might feel especially safe from the evil-tempered people since there were so many in their company.

Jonas Petter continued to shorten the fifty long miles by his talk. Robert was busy opening gates; he had by now counted thirty of them. The gates had lately been closer together—the travelers were nearing inhabited places.

The forest came to an end and they drove into a large village. They were in Eringsboda, almost halfway to Karlshamn. This was their first resting place. The wagons came to a stop in front of an impressive-looking building with iron rings in the wall for the horses' halter straps; this was the inn. The travelers came down from their seats, and the horses were unharnessed.

Big as well as little ones felt frozen, and their faces were blue from the biting wind. The children's noses were running, making tapers, as it was called.

"We must get inside and thaw out our young ones," said Kristina anxiously.

Her own children had on warm woolen mittens which she had knitted for them especially for the journey, but the children from Karragarde were barehanded. Inga-Lena's last-born, a girl only a few months old, began to cry. She was hidden somewhere in a huge bundle of woolen shawls. Through an opening in the coverings her mother spoke comfortingly to the baby. Danjel came by and nodded and smiled at the little one, the child conceived in the couple's true, God-inspired marriage, after they were living in the spirit. But not even the father could silence the crying baby. Then the youngest boy from Korpamoen joined in the crying, and the two children tried to outdo each other.

The company of emigrants entered the barroom of the inn with their two loudly crying children.

Nearly every day the maids in the inn saw peasants from Smaland with their loaded wagons stopping in on their way to Karlshamn, but never before had they brought along wives and children. Now a question could easily be read in the maids' staring eyes: What was the idea of dragging suckling children along the roads in this bitterly cold spring weather? But it was warm in here in the barroom, a tremendous fire was roaring on the hearth. The maids busied themselves heating milk for the children and preparing coffee for the grownups.

The emigrants found benches and chairs, sat down, and opened their food baskets. They cut long slices from their rye breads, and brought out their dried lamb quarters. Jonas Petter and the Korpamoen brothers shared a quart of brannvin. Kristina had baked a potato pancake which she divided among husband, children, and brother-in-law; as yet she would not open the butter tub.

The fire sparkled and all enjoyed the coziness of the inn after the cold road. Their senses as well as their limbs thawed. There was an odor of food and brannvin, snuff and chewing tobacco, greased leather and warm, wet wadmal, there was a fragrance of mothers' milk as the women suckled the children.

The people from Korpamoen and those from Karragarde were gathered around their respective food baskets, but Jonas Petter sat alone with his. He had left wife and children behind. It was said he had left without forethought: one tvening he quarreled with his wife and next morning packed his America chest. But no one knew how long this had been in his mind. He willingly told what he knew of other people, but about himself he never said a word.

Kristina sat and thought of how some in the company still were strangers to each other; as yet she had not exchanged a word with Ulrika of Vastergohl, nor shaken her hand. Before their departure she had told her Uncle Danjel the truth: she could not stand that woman. Must she endure her as a traveling companion? Danjel had opened the Bible and read to her about the meeting of Christ and the harlot. What the Redeemer had said to her, he, Danjel, had said to Ulrika: Sin no more! And Ulrika had obeyed him, she had discarded her old sin-body. Now it was Christ's body that lived in her, and anyone saying unkind words to Ulrika said them also to Christ. But Kristina could not help herself—she still could not endure that woman.

Nor did she notice any difference in Ulrika. She was good to her daughter; when the two spoke to each other she was sweet and careful in her words. Otherwise she was as foulmouthed as ever. And one could never misunderstand her manner of looking at men; there was always something of a come-and-let's-get-to-bed look in her eyes. Hadn't she today looked at Karl Oskar in that way? She had long taken advantage of Uncle Danjel, who fed and clothed her and her daughter and now paid their passage to America. Uncle Danjel was credulous and easy to take advantage of. Perhaps Ulrika still carried on her whoring in secret, whenever she had the opportunity. At least she *acted* like a sow in heat.

Good-looking she was, the bitch, no one could deny that. Now she was sitting in front of the fire, combing her daughter's hair and tying a red ribbon in it. The whore was as haughty as a queen, with her bastard a princess being decked to wed a prince. One could wonder what kind of virtues that woman had instilled in her child, poor girl who had to wear old women's cast-off clothing.

Sven was the eldest boy from Karragarde, and he had already torn his jacket on a nail—now his mother was mending the hole with linen thread and a darning needle. Inga-Lena and Kristina got along well together. But Danjel's wife was easily led, quite without a will of her own; she let her husband decide and rule in all matters. Kristina felt a little ashamed of her when among women.

Inga-Lena had suckled her baby, which was quiet now, after being freed from its bundle of shawls. But presently it began to cry again. The mother opened her blouse and offered the breast to the child once more. But the little one threw up what she had already eaten.

Kristina's thoughts turned to the impending sea voyages as she watched the child vomit.

"I wonder if we will be seasick on the ship," she said.

"Seasickness is no real ailment," said Karl Oskar.

"Nevertheless, one has to throw up."

Ulrika gave Kristina a meaning glance: "I guess it feels like being in the family way."

Kristina's cheeks flushed a flaming red. Ulrika apparently knew how things were with her. They had both gone to the outhouse when they had arrived, she must have noticed. And now Kristina was provoked by the color in her face. Why must she blush? She was married, and no man except Karl Oskar had touched her. She had a right to be with child a thousand times if she wished. Was she to blush because of that woman who had borne four bastards and given her body to hundreds of men?

The baby stopped suckling, and as Inga-Lena buttoned her blouse over her breasts, she said: "They say seasickness is painful."

"Are you afraid, Inga-Lena?" asked Danjel.

"No, no, of course not!" Her worried voice contradicted her. "But when one never has been to sea before . . ."

Danjel went up to his wife and laid his hand on her shoulder. "Don't you remember my words? Have you forgotten what I've told you?"

"No, I haven't, dear Danjel."

"A person who has Christ within him need not fear seasickness. He can endure the sea even the first time."

"Yes, I will have faith, dear husband."

And Danjel emphasized again to his wife that one reborn could sail on all the seas in the world without being seasick. One living in Christ's faith could endure the sea at any time; whether he traveled over narrow rivers or broad oceans, he would remain as sound and well as ever.

"Yes, dear Danjel, I believe it. I'm not afraid any more."

Inga-Lena patted her husband's hand affectionately.

"Don't you think you might get seasick, as well as we others?" asked Karl Oskar, who had listened in astonishment.

The farmer from Karragärde smiled kindly. "No! Because I believe Christ has died on the cross for my sins."

"You are a doubter, Karl Oskar," said Ulrika of Vastergohl, but there was no reproach in her voice.

"God will convince him when we are on the ship," said Danjel.

Ulrika wanted to help Danjel explain. "You know, Karl Oskar, it says in the Bible that Jesus had gone in a boat with His disciples and there was a horrible storm but no one was seasick. If Jesus or some one of His disciples had needed to throw up then, it would say so. But there isn't one word about it in the gospel. So you may understand, Karl Oskar, when a person has Christ's body within his own, he can never more feel rotten."

Karl Oskar snorted but said nothing. What use was there in arguing with the Akians?

To Kristina it sounded like blasphemy when the name of the Saviour was mentioned by Ulrika in this way; as if one were to think of Him lying in a ship, seasick and throwing up. He was God's Son, He could have no ills. But even if He had a toothache, or was footsore, or had other human ailments, He could heal Himself as He healed so many others. Ulrika used such vulgar words in spiritual things that no one in his full senses could believe in her conversion. Who could imagine Christ living in her worn-out old harlot-body?

Kristina turned to Danjel. "Berta of Idemo said the married women will get more seasick than the unmarried."

"Not if they live in the spirit."

"But most women do live in the flesh," interrupted Ulrika. "Bastards can be made in wedded beds, too."

She was hurt by the disrespect Kristina showed her, and now at the first opportunity retaliated. But Kristina decided not to answer the nasty words Ulrika threw at her.

Robert was disappointed because no one had asked him about seasickness. He had knowledge from books, and now he was able to get in a word: "Ship's fever and cholera are much more dangerous than seasickness."

He wanted to give a description of these ills, but his brother gave him a look that could not be misunderstood; he stopped short at the very beginning.

They were to rest a few hours. When all had eaten and were satisfied, Danjel kneeled on the floor and thanked God in a loud voice for the food. His prayer was so vociferous that it was heard out in the kitchen. The maids stared in surprise through the door: one of the peasants from Smaland was crying on his knees to God—indeed, a strange rabble that passed by today!

Kristina put the lid on her food basket. She was content that she hadn't opened the butter tub. It was supposed to be thousands of miles to North America, and as yet they had traveled only twenty of them; the butter would be needed.

4

Later in the evening the emigrants resumed their journey. The next road post was Moljeryd, where they intended to rest. From there the road went over Bredakra to Karlshamn.

Now the weather grew milder. The snow had melted, the air was moist, and soon a light rain began to fall. They could see that the spring was earlier in Blekinge than at home; the grass was high along the roadsides, the coltsfoot had opened in the ditches, and the buds on the trees were thick and swollen; the spring work could soon begin hereabouts.

Their horses were growing tired from the heavy loads, and

moved at a slow pace; even on small hills the men stepped off and walked; on Jonas Petter's wagon only the girl remained in her seat.

Robert could not help thinking of Elin. She thought she needn't learn English from his book. The language would pour forth from her mouth as once the languages of the Parthians, the Phrygians, and the Elamites had come from the tongues of the apostles, so that people thought they were drunk from new wine. Why did people think they were drunk? The more drunk a person was, the thicker his speech became, stammering, slurring, spluttering. But the girl must be given information about the land she was emigrating to. What did she know about the North American Republic? Its government, laws, religion, and railroads? Surely she needed more knowledge about the New World.

It would not hurt to show Elin what he knew about the United States—but before he had a chance to begin his discourse she said, almost confidentially: "You know—I'm afraid of America."

"Afraid? Why?"

"Because it's unknown—perhaps people are unkind to newcomers."

"Oh, no! I'm sure you need not be afraid. There are so few women in America that they treat them like gold and jewels. You'll be taken care of like a baby; you can have anything you want, you needn't worry about a thing."

Elin apparently did not know how well things were arranged for the women in the United States. He must cheer her up a little by telling her.

The Americans treated all women—were they old or young, ugly or beautiful—as if they were queens and princesses. They waited on them and guarded them as if they were costly pearls and diamonds. The women never need do heavy or foul chores, as here at home; they could go clean and white and with washed hands all day long; a maid in America was as well dressed as her mistress, because *all* women were allowed to dress in fine clothes. It wasn't a bit like here—all women had the right to wear hats, that right was written into the laws of the republic. It was strongly forbidden to mock or poke fun at a simple woman because she wore a hat like a gentlewoman. Moreover, there were no simple women, and no noble ladies—all were equals.

In the North American Republic it was the menfolk who served the women, not the opposite, as here. If a man were attacked and beaten by a woman, he had no right to defend himself. Because the law was not like here. Outside a house a man could go no closer to a woman than three steps, if she herself didn't allow closer proximity, or perhaps order him to come nearer. Inside a house the distance between the sexes was two steps, according to law. Any man who wished to be closer than two steps to an American woman must first marry her. The law was not like the Swedish law.

So Elin need not be afraid of America. If a man spoke to a woman in public, then she had the right to call for the police and request protection. Even if, in all friendliness, he only asked his way, she could have him arrested, or sue him for breach of promise if she was in need of cash, whichever suited her best. Women always had their own way in the United States, so she need not worry.

If a man in the United States betrayed a woman, then he was first decapitated and afterwards hanged; he would never repeat his deed. Nowadays there were no unfaithful, untruthful, or deceitful menfolk left there. They were exterminated and destroyed. She need not be afraid of America.

Thus while the wagon rolled along one of the future inhabitants of the United States was informed of the position of women in the new land. And Elin did feel more comfortable and happy and expectant. She relied on his words, she felt she would like her new country.

Robert and Elin sat as close as possible in the driver's seat. The wagon shook and rocked, the girl pulled her clothes tightly around her, she yawned and shivered from cold. And while Robert was busy describing the railroads of America, her head fell suddenly on his shoulder. He stopped short in surprise while her head sank down on his chest. What did it mean? What did she want? What was he supposed to do? He held his body stiff as a steering shaft, yet her head remained in the same position. Then he discovered that she had fallen asleep. She slept, her tender girl-body resting against his.

She had gone to sleep at a moment when he himself was carried away by his description of the United States—for her benefit. He was disappointed in her. But here she lay, practically in his arms; for the first time a girl's head rested against his breast. This could happen only on the chariot of adventure

—after just thirty miles on the road! How many miles were left? Many, many! This adventure would last a long time!

Little by little he too was rocked to sleep by the movement of the wagon. Jonas Petter did not have the heart to awaken him at the next gate, he opened it himself. Robert slept on, unmindful of the gates on the road to America, unable to count them any longer.

5

Early the next morning the three wagons drove into Karlshamn and came to a stop near the harbor. From the steeple of the town church they were greeted by a clock striking seven, slowly and solemnly. The harbor town was just coming to life for the day. The fishermen, returned from the sea with the night's catch, were busy mooring their boats at the pier where the town maids awaited the fresh herring with their baskets. A shop clerk with a long birch broom was sweeping the steps in front of a house with the sign *Sunesons Skeppshandel*. In the air was the odor of fish, tar, hemp, herring, salt, and sea.

The emigrants climbed down from their wagons, sleepy and frozen, stiff and aching in their bones after the long ride. The menfolk stepped aside and flapped their arms against their bodies to warm up. The women attended to the children who were whimpering and whining from lack of sleep. They were all rather depressed and dullish after the long night; no one felt morning-cheerful.

A sharp, cold, penetrating wind blew from over the harbor and bade the emigrants welcome to the sea.

For the first time in their lives they looked across water without seeing land on the other side.

They had reached the sea they were to cross—this sea now greeted them with its wind; it sent as its messenger this cold, severe wind as if to frighten them, to challenge them: Come out here! I'll teach you! The men turned up their coat collars and the women pulled their woolen shawls closer around their children and themselves. What an unmerciful wind they had in the coast towns! It cut through skin and bones, it penetrated their very marrow. Never did it blow so fiendishly at

home, not in fall or in spring, not in summer or in winter.
Even the heavy peasant wadmal seemed to give no protection.

The people of the earth met the sea, and they hardly had
time to behold it before the wind brought tears to their eyes.

The men in the fishing boats looked curiously at the group
of strangers who had stopped near the harbor with their high
loads and their crying children. Some men, gentry by their
dress, walked by in leisurely fashion and looked at the little
company in amusement: apparently honest-to-goodness gray
wadmal peasants with their simple shawl-wrapped wives and
their pale-faced, runny-nose children; a couple of farmhands
in new suits which were too large and puffed out in bags
front and back—jacket and trousers carelessly basted together by some village tailor. And whole loads of ancient
chests, flowery knapsacks, homemade baskets and boxes and
bundles—they must be backwoods people going on a long
journey across the sea. What kind of restless itch had got into
the poor devils?

Karl Oskar had arranged passage for them all, and it
seemed as if he was to be their head, also, during the whole
trip. No one undertook anything of importance without first
asking him.

He now went over to a herring fisher and asked about ships
in the harbor. He had paid passage to America—where might
their ship be anchored?

The fisherman peered at the peasant and sized up his solid
new boots. Yes, and America-sailer had arrived the night before last, she was a brig, the *Charlotta*. She was lying at anchor in the outer harbor—perhaps it was that old hull over
there.

The name was the right one. Karl Oskar looked toward the
outer harbor in the direction where the fisherman had
pointed.

"Is *that* the *Charlotta*? Our ship?"

All eyes were turned toward the ship indicated. They stood
silent, and gazed. It was a silence of disappointment, wonder,
anxiety, and bafflment. Could this really be their ship?

It was Kristina who expressed in five words what all were
thinking: "Is our ship so little?"

None among them had seen a sailing ship except in pictures. They had thought of ships as being much bigger than

this. And the ship that was to carry them across the enormous ocean they had pictured as *much* larger. In front of them was the wide expanse of the sea; and on this sea their ship seemed so minutely small. Compared with the water she was to cross she looked pitiful and puny.

"The boat is larger than you think. It just looks small at this distance," said Robert.

He attempted to choke his own feeling of disappointment at seeing the *Charlotta*, and wanted to encourage the rest of his company.

He pointed. "Look at the masts! Has anyone ever seen such tall masts?"

None had seen other masts on ships to make comparison. The small ship anchored landwards from the little island, in the entrance of the harbor, had two masts stretching toward the sky and seeming higher than the tallest tree in the forest. The masts were as tall as the ship was long. Robert thought that perhaps he himself had helped fell the trees which he now saw as naked, slender stems: perhaps he had cut the firs, helped remove them from their place of immobility in the forest to the sea, replanting them, as it were—thost mast-trees which for the rest of their lives were to sail the seas, were to be supported by water instead of earth.

Karl Oskar wondered when they might be allowed to go on board. The fisherman said that the *Charlotta* was to take on freight, and as the vessel had barely arrived in harbor nothing had been loaded yet. It might be several days before passengers could board the America-sailer.

They could not remain here in the wind with their freezing, whimpering children. They must find quarters while waiting for embarkation. The kind fisherman showed them to the Maja's Inn, located in an alley near the harbor. It was the house behind the Hope Tavern, right there, as they could see; they were sure to get accommodations.

The emigrant wagons pushed on to the indicated place. Only Robert remained standing at the harbor.

He stood there alone and looked out across the sea.

The others called him several times, but he did not answer.

PART TWO

Peasants at Sea

XIII

THE CHARLOTTA OF KARLSHAMN

1

The Ship

The brig *Charlotta*, Captain Lorentz, sailed from Karlshamn April 14, 1850, with New York as her destination. The ship's capacity was 160 lasts, her length 124 feet, and her width 20 feet. She had a crew of fifteen: 2 mates, 1 bosun, 1 carpenter, 1 sailmaker, 1 cook, 4 able-bodied seamen, 2 ordinary seamen, and 3 deckhands. She was loaded with pig iron and sundries.

She carried 78 passengers, all emigrants to North America, making the total number of people on board 94.

It was the brig *Charlotta*'s seventh voyage as an emigrant ship.

The Passengers

Through its very nature the globe offers two kinds of life to human beings: life on land and life at sea; life on one-quarter of the earth's surface—the solid ground—and life on three-quarters, the water; life on the firm land, life on the ever-moving sea.

The emigrants were people of the soil; their whole lives had been lived on solid ground. On the day when they boarded the brig *Charlotta* they first encountered the sea. For an indefinite period they were to be settled on a ship, exchanging their accustomed existence for one new and alien to them.

Their feet stepped for the first time on a ship's deck, having hitherto always tramped solid ground. With awkward, fumbling movements and clumsy, unsure steps they walked the deck. They found themselves on a plank floor, yet it was not the safe, solid floor of the peasant cottage; these planks were laid lower at the rail, higher toward the center of the deck. And the water under them moved constantly—a wave fell, a wave rose. No longer could they control their movements independently, they must obey the sea.

The emigrants had the earth's heaviness in their bodies,

clay from the field clung to their feet. And their heavy footgear—their shoes of rough leather, their impressive high
boots—were only a hindrance to them on the surface of a
slippery deck. They had stood broad-legged and sure on firm
land; there they ordered their own motions. But here on the
vessel they stood on insecure and treacherous footing.

They were accustomed to walk freely in the fields, unham-
pered. Now they were on a small crowded ship, fenced in like
prisoners behind the rail. For months to come earth's people
must live at sea.

The emigrants came from a kingdom of stones and junipers, their muscles and sinews hardened and strengthened
from breaking stones and twisting the juniper branches to wat-
tles. But their strong arms and powerful backs were of little
use on the sea. Here all of them stood equally helpless, the
most capable farmers and the handiest farm wives. The earth
was known to them, intimate, reliable, but they mistrusted the
sea; it was unknown and dangerous, and their mistrust was in-
grown and inherited through generations.

The passengers embarking on the brig *Charlotta* in Karlshamn this April day wandered about her deck uncertain, insecure, lost, bewildered. They felt they had surrendered
unconditionally to the unknown, were irrevocably in the
hands of a power whose presence left them impotent, a lord
whom they could not entreat—the Sea. This unfathomable
antagonist had taken them on its world-encircling back to
carry them to another continent.

It was a day of calm weather; haze and mist, when the
Charlotta sailed from Karlshamn. A light rain began to drive
in from the Baltic Sea. The ship's movement was only a weak,
slow roll.

A small group of emigrants had gathered in the stern. A
few peasants in their gray wadmal jackets and robust high
boots stood there on the ship's rocking deck and watched the
cliffs of Kastellholmen—that little isle in the harbor entrance
—gradually disappear into the April fog.

What they saw was the last outpost of the land they had rejected.

The travelers spoke in low voices while they cast their farewell looks on their homeland. Some spoke as if to themselves,
others stood silent, eyes peering landwards. Talking emigrants

and silent ones stood side by side; there were open words and hidden thoughts at this, their last glimpse of Sweden.

"I had a farm, foreclosed last fall; a homey place. It hurt me to see it go. But a farmer once fallen here at home can never rise again. I could never have got out of debt, not in a thousand years. Let the sheriff keep the place. Taxes were too heavy; when taxes are collected, that's the time we are good enough, we in wooden shoes and patched pants: then they come to see us. Other times we're peasant rabble. But I'll miss the old place. I'll miss relatives and friends, too; but never the country—no, never, never the country!"

Or—"I had nothing to lose. What could there have been? I slaved on the manor until I spit blood. Is that something to lose? I tired of the drudgery. I've stuffed the gullets of sluggards too long; I am through. The masters can be their own servants; that would only be fair. Perhaps one day they must be. The gentry's arrogance is the bitterest thing. They despise honest work, they despise us in our poverty. Let them do the dirty work themselves; it would serve them right. No one can stand it in the long run, to do the dirtiest and heaviest work, and be treated like a dog, looked down on. All poor people should emigrate to America; that's what they should do. So help me, all devils. That would serve the gentry right! Then they could do their own dirty chores! If only this ocean weren't so broad and big. . . ."

Or—"I couldn't stand the minister. We became enemies. I couldn't stay at home. Might as well go far away when you have to move anyway. Now the minister can sit and watch his sheep running off; he won't be able to shear them any more; he'll get less income, and a good thing, too. There are too many giving orders and commands—everyone must have some devil to torture. There are too many lords and masters to inspect and guard us; too many of the gentry for us to feed; too many useless lords. In the end it's unendurable. The gentry have smothered me long enough! It's over! I'm away from that country at last! But there's an ache somewhere. Why? I don't know. Perhaps I'll miss them, a little, the rest of them—only never the priest! I hated that priest. . . ."

Or—"I'll never regret it. I couldn't advance. It was hopeless: however I slaved, I stood in the same place. Labor brought nothing—I had to get out. But now land disappears,

I remember. Perhaps—perhaps . . . in the long run I'll miss —I don't know. One is born there: father and mother remain; I couldn't bring them, but I'll remember. It wasn't always sorrow. There was happiness too. I've been young in that country, been with girls on summer evenings, when it was warm and pleasant. I've danced at road crossings and dance halls. No, it wasn't always sad. I'll remember. And I'll never forget the old ones, toiling still. Much comes to my mind as I stand here, looking backward—things I haven't thought of before. But regret? Never!"

So thought those emigrants in the stern, as the rock islet melted into the April haze.

The Captain:

Back aft on the poop deck next the helmsman Captain Lorentz stood, near the wheel, where he would watch the easing of his ship out of the harbor. The wind was southeast and light, giving the vessel little speed, barely sufficient for steering.

"Starboard a bit. Steady. Steady as she goes."

His voice, trained in long service as ship's master, was far-reaching and powerful. The *Charlotta*'s captain was about sixty, and of stocky build. He had an ugly face with thick, blunt nose, protruding eyes, and weather-beaten red skin. His broad, sunken mouth with the outjutting lower jaw was strikingly like the snout of a large pike. He looked capable of biting as sharply as those beastly fish, too. From the pike-snout hung a pipe. Captain Lorentz had spent almost fifty years of his life at sea, and for the last ten years he had commanded this old sailing vessel that was his home.

At last, anchor had been weighed, and his ship liberated from her shackle to the bottom. The time in harbor always gave Captain Lorentz a feeling of discomfort and disgust. At sea was the decent place for a grown man; to the *Charlotta*'s captain, riding at anchor was almost degrading, to step on land a disgrace. The only occupation worthy of a human being in this world was to sail a ship. To this occupation, unfortunately, one repulsive duty belonged, one painful necessity he could not shirk: at certain intervals he must steer his ship into harbor.

But now this humiliating time was over again. Captain Lorentz had lain eight days in Karlshamn, and it had been a week of annoying tasks, trying the patience of the *Charlotta*'s master. More cargo had had to be taken on, provisions stored, new crew members signed on. But the biggest nuisance were these damned peasants. In her old age the *Charlotta* had been turned into an emigrant ship instead of a merchantman, and her most important cargoes nowadays were these people emigrating to North America: peasants—peasants from Blekinge, Smaland and Oland. Each time he had shipped such passengers across the ocean they had filled and overrun Catain Lorentz's ship. This time they had even chased the rats from their holes before they all found room. This time they had come dragging still larger chests, still heavier boxes, still bulkier sacks, more baskets, bags, and belongings. Not even God the Almighty knew what junk they contained. This voyage they also had brought along more women and children than ever before. Never were so many brats aboard the *Charlotta* before—whole families, from old white-bearded grandfathers to suckling cradle-infants; cradles, yes, the number that were dragged on board this time! Devil take the captain if his ship wasn't a nursery this trip!

And all these people his old ship must transport to the other side of the globe. The *Charlotta* was getting somewhat squeaky and ancient and sour in her hull, but was still seaworthy. Captain Lorentz loved watching her ride the sea, taking rough weather, curtsying to the waves like a court lady to a queen. She had only one fault, the old ship: she sweated. Perhaps she hadn't been quite dry when launched—and such ships remained moist in their hulls as long as they lasted; only usually they didn't last long.

Skipper Lorentz thought back in regret to the years when the *Charlotta* had been a simon-pure merchantman. The captain on an emigrant ship had many heavy new duties, and much greater responsibility. Nor did Lorentz like the idea of taking so many people out of the country. With each voyage he asked himself: Why did these peasants with their wives and children cross the sea? What did they expect to find in North America? In the captain's mind all countries were equally good or bad. Dry land was dry land the whole world over, in North America as in Sweden. The sea was the part of the globe where sane people lived. He could never understand these peasants who undertook a long and costly voyage to the other side of the earth just in order to find another patch of soil to till! They might as well keep turning their patches in Sweden as in America; to poke and dig in the earth was the same degrading prison-chore everywhere. These peasants traveled from one field to another, from one dunghill to another—for what?

A seaman ought to spend his time at sea, a farmer on the farm. But strangely enough, it was actually the farmers, the homestead people in Sweden, who crossed the seas to change their country. Why? They were of course crowded in their bunk-beds over the fireplaces. There were too many around the potato pot. But it was their own fault: they begot too many children. If these peasants had been as busy in their fields as in their beds they would never need to emigrate. Apparently they used their wives every night of the year—except Christmas night; that night they abstained for fear of getting thistles and weeds in their fields next summer, for these peasants were as superstitious as they had been a thousand years ago.

Oh, well, some of them came from good stock in Sweden, and they might find a better lot in North America, where they would at least have elbowroom. He himself had never been farther inland than the harbor town of New York. And no decent soul could enjoy that dirty hole. When for the first time, some ten years ago, he had touched at that port, he had seen pigs poking in the stinking filth of the town streets. Some quarters were veritable pigpens. Cholera raged then, with hundreds dying daily, and most of the inhabitants had moved inland to uncontaminated regions. The town of New York had looked dead, stinking of corpses. Now it was lively again, and noisy, and beautiful women in white silk dresses drove in stately carriages through the streets. But it wasn't a town where a seaman felt at home, not even for a few days. On Broadway there were some taverns, but none could offer a traveler the comforts he was accustomed to in the harbor towns of Europe. New York, after all, was a town for peasants.

The brig *Charlotta* had at last cleared the harbor and was in the open sea. The captain sniffed the wind—it seemed even calmer than before; all sails were set but hung limp and dead; they were depressed and wrinkled, waiting for the wind.

The second mate, a Finn, approached the captain. He was responsible for the passengers in the hold, and in his Finnishaccented Swedish he reported that they all had found their allotted bunks and turned in; all was well. There had of course been the usual complaints that it was too crowded and too uncomfortable down below. It was always so at first. They kept on jostling each other in the hold, until they realized that they couldn't make the ship roomier or gain more space by pushing with their hands and elbows. As soon as they understood this they tired of their noise and settled down. And it looked as if they had fairly decent folk on this voyage; only one of the peasants appeared refractory, a man with the biggest nose he had ever seen. He and one other married man had been unable to find sleeping room within the partition set aside for families. Perhaps new bunks could be built for them near the family bunks, but for the time being they had been put up with the unmarried men, and this made the big-nosed man furious and hard to handle; he insisted on staying with his wife and children. He—the mate—had told him to pull in his big nose if he wished to remain on board with his huge elephant feet. My God, the boots these peasants wore! That man had such big underpinnings he no doubt could sail dry-shod across the Atlantic in his boots.

Captain Lorentz chewed his pipe while he listened to his mate. The peasants crawled over his ship this time like grasshoppers in the fields of North America. Hell and damnation! Perhaps he had allowed too many of them aboard. He hoped they would be manageable, as his mate predicted. The first few days of the voyage, while they were still on inland seas and had calm waters, the emigrants usually kept quiet enough and busied themselves in their curious way inspecting the ship. But when they reached open waters and began to feel the sea, even the most tractable of men sometimes went berserk. A peasant who on land was the most docile of creatures could, in a storm at sea, become the most ferocious beast, impossible to handle.

The *Charlotta*'s captain felt sorry for the pathetic earth rats who had been lured from their safe holes to spend weeks at sea. Perhaps these poor devils had never been in even a flat-bottomed skiff, or seen a larger body of water than a wash pan; and now suddenly they were off on an ocean voyage. The poor creatures could never take to the sea, and were as much afraid for their lives as old maids. But after all, what business of his was that? It was not his fault. He hadn't advised these farmers to leave their peaceful cottages in their home parishes, he hadn't persuaded them to exchange the sturdy fold-bed of the farm for the rolling bunk of a ship under sail. They could blame only themselves.

The drizzling rain thickened, the southeast wind died down. This time of year the winds shifted suddenly in the Baltic Sea, and even an old skipper would not predict the weather; but it seemed at the moment that the night would be calm. Captain Lorentz might as well turn in and rest for the remainder of the evening watch.

On the way to his cabin the captain almost fell over one of the passengers, who was down on his knees near the rail. Lorentz grabbed the man by the shoulder and raised him up. He was a rather short peasant, his face covered by a bushy, brown beard; his long, round-cut hair fell on his jacket collar.

"Keep your eyes open," warned the captain. "Don't fall overboard!"

The little peasant kept his hands folded across his chest, as if he were protecting something under them.

"I did not fall. I was kneeling and praying to God."

"Why do you pray your prayers up here?"

"It's noisy down in the ship. I wish to thank the Lord in peace."

"Oh—so that's it, my good man." Lorentz looked at him and added: "You'd better wait awhile to thank God for a safe voyage."

The farmer looked up and met the captain's gaze with two mild, frank eyes. He wished to thank the Lord already—he had been permitted to board a good ship, sailing under an honest, conscientious captain, manned by a capable, orderly crew. Now he could leave all to God. He knew the Almighty would do what He could to help them cross the dangerous sea.

"Hm—hm," mumbled the captain. "Be careful you don't fall. The deck is awash and slippery."

Lorentz continued toward his cabin, musing over his discovery. So he had religious cranks aboard. He knew that sort and didn't like them. A few years ago he had sailed to North America with fifty of the creatures. They had embarked at Gavle; some of them had been so sorely taken by the religious bug that they had tramped on foot from their homes to the harbor town, walking many miles, day and night, to board ship and escape the country. Their feet were bleeding when they arrived, and they had compared this to the blood in Christ's wounds.

Immediately he had recognized them as fantaics, and these sectarians had, indeed, been the most difficult passengers he ever had had on board. They did not consider him master of the ship, but insisted that the Lord God was in command. What is more, as soon as they reached the open sea they insisted that God ordered them to steer; the crew were hired by the devil, they said, and steered the ship to destruction. Many of the peasants, from Helsingland and Dalecarlia, had never seen the sea before, much less been near a helm. If God had meant passengers to steer, He no doubt would have chosen someone accustomed to the sea—even Captain Lorentz relied on the Lord to that extent. But when the sectarians had interfered to the extent of wanting to change the ship's course, he had at last been forced to read the law of the sea to them. To be on the safe side, he also had had to tell them he had guns on board. They were full of crazy notions. It had been a hellish trip with them aboard.

But he had done his fatherland a great service that time, when he shipped out fifty crazy Swedes and deposited them in North America. There were so many madmen there before them that this new load would be lost in the mob.

This brown-bearded fellow he had just encountered praying on deck seemed, however, a decent soul. He had thanked God for the capable captain; and as long as his religious nonsense took such expression, he might be considered harmless.

In his small cabin below the poop deck Captain Lorentz now brought out a jug of Bavarian ale which he kept wedged beside his table. He poured the foaming drink into a tremendous earthen stoup which held almost half a gallon. The handle of the stoup was in the shape of a female figure, the naked body of a young girl. She hung over the edge of the mug and dipped her hands and arms into the ale, bending her head as though she were drinking. Her back, a slender young girl-body, formed the handle.

This drinking stoup had been the gift of a ship's chandler in Barcelona to his good friend, the *Charlotta*'s captain. Many times the friend had helped Lorentz find girls with softer bodies than burnt clay; but that was long ago, that was when this old bachelor was younger and livelier. Now the siesta in a woman's arms—if one called it siesta—belonged to needs which Captain Lorentz had gradually left behind him. He led a quiet life, these days, where women played no part. But the big earthen mug with the girl's body he used daily in his cabin. Many a time he had satisfied his thirst with ale from this vessel, his hand holding the young, well-shaped woman. At regular intervals during the day he would caress her waist with his old, rough, seaman's hands. Nowadays she was his only girl, and she remained his constant and devoted mistress whether the brig *Charlotta* sailed inland seas or the open oceans.

The captain took a firm hold of the girl's body and raised the ale stoup to his mouth. When he had drunk he stretched his legs out under the cabin table and sighed deeply with pleasure: good thirst and good ale, two exceedingly fine things when one had both at the same time!

The captain was mellow this evening—he had the keel in clear water. Long days of open sea lay ahead; the entire spring would be spent at sea. He would not give the slimy Hudson—the entrance to New York Harbor—a single thought until the day he was actually there. He had set his ale stoup on a piece of paper, and the foam had wet it. He now picked it up, holding it close to his eyes. He recognized a comic prescription, written in a neat hand and given to him last night by the Karlshamn apothecary, at their farewell drinking party in the Hope Tavern.

"For Cholera
"(To my friend Captain Lorentz of the *Charlotta*)
"Temperately you must live.
  Not be afraid, nor worries give.
  Cheerful be, and every day
  Throw all your medicines away.
  Downhearted you must never be
  Nor let your tempers disagree.
  Eat a little, drink the more,
  Forget the girls and let them snore,
  Sleep every night and work each day.
  This is the rule that keeps you gay."

The apothecary had wanted to cheer him with these verses, which he had copied from some paper. But Lorentz was not cheered by them tonight—quite the contrary. And this because twice during his long voyages across the ocean he had been visited by the disease for which the verses suggested advice. Now, sitting in his cabin with his evening ale in front of him, these lines reminded him of all the troubles and difficulties he had encountered as captain of this ship during earlier voyages with emigrants to North America.

In front of him on the table lay the ship's *Medical Adviser for Seafarers,* printed in Danish; as yet there was no good Swedish handbook for captains sailing without a doctor. This *Medical Adviser* was a most useful book. On one of the very first pages he had underlined in red pencil a few sentences: "If so many passengers are aboard that they must be treated as cargo, this is of course the most unhealthy cargo possible. A great deal of attention is then required of the captain. . . ."

Attention—in that one word was included all the responsibility resting on the captain of an emigrant ship like the brig *Charlotta.*

Captain Lorentz sighed again, this time not from the satisfaction which came from good ale. What did a captain's attention avail? Lorentz was sure he could sail his ship to her destination in North America. This time, as always before, he would sail her undamaged into port. But he was equally sure that not all of the passengers who had embarked today would still be aboard when he tied up at the pier in New York. Before the voyage was over he would have to read funeral prayers for one or more of the emigrants; one or more would have to be lowered into the sea.

What was printed in the book was true: he was ship's master to the unhealthiest cargo imaginable—human beings.

He had reason to regret that the *Charlotta* no longer sailed as freighter only. He preferred dead cargo in the hull to this unpleasant, living cargo; there was never need to read funeral prayers for ordinary freight. Of all his duties as captain, the one of minister was most repulsive—burying those who died. A freighter captain need seldom perform this duty, which the master of an emigrant ship on an unfortunate voyage might find almost a daily task. How many days had he been on deck and acted the priest that time when they had the cholera aboard! How often during that voyage had he thrown the three shovelfuls of earth over the canvas-shrouded bodies— only he had had no earth in the hold, not a handful, even. At first he had been at a loss what to use for the funerals, but finally had taken ashes from the galley—there was, after all, little difference between ashes and earth.

That was the time the idea had come to him to take along Swedish earth to be used at funerals: a bushel of Swedish earth. It was little enough.

The *Charlotta*'s captain had thought: I will take along earth for these emigrating peasants. They are covetous of earth, they are bound to the earth, they love the earth above all in this world. And when they die they will want their mouths full of earth. Let them have it. Their mouths are filled with earth when they rot in the churchyard. To die on the ocean is different—then they are lowered into water—so why begrudge the poor devils three shovels of earth over their bodies when they have to be buried at sea, far from home—just three shovelfuls of their own earth?

After that voyage Captain Lorentz did not use ashes from the galey for his sea burials. He had a bushel of Swedish earth ready on his ship. One provision for the passengers of which they had no knowledge—a bushel of earth to be used when needed at sea.

And he knew that bushel would be used on the brig *Charlotta*'s seventh voyage to North America.

XIV

FORTY PACES LONG AND EIGHT PACES WIDE

1

In the hold enormous pieces of canvas had been hung to separate the space into three compartments: one for married couples and children, one for unmarried men, and one for unmarried women. The family bunks were toward the stern, partitioned off by bulkheads of rough boards nailed together. The small cells looked like cattle pens or horses' stalls. Beds were made on the deck of the hold with mattresses and loose straw. Unmarried passengers slept in bunks, strung longships between the stanchions. There were one-man and two-man bunks, "upper and lower berths."

Dust rose from unaired mattresses, blankets, and skins as the emigrants spread their bedding and made up their bunks in the hold of the *Charlotta*—berths for seventy-eight people. Each passenger kept his belongings at the foot of his bunk. The overhead was low, and the air thick and choking. The three small compartments with canvas bulkheads seemed even smaller than they were, with this cargo of knapsacks, food baskets, bedding, and bundles. Here and there stood crude little tables or food boards, where people could sit and eat. These also were crowded with baskets and tubs, which must be put somewhere. At last there was hardly a spot left for the people to step on.

Only through the main hatch did light filter into the hold. After dark a few weak, smoking, kerosene lanterns were lit and hung along the sides of the ship.

As there was no room for Karl Oskar in the family pen, he must share a two-man bunk with his brother Robert, in the unmarried men's compartment. Above the two brothers slept Jonas Petter, and Arvid had his bunk next, on the same side. The men here had about as much space as pieces of kindling stacked in a woodpile: there was hardly a foot's width per person.

"They must have meant us to sleep on our sides," said Karl Oskar. "There isn't room for a man to sleep on his back."

Jonas Petter held his nose: "It smells of piss!"

Robert too thought the hold smelled of night-old urine. "The air is so foul," he said to Arvid, "let's go above."

The hold was dark as a cellar. He felt as if he were in a sack.

By using their elbows the two boys were able to force a way between fellow passengers and their mattresses and sacks and bundles, through the narrow passageway along the ship's side, to where they could struggle out through the hatch. Robert looked more closely at the hatch covering, which was pierced through by a number of small holes, like a milk strainer. The only entry for fresh air was through these pitifully small openings. No wonder the atmosphere below was thick and stifling.

"Why don't they make bigger air holes in this ship?" wondered Arvid.

On deck they breathed clear, fresh, spring-cool Baltic air. It was calm at sea, and the ship rocked with a slow roll which they hardly noticed. The water purled softly against the hull, like water from a slow-running spring.

Robert wanted to walk about and inspect this ship which was to be his home for a long time. At the embarkation yesterday there had been such hurry and disorder he had been unable to see anything of it. Their sleeping places had had to be found, chests and knapsacks, boxes and kegs, tubs and baskets carried into the hold. Wherever he had turned he had been in the way of someone. Today he was more at home.

Only he was a little afraid to get too close to the captain. In Suneson's chandlery in Karlshamn one of the clerks had shown him the newspaper *Karlshamns Allehanda*; there was a notice about their ship under "Arrived Ship Masters." At first he had thought it must be a misprint in the paper; it actually said "Ship Masters," not "Ships." It was the ship masters who arrived in harbor, not the ships themselves. Then the little man whom he saw yesterday, back aft among the crew, was more important than the whole ship. It would not do to get in his way.

The boys looked cautiously around. Arvid inspected the ropes, thick as a man's arms, coiled here and there on deck like giant snakes. He had seen the same kind of ropes at the ship chandler's in Karlshamn. When he had asked if these ropes were meant for huge ferocious bulls, the clerk had laughed and said they were to hold something much wilder and much more difficult to handle than all the bulls in the world. Robert had then nudged Arvid in the side and explained that the ropes were used on ships to tie something with.

Robert had tried to learn all he could about ships and sea life, and already he was instructing his fellow traveler: Their ship was called a brig; a brig could easily be distinguished from other ships because she had a gaff sail on the aftermast.

"A gaff sail? What in the world is that?" asked Arvid.

Robert couldn't answer this as yet; but he thought it must be a sail put up with gaff (whatever that was). The aftermast, anyway, was the one farthest back on the ship.

"Someone talked about a yard sail today," said Arvid. "What might that be?"

This Robert thought he could answer accurately: a yard sail, no doubt, was one made right in the shipyard.

The boys looked up toward the ceiling of sails; they counted eleven of them, breeze-tightened: three on the bowsprit, four on the foremast, three on the after- or mainmast, and one small square sail on the stern. The masts were many rods high: they seemed taller than a church steeple. The mainmast was a few feet higher than the foremast—hence its name.

Robert noticed the masts were of pine; he thought again, as he had on first seeing the ship, that perhaps he had helped cut down the very trees which made them.

"Is it all one tree?" asked Arvid. "They are equally thick all the way to the top."

Robert thought several trees had been joined to make up a mast; one pine could never be that tall.

Thus the two farmhands contemplated the riddles of sea life, staring at the mast-tops until their necks ached. Those pines from the deep forests had traveled far across the ocean. Trees which had been next neighbors to them were still rooted in the woods. They might never get out to sea. Fate dealt unequally, even among the trees of a forest.

Up in the masts hung strange nets of heavy rope; they must be intended for huge fishes, such large meshes they had. A few of the sea folk were climbing up there, shouting to each other. The farm boys went dizzy watching them suspended above. The seamen had nothing to hold on to, as far as the boys could see, and they feared that any moment the men would lose their foothold so Robert and Arvid would have to witness the bodies of these daredevils fallen to the deck, crushed into bloody pulp.

The boys continued their inspection of the brig *Charlotta,* and were astonished at the small space the passengers had in which to move about. They paced off the length of the ship and her width, and even though they shortened their steps somewhat, they found her length to be no more than forty paces, and her width eight. The floor in some farmhouses was as large as this deck. Their ship was small—not only at a distance. Forty paces long and eight wide—for almost a hundred people, for them to live, to sleep and eat and perform all the necessary functions of life. If everyone came on deck at once it would be so crowded they would almost push each other overboard. Overboard—and suppose something should happen to their small ship, out on the great ocean: what would they do? There were a few rowboat-like rafts, here on deck, but by no means enough for the passengers. Well, perhaps such gear was not considered a necessity by sailors.

As far as immediate necessities were concerned, Robert had asked a seaman today where the outhouse was located. He was told it was the roundhouse forward, just aft of the port bow. Robert didn't know where the port bow was, but he had found the house anyway—though it wasn't round, but square. He didn't understand why it was called the roundhouse. It was true, the hole one used was round, of course, but so were all such holes. Who could solve the riddles of the sea?

The America-bound boys looked at the anchor winch and felt the heavy chain. What gear! But naturally heavy chains were required to tether a ship to the bottom of the sea.

"Look at the man in the fore end!" said Arvid, and pointed to the bow. The "man" was a wooden figurehead. They went closer and saw it represented the head and neck of a huge bird: an eagle stretching out over the ship's bow. The long beak of the bird was open, and pointed over the water like a spearhead, as though he would guide the helmsman across the seas with his beak. The eagle looked ravenous and ferocious, his black, immobile wooden eyes scanning the waters of the Baltic Sea.

A bent old man with a long beard sat leaning against the foremast, busy with pieces of rope and such. He grinned in a friendly way at Robert, who asked him what he was doing.

"Can't you see, boy? I'm splicing."

Robert had picked up a new word—"splicing." The bearded old man was the ship's sailmaker. In his younger days he had been a bosun. Robert asked him about the *Charlotta*'s figurehead, and the old man explained it served no purpose except decoration.

At the railing the boys looked down into the water rolling softly a few feet below them. Robert thought it might be a couple of miles to the bottom. Arvid shuddered—he had thought it would be a hundred rods at most.

The sea lay perilously near, and he was seized with terror. "If the sea should rise only half a yard, it would drown us!"

The possibility loomed before Robert for a fleeting moment, then he said there would be no danger: should the sea rise, it would only lift the ship higher. Arvid shook his head, unable to follow this.

A fellow passenger came up to the boys. He wore a broad-brimmed hat, a light brown, loud-checked coat, and trousers that fitted his legs as tightly as skin. From his hip pocket dangled a white handkerchief, swishing his thighs like a horse's tail; his shoes were of the finest patent leather. Robert had noticed this man earlier, on account of his colorful clothing. He seemed a gentleman among all these farmers.

The stranger looked down the side of the *Charlotta*'s worn hull and waterlogged planking, which had begun to soften and splinter. He grinned contemptuously and spat on the old hulk.

"God-damn her! Damn this sour old washtub!"

He spat a second time for emphasis.

"This is a rotten, stinking ship! Do you understand, peasants?"

In some resentment, Robert answered that he had felt the same when he boarded the ship. She was damp and un-healthy.

"Her bilge water stinks like the devil," said the man in the checked jacket. "I've sailed on many ships, and I must say this old hulk is unwholesome."

"Are you a seaman, sir?" asked Robert with new respect.

"I should say so! Was for ten years."

Arvid was bending over the rail, and now he made a discovery. He pointed and said: "Look! There's a hole! Our ship is leaking!"

He pointed to a hole at the water's edge through which a stream ran in and out continuously. The man in the checked coat laughed.

"That's the scupper hole, my boy! But the ship *is* leaky, anyway."

Robert caught the word "scupper." Of course, it was the hole through which the passengers scupped, or vomited; Arvid ought to have known this. He noticed now the hole was lined with iron, no doubt to prevent waste from clinging to the wood and smelling. The presence of the iron convinced him that the hole had been made with a purpose, was not caused by rot.

"Yes," resumed the stranger, "now I sail to the North

American Republic again, if this old tub keeps afloat that far."

"Have you visited America before?" asked Robert.

"Many times, my friend, many times. I have lived in America for years."

Robert viewed his fellow passenger with new interest. For the first time in his life he was face to face with a person who had been to the New World. What he beheld was a red, flushed face, swollen as if the owner had the mumps; a flat nose; and bloodshot, thick-lidded eyes. It was difficult to discover any redeeming features in this countenance, but the owner had been to America, and spoke of this without bragging, as if he merely mentioned that he'd been to the outhouse.

"What did you do in America, sir?"

"Various things."

The stranger's eyes scanned the water as if his memories of America were floating on the wave crests.

"This last year I helped a Mormon priest with odd jobs."

The man in the loud coat and the snakeskin-tight pants spat again, this time straight out to sea. Robert need not urge him further, he continued now of his own volition.

The Mormons were the Latter-Day Saints in the United. States, and he had been allowed to assist one of their greatest and most saintly prophets—or so he had thought when he accepted the job. Later, he might as well admit it now, it turned out that the priest was no Mormon at all! Things were not always what they seemed. But he would tell the story as it happened to him.

The Mormon priest (it was easier to refer to him so) had journeyed on the railroad from town to town, and he had gone with him to help with various things. It had not been a heavy or arduous task. When the supposed priest held a meeting in a town, then he, the assistant, had mixed in the crowd as one of the listeners. When the priest's sermon was over, then it was his duty to step forward and ask leave to say a few words: that this evening, in this room, the spirit of revelation had filled him. It had been granted him to see with his own eyes the returned Lord's prophet. And deep in his heart suddenly he had realized that he himself belonged to the lost tribe of Israel. His memory of long-gone-by times had returned to him so that it spanned even the days of Father

Abraham. He wanted now to be a member of the Holy Sons of Zion.

He would be received immediately, the bogus priest would open his arms to him, hold him to his heart, and in the presence of the whole congregation call him his long-lost brother. And then many of those sitting in the audience, till now somewhat doubting and undecided, would come up to the priest and testify to the same thing: they too belonged to the lost tribes of Israel, and they too had this evening seen the prophet. All would be received into the church, and a collection would be taken up.

Evening after evening this was his sole occupation; he acted again and again the son of Zion, a brother of the Lord's prophet, and for his services he received a dollar a day in cash, two free meals, free journeys on the railroad, and beautiful clothes lent him by his boss.

Almost every evening some woman in the audience would remember that she had been a daughter of Zion. The priest would take the most tender care of the prodigal sister, and marry her immediately, as, he said, the Lord commanded him to do. This was the one and only salvation of a woman's soul: she must be taken to wife. There was no other road along which a woman might reach the glories of heaven. She must be sealed by a man who fulfilled his duties as bridegroom.

Sometimes it happened that more than one of Zion's lost daughters were granted their memory, and returned to the church. Then the boss was not able to marry all of them. Neither his time nor strength was sufficient for such a task; moreover, he was a little ailing at times—especially on Saturday evenings—and then he wished to have a little time off. On those days he seldom married more than once or twice. Sometimes he actually needed a little peace, particularly as his health was not rugged. Then he would order the speaker, his paid assistant, to help: he too, at the priest's order, would marry one or two of the lost daughters of Israel. He was not one to bar the road to heavenly glory for good sisters in Zion. Furthermore, he had been engaged to help in all matters.

The boss himself chose his brides from among the youngest sisters. Tender, helpless women were, of course, most in need of a skilled helper who could guide them to the Lord, who could lead them with experienced hands. It was the assistant's duty to marry older, riper women, many of whom had never before known a man. But the more advanced in years the bride, the more shy she appeared—sometimes dressed in innumerable undergarments for the marriage consummation. Then the bridegroom's first occupation might be likened to the patient, reverent turning of the leaves in the old family Bible—one of those really old ones, with big pages. So there was, after all, an air of religion in the wedding night.

But this job had lasted only half a year. The boss had had a most unpleasant accident one dark evening in the fall. The two of them had come traveling on the steam wagon to an out-of-the-way little town far in the West, in which place little was known about God and His Ten Commandments. The people in the town were heathenish and wild, sometimes attacking strangers—before they had said a single evil word, or even had time to fire a shot at the inhabitants. And as the fake priest and his assistant stepped off the railroad car in this town they were attacked without warning by a group of god-forsaken hoodlums. They were infuriated by the idea of Mormons, it seemed, because in the past so many of the town's women had become daughters of Zion. There were scarcely any women left for wives and cooks among the settlers of the district. Now of course he, as a hired assistant, had little to do with this, he had only done what he was told to do. And luck was with him, too: he was able to get away from his boss as the mob surrounded him. As it happened, he had just that day received his weekly pay, so there was no reason to speak further to the priest. He had left the town as fast as his legs could carry him, and reached another village where people were more humane and refined.

Meanwhile the infuriated mob took charge of his boss, and the following day the assistant read in a paper, with great sorrow, that the poor man had been found dead, dangling from a tree. He had really had bad luck, encountering such uncivil people. He had been a just employer, too, and deserved more friends—or someone, at least, to help him in his hour of need.

It had also said in the paper that many were anxious to locate the supposed priest's assistant. This he couldn't understand, as he himself had nothing to do with the Mormon religion, real or pretended: he was a Lutheran engaged merely as servant to the priest—simply employed to help him with various things. And if the priest was not a priest anyway, and not a Mormon—well, it was not in any sense reasonable.

The passenger in the loud-checked suit finished his tale. He spat once more over the rail, pulled out the large handkerchief from his hip pocket, and dried his eyes. Robert and Arvid silently stared at him, thinking he was shedding tears over the fate of his employer. But it appeared he was only drying spray from his face. Then he nodded to the boys, left them, and resumed his leisurely walk, his big handkerchief dangling behind like the tail of a skulking dog.

Arvid was unable to solve the stranger's mystifying occupation in North America.

"Was he an assistant pastor, do you think?"

"Something of the sort, I suppose," said Robert.

"Are they allowed to hang ministers from trees in America?"

"Perhaps—if it is absolutely necessary. Otherwise I don't think it's permitted."

The two America-bound farmhands continued inspecting the ship from stem to stern—forty paces long and eight paces wide. They would prefer to stay on deck both night and day. They did not look forward to going back into the huddle below, to the dark space under the deck, the moist, smelly hold filled with dust from mattresses and straw, stinking of urine and vomit.

When on land Robert had always imagined a sailing ship as something immaculate and shining. He had thought of sails as being like white angels' wings. But the *Charlotta* of Karlshamn had dark gray sails, dirty from wind and weather, gray as potato sacks in a muddy field in autumn. The brig *Charlotta* had no angels' wings. She was no yacht with white sails, flying lightly over the sea. She was a lumbering cargo ship, deep in the water, her lower holds loaded with pig iron, plowing her way heavily along. She wasn't Robert's dream ship, she wasn't the ship he had seen for days and nights in his expectant longing. Yet he felt pleased, nevertheless, as he walked about on deck, looking up at the rigging where seagulls swarmed with their wings white and clean against the gray sails.

He was participating in a great adventure. If only he didn't have to go below. . . .

2

The passengers had been called on deck and gathered around the unbattened main hatch, where the second mate announced in his sing-song Finnish-Swedish: "The first week's provisions!"

Two of the seamen were busy rolling barrels and tubs from the storage hold. Lids were removed from the provision vessels, and the smell of food, combined with the sea air, made the emigrants hungry.

During the passage they were to receive their food and water at the ship's expense. Curiosity about the fare was great, and all passengers—men and women, children and adults—assembled to watch as the provisions were handed out. But the mate told them it would not be necessary for every passenger to come up and crowd around him; one person from each family should fetch the food, the head of each family only.

He further said that definite portions of unprepared provisions would be allotted to each and every one weekly. They must manage so that their provisions lasted the intended time. They could not return after a few days, said the mate, to tell him they were hungry, and demand larger allotments. He wanted them to understand, once and for all, that this was a whole week's supply. Each in turn could prepare his food in the galley on deck, and use the ship's utensils if he didn't have his own. The passengers must agree among themselves on time, and take turns at the galley so that everyone's right was respected. Refuse, bones, dishwater, and sweepings must be thrown overboard—leeward, not windward. It was strictly forbidden to throw anything windward.

They could obtain fresh water from the ship's supply once a day, half a gallon each for drinking and washing; they must economize on water. They themselves must keep the hold clean, and every morning remove vomit and other dirt. Water would not be issued before the hold was cleaned; that would help them to remember this chore. Sick people could obtain medicine: drops, pills, balsam, and such from the ship's medicine chest. And if they needed to buy something during the voyage, goods were sold from the slop chest which the captain had charge of. Among supplies available at a fair price were soft soap, combs, brushes, Bibles, hymnbooks, snuff, chewing tobacco, knives, games, playing cards.

The passengers were admonished to handle fire with the strictest care. Below deck it was forbidden to smoke, or to carry or use unprotected lights. In general, it was the duty of everyone to obey the rules and orders of the ship's command. All must realize the necessity for order on shipboard during a long voyage, for their own protection and safety. The law of the sea was in effect, and the captain would punish those who did not obey instructions.

The emigrants listened in silence and awe to the second mate. Some wondered what sort of punishment was to be meted out according to the sea law—was there an altogether different law at sea?

Near the foremast stood Inga-Lena and Danjel Andreasson. The wife held her husband's hand and looked inquiringly around the deck. "Danjel—where might it be, that which he spoke of—windward?"

"I don't know, beloved wife."

"The place—where one is not allowed to throw anything? One must know where it is. I don't wish to do anything that is forbidden."

The old sailmaker standing near by explained to the peasants: "The mate meant that nothing must be thrown into the sea against the wind. Then it would blow right back onto the deck again."

"Goodness gracious!" exclaimed Inga-Lena. "That much sense anyone must have, without orders. I thought windward was a special place on the ship."

The second mate took out his wooden *betsman* and weighed the provisions, dividing them among the emigrants waiting around him.

Danjel Andreasson folded his hands. "God is feeding us for the first time on board ship."

There were many kinds of provisions which the Lord God now offered through the mate: ship's bread and ship's biscuits, salt pork, salt beef, butter, rice, barley grains, peas, salt herring, flour, sugar, syrup, mustard, salt and pepper. The emigrants crowded around the mate, they brought crocks and pans and vessels of all kinds in which to store their portions.

Some couldn't find containers, and tied their herrings, or peas, or salt pork, in towels or aprons. Others received their allotment with their bare hands.

The mate repeated: "Remember, now—economize, good people!"

His was a chore which required patience and skill. The smaller portions caused him endless figuring. Only pork and bread were allotted in sufficient quantity to enable him to figure in whole pounds; for the rest he had to count in ounces on his *betsman*: six ounces of butter, six ounces of sugar, thirteen of flour, four of salt, four of coffee, half an ounce of mustard, and a tenth of an ounce of pepper. And the vinegar too was measured, two ounces for each passenger. It was degrading work for a mate, to stand here and weigh and count and divide; and the second mate on the ocean-sailer *Charlotta* thought, as he stood arguing and weighing and measuring and counting ounces: This is a job for a shop clerk, not for a deep-sea sailor.

It took several hours before the provisions were distributed and the second mate could throw aside his *betsman* and measuring vessels. He sighed in relief: now it was done for a week. All had received their week's rations; but of course, as always with these peasants, they didn't have enough containers. A couple of women had received their flour in shawls, and the barley grains and peas in turned-up petticoats. However, they were never finicky, these passengers to North America.

Soon the smell of frying pork and boiling peas in the galley permeated the whole ship, but it would be long before each had his turn at the galley stove, and while waiting for the prepared meal the herrings and bread and such were taken out and eaten.

Arvid and Robert stood in the stern, each chewing on a ship's biscuit, hard as a stone chip. Arvid broke one of his front teeth on the very first bite; after that he was more careful, crushing the biscuit with his hands and eating the small pieces. He had often eaten month-old bread in Nybacken, but never had he broken a tooth on it. He thought if it was to continue this way, he would be toothless before reaching America.

It was growing dusk. The water around them darkened, rigging and sails were shrouded in mist as if the clouds had descended upon the ship. Their world seemed to shrink, no other ships were in sight, and their little sailing vessel seemed alone and lost on the darkening sea, with land no longer visible.

Robert shivered. It was a horrible depth there under the ship's bottom—and here he stood on a pile of old, half-rotten planks. He was inside a sour old wooden bucket which was intended to carry him across these depths; he felt infinitely helpless. Into the youth from firm land crept fear that bit and tortured him like a multitude of ants: the seafarers' life was precarious, it was not like life on land.

Perhaps it would be best after all to crawl down below and hide himself tonight in the dark bowels of the ship.

3

Kristina stood by the place where she and the children were to sleep, this bunk or bed-pen nailed together of roughly hewn odds and ends of boards. She had placed her mattress on the floor of the hold and spread her quilt, her bridal cover, over it. On top of the bunk stood the big willow basket, their food box—they had found no other place for it. And in this bunk tumbled and tussled the children; there was no other place for them, either. The bunk was their only room, and in it was gathered everything.

Kristina had slept the first night in the family bunk. The compartment was too small for her and the children—even without Karl Oskar. Almost every time she had been about to go to sleep, a child's knee or foot had poked her in the stomach or face and awakened her anew. She had lain there like a setting hen, unable to find space under her wings for her brood. In between she was kept awake by noise from the other passengers, and by the many sounds of the ship. So she had dozed uneasily and started awake through the whole night, and when she arose in the morning she was more tired than she had been the night before.

In the family compartment more than thirty people lived, men, women, and children, jammed together in one room that was no larger than Kristina's own room in Korpamoen. As soon as she stepped out of her bed she bumped into someone. And Kristina was shy in the presence of all these strangers crowding around her. All she did must be done in full view of these people. How was she to suckle little Harald? She felt uncomfortable opening her blouse to expose her breasts in the presence of strangers; she did not like to suckle her baby while other wives' husbands looked on. She was shy even in the presence of Karl Oskar, her own husband. It was dreadful that she had to dress and undress among all these unknown folk.

Lill-Marta had caught a cold in the windy harbor town, and was now in bed with a fever, perspiring, an alarming flush in her cheeks. Kristina wished she could obtain a mug of hot milk for her. But there was no milk on the ship. She must now mix honey in water and warm it for the child. And what was she to do with Johan? He was well enough, but he wet his bed nearly every night; that dripper ought to have had his own mattress. And the amount of clothing which the children already had dirtied—how was she ever to wash and dry it here on the ship?

She was now enclosed in a small pen, among all these strangers, with three children, one of them sick—never in her life had she felt so lost and helpless.

The children had no place down here to play and entertain themselves, and they hung on their mother. Johan kept pulling at her skirts.

"I want to go out, Mother!"

"We cannot go out here, little one."

"But I want to go out and go home."

"We are on the sea now."

"I don't want to be on the sea. I'll go home. I want milk and cookies."

"But we cannot get off. I've told you."

"Mother—I don't like it here!"

"Keep quiet now! Be a good boy!"

Thank God, she had some sugar. She opened the knapsack at the foot of the bunk, found her bag of sugar, and gave the boy a lump. He kept quiet awhile—this was her only way to silence him. Lill-Marta ought to have had a piece, too, but she slept in her fever. Kristina felt the child's forehead tenderly; she was still burning hot.

Karl Oskar came down from deck with a jar of water in his hand. Now they had obtained their weekly rations, but had not received potatoes; he missed potatoes, he was used to potatoes every day. Instead he had been given sour cabbage —but this he liked. Kristina thought that perhaps potatoes wouldn't keep on the ship, they would sprout and spoil, though she was not sure if this was the reason for their absence. Karl Oskar said they would eat just so many more when they planted their own in the rich soil of North America.

Soon it was their turn to use the ship's galley. But Karl Oskar said there was little room up there—it was as crowded in the galley as it was in church pews on a Christmas morning; the women stood and sat on top of each other. This did not cheer Kristina: was she now to elbow her way among strange women while she prepared their food, also?

Each time Karl Oskar came down from the fresh sea air on deck he would grin and sniff the air in the hold. "One needs a nose clip down here! The air stinks!"

Kristina had almost collapsed the first time she came into the hold. All evil smells that used to make her sick streamed toward her: rancid pork, old herring brine, dirty socks, sweaty feet, dried vomiting. In one corner she had espied some wooden buckets, and she could guess their use. She had felt as if she had been pushed into the bottom of a smelly old herring barrel. She had felt nausea, had wanted to turn and run up on deck—had wanted to get off the ship at once.

Little by little she was accustoming herself to the evil odors. But she still went about taking short breaths, trying not to inhale the bad air.

Karl Oskar explained that the bad air was caused by poor ventilation. The people took the air from each other's mouths down here. But as long as calm weather lasted they might go on deck and breathe fresh air during the daytime.

He was dissatisfied with their ship; he felt he had been cheated in his contract for the passage. And yesterday—when he had been denied sleeping place with his wife, and been put with unmarried men—he had spoken plainly to the mate: he did not ask to sleep like a king on silken sheets under eiderdown in a gold-plated chamber; but neither had he imagined they were to live crowded and jammed together like wretched sheep in a pen. At least twenty people too many had been packed in down here. The shipowner had only been interested in getting their money. Each grown person paid one hundred and fifty riksdaler for his passage—forty-three and a half dollars, he was told it was, in currency of the new country they were bound for. Yet they had to lie here and suffer in a dark unhealthy hole so the owner might grow fat on their money. That was what Karl Oskar had said to the mate, and the most outspoken among the emigrants had agreed with him. The mate had threatened to call the captain, Kristina had become frightened and prayed him to keep quiet—but Karl Oskar was like that; he could not keep his mouth shut when he felt an injustice.

Moreover, they had had to lie and wait in Karlshamn a whole week, and their quarters in the harbor town had cost many daler which he had had to pay unnecessarily; they should have been notified in advance about the exact date of the ship's sailing.

One of the seamen, who looked decent and wasn't quite so haughty, had admitted that the ship was overloaded with people. But he had added that it usually thinned out in the hold as they got out to sea.

If that hint was meant as a comfort, then it was indeed a cruel comfort; as a joke, Karl Oskar liked it even less.

This much he knew by now: that their life on board ship would be neither comfortable nor healthy.

There were already sick fellow passengers. In one family compartment, on the other side, lay a young girl who had been ailing when she embarked. She had fallen ill with a throat abscess while they were staying in Karlshamn. Her parents boiled porridge in the galley and tied this as a warm compress around her infected throat. But it had been of no help as yet. The girl lay there breathing heavily, with an unpleasant rattle. Karl Oskar had suggested to the father that the abscess in the throat be opened. He himself had once in his youth had such trouble in his throat, and porridge compresses had been useless—only the knife had helped.

The enclosure next to Kristina was occupied by an old peasant couple from Oland. The husband's name was Mans Jakob, and the wife was called Fina-Kajsa. They had told Karl Oskar that they were emigrating to their son, who had been living in North America for many years. Karl Oskar had noticed the old Oland peasant when they embarked: he had brought a huge grindstone with him, and the mate had objected, wondering if it were necessary to drag that thing with him. Couldn't they just as well heave it overboard? He would no doubt get along without the grindstone in America. But Mans Jakob thought a great deal of his stone: he would take it with him on the ship, or demand the return of his money. He was so insistent that the mate finally gave in; and the grindstone was now in the hold. Mans Jakob had heard from his son that good grindstones were expensive in America. They were cheap on Oland, and he wished to bring this one as a present to his boy.

Karl Oskar recalled that he had practically given away a new, even grindstone at his auction, because he had considered it too cumbersome for the voyage. Perhaps it would be difficult to find an equally good stone—he would surely need one to sharpen the scythes that were to cut the fat, rich, tall grasses in America; a sharp scythe did half the haymaker's work.

There were also other implements they should have taken along.

"Did you see, there are those who drag along spinning and spooling wheels and such?"

"Yes," admitted Kristina. "I regret leaving my spinning wheel."

Seeing what others had taken with them, she regretted having left behind so many necessary household articles.

But they must reconcile themselves to the thought of what they should have taken and what they would miss in America. Kristina was much more upset by the fact that they must travel in the company of one person who ought *not* to have been taken along.

She pointed to the canvas bulkhead at the foot of her bunk: in there slept one who ought not to have been in their company on this voyage.

She whispered: "She sleeps right there—the whore!"

That disgusting woman was as close to her as that; Ulrika of Vastergohl had her bunk right next to Kristina's—only a thin piece of sailcloth separated the beds. Kristina could hear every move of the Glad One, every word she uttered—and those were words she would rather close her ears to.

Kristina pointed, and Karl Oskar looked. There was a small hole in the hanging, through which he caught a glimpse of Ulrika of Vastergohl; she was busy undressing, and he noticed something white: her bare, full breasts. He turned quickly away, embarrassed and a little irritated, and he became even more irritated as he saw Kristina's vexed look: did she think he was in the habit of staring at undressed women? She herself had pointed out Ulrika's place. But Ulrika ought to hang a cover over that hole before undressing. Still, among all these people on the crowded ship one must apparently grow accustomed to incidents never before experienced.

"Why do they call her the Glad One?" asked Kristina.

"I suppose because she is never sad."

"If ever a woman needed to be sad, she is the one. She should weep tears of blood, that woman."

"Don't pay any attention to her," said Karl Oskar.

"Attention! Certainly not! I have other things to do."

Kristina wondered if he could find her a bucket of water. She must wash their dirty clothes. She intended to keep herself and her children as clean as if they were on land, both underclothes and outer garments.

But Karl Oskar thought they could not obtain more water today—not before tomorrow morning, after the hold was cleaned.

"Too bad you can't ask the mate for an extra portion; he is angry at you."

Karl Oskar did not answer. He was a little hesitant and lost here on the ship. He always knew what to do when on land, and if he needed anything usually managed to get it. But here at sea he didn't know where to obtain anything, he was not allowed to go where he wanted, he could not do as he wished. And if he complained, he was threatened and talked down to by the ship's command. He felt that these seafaring people looked down on peasants as some order of lower beings. They treated them almost like cattle. Here he went about like an animal tethered to its stake; he could go as far as the chain permitted him, around and around, but not an inch farther. It was the sea that tied him. The sea outside the ship's rail closed him in. The sea was not for anyone who wanted space in which to move freely.

He was disappointed mostly for Kristina's sake that their ship was so crowded and their quarters so dark and moist and unhealthy. It was he who had persuaded her to emigrate, he was responsible for their being here. And from her countenance he knew what she thought—he had avoided looking her directly in the face since they came on board, but he knew what her expression was. Still, she was not one to complain and blame him, even when she had cause; that was one reason he had wanted her as his wife.

He would try to cheer and comfort her: "We have fine weather at sea! We can be happy for that!"

He had hardly finished speaking when the ship lurched heavily, the result of tacking. The movement came so unexpectedly that Kristina lost her footing and fell on her side, luckily on the made-up bunk.

"Our ship is leaping ahead!"

Karl Oskar gave Kristina a broad smile. "You should feel at home here at sea—you have always liked swinging!"

The ship had lurched and knocked over Kristina from Korpamoen. She did not smile. The young wife looked about her in the dark, dusty, smelly hold of the *Charlotta*, overfilled with people: these were to be their quarters during the long voyage to North America; here she was to live for weeks, maybe months, with her children. Here they must eat and drink and sleep, here they must live and breathe and be awake. Here they must remain in their bed-stall, like imprisoned animals in a byre during the long, dark winter.

And as she looked at her home at sea, the thought returned to her—a thought she had had the first moment she had put foot in the hold: I will never get away from here alive. This looks exactly like a grave.

XV

A CARGO OF DREAMS

Sometimes during the nights the emigrants lay awake and turned in their bunks, listening to each other's movements and to all the sounds of the ship.

Karl Oskar:

We are on the voyage and very little is actually the way I had thought it would be. But whether it goes well or ill, I'll never regret my step. The stupidest thing a man can do is regret something that's already done, something that cannot be changed. Perhaps I have brought unhappiness upon us—we may have to suffer a great deal; and all is on my shoulders. I insisted on the emigration—if it turns out badly, I can blame only myself.

If only we can get across this ocean, and land with our health.

Everything I own is in this venture. With bad luck all can be lost. At home they ridiculed me. They thought I had a crazy notion. This irritates me, but I won't let it get under my skin. Why should other people necessarily like what I do? Only cowardly dogs hang about lapping up praise, waiting to have their backs scratched. I'll have to scratch my own back. And I'll never return with my wife and children to become a burden to my parish—whether our venture turns out happily or not. That pleasure I won't give anyone. No; however it goes, no one at home shall suffer because of us. There are many back there who wish me bad luck, so I must watch my step. The home folk are envious and begrudge each other success, wish hardship on each other; they would be pleased if things went wrong for me.

I don't think things will begin easily for us in America. It's hard to start anew. But my health is good, and if it stays with me I can work enough to feed us. Hardship is not going to bend me; with adversity I shall work even harder, from pure anger. I'll work, all right, as soon as I have my land. And no one is going to cheat me—I won't put trust in the first soft-spoken stranger I meet.

As I lie here with my money belt around my waist I like to touch it now and then. It gives me a sense of security to touch it when I want to. It holds all I have left of worldly possessions, changed into silver coin. It's all we have to lay our new foundation; I carry that belt night and day—no one can steal it without first killing me. Of course, all the folk here in the hold are simple farmers, and perhaps as honest and decent as I; but I never did trust strangers. I suppose the other farmers are also lying here with their money belts around their bellies. But who can know for sure that there isn't a thief on board? He wouldn't go around saying: I'm the one who steals! And in the jostle down here we are so close to each other we can look under each other's shirts. The way we lie packed together one couldn't hide even a needle from the other fellow.

I have never relied on any person, except myself—and on her, of course. God be praised I have such a fine woman, industrious, thrifty, and careful of our young ones. A farmer with a wasteful, lazy, slovenly wife never can get ahead. And she came along with me, she did as I wished. But I'm afraid she will regret it, although she will say nothing. Perhaps she would rather see the whole thing undone; at times I think so. If she should begin to look back, and wish to return, what might I do then?

No. She has agreed, once and for all. She is a woman of her word, she'll stick to her promise.

It's bad luck she got with child at this time—it looks as though it had been planned—the very moment we left. Now she is sensitive—and I'm afraid the sea will aggravate her further. But I shall take care of her, and help her with the children where I can. Luckily, she too is in good health.

We can't expect much joy on this ship. Not in any way. It may be long before things go well for us again—for her and me. I don't even know how soon I can move over to her bunk. Lying here this way, separated at night, I can never touch her. Here I lie with the unmarried men—like a castrated steer. Here I lie in "the ox pen." I can't get what I need, what I long for. This can't go on too long. Why should one suffer just because one travels on a ship? They say one gets horny at sea; but of course, one gets that way on land too. Perhaps it's worse here because I see so many women. There are those who are young and shapely too. Oh, well, I don't care for any others as long as I have her. Nor have I ever had another one. But Ulrika of Vastergohl strolls about and shows what she has—to the men. That woman couldn't think that I—Oh, no. Not even if I were single. Not any more. Too many men have used her. But she is tempting; that I cannot deny. She is nicely shaped, and I believe there are men here who wouldn't hesitate. And she herself would no doubt be agreeable. Even though she is said to be "reformed," and Danjel thinks she won't sin any more.

Life at sea is dreary and monotonous. I must cheer her, my wife. I must tell her what we are going to do, once we are settled over there—a few years from now. When the earth in America has given us abundant crops. When I have built a big house. When the children are grown and can help us. When Johan can go with me out into the fields. When Lill-

Marta can help her in the house. When we have a farm without a mortgage. When we won't have to worry about the mortgage interest when we go to sleep and when we awaken. When we are independent in our own home. When we have begun our new life. When we live cleanly and comfortably in a house where it doesn't smell so damn bad as it does in this stinking hole. Yes, I'll tell her everything, as I have imagined it.

If only I could get near her; only once, at least. There ought to be a change soon.

One has such foolish thoughts. No one knows what we may have to go through. The old ones think that all is arranged before one is born. Then it doesn't matter what one does—what use would there be in labor and struggle? But I don't agree with the old ones. I think one must put one's strength into everything, and use one's head as well as one can. Always I have done it at home—I'll do the same over there. And I intend never to regret it.

But our welfare and maybe our lives depend on this emigration. If only we were safely across the sea. . . .

Kristina:

I should never have given in; I should have talked him out of it; I feel it can never go well. Something has warned me all the time: this venture will turn out badly.

And yet—if there were a bridge back to land, and I could take my children and walk back, I would not do it. Even if I knew for sure that it would turn out ill for us, I could never return. I have told him: I want to follow you! And this cannot be revoked. He is my husband and the father of my children; what else can I do but follow him?

I wonder if he is thinking it over, perhaps regretting it, now that we are on the sea. He is much more serious. He seemed concerned as long ago as when we lay at Karlshamn and waited. I wonder if it has dawned on him what we face. This notion came to him, he had to carry it through, he is so stubborn. But how far had he thought it through in advance?

We must stick together, even so. I've promised to stick to him as long as I live.

What a pity we can't sleep together here on board, and be more cozy. I must always be so careful when I'm not pregnant, I never dare give in—as I want to. I don't wish to be with child every year if I can help it. We must skip a year now and then. But now there would be no danger—I can't become pregnant when I am already with child. That's one reason why it's so disappointing and annoying, this sleeping arrangement.

I can see he wants me all the time. He has a strong nature and he can't help it. Sometimes I've blamed him when I myself was equally weak; it's not easy to admit your own weakness. When he wants me it's almost impossible to resist—he can always have me. Because deep within me I want just what he does—even though I've never actually admitted it to him. I'm ashamed to appear weak; my mother said a woman must not let her husband know how weak she is. She must be master of her desires—she mustn't be like the menfolk. That's why I never admit the truth. He must believe that I'm willing only for his sake, for his satisfaction. It may not be quite honest of me, but it is right.

Perhaps sometimes—inadvertently—I may have shown him how much I like it. Perhaps once or twice, when it was at its best, I've let out sounds. But nearly always I've been filled with anxiety and the thought: Now—in this moment—now it's happening, now I am becoming pregnant again. Then it has never been the same.

He pats me sometimes. I think he pats me more often since we left home. That last evening at home—how foolish of me. I regret it. I feel ashamed to remember the way I acted. But I've never misbehaved since then—nor has he used an ugly word since then.

I wish he could come to me tonight, now, when we don't need to worry. Now I could give in completely; then everything would be so much better. It's not right, and I feel ashamed of it, but my desire is much greater when I am with child than otherwise. A pregnant woman ought not to feel that way. I wonder if it is that way for sinful human beings only, not for animals. It must be the original sin within me.

But when you are a married woman, then it is permitted by God. And when you have your husband so near you—

It couldn't be done, of course. People are lying so close all around, listening in the night. It would be difficult here on the ship, probably impossible. No eyes can see in the darkness, but all ears can hear. Some people seem to lie awake all night long. And if one did try, one would have to forget all shame. There are those who do it—that young couple in the corner last night. They could be heard, I must say. They did not even try to keep quiet. I wanted to keep my fingers in my ears, but I didn't.

It is much worse when one has to lie here and listen to all sounds on the ship. One is aroused. And I dream so much. Last night I dreamed he was here with me. I'll go to sleep and dream that again. I've lost all shame here.

It will be a long, long voyage. And we don't know where we are headed. I'm afraid we may drown in the sea. And I'm afraid of the new country. All the little ones crawling about me. Those three creatures know nothing. Every time I feel fear, I take all three of them into my arms. But then I still miss him.

Karl Oskar—what a pity we didn't—that we didn't—I wanted—I should not have let you—I should have been against this venture—

Robert:

I wonder if the captain has any drops for earache in his medicine chest.

My left ear aches again tonight. At times I'm almost deaf in it. Inside, it feels like a weight. My hearing is much worse. I've become hard of hearing because I didn't listen to my master, and obey him. But when I get to North America the ache will disappear. There is another air there, healthy for sick ears. Those hard of hearing in the Old World will get their hearing back in the New World.

The roar in my ear is stronger at sea. Perhaps it is the wind that causes this. It feels like a sea closed up inside my head—boiling, hissing, booming. The sea is bursting, pressing, trying to get out. This causes me pain, great pain. I awaken from the ache and find my ear is wet—my pillow too: a few drops of the sea have escaped.

I am afraid of the sea—outside there—but I try not to show my fear. I am particularly afraid in the evenings, while I lie here in my bunk. Outside the wall—on the other side of the hull—I can hear the sea with my good ear. It is not very far away. The side of the ship is only five or six inches thick, perhaps a little more, perhaps a little less. There is no great distance between me and eternity. The ship might sink tonight —the sea has only five or six inches to travel. The sea can break in and reach me, fill my ears, nose, mouth—penetrate my throat and fill up my stomach. It can fill me and pull me down to the bottom. I would hardly have time to cry out—I would sink like a stone. I can't swim—hardly anyone here can swim. I'm afraid of the sea late at night.

Once I wanted to drown an old cat in the brook; I put her into a sack, not realizing that I should have put a stone in, too, before I threw it into the water. It didn't sink, the cat was alive inside and swam about with the sack. It floated there like a horrible hairy water-animal. The sack kicked and moved but would not sink. I threw stones at it to make it go down, I must have thrown ten before it sank. It was gruesome, I was afraid, and I remember I cried. I was about ten, I had no better sense then. I have many times regretted it. I have never drowned a cat since.

Why is it that I always think of that cat, every evening after going to bed? It frightens me. My brother is not afraid or worried. I have never seen him afraid of anything, on land or sea.

I wonder if Elin is afraid when she lies like this, and listens to the sea outside. I was often alone with her in Karlshamn, but here on the ship I have hardly a chance to speak to her. Yesterday when we sat together on deck her mother called to her: Come here, girl; hurry up! She sounded angry. She couldn't be angry at me.

I said to Elin once, I feel sorry for your mother. Then she seemed hurt—I can't understand why. Feel sorry for yourself, you, living in the flesh, she said. What did she mean? I did not say a word against her mother, I only said I felt sorry for her. But Elin got angry, and I was embarrassed. I must have said something foolish, though I don't know what it was.

I wonder if Elin sleeps with her mother behind the sail-cloth. If she sleeps alone, I might crawl across to her. No, I would never dare to. One only thinks about those things—I would never dare. But it is not forbidden to wish, no one can stop you from wishing. I can wish to crawl into bed with a princess. No dean or sheriff can do a thing about it. In the catechism it is forbidden even to wish for things, to covet—to covet a woman to whom you are not married is the same as to commit adultery with her in your heart.

But one has to desire a woman before one can get her, before one can marry her.

I don't wish to touch Elin in that forbidden way. I don't

wish to commit adultery with her. If I crawled into her bunk, here on the ship, I would just lie quietly and hold her, hold her in my two arms—as I did when we sat and slept together on Jonas Petter's wagon. What a wonderful ride! If I were near her now I could comfort her when she is afraid, when the storms come and our ship might sink.

Today she told me she is afraid of wild Indians in America. I have told her before that the Indians might at times be a little treacherous and evil and unreliable—they are known to have attacked white people who have tried to kill them. But otherwise they are docile and peaceloving.

My ear aches as though it would burst tonight. It will soon be two years since I got that box on the ear from Aron in Nybacken, and I still feel it. The ache tonight is from that box. It must have been a "big" box—I have nearly lost my hearing in that ear. This is not so good. One cannot know what people are saying if one doesn't hear. But I know my ear will mend as soon as we arrive in America.

For every wave I hear break against the ship, I am coming nearer to the United States. I am participating in an adventure. I will learn how big the sea is. There are few boys from our neighborhood who can sail the sea and find out how big it is. And when I arrive and step on shore I will be free for all time. On America's shore no old farmers will be waiting, calling me their "little hand." Never more will I be a servant to anybody. I shall be my own master.

It hurts awfully in my ear tonight. If only we could move a little faster, if only the ship could sail with higher speed, then we would soon arrive in the land where my earache will disappear.

Arvid:

A hell of a good thing that I could come along. I must thank the pious farmer for that. I think there never was such a kind couple as Danjel and his wife.

I am a passenger now. I've chewed that word over and over. Robert thinks I can read, and he tries to make me spell it. He says it has a che-sound in it. What the devil is a che-sound? I went to school a while but I never heard of a che-sound. No other sounds either, as I recall. I never let on to Robert, of course—he thinks I can spell and read. It is the same sound as in a chunk of dirt, he said. But I didn't understand it. You must mean shit, I said. I think they call that a piece of dirt in school.

Robert is a very learned man who has read much. I would like to have his eyes to read with and his head to think with. He is a clever devil in thinking, finished before I even get started.

Anyhow, now the Bull of Nybacken is a passenger and walks the ship and lives a lazy life. Sundays and weekdays the same. I don't earn my food, but I get it anyway—three meals a day. I can hardly believe it. Never in all my born life have I had it so easy and comfortable. Ever since I was a small child I have slaved every day—Sundays too. Even when I had my free-week, and came home, I had to help with chores. If I sat down and rested my mother used to say: "Go get some wood! Get a bucket of water!" Or my father said: "Come and crank the grindstone! Help me make this broom!" Never in hell did I have a free week. No, never. But here on ship no one says: "What are you doing, lazy dog? Give me a hand!" I haven't done a damned thing since we left home. I have been fed just the same, eaten three meals every day—and how good I feel!

I haven't been seasick either. A couple of times I have felt like spewing a little, but it went away. I think I have too much food in my stomach. I haven't missed a single meal yet, and I'll eat all I can get.

Christ, yes, what a good life! No damn farmer gets me up in the middle of the night to feed the horses. No devil gives me hell because I work too little. No one says a word because I take it easy. It's a hell of a fine thing. I am a passenger with a che-sound like in shit!

Our boat holds together—not a drop of water has come in through ceiling or walls. That hole on the side—that was made, it's good with water running through it. But the boat does wobble at times, and I feel it might turn over. It looks warped, up on one side and down at the other. Happily, it gets back in pôsition. But if it did fall over, and sink in the sea, one would never get up again.

When I think that the boat actually can drown, I feel a kind of sickness in my breast. Mother gave me the prayer-book and she knows I can't read. "You must take God's word with you to America, in any case," she said. "You can read those prayers by heart which I taught you when you were a little tyke." Oh, yes, I do know prayers by heart. The book has one prayer for each morning and each night, the whole week. I try to read as best I can remember—I am out at sea and the ship is rickety and totters at times, and I don't know how to swim. I know neither cat-swim nor dog-swim, and it may be useful with God's word: ". . . help me sweetly to go to sleep this night . . . help me this night that my soul does not go to sleep in sin, and no calamity befalls my body . . . if I live on land or sea . . . receive me at last in the safe harbor, my dear Father. . . ."

Perhaps I mix the evening prayers. But God wouldn't care if I said a few words from the Tuesday prayer on Monday evening. He couldn't be that persnickety, not with me who only read by heart. But it feels safer and easier in my chest when I have said my prayer and put myself in the hands of God. What luck that I can leave myself to the Lord on this wild, un-Christian sea.

We must have been traveling very long on this boat. Today I asked one of the seamen how much was left to sail. He said it was nearly as far from here to North America as it is from North America to here, perhaps only fifty miles' difference. I thought a lot about that, it seemed so far. Then he laughed, the devil, and the others around him too, and I got so mad I wanted to give him one in the snout so his shit would run out. I told him it was the same to me how far it was. If a seaman who had traveled that way before couldn't give information, then he needn't poke fun at honest people. "You must not think, you sheep-coint," I said, "that we who come from the farm country are any dumber than you who fare around on the sea. We understand when anyone tries to make a spectacle of us."

However far it is, I think we'll get there, for the boat sails every day, Sundays and weekdays, and Danjel says that God's breath blows on the sails. And when I get to America I shall ask all those old, tight peasant shits at home to kiss my ass. No one has ever had such luck as I on my America journey— a free-week in April, a free-week in May, free-weeks throughout the whole damn spring! And three meals on every one of God's days!

I am damn lucky to be here.

Danjel Andreasson:

The Almighty has so far given us fine weather at sea, and He helps us all He can.

Our ship sails with the Lord's chosen ones to a land which He has designated. She is a little, fragile ship, the work of faulty human hands, but she is the Lord's vessel. One night I saw two of God's angels standing at the helm. They helped the seamen steer the ship on the right course.

I was dubious at first, I worried about the great undertaking: to leave my land and all my kinfolk and voyage with my wife and children over the sea—when I am no longer in the days of my youth. But I drove fear away from my heart, and followed the call of God: His word is the lantern of my feet and a light on my path.

But I observe that doubt and fear assail my little flock: Inga-Lena, my beloved wife, our four dear children, and Ulrika of Vastergohl, and her tender daughter. The Evil One whispers tempting words in their ears to test their faith. My beloved wife fears the language of North America. She is afraid she will have to go about like a deaf-mute among the people of the foreign land. But I assure you, Inga-Lena, as I have done so many times, as soon as we arrive in the land the Holy Ghost will fill us so that we may speak the unknown tongue at once, as if we were born children of the American hamlets. We have the Lord's promise and the Bible's words about the miracle on the first Whitsuntide. I have read it many times for you, Inga-Lena: "And there appeared unto them cloven tongues like as of fire, and it sat upon each of them. And they were all filled with the Holy Ghost, and began to speak with other tongues, as the Spirit gave them utterance."

You must remember what I have so often told you, my dear wife: the Galileans, too, were simple unlearned men and women; yet they were able at once to speak Greek and Arabic, and the languages of the Medes and Elamites, Egyptians and Parthians and Libyans. They arose and spoke these tongues and praised the wonderful works of God. And according to God's promise, the same miracle will happen to all who are reborn in Christ. As soon as we land on the North American shore, the words of the Holy Ghost will shine over us and our tongues will leap as if we were drunk and the American language will be as accustomed to our lips as if we were children of that land. Sinners and nonrepenters may suffer hardship with the strange language. But we shall be able to stand up at once and praise our new land in our new tongue. And however far we may travel among other races—black, red, or mixed—the Spirit shall have power over our tongues so that we can use their languages.

Yes, no one in my flock need doubt that over us—the Lord's chosen—the prophecy will be fulfilled about the Spirit filling all flesh: ". . . and your sons and daughters shall prophesy, and your youth shall see visions and your elders shall dream dreams. . . ." And mockers and deriders will say of us that we are drunk from sweet wine.

The Lord has taken us away from evil spiritual powers at home. The church, that wicked harlot, snatched at us, wanted to swallow us in her sour, stinking mouth. But now we sail on the Lord's ship, and the ministers in their black capes cannot reach us with their talons here at sea. Evil has passed, my heart is joyous, and my tongue is glad.

All lands in North America will open up to me and be given to me and my seed. There we shall build our new church, which will be like the one of the first Christians. We shall gather together and break bread and drink wine, as the apostles used to do. And we shall have everything in common, as it is written: "They sold their chattels and divided, each what he needed." And no sheriff will bother us—we shall live in peace.

In the land of North America I shall build an altar of thanks for you, my Lord! And I will sing and play and praise Thee with my tongue and my strings, as once King David did. I am a simple man, I have no gilded harp, but I know You will listen to me when I string my old *psalmodikon*.

You give us good weather, Lord, and us old onees, all your chosen ones, you have protected from the evils of seasickness—for the sake of our faith. The unbelievers and the lost ones you have punished with this plague.

Last night I beheld one of your angels at the mainmast, and two at the helm. The angel at the mast greeted me before he vanished—I do not fear. You are carrying us in this night over the dark depths! The Lord is our captain, no want shall we know.

Blow, Lord's wind, fill the sails of the Lord's ship!—"And your elders shall dream dreams. . . ."

Inga-Lena:

Tomorrow I must darn his socks. He wears out so many socks; he always has—during our whole marriage. I don't know why. He doesn't walk heavily on earth. Perhaps it is because he has foot-sweat. Yes, that has always been a nuisance to him—and he doesn't bother to wash his feet. I always have to tell him to. He had three pairs of newly mended whole socks when we left home—besides the pair he had on. All his socks now have holes in them, and I haven't had time to mend them; and today I noticed he had a hole in the ones he wears with his high boots. Children must be chastised and holes must be darned while they are small; a hole should never be larger than the width of the little finger.

I must see to it that he has socks on his feet in North America—they say there is a scarcity of woolen things there.

They say that the Saviour always went about barefooted when He preached here on earth. But I suppose the ground is warm in the Holy Land. Figs and vines and sweet fruits grow there, they say. I can understand that the Saviour and His apostles didn't need socks. But my dear husband always gets an ache in his throat when his feet are cold. And he doesn't attend to his bowels the way he ought to. He says he doesn't have openings every day. "Empty your guts, keep your feet warm!" That's a wise saying.

Today when I was sitting on deck with my darning needle and my woolen yarns, trying to mend my black jacket, he came to me and said: "Come with me downstairs—we must pray together." "I'll only fasten the lining," I said, "there are but a few stitches left." Then he looked at me the longest while, without saying a word, and his eyes were so sad I suspected I had done something wrong. I had preferred worldly duties to the Lord's service, I was thinking of darning and mending. I could feel his sadness, and I did not want him to speak to me while in that mood, so I went down with him at once.

I am a poor creature when it comes to faith. I only understand a little. When I think and muse on spiritual things I must quickly stop. I get so astray and involved, and I mix the spiritual and the worldly.

I am afraid we will be poverty-stricken if this continues. He gives away what we have, to feed and clothe and take care of so many. I am afraid in the end he may give away everything we own, and we will be left there, with our four children, in dire need, without food or clothing. When I think of this— that's when the doubt assails me. Yet I know that doubt is the bloodiest of sins.

Once I made him very happy. It was when he told me he would go to a new land which God had shown him—after the court had exiled him. He said nothing about his wife and children, but when he looked at me his eyes were as sweet as those of Christ in the altar picture. He asked me with his eyes, and I answered him. I answered and said, with Ruth in the Bible: "Whither thou goest, I will go; where thou diest, I will die, and there will I be buried." Then his face lit up and he said: "My beloved wife, we will stand together in Christ's presence on the day of judgment!" And then I cried, and the children cried, because they thought their father was unkind to me and made me sad. But it was the opposite, and I told the children that Father had promised to keep Mother company on the day of resurrection and lead her to God the Father's right side. And I told them they must never think ill of their father.

And I try to believe that however he acts and whatever he does, he is carrying out the Lord's errands.

I get so depressed at times, worldly worries take hold of me, I cannot help it. As I count and count I discover we have hardly anything left to begin life with in America. If only I could rely on the Almighty helping us, then I wouldn't worry. But I do worry, I can't help it. There are so many things I must look after—I and no one else. If I don't attend to them, no one else will.

I asked him today how we were to get a house and home in America. "Before I put nail in wall," he said, "I shall build an altar for the Lord. Before I lay a plank for our floor, God must have His altar." And then he looked at me as if to reproach me for being so worldly; and I left him for a while. I won't talk to him when he is in that mood.

I am such a wretched, forgetful creature—I know that. I forget that my beloved husband is the Lord's new apostle on earth.

Now he has worn out the last pair of socks—I saw it when he pulled off his boots this evening. I must get up before him in the morning, and darn them. The holes must not get too big. Oh, oh, oh, he wears out so many socks!

In the old days, when the apostles went barefooted, there was much less to worry about and attend to.

Ulrika of Vastergohl:

I felt at once that this is a devil's ship. I could smell the stink of the Evil One in my nose. The devil is on board. Round about my bed are females who do not have the Spirit. Round about me crawl the brood of Satan. And among the menfolk—it stinks billy goat! I know that odor. But no one shall bite my rump, for I am under the Lord's protection. The mockery of sinners can't harm Christ's body. But I shall pray the Lord to remove the smell of billy goat from my nose—I cannot stand it.

Christ is in me and I am in Him. I've eaten His flesh and drunk His blood. That's why I was punished with bread and water in jail. A priest came and wished to preach to me in prison, but I spat on his black cape—I know those who come in black garments. I ate my bread and drank my water, and I wanted to be left in peace. The priest didn't come back, either. The last day the jailer brought me a bowl of barley porridge, but I pissed in the bowl while he looked on, and then he had to take it away. I said I was sentenced to water and bread. I did not want to receive favors from the children of the world; I accept no porridge from the devil's viper-brood, I said. They have no grace to give us, that's what our apostle says.

Now I have got away from Sweden, that hellhole, where anyone who receives Christ's body and blood is put in jail on bread and water.

With my old body, my sin-body, I practiced much whoring in my days of error. But I was taught to do it as a child, by my foster father, the peasant in Alarum. I never forget anything. I remember everything, and have since I was four years old, when I was sold at auction. After my parents died, the brat had to be farmed out to someone who was willing to clothe and feed her. A peasant couple in Alarum got me— they offered to take me for the lowest charge, eight daler a year. The farmer regretted afterwards that he had bid so low: I ate too much, and wore out clothes worth more than eight daler a year. So my foster father made me pay for his mistake. When I was fourteen years old he told me I should pay for myself. My body had developed so I could, he said. And

what a fourteen-year-old girl, sold at auction, to pay with?
I should spread my legs and lie still, he said. I didn't want to,
I cried and begged him to let me go, but I was only a slight
child and he was a big strong man. He knew how to make me
mete out pay. The first time—I can never forget it. He caught
me in the calf pen in the byre one morning when I was there
milking. The farm wife was in childbed, and the farmer himself had been lying in "the ox pen" for so long—Then he
reckoned up the pay: I owed him for food and clothes, therefore I must spread myself to him, and lie still. It was like
being cut with a slaughter knife, and I cried and prayed to
him to let me go. But he said that was out of the question.
Afterward, the peasant of Alarum stood there on the stable
floor and buttoned his pants, as if he had only been pissing,
and mumbled and said: "That's that, well, now that's over."
Then he picked up his bucket with the slops for the pigs and
went on with his chores.

In his way he requested payment many times, and I grew
accustomed to it. But as soon as I could I ran away from my
foster home, and soon I met menfolk and found company. I
received food to eat, and other things I needed, and when I
had to pay I gave the only thing I had—I understood no better. I had been trained by the farmer in Alarum. Since he had
insisted on payments so many times, there was little left to
save. At last I became Ulrika of Vastergohl; I whored, as
they called it. I was excluded from the Lord's table, and those
who had taught me, and used me, passed judgment on me and
thought it right that I was under the ban of the church.

But the rich farmer of Alarum, my foster father, was a
great friend of the dean, and went to parties with him. And
when the devil at last fetched him home, the dean gave a
pretty oration at his funeral and praised his good deeds on
earth. You may be sure nothing was mentioned about the
time in the calf pen when he had raped a fourteen-year-old
orphan girl whom he had bought at auction. Perhaps that
deed was considered a part of all the others he had performed
to get into heaven. But there is one who knows where he
landed! And when his coffin had been lowered into the grave,
and all the people left the churchyard, there was one who
stepped up to the graveside and spat on his coffin. It felt
good; damned good.

So I kept up my whoring, and in time I bore four bastards.

Three were taken home while they were little—the Lord was good to them. And my Elin is no longer a bastard, she is received among those reborn, she has been confirmed by the Lord's apostle.

A leprous person can be hated no more than I was in that old peasant village. The women shoveled most of the dirt on me; women never have been able to tolerate me. They cannot forgive me, that I have had more men than they themselves, that I have felt the rod of more men than any other woman in the parish. Go to Ulrika of Vastergohl! they would say; she will grind your seed! And it was true—in my mill everyone could grind. It was true that many women had to share their husbands with me. But why should I turn away those who came? They needed to come to me, it was good for them. It is dry and barebitten in the meadow for married men, when their wives get on in years. Some women grow fat as filled grain sacks, so no man can reach them; others grow skinny and bony and sharp as a swingletree, so the men cut themselves on them; and all become as large and bottomless as a peat mine. So one can easily understand why the men are not satisfied in their wedded beds.

I have heard men talk of their wives' shortcomings. That's one reason why the women hated me. But I have only pitied the menfolk, and let them in—as one opens a gate for hungry, thirsty cattle, and lets them into the clover field. God has given me a shapely body, and no male has complained. Many men who were forced to chew dry old hay at home have been given juicy clover with me. And I enjoyed it myself, many times. Excuse me, dear Jesus, but I did! My dear little Saviour, forgive me the joys I had while living in the flesh. Because one sins mostly when one has most joy from sin.

But if the sins of Ulrika of Vastergohl were blood-red before, they are snow-white now. I live now in Christ's body, and He lives in mine. And this body of mine is still white and soft as a snowdrift on Christmas night. I am not afraid to show it to anyone who wants to come and stare at it—it is a wondrous work of the Lord.

Tonight as I lie here in my bunk I smell billy goat worse than ever. My old body is nudging me, it wants to crawl back into me again. There are so many men around—I can't endure men so close; then my old body wants to come back. There are men who walk around here so hot their pants nearly burst. They can't get their seed ground here on the ship, they walk about and squeeze and suffer. I recognize them, I know how they act when that itch gets them. Who should know better than Ulrika of Vastergohl?

I can't stand Kristina of Korpamoen, that proud piece. She goes around staring at me as if I were an old whore, when in fact she is the one living in the flesh. She has no respect for Christ's body—the bitch! She thinks she is pure because she was married by the dean. But the Lord's apostle says that whoring goes on inside a marriage as well as out. Her husband is young and husky, and no doubt he can use his rod. But now he can't get what he wants because he has to sleep with the unmarried men. I can still please any man, if I wish. If I lived in my old body, I would try to help him.

I have no use for his brother, the young fool. He hangs about and sniffs at my girl the minute I turn my back. If he thinks he can pluck that little chicken, he has another think coming. What has such a whelp to offer? All he owns he carries in his servant bundle. And what little he has in his pants had better be left growing. Yet here he snoops around and fishes for my Elin. He wants to taste the brew, taste it and leave it, like all men. Oh, no—I know you wolves! Oh, no— you little snot-Joe! You walk about here like a wolf, stalking God's pure lamb. But you won't get to her! You shall never enter that door, you wretched farmhand. It is saved for some-one more important than you.

My child is my only joy in this world. Elin was allowed to remain with me when the others went home to God, so I know she is meant to have a beautiful life here on earth. North America is teeming with rich men greatly in need of wives. Capable, beautiful girls have proposals before they can step on shore in America. Over there my girl shall marry a man of high station, prominent, and kind to boot. It will be her portion to eat eggs in a silver bowl, and sleep every night in a silken nightgown. She will not forget her old mother then, who once upon a time, among the peasants at home, had to whore in order to feed her.

Yes, but I can't get the smell out of my nose tonight—billy goat. Young and old bucks jostling. My old body is hard on God's chosen one. Dear Jesus, give me strength to withstand it! Because at times I don't know what I might do. But You must know of this Yourself—You Who live in my body. You must not let me be tempted too strongly. I am a wretched creature at times, You must have noticed that. And it is not always easy to be reborn. Yes—my dear little Jesus, You are so very good and kind to me.

But this is a devil's ship—I knew that at once.

Elin:

One has to think of something when one cannot sleep.

He shouldn't have said what he did about my mother. I haven't forgiven him for that yet. He didn't know how much he hurt me. He can pity himself. He knows nothing about this world. But he should learn. He need not have said anything. I know I am Ulrika of Vastergohl's bastard; I have been reminded of it every day since I was very little. I have known everything since I was very little.

Only men came to visit my mother at home, never women. And when visitors came I was sent outside, and my mother locked the door. In wintertime I had to sit in the woodshed and wait till she let me in again. She always tied me up in a warm sheepskin, so I wouldn't get cold out there—she has always been a good mother. Most of the time we had little to eat, sometimes nothing. When we were short of food, and a man came to visit, then I was very glad, for I knew it wouldn't be long before we had food again. And I liked many of the men. They were never unkind to me. Some were unkind to my mother. One of them hit her with an ox-whip once. I threw the pressing iron at his head—then I helped Mother push him outside. He fainted and lay outside for a long time.

I wondered at times why no women came to visit us—only once in a great while some very old hag. But as I grew older Mother let me know why only men visitors came—I was told their errand. I never thought Mother had done anything wrong.

One time I wakened in the middle of the night when Mother had a visitor. I had a kitten which one of the men had given to me, and I thought it was the kitten who cried and made sounds. But it wasn't. I think that was the only time I had bad thoughts about my mother. I spoke to her about it, and she forgave me. Then she cried, the only time I ever saw her cry. I'll tell you, she said, what people have done to me. And she told me everything. Since then I have never thought ill of my mother.

That poor, childish boy—he thinks I don't know anything. He speaks to me as if I were a little child, needing milk and swaddling clothes.

Mother thinks my father was a tramp who once stayed overnight in our cottage, and never came back. He was a happy soul, she says, and he could play the violin. I'd like him to be my father, as long as some man must be my father. Mother says it could also be the churchwarden, Per Persson of Akerby. She doesn't want him to be my father—nor do I. He is an evil man, and has called mother a whore—even though both she and I are reborn in Christ and washed pure in His blood.

Last night I dreamt that Mother made a little hole with her fingers in the flower bed in our garden outside the cottage. Then she put a plant in the hole. She pressed down the earth around it to make it stand up straight. Then she patted the earth around the roots as she pats me. The plant began to grow, and before I knew it it had grown taller than I. I stood there and stared at the flower as it grew and became taller and taller. It grew all the way up into the sky. At last it reached heaven, and then the crown opened up. The flower was white, and I noticed it was a China lily. And when it was in full blossom, a window in heaven was let open, and God peeked out. He was old and had a large head, white flowing beard, and a serious and wrinkled forehead. He looked thoughtful. God broke off the flower and took it—then He closed the window again.

The stalk began to wither, it turned black, like potato stalks in fall after a few nights' frost—they get black and slimy and stick to the fingers when one picks the potatoes. The stalk withered and I could see it lying in the flower bed where my mother had planted the flower shortly before. As I stood there and looked at the hole Mother had made I could see the black stalk lie there, rotten, smelly, and coiled like a horrible, slimy worm. I became terribly frightened, because the hole in the flower bed became deeper and deeper and more frightening. It looked like a grave in the churchyard. I began to cry aloud, for suddenly I knew where I was: in the churchyard when my little brother died. And a voice said: "She lies down there, her body is in the grave."

And as I awakened I understood that I myself was dead, and that it was I who lay there in the churchyard.

Mother had awakened when I cried, and I was so frightened that I told her my dream. She explained it to me: I was the flower she had planted. But the stalk that blackened and withered and rotted and was eaten by worms—that was my sin-body. The grave where my body rested was our home parish in Sweden, that hellhole, said Mother. But the crown of the flower that God picked and saved, that was my soul.

When Mother comforted me I lost my fright.

And now she and I are traveling to the promised land. There we shall live forever. And the way Mother explained my dream, I shall now grow up and blossom and open like a flower in that land.

Mother has told me that. . . .

Jonas Petter:

Sometimes I don't rightly know why I am lying here on this ship. I must be traveling somewhere, I think; I am after something, I believe.

Anyway—I have freed myself of her. She never thought I would do it, but there are already many miles between us. There will still be many more—so many that I can never travel them again.

I woke up one morning and made my decision. We had quarreled the night before. It began with the grain shovel. I wanted to get some oats from the attic bin for the mare, but I couldn't find the shovel. I asked her if she had seen it. Must I keep track of your shovel? she said; am I your maid? That's not what I said, I answered; but I need the shovel to get at the oats for the mare. For that gluttonous creature! she said. Your mare stands there with her fat belly like a barrel, and eats all our oats. My mare? I said. Yes, she said, you have most use of her, for you drive around the roads on your own errands. Then I began to get angry. I said, I want the shovel! Have you used it? Have you shoveled oatmeal for the cows? Never, she said. My wretched cows never get oatmeal. Your cows? I said. They are mine as much as yours. Have you forgotten that I brought two cows in my dowry when I moved to this farm? she said. No, I said—and now I was really angry— that I have never forgotten. How could I forget something you have reminded me of every day for twenty years?

It had started with the shovel. The quarrel lasted the night through, and the next morning I had made up my mind.

We have been married for twenty years, and during those years we have had about two small quarrels every week and a big fight every month. All together there must have been several thousand quarrels, over the years. But the shovel one was the last. I couldn't stand it any longer. I prepared to leave. And in order to have peace and quiet while I got ready, I sharpened the knife and let her crank the stone. That was the only way.

I found the shovel next day. It had slid so deep in the bin I couldn't see it. And I was grateful to the shovel that it had hidden itself—it helped me get started on my way to North America. I pressed the handle, as though I shook hands with the shovel: Thanks for the help!

I have quarreled away one whole year of my life. Now I am so old that I cannot afford to give up any more years in quarrels. I will be careful with the days I have left. I wish to live in peace with all. And I have lived in peace with everyone but her. Why should I live with the only person with whom I can't get along? Why should I dwell under the same roof with someone who only criticizes and irritates me? Why should I live in a house where I never can have peace?

We should never have married. But our parents thought we were suited for each other—we were equals as far as possessions were concerned. And God tells us in His Fourth Commandment that we must obey and honor our parents so that things may go well and we may live long on earth. I obeyed my parents, and she hers, and we were married. Her outward appearance was shapely enough, she was young and healthy, but otherwise I knew nothing about her. Not what she was like inside, not her disposition. That I got to know by and by.

The first years I had some pleasure in bed with her. But it became less and less, I couldn't understand why. I became indifferent and lost my desire for her—I couldn't help it. Now when it was too late I realized that I had never really liked her and would never do so in the future, either. Nor did she care for me or for what I thought. She was more married to the farm than to me. But as my desire for bed play lessened, then hers increased, and she mocked me and wondered if already I was impotent, young man as I was. Then of course I had to show her. I preferred not to touch her, it became merely a sort of habit; I could take it or leave it, without enjoyment. I never dared tell her this, of course. It was the only thing I couldn't tell her. I was a coward, I know, but I suppose she guessed my thoughts: I take part in this because I dare not refuse. Yes, I think she knew I had lost my desire for her, so she began to hate me. And she acted in such a way that I began to hate her, too. Perhaps I hated most that which could not be changed: the fact that I was married and tied to her.

It should never be between married couples as it was between us.

Our quarrels came more often and lasted longer. There was no peace in the house. And as the children grew up they took her side. They turned against me, because she spoke to them and said: Such is your father! Such has he always been to me, your mother! And then she told the children all I had said and done when I was angry and upset. At such times a person often does things he later regrets, he should not be condemned for what he does or says in those moments.

She turned my children against me, and I had to quarrel with them also. They lost respect for me, they obeyed their mother and believed her but they never obeyed their father or believed in him.

These last years we were seldom together in bed. Once in a while I pleased her when I realized I couldn't get out of it. I dared not refuse, I was too cowardly. I have been a coward many times in my life, and I would agree to do it for the sake of peace—when I satisfied her in bed she was milder in her mouth for a few days and it was more bearable at home. Sometimes I thought I would tell her: This is the last time! But I was afraid of her, afraid that she would take revenge in some way if I said no to her. Then she would have plagued me worse. Many times I had to swallow a few drinks before I could make myself go near her. Yes, the brannvin helped many a time, without the brannvin I would not always have been able to. But afterward I felt sick with myself; I felt more wretched than any creature in the whole world, worse than the animals. They don't drink brannvin in order to be able to—they do it only when they have desire. I lay with the one I hated, the one who hated me. Animals don't do that.

We were a married couple, joined together in Christian and holy bond—matrimony—wedded together as God has ordained. But it should not be so between married mates, not as it was with us.

One time during a big fight I said I would go and cut my throat. It would take more of a man to do that, she said. She mocked me, she didn't believe me, but that time I did mean it. I went after the sticking knife, I wanted to kill myself. I stood there and felt the edge of the knife, to see if it was sharp enough. I felt the bite with my thumb. And I set the knife against my throat. But then I couldn't do more. When I felt the cold edge against my skin, I couldn't. The knife cooled me so that I felt chilled through my whole body; I had no more strength left in my hands, I couldn't press, I couldn't cut. I have stuck and killed many hundreds of animals in my day, I have seen the blood gush from their throats, and I knew where to put the knife to myself, I know where the big blood artery is. But I could not make my hand perform the thrust, I couldn't force it to cut my own flesh, make my own blood gush.

I had a wish to do it, but my hand did not obey—I was too cowardly.

Then I discovered something—she had lied, because she *did* believe me, she thought I was going to kill myself. I noticed that she hid away cutting tools from me. She was afraid, after all. And for a long time she was quite bearable and kind to me, and we had no quarrels.

I had thus discovered one way to get peace, and I used it a couple of times—I sharpened my knife and let her crank the grindstone.

But it shouldn't be that way between mates in a union which God has ordained—one shouldn't need to sharpen knives to get peace.

Perhaps she did see through the knife trick in the end; because when the day came that I told her I intended to emigrate to North America, she didn't believe me. You are too much of a coward, she said. You are afraid of getting out on the sea. You dare not, you poor coward! You have never dared anything. You dare not sail on the sea!

But that time she was mistaken.

When at last she realized that I wasn't the coward she had thought—when she saw my America chest packed on the wagon—then she began to cry. She cried very often from anger, but this time she cried in another way: she almost moaned, slowly and softly, as some animals do when they are in great pain. Perhaps one should feel sorry for her; she is as

God created her, she can't help it. She can't change herself. Yes, one should feel sorry for her; but I know it has given her pleasure to torture me, and *that* I haven't as yet forgiven her.

Now I lie here out at sea, and I am free of her. I lie here and muse over what I have missed in life. It is bitter to think of this. There are men who are good to their wives, and wives who are good to their husbands. How would it be to have a wife who was kind and thoughtful and wanted only to do good, who could understand that one can mean well even when one does wrong, a wife who may criticize and scold, yet interprets all for the best—not for the worst, as my wife did? Well, how would it be? I turn here in my misery when I realize what I have missed in this world.

I feel ashamed of myself. But old as I am, there is still something left inside resembling hope, a very small hope. There is something that whispers: Perhaps good luck awaits you somewhere in the world. Perhaps you need not die before you have tasted some of that which you so sorely missed. You have lived like a dog on your farm, a dog without a master, a wretched creature who doesn't belong to the house—so have you lived, Jonas Petter. You have sneaked about, searching, silent, hungry in your own home. It is true—who can be more hungry than you for that which a woman can give to a man?

Yes, I am ashamed, a little—but mustn't a wretched human being have at least this left—a little poor and puny hope?

One can seldom sleep well here on the ship; I lie and fret too much. I am on a voyage to another continent. I am going somewhere, I don't know where, but one thing I do know: I search for peace.

XVI

HAPPENINGS ON BOARD THE SHIP

1

The brig *Charlotta* sails through night and day in the mist and drizzle of the April spring.

The sails in her two full-rigged masts hang limp and lifeless —the wind is still light. The ship's heavy body lies deep in the sea. The sea's beast of burden, a camel in the water desert, she plows her way slowly through the soft, blue-green billows. The figurehead on her prow—the eagle—incessantly scans the sea with his piercing eyes. At times foam sprays his neck and washes his open mouth; it drips from his beak, ever ready to taste the salt water; it runs from his eyes, ever washed clean by the sea. The neck of the bird rises proudly: the eagle's eye searches the width of the ocean as though trying to find the path of those who sailed this way before. Here ships have sailed for thousands of years, but on this path wanderers leave no footprints.

The last time the emigrants saw land it was the outermost point of Denmark, appearing at a great distance. But sometimes they saw other ships, larger and smaller than their own; they saw faster sails, and slower ones. Either way, the *Charlotta* soon was alone again on the sea.

For several days the weather had been so cloudy that Captain Lorentz had been unable to take their position by the sun. He measured distances and figured his course by dead reckoning. The speed was slow, the ship moved at a snail's pace across Kattegat.

The little peasant with the wild brown beard came up to the skipper near the helm and smiled in his quiet way: God was giving them fine, calm weather on their voyage. Lorentz replied that if God wished them well, He ought to give them stronger wind.

If this damned peasant only knew how long he would have to stay on board if this weather lasted the whole crossing! Then he would no doubt throw himself down on his knees and pray for wind.

But these poor farmers had no idea about anything at sea. They acted as if their ears and eyes were full of earth. They had only traveled on manure wagons, never before been carried by the waves. And they had one reason to be satisfied with the calm weather—up to now they had practically escaped seasickness. Nor was there any hurry, apparently, for these earth rats to reach North America. They were only traveling from one piece of land to another, from one field to another. They would reach their destination soon enough, and begin to poke in the turf on the other side.

Day after day, for days on end, the first mate wrote in the *Charlotta*'s log: Wind light southeast. Cloudy. At times rain and fog.

2

In the daytime the emigrants were on deck. It was bitter cold and they wore all their garments—coats, shawls, blankets, sheepskins. It was more comfortable on deck for those who stood the sea poorly and were afraid of nights in the hold. Here there was fresh air—in the hold the air was fetid. In their bunks at night seasickness stole over them, as though the illness kept itself hidden somewhere down there and crawled out at night. Then it might happen that there were too few wooden buckets, or that someone couldn't find a bucket in time in the darkness; lights were not allowed after ten in the evening. Then, when daylight began to creep in, it revealed the long night's happenings.

The emigrants began their day with a cleaning of their quarters. Men carried water in big buckets, and women scrubbed and scoured and washed and hung wet clothing to dry on deck. This chore must be completed before the thirsty were allowed to drink, before the dirty could wash themselves. Now they understood why the day's portion of drinking water was withheld until they had cleaned up after the night.

There were complaints among the passengers that half a gallon of sweet water a day per person was too little. This half gallon must last for preparation of food, for drinking water, for washing themselves and their babies. And they were accustomed to draw water from full wells. The second mate tried to explain to them that this amount had been decided, once and for all, that the ship's total supply of fresh water did not allow greater rations: they were on a long voyage, it might take three months if they were unlucky with weather. There might even come a day when they would have to manage with less. They must learn now to save the drops.

The women tried washing their woolen things in sea water,

but the soap gave no suds. One morning a heavy rain fell. Then the seamen stretched a sail on deck to gather rain water. The sailors washed themselves and their clothes in this, and the passengers stood by looking on, some following their example. Danjel Andreasson said that the Lord had remembered them with good washing water from His heaven.

The emigrants talked among themselves about sending someone to the captain to ask for more water. But who? No one volunteered. There was respect for the captain among them. Whenever it was mentioned that someone should go to him, invariably the reply was: The captain is asleep now, or, The captain is taking his siesta, he cannot be disturbed. It seemed as if the commander of the ship slept in his cabin the clock around. Yet they all knew he took his siesta only in the afternoons.

As early as on the first day, Karl Oskar had told the second mate the truth about the crowded situation on the ship, and since that time he had been considered a particularly fearless person by his fellow passengers. Several of them now urged him to see the captain about the water. But Karl Oskar flatly refused; he was not going to be used as a shield for others.

Neither Karl Oskar nor Kristina made friends easily. Of all the people in their quarters they were most friendly with Mans Jakob and Fina-Kajsa, the old peasant couple from Oland. Those two were kind and helpful people. Only, thought Kristina, they seemed somewhat dirty—perhaps because she herself was trying so hard to keep clean. She had never seen Mans Jakob wash himself, he always had some water left from his half gallon, and she asked to use this. Yet she thought that more than anyone else, he needed it. His clothes and everything around him he dirtied with snuff spittle and dribble which ran in two horrible rills from the sides of his mouth. And Fina-Kajsa had black cakes of dirt in her ears, and the furrows on her neck were like black ribbons. She must be afraid of losing them, as she didn't wash them away! Mans Jakob and his wife each carried more Swedish dirt to America than any other passengers on the *Charlotta*.

Soiled and worn, too, were all the things they carried in their homemade knapsack, made from old, gray sailcloth, fastened at both ends to pieces of one-inch boards. Narrow woodoen laths kept the end-pieces apart. The Smaland farmers sewed their knapsacks; the Oland farmers apparently hammered theirs together. But all were on the same long journey and in time would become equally experienced travelers.

Mans Jokob kept worrying about the grindstone he was bringing to his son. He was afraid that it might be damaged in he hold, that it might be broken on this long voyage. And how was he to transport it to his son when they landed? Perhaps it might cost too much money in freight to send it on in America. The grindstone weighed heavy on the old Oland peasant as he lay in his bunk and suffered from the sea. He didn't seem to care so much whether or not he himself arrived in America, if only the grindstone reached its destination whole and sound. The grindstones over there were expensive and poor; his son had written he was unable to sharpen his axes well enough on the American stones.

Since their embarkation Karl Oskar had more often mused over the question: Where would they go once they landed in the town of New York? No one in their company had any idea, not one of those from Ljuder Parish. And he must plan for himself and his family, think about it in advance, arrive ahead of the ship, so to speak. Now he heard the Oland farmer talk about his son, who had taken a homestead in a place called Minnesota.

He asked Mans Jakob: "Is there good farming land in that place?"

"First-class, according to my son. The topsoil is much deeper than at home. My boy has taken one hundred acres."

"Our boy is able, that's what he is!" said Fina-Kajsa, with a questioning look at Karl Oskar, as much as to say: Would he be able to clear land?

And while the two narrow rills continued their peaceful course down the chin of the old peasant, he went on: His son had written him that there were such extensive, fertile plains that all the farmers in Smaland and on Oland could have their own farms there if they wished to emigrate. The ground only needed to be turned. And the place was healthy: in the summers the air was somewhat humid, but at other seasons it was neither too cold nor too warm—about the same as at home. A likable place for simple folk. In other places in America the emigrants died like flies, they couldn't stand the foul climate—yes, the climate was evil in some places, wrote his son. He himself was a little afraid of this, he was ailing somewhat in his old age, he had a wicked pain in his heart—that was why he used so much snuff; snuff was supposed to comfort his ailment. The heart—inside him—wanted to stop at times, but it always started again as soon as he took a couple of pinches of snuff. It might stop for long times when he had no snuff at hand. This was very inconvenient. Because of his advanced age he had hesitated about the emigration. He had never moved before in all his days, he was born on his farm at home. But his son had paid for his voyage, and he was anxious to see the broad fields his son owned in North America.

Karl Oskar wondered if that place, Minnesota, might not be the right one for his family to settle in. He asked Robert about the type of soil there, but his brother could not find the name in his description book. There was no such state in the Union, of that he was sure, but he thought maybe the great wilderness around the upper end of the river Mississippi was named thus. This was the biggest and most useful river in the whole world. It had more water than any other river. Its shores were fertile and healthy, covered with forests and meadows, abounding in fish and game and Indians and all that people could need for their existence. On the fair shores of the Mississippi it had happened that a settler in five years had earned a bushel of gold.

"I'm not interested in bushels of gold," said Karl Oskar. "I asked about the soil."

But the information sounded favorable. And Karl Oskar kept the name, Minnesota, in the back of his mind. It was easier to remember than any other word because the first half was *Minne* itself, memory.

3

Kristina was in the galley and had just finished preparing dinner for her family. The women stood in a long row near the door, awaiting their turns to use the stove. As soon as one pot was taken off the fire another was put on. Kristina was looking forward to the day when she could cook and fry over her own fire again, when she could leave a pot standing as long as she pleased. No one could prepare food aright in the rocking cookhouse on the ship, which had to be used by so many.

When her peas didn't get soft fast enough, there was always some woman at her elbow impatiently wondering if she weren't soon going to remove her kettle. As if she could help it that the old ship's peas became harder the longer they boiled! And oftentimes the water splashed over and killed the fire. She hadn't known how well things went for her in those days when she parpared food on a stove where the kettles didn't dance.

After the meal Kristina picked up her knitting and went on deck, as was her habit in calm weather. Little Harald was asleep in the bunkpen, and Johan and Lill-Marta were playing up here with other children. Karl Oskar watched to see that they didn't climb the rail. Lill-Marta had—God be praised—thrown off her cold, and the other two children were hale and hearty.

It was a blessing she had taken along her knitting needles and some balls of woolen yarn—now she had something with which to while away the time on the ship; her hands were not happy when still.

Now, as Kristina sat there knitting, she discovered a small speck on the sock, a grayish yellow something on the white wool. She picked it up between her thumb and forefinger, and placed it in the flat of her hand and looked at it. She sat there and stared at it. She could not be mistaken—the speck moved, the speck moved about in the palm of her hand.

There was no doubt about it: she had in her hand a big fat, proud, body louse.

While her eyes followed the little animal that moved so valiantly across her hand her anger rose within her. Lice! Big, fat, body lice! And now she recalled that she had felt a peculiar itch the last few days.

With the thumb of her other hand she quickly killed the creeping creature. Then she rushed down into the hold, to her bunk, where she stripped to the skin.

All her garments were filled with lice. They were in her vest and in her petticoat, she discovered them in every seam and hiding place of her woolen clothing—the living, gray-yellow little specks were crawling all over the warm, soft, woolly cloth. And the pleats and creases were filled with nits. In the armholes of her vest there were veritable nests of them. And as she stood there naked she could see in the poor light that her body was covered with small red spots—her shoulders, stomach, and chest were dotted with louse-bites. She had felt some pricking and itching, but in the dim light when she dressed and undressed mornings and evenings she had not seen the disgusting marks.

Kristina sank down on her mattress and broke out crying.

Karl Oskar wondered why his wife had left the deck so suddenly. He went after her and found her lying there naked. Was she sick?

She turned away her face and sobbed: "I'm full of lice! Body lice! Oh, Lord my God in heaven!"

He stood there, awkwardly, and stared at her.

"Don't look at me! It's horrible!" She pulled the bedcover over her. "Such a disgrace!"

"But, Kristina dear, we have never had vermin."

"No—I've always kept us clean. The children and all of us —you know that. And then I come here—to sea, to get filled with lice!"

"But, dear sweet, don't cry!"

He had not seen her cry since the night before they left their home, she had been in good and even temper until now.

She cried out between her sobs: she had never in her life had a louse on her body. Once only, when very little and going to school, she had picked up a head louse from one of the children, but her mother had immediately cleaned her with a fine-tooth comb. And her own children had always been kept clean, she had taken pride in it—even though head lice in children weren't actually considered vermin.

"It's an eternal disgrace!"

In her parents' home it had been instilled in her that it was disgraceful for people to have vermin. Only bad people— tramps and whores—bred vermin on their bodies. Vermin on the body were the outward sign of a person's soul and disposition: lice made their nests on lazy, indolent, and dishonest people. Vermin did not feel at home with industrious, honest, decent people, and the absence of them was their mark of honor. Kristina felt dishonored and debased.

Karl Oskar tried to comfort her: she mustn't take it so hard, she herself had not bred lice on her body, she had received them from somebody on board. The vermin were not her disgrace, they were the disgrace of some fellow passenger. There must be someone here in the family compartment who had brought the lice along with him. And the unpleasant creatures spawned and multiplied very fast. A night-old louse was already a grandmother.

Karl Oskar looked at the bed-pen next to them, where the old couple from Oland slept, Mans Jakob and Fina-Kajsa—perhaps Kristina's next neighbors were the guilty ones. He had definitely heard that the people on Oland had more lice than those living on the mainland.

As he was about to confide his suspicions to Kristina, Inga-Lena and Ulrika of Vastergohl came down from the galley with their noon meal in their baskets and crocks. Inga-Lena noticed that Kristina had bloodshot eyes, and she approached helpfully to ask how things were.

But Kristina's eyes fell on Ulrika: there—on the other side of the hanging, at the foot of her own bunk—there that woman and her daughter had their sleeping place. It was not a foot's distance between Ulrika's mattress and her own, and the opening between the hanging and the wall was an inch wide—that was the easiest way for the vermin to get through, there they could march through unhindered and carry each other on their backs.

Without hesitation, Kristina shouted to Ulrika: "It's you! No one but you, you old whore! You have infested us all with lice!"

"Kirstina!" Karl Oskar cried out in warning. But it was too late.

His young wife went on: "It's you, you slut! You always had your louse-nest in Vastergohl. All men running after you spread your vermin over the parish. Now you have infested the ship with lice! And you are on your way to infest all of America, too."

Kristina's eyes were flaming. But the accusation she threw at Ulrika was only part of what she felt. She had long endured biting words from that woman, now she shook with suppressed hatred—the decent woman's hatred for the harlot.

Ulrika winced and narrowed her eyes till they seemed like small, white, gleaming slits. Those who knew her would have understood: she would not be easy to deal with now.

But she did not answer Kristina directly, she turned first to Karl Oskar: "So that's it—your wife brought along her lice from her home? I guess they didn't want to part from so fine a woman!"

"Be quiet now, Ulrika!" he said harshly.

"You would do better to admonish your wife!" And Ulrika's eyes narrowed still further, and her mouth twisted in a grimace as was its habit when it spat fury.

"She must take back her accusation! This moment! I'll go up and get Danjel!"

She ran up on deck.

"Now you have started something," said Karl Oskar with concern.

Kristina had stopped crying. A sudden fearlessness came over her, as if she had made a decision. "I called her whore and slut. Those are her right names. I take back nothing!"

"But here we must let bygones be bygones. We must be friends as long as we share our journey to America."

"I have not asked to be in the company of that woman!"

Ulrika returned with Danjel Andreasson at her side.

"Now we will hold our reckoning, Kristina of Korpamoen!"

And as she went on her voice rose to a shout: "Kristina accuses me of having infested the ship with lice! She accuses me of having vermin! She has derided Christ's body and His pure, innocent lamb!"

Most of the passengers were on deck, but those in their bunks came near to listen to the commotion. Karl Oskar looked at Danjel, appealing for his intercession.

"Let there be peace among you, women!" said Danjel beseechingly.

"She accuses me when she herself is full of lice!" cried Ulrika. "I want her to ask my pardon on her bare knees!"

"Bend my knees to you?" exclaimed Kristina in uttermost contempt.

"You must ask Christ's body for forgiveness!"

"I would rather kneel to the devil himself!"

"Do you hear, Danjel? She blasphemes!"

"Be calm, dear sweet ones! Keep quiet, both of you," entreated Danjel persuasively. "We all wander together on the same road and the Holy Writ says: 'Quarrel not on the road.'"

The peasant from Karragarde looked on the two enraged women with compassion, his eyes wandered from his sister's daughter to his sister in Christ, and his eyes were even more entreating than his words.

"She must take it back!" shouted Ulrika furiously.

And she turned to Danjel and went on. She, Ulrika, was innocent. As sure as the Lord lived on high, she had never seen a louse on her body since she could remember. In the old days while she still lived in her old, sinful body, she might at times have found something crawling that had lost its way in her underwear, for lice did feel at home in woolen underwear. But since she had been reborn through her faith in Christ she had been clean and free of lice. And he, Danjel, must know this better than anyone else, he must know that no vermin would cling to Christ's body. He must know that neither Christ nor any of His disciples had lice while they walked here on earth—possibly with the exception of Judas, the betrayer, she could not answer for him, he was no doubt a vermin-infested shit-heel. But lice could live and thrive only on an old, sinful, rotten body—not on God's pure, innocent lamb.

And Ulrika began to unbutton her blouse. "I shall strip to the skin! No one will find a single louse on *me!*"

"Have you no decency?" Kirstina's face flushed red. "You disgrace all womanhood!"

"You have accused me! Anyone who wants to can look for himself!"

Her bare, full breasts were uncovered as she unbuttoned her bodice. Karl Oskar turned away, a little irritated that the sight of the white breasts somewhat disturbed him.

Ulrika would have undressed and bared her whole body if Danjel had not taken her by the arm and dissuaded her. He now spoke to her about a Christian's true behavior in the presence of worldly people. He warned her of the dangerous temptation of vanity which might entice her to show her body, a wonder of God's handiwork, which she must not use for the purpose of arousing sinful desires in menfolk.

"But I must clear myself!" insisted Ulrika. "Inga-Lena must examine my clothes—she must be an unbiased witness for me. Come and look, Inga-Lena!"

Ulrika and Inga-Lena withdrew behind the hanging to the unmarried women's compartment. In there, on the other side of the sailcloth, Ulrika completed her undressing.

After a short moment the two women returned. In Ulrika's gleaming face one could immediately read the result of the inspection.

"Speak up, Inga-Lena! Did you find any lice on me?"

"No-o."

"Did you find as much as one single nit?"

"No-o."

"There, you can hear, all of you! I am innocent! Kristina must get down on her knees to me! She must ask my forgiveness!"

"Never while I am alive!" exclaimed Kristina in disgust. "I would rather jump into the sea!"

"You and your man can undress each other! You two can pick the lice off each other! But now you hear that I am free of vermin, and you must ask my pardon! You have blasphemed God's pure, innocent lamb!"

"Shall I ask *your* pardon, you old, inveterate sinner?"

Down on your knees with you!" Ulrika's eyes spat fire. "If you don't, I'll tear your eyes out!"

She was ready to spring at Kristina, as Danjel and Karl Oskar grabbed hold of her arms and held her back.

Kristina did not ask her forgiveness. But another woman stood by, ready to bend her knees: Inga-Lena was sad and ashamed and almost ready to cry. All turned to her. She held something between her thumb and forefinger, she held it up to her husband's eyes. It was something that moved, something gray-yellow—a big, fat, body louse.

"Danjel—dear—look, I too—I have—"

Ulrika was innocent, but Inga-Lena had found a louse in her own undergarments. And now she stood there and fumbled for her husband's hand, as if she wished to ask his forgiveness.

Danjel Andreasson examined the louse which his wife held up to his eyes. He said softly: This animal, too, was the created work of the Lord. They must therefore not hate and detest the creature, but accept it in quiet submission. It must remind them that they should wash themselves and keep clean here on the ship. The vermin were sent as a trial for them— for everyone's betterment.

Karl Oskar could now feel a crawling along his spine. He went to his bunk, among the unmarried men, and began to undress; he soon found what he was looking for.

It turned out, by and by, that all the passengers in the hold were infested with lice, all except one. The only one to escape the vermin was Ulrika of Vastergohl, the old harlot.

4

Kristina at once began the extermination of the small crawling creatures. She saw other women sit around and pick lice from their clothes and kill them one at a time with their thumbnail against a wooden plate. But this required too much time and was, besides, not a reliable extermination. The soft soap she had taken along now came in good stead. In the galley she boiled all their underwear in a strong, seething soap-lye which no louse could survive. Then she took a quicksilver salve and rubbed it over the whole bodies of herself, her husband, and her children. With her splendid fine-tooth comb she went after the children's hair so thoroughly that their scalps bled from the brass teeth.

It irritated her deeply that Ulrika of Vastergohl could walk around in malicious joy and feel superior to everyone on the ship. But Kristina did not believe that Ulrika had escaped the vermin because Christ lived in her. Uncle Danjel, no doubt, was more pious and Christian-spirited than Ulrika—yet the lice had not spared him.

She had accused Ulrika wrongfully, and she regretted it, but she could never force herself to ask forgiveness of that woman; that would be to admit that she was lower than the Glad One, the infamous whore. The one to ask forgiveness was Ulrika—she ought to ask forgiveness of all those women at home whom she had insulted when she gave herself to their husbands.

And Kristina half admitted to herself what had driven her to the accusation: she had watched Ulrika strut about in front of Karl Oskar; one could easily imagine how she would act if she were alone with him in a dark corner. Of course, he would never let himself be tempted, but Ulrika had a strange power over men. Karl Oskar had a strong nature, and he had slept alone here on the ship for many nights. So one could not be sure, not absolutely sure . . . The look which crept into Ulrika's eyes when she turned them on the men, on both Karl Oskar and others, those disgusting eyes, radiating seething lust —in those eyes whoring gleamed.

And Kristina sought comfort in the thought that as soon as

they landed in America, they would be rid of Ulrika of Vast-ergohl.

It turned out that the number of "free passengers" on the brig *Charlotta* was infinite—the greatest number of which probably were created on board. There was a great demand for quicksilver salve for their extinction, from the captain's medicine chest—so much so that after a few days the second mate reported the ship's supply was dangerously low, so many jars had been distributed.

It was never determined who had brought the disgusting vermin on board, but Captain Lorentz said to his second mate that he wondered how things actually were in old Sweden when even the lice emigrated to North America.

5

Robert went everywhere on the ship, and was a keen observer. He listened to the orders of the ship's officers, and he watched the seamen execute them. He learned what it meant to "sheet home" and "hoist sail"; he learned to distinguish between tackle, boom, and stay; he knew what a block was, and he could point out to Arvid the spar, the hawse, the bollard, the shrouds, the bolt, and the winch. He knew that luff meant the ship went more against the wind, and fall away was to have the wind more to the side. He had made friends with the old sailmaker, who gave him all the information he might want. He was told that the ship's earth-gray sails were never washed—except when God the Father Himself cleansed them with His rain and dried them in His sun and wind. He was informed that the strongest sails in the world were made in Jonsered in Sweden, and were known on all seas as "Jonsered sails"; he was told that the *Charlotta* carried her cargo of pig iron in her bottom, to make her lie deep in the sea; he was advised to eat all the peas and sauerkraut he could get—then he would not become sick of scurvy; scurvy was the most dangerous disease for emigrants—many succumbed to it during ocean voyages. But he must be careful and eat meat in small quantities—though salt pork was probably least dangerous.

Robert also kept close to the man in the broad-checked

jacket and narrow pants—the one who was referred to on the ship as "the American." Robert questioned him endlessly about things in the United States. To some inquiries he received an answer; others were ignored. The man said that the American President had forbidden him to tell all he knew about the country. He had held such posts over there that he was in possession of important secrets concerning the country's government, and if he divulged them to outsiders he would never be allowed to enter the republic again. Robert wondered about this statement.

So far he knew only that the American's name was Fredrik Mattsson. And now he thought of another man with the same first name—Fredrik of Kvarntorpet, who had made the famous America journey to Gothenburg and had afterwards disappeared. Robert thought that the stranger on board might be Fredrik Thron—it was rumored that he had gone to sea. Robert confided his suspicions to Jonas Petter, who had know the Kvarntorpet boy while he was growing up. Jonas Petter looked carefully over his fellow passenger when unobserved, and finally said that this man could be Fredrik Thron, the escaped farmhand. He was about the same height, and his face was similar. But he hadn't seen the rascal in twenty years, and a person can change much from youth to manhood. He could not say for sure. Now, the American had said that his home parish was in Blekinge, and that might prove that he came from Samland, for Fredrik Thron lied at all times, except when he told the truth in momentary forgetfulness. But at such moments he always used to blush, he was so ashamed of it, said Jonas Petter.

Robert recalled that he had read somewhere about a President of North America—George Washington—who always told the truth and even confessed that he had cut down an apple tree; they now celebrated that day in the United States.

He decided to try to find out the truth about Fredrik Mattsson, the American.

After one week at sea, Robert was convinced that his place was on land. Nearly every chore of a seaman was dangerous. The farm service on land was hard, but it was never dangerous. How could the ship's officers make the seamen climb up there in the mast-tops? The seamen worked their regular watches and were free in between, but real peace they never had; neither day nor night could they rest completely. One who served as seaman on board a ship was no more free than a farmhand. The farmhand must look after the horses night and day, Sundays and weekdays, without letup. And the seamen must lie there in their bunks in the forecastle, as closely packed as salted herrings. He and Arvid had had better quarters in the stable room in Nybacken, even though there was an abundance of bedbugs there.

A farmhand must eat salt herring all the time, but a seaman must eat rancid pork at every meal. And the seamen must live here year in and year out, imprisoned inside the rail; they couldn't take a step outside—only forty steps lengthwise, and eight sidewise.

A farmhand on land had more freedom than a seaman at sea.

There were also moments when the farmhand Robert Nilsson from Korpamoen was filled by other thoughts than those of the dangerous, chained life on three-fourths of the earth's surface, the sea: ". . . but he who learns to understand why the water takes so much space shall therein see a proof of the Creator's omnipotence and kindness." For hours on end he would stand and gaze toward the mast-tops. Up there—in dizzy heights above the deck—the forest pines stretched their heads: those widely traveled trees, those debarked stems of the large, prolific family of evergreens. These pines had lost their branches and crowns, and instead had been decked in clothes of sail. Dressed in these, they rose here at sea higher and more proudly than ever in the forest. From their fenced-in wood lot they had been let out on the world ocean, there to sail for life. But for each fir cut for a mast, one hundred remained rooted, sentenced for all time to the drab and dreary life at home. There they stood—fifty, sixty years—then they were cut down for rafters or used as timbers in a house, byre, or barn. Then there they lay, in their deep disgrace for a hundred years or more, growing hairy with moss and green with mold, brown-spotted from cow dung, hollow and filled with cockroach nests. Slowly, very slowly, they would rot down in the unromantic stable wall, and when the old building at last had served its time and was torn down, they would be thrown away with odds and ends on the woodpile, to end their lives in the fire—to succumb at last under a peasant pot in which potatoes for the pigs were boiling.

Such is the fate of pine trees which remain at home.

But the chosen mast trees fly the sails which carry ships across the oceans. They help people emigrate from continent to continent, in search of new homes. Their graceful heads carry the winged sails, they are the wingbones of the sailing ships. They may be broken in their youth by storm and shipwreck, or they may sink with their ships in old age, but they will never end in smoke and ashes under a pot filled with potatoes for swine. And when the ship goes down, the masts follow her to the bottom of the sea and proudly lay themselves to rest in the roomiest, deepest grave in the world.

Such is the fate of seagoing pines.

One hundred remain rooted while one is let free to sail on the sea that covers three-quarters of the earth.

And for each farmhand who emigrates across the sea to the New World, hundreds remain at home. There they sit, in their dark stable rooms in the Old World, and gaze through the small fly-specked windows during dreary Sunday afternoons, rooted in their home communities, in their service, until one day they die an ignominious death in bed in a corner of some moss-grown cottage, or as a pauper in the home of some charitable soul.

Such is the lot of home-staying farmhands.

XVII

" . . . THE SHIP WAS COVERED WITH WAVES . . ."

On the North Sea the emigrants encountered their first rough weather.

It began to blow in the evening—at midnight the captain judged the wind to be the ninth grade, according to Beaufort's Scale. The *Charlotta's* topsails were now bottom-reeved, and in the log the first mate wrote: "Storm."

Robert:

He awakened. Something heavy had rolled on him—his brother's body.

He had gone to sleep as usual in his bunk next to Karl Oskar. He had already had time to dream. His dream had been about a word, "Dead sea."

He had stood on the afterdeck at dusk when one of the seamen had said, they were almost in a dead sea. It had sounded horrible—as if they were sailing over a sea where they were to die. The sailmaker had told him what it meant: waves that were remnants of an old storm—afterwaves, so to speak. They were the ghosts of the sea, threatening billows that came from some place where a ship shortly before had gone down. They came with a message from the drowned ones—the dead ones told about their shipwreck.

Someone had said: Dead sea is a foreboding of storm; the wind has shifted to northwest.

Round the ship rose steep, high knolls—white-topped— swelling like rising bread in the oven. Suddenly a wave had broken over the deck where Robert stood, soaking his trousers to above the knees. He had become frightened, and had wanted to run away, when he had heard one of the seamen—a young boy of his own age—laughing at him and his wet pants. Then Robert had pretended that it didn't matter, and had remained there.

Until now he had known the sea as a pleasant splash against the hull at night. But the kind, friendly sea was changing: a beast with thousands of high, seething humps coiled around the ship. He heard the first mate's command: Batten down the main hatch!

He had been about to wring the water from his wet trouser legs when suddenly the whole deck became a steep, slippery downhill. The brig *Charlotta* listed to one side. He grabbed the rail with both hands so as not to slide away, and there he hung, waiting anxiously for the *Charlotta* to get back on an even keel—which she did, only to roll over on the other side: downhill became uphill.

Robert wanted to remain on deck, he didn't want to appear cowardly. But a feeling of dizziness took hold of him, and he had a sensation as though his stomach were rolling about loose inside him. What was this? What was the matter with him? Hadn't he read in his *History of Nature* about that which overcame him: "This rolling movement of ships at sea causes inexperienced people who voyage on them . . ."? And now he noticed that only a couple of passengers were left on deck; he was not the most cowardly. Then he had gone below and lain down in his bunk.

A great hue and cry was heard from the other side of the sailcloth, where the women were. One of them had been badly burned by scalding water while she was preparing her evening meal in the galley. A pot with boiling water had fallen over her foot as the rolling began. The woman had cried out loudly: "I shall complain to the captain! The captain shall hear about this!" But from the men's side was heard a rough voice: "Damned hens, those women! Must the captain hold their pots? Why in hell can't they be more careful?"

The young girl who was ill with an abscess in her throat often moaned softly—tonight Robert could not hear her.

Then he had gone to sleep, but the word had penetrated his brain like an auger, working away inside: dead sea—*dead sea* —*dead sea!*

It was night, and the darkness impenetrable. He lay on the inside of the bunk, and his brother's heavy body had rolled over him so he could not move. Karl Oskar slept. Robert could hear men turn in their bunks—snore, groan, puff, vomit, fart, talk in their sleep, pray, swear and curse.

Karl Oskar rolled back to his place, their mattress seemed to sink. Robert grabbed hold of his brother's shoulder—their bunk was sinking! Nothing stopped it—now he was lying on top of his brother and they sank together, toward the bottom of the sea!

He clung to his brother's shoulders and was able to whisper: "Karl Oskar—"

Then their bunk stopped sinking—it rose. And again his brother's body rolled over onto his. Now it was his turn to sink, with his brother on top of him. No bottom hindered— they sank and sank. Now they must be deep under the water —*they must be going down!*

He heard himself cry out: "We are sinking!"

Karl Oskar seemed to waken—he mumbled, half asleep: "It's only storming. Keep quiet!"

It stormed. An uninterrupted roar was heard from the sea on the other side of the hull, like thunder after a bolt of lightning. The mass of water outside, which until this evening had carried their ship on its back calmly and patiently as a docile beast of burden, had now become a wild beast with frothing, foamy jaws, and it heaved with all its pliant humps as if to throw off its burden. Already it had snapped at Robert—his wet trousers hung near the bunk: the sea had licked him with its wet tongue.

And now he lay there and sank: the sea had swallowed him. It had licked his legs in the evening, tonight it had swallowed him.

He wanted to throw up. There seemed to be no air around him, he could not breathe.

"Karl Oskar! Have we sunk? Has the ship gone down?"

The water had not yet come in to them. But as soon as the hull broke, when the planks splintered, when there were holes in the bulkhead—then the sea would rush in and drown them.

"Karl Oskar! Can't you feel we are sinking?"

"It's only seasickness."

The two brothers kept rolling over each other. Their bunk went up and down. The older one explained: in a storm a ship rocked like a cradle.

"But it is stifling in here tonight," panted Karl Oskar, and turned over on his other side.

One could hear that he, too, suffered. He had not yet been seasick, every morning regularly he drank his wormwood-seed brannvin on an empty stomach; he was sure this kept his body in good order.

Now the crew had battened down the hatch, as the waves were constantly washing over the deck. In so doing they had also closed all the small holes which let air in to the hold. That's why it's so stiflingly thick in here tonight, Robert thought. The air he inhaled had already been used. His fellow passengers had used it, men and women had sucked it in through their throats, old men and hags had held it in their filthy mouths. It was not air any more, there was no air. Robert inhaled—this is the last, is no more air—it does not suffice for all, there isn't air for one more breath, this is my last one in life. Perhaps one more—if I use very little only. This is my last breath—next time I cannot . . .

The air dried in his throat, and he became faint from fear: he was dying.

He gasped for breath in short, weak jerks: "Karl Oskar—I'm choking to death—"

"You have as much air as I. Keep quiet!"

A light fluttered above them; Jonas Petter had lit a tallow candle.

An angry voice was heard through the darkness: "Don't start a fire, you bastards!"

"I can't see to puke," panted Jonas Petter. "It runs beside the bucket."

But he blew out the light before he was through vomiting.

Robert kept on breathing; the air seemed to give out at each breath he took, but there was always enough for one more. People around him puffed, groaned, swore, vomited, prayed, moaned, and cried.

The brig *Charlotta* sailed on with them all, through the night, over a sea with hissing, wet tongues licking the vessel on all her sides. The night was dark and starless with low sweeping clouds. Two lanterns were burning on deck: the green on starboard and the red on port. But they gave out poor light, these kerosene burners, hemmed in by darkness and the storm. Two fragile little lanterns on a black, raging sea, two lights in a little world that moved above the depths of a great tempestuous water.

Yet in this little world lived nearly a hundred people, cramped and crowded.

Robert listened to the sounds of the breaking waves: they roared, splashed, and flowed as they broke over the deck above him. Mighty masses of water came rushing, crashing tumultuously, and falling. When a wave broke against the deck the sound increased to a thunder-roar, deafening as a big box on his ear. Surging and splashing, the water ran in small runnels over the deck planks, flowing, like a swollen spring back to its home. A wave rose, broke itself against the ship, and fell back into the sea. The next one followed—a hard thud, the water threw itself over the deck, then followed the roar, the soughing, the purl of running water. He lay there and listened to wave after wave, and each time he could hear how the ship freed herself from the lashing tongue of the sea, and escaped the yawn of the wild beast. The brig *Charlotta* was still afloat.

A baby cried incessantly on the other side of the hanging. It sounded like the mewing of a tortured cat. A cat—it wasn't a child he heard cry, it was a cat! It was the old cat which he once had drowned in the mill brook, the cat in the sack that wouldn't sink. The cat was in here and she was being choked slowly, she mewed pitifully, the sack would not sink before he had thrown many stones at it. And the cat mewed, she mewed incessantly, she had mewed for many years, ever since she was drowned. And now she mewed here, behind the hanging, while he himself lay here and was being choked, tied in a sack, sinking—

His punishment was inescapable: *he must die in the same manner as the cat.*

Perspiration clung to his whole body, like a cold, wet cloth against the skin. He folded his hands, he had not said his evening prayers last night. When he had finished he took hold of his brother's shoulder again. "Karl Oskar—please. I'm afraid."

"Keep quiet! It'll blow over."

"But I'm afraid I'm going to die—"

"No one can do anything for you—you understand that much."

No. No one could do anything. All the hundred people inside the hulk of the ship were forced to lie and wait, they could do nothing else. The ship might sink with them all, and no trace would be left on the water's surface, no one in the whole world would know how they had died, no one would be able to find their grave. In the space of a few minutes they would all disappear from the world, remain lost for eternity; and soon it would be as if they had never existed. And not a soul could do a thing about it. No one could bend a finger to help them. Here they would lie, inside the sack when the sea broke in, filling their mouths with water, filling their eyes, their ears and throats, choking them as the cat was choked in the mill-brook sack.

There was no one but God to turn to.

"Karl Oskar—"

"What do you want?"

"I drowned a cat in the brook when I was little. She suffered terribly before she died. Do you think I can—can be forgiven?"

"What nonsense is that?"

"I can hear the cat mewing—in here."

"You are out of your head!"

But Robert prayed God's forgiveness for what he had done to the cat in the mill brook. After that he felt as if his fear had eased.

His breathing came in short gasps. But suddenly his nose and mouth felt clogged: a slimy, sticky fluid was covering his face; something from the bunk above him dripped onto him. In the dark he could not see what it was, nor need he see it— the smell told him all.

The stench of the vomit overwhelmed him. He rose, and tumbling over his brother's body he got out of his bunk. Out . . . Out! He would die, this very minute, if he didn't get out at once. He felt his way through the darkness, between the close bunks of his fellow passengers. The floor beneath him fell away—the floor rose, and he crawled uphill. He reached the narrow passage longships as if walking on stilts. He skidded in the vomit, it splashed in his face, he spat, he dried himself with his hands, he groaned. Out—out in the open! Here he would die. The filthy stench forced itself into him, it went deeper into his throat, it filled and choked him. Up—up on deck!

He reached the ladder in the hatchway, he tried to crawl up on hands and feet. But the hatch was fastened solidly, he pulled and pushed, he could not move it, he could get no farther. The sack was well sewn together, he could not get out, he must choke to death down here. He could hear the seamen on deck shout to each other: A hell of a gale! Batten down and secure! What a bastard!

We are in a dead sea—*dead sea—dead sea.*

Robert remained clinging to the ladder, vomiting. He clung there until he felt a pair of strong arms around his body, a pair of arms that dragged him back to his bunk.

"It's only seasickness," said Karl Oskar.

But during the horrors of this first stormy night Robert felt, for the first time in his life, that he was participating in death.

Kristina:

The swing here in the barn was ready. Both ends of the ox-thong were fastened high up in the roof beams. The swing was so high she felt dizzy when she looked up. They used to sit, two of them—two girls together—and hold on to each other. It felt safer that way; but they cried out each time the swing went high. If you were afraid, you jumped off. Now she would ride the swing alone, and that was dangerous.

She crawled up and sat down in the swing, grabbed hold of the ox-thong with both hands, and held on. Then she kicked against the barn floor and started.

You have always liked to ride on a swing, said Karl Oskar.

But once she fell off the swing and broke her knee, and gangrene had set in and she was sent to Berta in Idemo. Karl Oskar came into the kitchen; he was a tall man with a big nose. She remained in her chair the whole time he was there, because she limped when she walked—and for some reason she didn't want him to see her limp. But now we shall get married, he said, and then she sewed her blue bridal quilt.

If she hadn't fallen from the swing she wouldn't have been sent to Berta in Idemo, where she met Karl Oskar, nor would she have been with him in the ship on their way to North America. The happenings of her whole life were decided that day when she made a swing of the old ox-thong in the barn.

Nothing must spot our bridal cover here; our quilt must be kept clean—we must use it in America, when we build anew.

She was riding her swing—at last she could ride as much as she wished, and no one said a word about it. But she must hold on with both hands, she rode higher and higher, she rode backwards up against the roof, and the ground was so far under her that she felt dizzy—she rode forward again, down to the floor. If she fell out she would surely kill herself. She held on harder to the ropes, they cut into her hands, it hurt.

It was dangerous to swing as fast as this—it hummed at her ears, she must slow down. But that was impossible. What should she do? She could not get hold with her feet; she might easily fall out. It was much safer to sit two in the swing, then they could hold on to each other. Why didn't Karl Oskar come? She wanted to hold on to Karl Oskar.

Here she sat in the clouds—and there, deep below her, was the barn floor.

She cried out; she must stop the swing.

She was awakened by her cry. Lill-Marta lay on her arm and moaned in her sleep, like a little whelp. Her small hands and cheeks felt warm and soft. Children were always warm, they warmed their mother's hands. Her babies were healthy, God be praised. And they were all on their way to America, where they would settle and build a new home.

She must be careful not to let anything drip on her quilt. But she had nothing more to vomit—the last time it had been green, like the cows' cuds, pure gall. Now it was finished, some time it must come to an end—though as long as she still had something to throw up, she felt better. Now she would not feel better.

Children were crying, but they were not her children. It's probably Eva, Inga-Lena's little one. Poor Inga-Lena, her little one is so sick. She is not six months yet, it is difficult at sea with such a little one. Poor Inga-Lena—she has much to look after, and no help from Danjel. She is killing herself for his sake.

Now Kristina was riding the swing again. She flies up through the air, she falls down, back and forth she rides. She is thrown through space, back and forth. She holds on with both hands, in panic. She wants to jump off, she wants to get back on the floor again.

How far was it to the floor? She looked down. *The floor was gone!*

Horror seized her, her hands grabbed hold of the rough boards of the bunk-pen, desperately—while the ship rolled and she sank, sank. There was no longer any floor to receive her feet—she fell, and nothing stopped her.

For there was no bottom.

Oh—she must get down, she must rest, she must lie down and rest against something, something onto which she could jump, something soft and warm—arms that would embrace her. She must get to the floor.

How thirsty she was! Her throat burned, in her mouth she chewed embers and ashes. But she was unable to reach out her hand for the water jar which stood near the bunk. She had no power to move her hands, to move her feet or her head. She would never be able to move again.

"Seasickness is harder on married women . . . and when a pregnant woman goes to sea, inexperienced with sea and sailing . . ."

But it didn't matter, nothing mattered any more, nothing could happen to her any more. And whatever happened, she would never attempt to raise her head, or her hand even. She had only one wish: to lie here, still, still, still. Never to move any more, never move in all her life, just lie here, until it was all over at last.

Wives who were with child suffered doubly because they were with child. He shall travel free of charge, the little tyke, Karl Oskar had said; he will cheat the skipper. But she paid the fare in her suffering. Three children around her, one inside her—that unborn one—what sort might he be?

But it didn't matter. Now she only wanted to reach the bottom. She must stop the swing, she wanted to sit on solid ground, she wanted to rest on something soft. But there was no bottom.

Except the bottom of the sea.

The sea was deep, the water was soft, the bottom of the sea was soft. Oh, how she would rest there!

The one who was afraid when the swing went too high could jump off. Other girls jumped off. But she had always liked to ride high. She never used to be afraid.

Kristina of Korpamoen rode on a swing. She was thrown into the clouds, she traveled through space without end or beginning, she sank into depths without bottom.

And from this swing she could not jump off.

Inga-Lena:

It had happened when she stood in the galley and fried pork. She had cut up a side piece, and laid the slices in the frying pan. Then the devil came to her and whispered: You mustn't rely on that, don't think for a moment it is true. You mustn't think that you more than anyone else . . . and suddenly she had become dizzy and exhausted and weak. She had rushed to the corner where the buckets were, and thrown up.

Perhaps it was the smell of the pork, sizzling there in the pan. The fat was yellow and had a rancid odor when it was placed over the fire.

She had been forced to go below and rest her head for a moment. All around her people were sick. Men and women vomited like cats. But they were children of the world—the believers were saved from seasickness. Yet now she had been seized by the same illness as the unbelievers. She prayed God for help in her bodily weakness, then she put some more camphor in the pouch she carried against her stomach—a remedy for seasickness—and took a spoonful of medicine—The Four Kinds of Drops.

At supper she was unable to eat a single bite. The rancid fried pork grew and became larger in her mouth. The ship's pork had never tasted good, today it was inedible. But she dared not tell her husband how things stood with her, he must not notice her bodily ailments, she must keep her seasickness a secret.

Danjel asked why she put her food aside. She answered

that she had eaten some in the afternoon when she prepared a bite for the children.

She thought that it must soon pass. She must be well for the sake of her husband and children. And her littlest one so ill—no one knew how it might go with her.

But when she wanted to rise from her bunk, to take the utensils back to the galley, her legs refused to carry her. She lay down on her bunk again.

Ulrika of Vastergohl came up to her and looked at her questioningly.

"You are green in the face! Are you ailing, Inga-Lena?"

The wife from Karragarde kept her silence. How could she tell the truth?

Ulrika felt perfectly well; she enjoyed the sea as much as solid land. Now she was practically the only woman in the hold feeling completely well. There lay Kristina of Korpamoen and suffered sorely, there she lay and grunted in her bunk like a farrowing sow. All who lived in the flesh became sick, the Lord had no mercy on sinners. But she, Ulrika, went free. One who lived in the true faith could stand the sea in any weather. One with Christ's body in him could never feel sick.

Only how was it with Inga-Lena? Was not she one of the Lord's chosen?

"Have you fallen seasick?"

"I'm afraid so," whispered Inga-Lena.

"Can this be true?"

"Yes—and what will Danjel say if I cannot get up? What shall I do?"

Ulrika was well and full of health and happiness. She could comfort an unhappy one, and now she told Inga-Lena to keep up her spirits. Perhaps there were some remnants of the old body left within her, and these she must give up. They were sinful parts anyway, good to get rid of; it would be well for her to vomit a little. She would feel cleaner and lighter and happier afterwards. When not the slightest piece of the old body was left in her, then Christ would feel much more at home inside her.

Ulrika left Inga-Lena to view the devastation of the seasickness among the children of the world. Inga-Lena remained in her bunk and cried—cried from sorrow that she had been unable to withstand the seasickness and thereby please her husband.

Soon Danjel could see with his own eyes what had happened to her. As he approached their bunk a few moments later, the illness overpowered her and she had to make quick use of the bucket.

"My dear wife!" he exclaimed in consternation.

"Yes, dear Danjel—"

"Was that why you put your food aside?"

"Yes, that's why, dear Danjel."

"You have gone to bed? Is your faith weak?"

"Dear, sweet husband, forgive me."

"Have you listened to the Enemy? Have you doubted . . . ?"

But the reproach in Danjel Andreasson's voice was only a mild, kind reproach.

Inga-Lena lay on her bunk and groped for her husband's hand, crying in despair. She sobbed out: yes, it was true, she had doubted.

Danjel bent his head as after a hard blow: in every unguarded moment the devil was near, trying to entice and tempt and cheat a poor sinner, making him doubt that God could help in trouble and tribulation.

His wife now admitted the whole truth: in her simple mind she had sometimes wondered if it were really true that those who adhered to Ake Svensson's teachings would escape seasickness on the American voyage. She had thought it sounded a little strange, and she had not believed it a sin to wonder. And today when she stood in the ship's cookhouse, and saw the tremendous waves, and heard the storm carry on so that their vessel jumped like a cork on the water, then she had become afraid. She had felt sick at her stomach. She was standing at the stove, turning the slices of pork, when doubt at its worst assailed her. Again she had wondered if it could be true—that about the seasickness. She didn't know what to believe any longer, she couldn't rely on not getting sick, for she felt in her body that she was about to vomit. That was why she had started to doubt.

Now Danjel understood that it was the devil who had come to her when she was frying pork. But she had not at first recognized him.

"He is always difficult to recognize," said Danjel. "But

don't you rely on our God, Inga-Lena? Don't you think He has power to save you from the seasickness, if He wishes?"

Yes, that she believed fully. She had only wondered a little, in her simple mind, only a very little. She had not thought that this could make any difference—if she wondered and questioned, just a little. . . .

"But you must know that man should not wonder and question! Why didn't you close your ears to the soul-fiend?"

Danjel's voice grew more severe; but his sorrow was still deeper, and he gave his wife devout admonitions: she must never never let go of her hold to faith, she must always cling to it. A little carelessness, and she might fall and be lost; and she had been careless while she prepared the meal in the storm. But he could understand this.

Inga-Lena needed to vomit again, and her husband held the bucket for her.

When she was through she said, as if to excuse herself: "The sickness may have started because my bowels are so hard. I have not had an opening for several days."

"Isn't that a sinner's defense, Inga-Lena?"

"No, dear Danjel, I know I would feel better if I could cleanse my bowels."

"If it were God's will, you would have openings," answered her husband.

"Yes, that I believe, of course."

"But you do not rely on the Lord your God!"

She wanted to. But she wished, so much, that she had a quart of buttermilk to drink here on the ship. Buttermilk had always helped her when she had hard bowels on land. By drinking half a quart a day she could always keep her bowels in good order.

"Do not worry and think of worldly things now, my dear wife," admonished Danjel, and softly patted the hand of his seasick wife. "Now you must reconcile yourself with Jesus. Do as Ulrika does. She feels hale and well. She believes that the Lord helps His devoted ones on the sea. She holds on to her faith."

And Inga-Lena felt a deep repentance, and prayed her husband to forgive her for having wondered and questioned and doubted: she hadn't known any better. But when she got well again, and free of the seasickness, then she would never doubt again. She knew very well that Christ had calmed the storm and walked on the sea and turned water to wine when He lived here on earth. She knew He could save her from any ailment He chose.

Danjel Andreasson kneeled at his seasick wife's bunk and prayed to God that He might give her more strength to adhere to faith in her Saviour.

Meanwhile Inga-Lena's head was filled with anxiety: she must improve, she must be able to get up on her feet again. Who, otherwise, would prepare the food for her husband, who could neither boil nor fry? Who would look after his clothes, and keep them clean? He was so sloppy, and dirtied himself so, he wouldn't care if he finally went about in rags. If she were to lie here—who would feed her children? And the baby who was ill, with something in her chest: who would take care of her? The milk in Inga-Lena's breasts had gone dry here at sea and she had been forced to stop suckling little Eva; someone had to feed her now by chewing her food. Who would chew for the toothless child, if her mother lay here abed? And who would see to it that the other children were washed and combed and dressed in the mornings? Her husband couldn't handle children, he was too clumsy with them. And who would watch the children when they played on deck? They might run too close to the rail and fall into the depths of the sea. There was no one to look after the poor little ones. Her dear family required her health and strength; if she were sick day after day, her poor husband and their poor children would be helpless and lost.

And while Danjel prayed for stronger faith for his wife, she herself prayed for strength so that she could do her daily chores and help her loved ones—she prayed for strength to get up the following morning.

Danjel Andreasson:

His feet sought a hold on a fragile little ship—a few brittle planks tossed about like shavings by the storm on these terrifyingly high waves. But each plank he stepped toward seemed to escape his foot and sink away. Darkness reigned over the great water, and darkness ruled the depths. And he could hear the cries and complaints of his fellow men, when the claws of pain tore their stomachs and bowels and emptied from their insides all they had consumed for their bodily sustenance. And they were all afraid they might drown on this ship, in this storm at sea. The sinner's fear of death penetrated to his ears, the unconverted's anguish at the thought of the resurrection and the Day of Judgment, when the King should sit on His throne of glory and separate them, one from the other, as a shepherd separates the sheep from the goats, saying unto those He did not recognize: Depart from me, ye cursed, into the everlasting fire prepared for the devil and his wicked angels! Danjel looked for the Lord's angels, but saw no sign of them. No white wingfeather gleamed through the darkness; and he feared there was no angel at the rudder guiding the hand of the helmsman.

Fright was about to overtake him, the weakness which shortly before had seized his wife. He knew the danger of doubt was lurking for him too. Where are you, my God? Are you near by? But the fright came closer. Why need he ask? Why must he question? There was no need for him to ask; he must know, he, who believed. It was not allowed for man to question and doubt. He must not let himself be overtaken by questions and doubts; they must be suppressed. God was surely here on the ship. Danjel could seek Him out, he could go to Him and throw himself on His bosom.

And Danjel now fled in this late moment to his God—he opened his Bible, the Almighty led his hand to the ninety-third Psalm: "The floods have lifted up, O Lord, the floods have lifted up their voice; the floods lift up their waves. The Lord on high is mightier than the noise of many waters, yea, then the mighty waves of the sea."

From the words of the Bible, confidence was restored to his heart: ". . . the Lord on high is mightier . . ."

What harm will you do to me, you high, horrible billows out there? The Lord is greater than you. And you noisy, roaring wind, blowing at us tonight—I fear you not! The Lord is stronger than you! And what evil can you bring, you great, wide, dark sea, embracing our ship? The Lord is mightier than you!

God had shown His presence to Danjel Andreasson in the words of the Psalmist: they were not alone on the brig *Charlotta* in this terrible storm. God sailed with them. God was as close to Danjel here on the ocean as He was on dry land at home in Karragarde. They could walk as safely on this little rocking ship as they did in solid, timbered houses set on rock and earth-fast stones.

And while this knowledge filled his breast he hurried to tell suffering, frightened people in the bunks around him that God was here among them on the ship—they had brought God with them, He was sailing with them to North America. And the storm He had let loose was a storm of trial—He wanted to try their faith and their belief in Him.

As a comfort and help for his fellow passengers he read for them from the Gospel of St. Matthew: "And when He was entered into a ship, His disciples followed Him. And, behold, there arose a great tempest in the sea, insomuch that *the ship was covered with the waves*: but He was asleep. And His disciples came to Him, and awoke Him, saying, Lord, save us: we perish. And He saith unto them, Why are ye fearful, O ye of little faith? Then He arose, and rebuked the winds and the sea; and there was a great calm. But the men marveled, saying, What manner of man is this, that even the winds and the sea obey Him!"

The Bible reader's voice rose so as to be heard above the roar of the waves that broke against the ship. But the Gospel word could not penetrate the indifference of the seasick ones: they were too deeply involved in their own pain and discomfort. They heard the story of a tempest at sea once upon a time, a storm in the time of Christ, blown out and dead many hundreds of years ago. What had that storm to do with them? They were seafarers on another sea, in another time, on another ship. Another storm had arisen, but Christ had not boarded their ship to still this storm. He let them lie there in their suffering. Ye of little faith, He reproached them. But He lived no longer on earth, He did not now come to help them —how could He accuse them of little faith? And their sickness in itself protected them against fear: those very sick had neither great nor little faith, they were neither afraid nor brave: they lay there in their vomit, unable to believe or to doubt. They were in a sort of beyond—coiled up in their indifference, completely insensible.

Danjel Andreasson, who, for the sake of his belief, had been exiled from his home, could now hold his Bible explanations wherever he wanted—in houses or in the open, on land or at sea. No sheriff would close his mouth, no minister would accuse him of being possessed by the devil. So he explained the Bible story to his fellow passengers: Keep quiet and be calm, Christ had said to the sea. And the waves subsided and the sea became calm, as an obedient dog crouches on the floor at his master's command. All these horrible waves on the sea, all roaring waters and noisy winds, all could be compared to God's creatures, who were allowed to bark and low and roar and bellow, but would instantly keep silence at their Master's command. How then could a person who believed in the Saviour be frightened by a storm? Even in this little fragile, rocking ship, he could rest safely and sweetly in his Creator's hand. The whole world rested in that hand, like a bird in its nest.

In a bunk near Danjel lay Mans Jakob and his wife Fina-Kajsa, the old peasant couple from Oland, and they were suffering much from seasickness. They lay on a worn old mattress with the straws pricking them like spears. The husband was the sicker, he shook as in fever and did not answer when spoken to, but only moaned. In his delirium he talked of the grindstone he was taking to his son in America. He thought it had been broken and was now useless. The grindstone worried him even now, in his delirious seasick dreams. The old man's face was drenched with perspiration and lined with black runnels from the escaping snuff in his mouth, which Fina-Kajsa tried to dry off now and again with a piece of cloth. She was still clear in her mind, and waited on her husband, although she was weak and suffered much from seasickness.

Fina-Kajsa listened to Danjel's explanations about Jesus on the ship in the tempest, and now she wished to talk to him. They should never have attempted the voyage, she and her husband, old and ailing as they were. When people had walked safely on land for more than sixty years, they ought to remain there for the rest of their days. She herself had wanted to remain on their farm, but something had got into the old man—he wanted to go; and their son in North America had written them persuasively. Now no one could tell if there would be enough left of their lives to last them to America. Mans Jakob's condition was bad, hers was not much better. Hers was a worn-out rickety old body, she could feel she would soon lie there dead with her nose in the air and smell cadaver. What was the meaning of her going off to sea, old woman that she was, now to lie here and suffer? Was this God's will?

If she were to face God the next moment, she would not be

afraid: she could look God in the eyes, she had long ago confessed her sins to Him.

She listened for a while to the uneven breathing of her husband. A few words escaped him: "I wonder if the—grindstone—will hold together—all the way—"

In the old woman's unwashed face dirt had gathered like
seed corn in her wrinkles—from her sour eyes a yellow fluid
ran. She lifted her head from her pillow, and turned to Danjel, who was sitting near the bunk with his Bible on his knees.

She wondered about that sea in Palestine, the one he had
read of, the Galilean Sea on which the Saviour had sailed—it
couldn't be nearly as big as this sea, could it? Was it possible
that the billows on Gennesaret were as high as these? Perhaps
it was easy for Christ to perform a miracle on that sea, it
would be nothing to still the storm on such a little sea. She
wanted to know what Danjel thought: perhaps the waves on
this North Sea were too strong, too overpowering for Christ,
so that He would be unable to handle them. Otherwise she
couldn't understand why He hadn't stopped the storm—so
many had prayed to Him, it had been raging for hours. . . .

"God have mercy on you!" exclaimed Danjel in terror.
"Are you prepared to die? If you don't think God is almighty—"

"I am only wondering why He doesn't help us—when we
lie here and suffer so."

"He has let loose the tempest for the sake of the unbelievers, because of the doubting ones."

From Mans Jakob came a groan of anguish: "Fina-Kajsa."

"Yes, my little man?"

"Some water—"

Fina-Kajsa picked up the water jug and held it to her husband's mouth. She straightened the pillow under his tousled
head, removed her kerchief and dried off the perspiration and
snuff from his face—she had nothing but her headcloth
handy. The snuff had mixed with the sweat into a slimy mass,
her kerchief became wet and soiled, but she used it to dry her
own face as well, as she turned to the Bible explainer. "Those
who doubt?"

Danjel Andreasson was sitting close to the old people's
bunk, his Bible lay open on his knees, and he wanted to admonish the sick old woman who lay here suffering because of
her disbelief. But before he could get another word across his

lips the Bible fell from his knees onto the floor of the hold—he let go of Holy Writ in order to grab the bunkboards with both hands, and a swaying sensation of dizziness cut through his whole body, from the top of his head to the heel of his foot. Danjel was suddenly lifted into the sky, and the whole hold rose with him.

What is happening to me, O Lord? The ship is losing her grip on the water, and with all her sails like wings is taking flight toward heaven! Dear Lord—is my hour near? Has it already arrived? Shall I, like Elijah, travel to Thee fully alive as I sit here at this bunkside and explain Thy word to this old woman? Dear Lord, is this ship the chariot Thou offerest me for my ascension? Yes, Thou art lifting me on high, I feel it—I am blessed—but I dropped Thy Word—Thy Bible. Forgive me, O Lord. I flee to Thee—I come!

But the ship quickly sank down again, and with her Danjel, and his soul and body. His heavenly flight led him back down to earth, he was not to follow Elijah. And on the journey downward he was suddenly seized with a cruel pain; at first it seemed as if his intestines were being strangulated, then as if they were all swelling up inside, as if they did not have sufficient space in their allotted place in his body. They were all crying to get out, to force themselves out. They craved new space, were relentlessly finding their way out.

He was at once overpowered: he fell, face down, on the floor, vomiting violently.

The ship was again sailing on water—the earth journey was resumed.

And next morning Danjel Andreasson lay in his bunk writhing in the unrelenting embrace of seasickness. When his agony left him for a moment, and his thoughts became clear, doubt and prostration assailed him. Then he stammered again and again, the same prayer. He prayed with trembling lips, prayed God for forgiveness for the greatest of all transgressions, the greatest of sins. With the remnants of the night's vomit still in his beard—like many-colored roses and red blossoms—he prayed his prayer of mercy: O Lord, Thou didst push me down again, from Thy Heaven—O Lord, who can endure Thy presence?

A seasick man prayed, and the prayer came from one stricken by God.

The brig *Charlotta* sails through the great tempest which the Lord has let loose over the North Sea, in the path of the emigrants, this April of the year 1850. In the ship's hold, in her narrow stomach, lies her living cargo, closely packed human beings strangled by the sickness that is caused by a ship's swaying motions at sea—emitting all the sounds that witness the disease. The ship has only one stomach, but inside this one are many stomachs—healthy and sick, old and young, children's and old people's; stomachs belonging to converted and unconverted, sinners and repenters, good and evil. In all of them the pain digs deeply with her multitudinous talons—in all these wretched bodies are nausea and loathing.

The brig *Charlotta* sails through the storm with Indisposition as guest and passenger, with Wretchedness in her bowels.

XVIII

A BUSHEL OF EARTH FROM SWEDEN

1

Karl Oskar Nilsson was one of the passengers in the ship's hold who could best stand the sea. He felt as well here on the ocean as he did on firm land. As yet he had not missed a single meal. The food was supplied by the ship, and he liked to get his due; many of the seasick peasants lay and fretted because they couldn't swallow a bite, although they had paid for the fare, and no money was refunded.

During the storm most of the emigrants remained in their bunks, day and night, without consuming anything except the half gallon of water which was their portion. Of all the grownups from Ljuder Parish, only Karl Oskar and Ulrika of Vastergohl were able to be up and about. While Kristina remained in bed, the father alone looked after the children. They were well and lively and did not suffer from the sea. Karl Oskar prepared food for himself and the children up in the galley, as best he could over a fire that rocked like a cradle with the ship's rolling and pitching. He had to stand and hold the handles of pots and pans to be on the safe side; once when he left them unguarded for a moment he had to get down on his knees and gather the food from the galley deck.

He had long ago given up trying to make Kristina eat; she had asked him not to speak of food, as this made her still more uncomfortable. Butter and pork he was particularly forbidden to mention: one was as rancid as the other, and if she heard either referred to she was immediately seized by convulsions.

The storm was still raging on the morning of the third day, when Karl Oskar stood at Kristina's bunk and asked the usual question.

She tried to move her head enough to meet his eyes. How did she feel?

Did he have to ask? She didn't have enough strength to answer.

He held the tin cup to her mouth, water he had saved from his own portion. The ship's water had become old, it was murky, as if it had been taken from some swamp or peat bog —slimy, and full of sediment. It stank, and had the taste of old laundry tubs; all edibles on board now had an old taste— of chests, cupboards, and barrels. But the water could be somewhat refreshed by a few drops of vinegar, which the emigrants were accustomed to add before they used it.

Kristina drank, and some water ran down her chin and neck. Karl Oskar dried her with his handkerchief.

"The storm will soon be over."

But Kristina did not care about the storm—it could do what it pleased, die down or rage on. She had only one wish: to lie here, still, still.

When her indifference left her for a moment, her first concern was for her children. Harald crawled about in her bunkpen and could not get outside its fence—she need not worry about him. But when she didn't see Johan and Lill-Marta, she wondered where they were. Sometimes they stood at the edge of her bunk and prayed and entreated her, pulled at her arms and clothing, persistently, stubbornly: "Mother, get up! Why don't you get up, Mother? You can't stay in bed any longer!"

And now she asked her husband, as she had asked him twenty times a day: "Are you able to find some food for the little ones?"

"They get enough to manage."

"I'm glad they are well—glad you are well."

Suddenly she broke off: "Karl Oskar—the bucket!"

The water she had just drunk came up, mixed with greenish slime.

"Do you want a spoon of The Prince's Drops?"

"No. I want nothing—nothing."

Neither Hoffman's nor The Prince's nor The Four Kinds of Drops seemed to relieve her. She had tried all the kinds that were obtainable from the medicine chest. And why should she take medicines, only to be tortured in throwing them up again?

Karl Oskar bent anxiously over Kristina: her face was green-white, pale and wan in the meager daylight down here. She could keep down neither food nor water, and these vomitings night and day were weakening her. Her pregnancy added to her discomfort. He had become seriously concerned about his wife—she could not stand this for very much longer.

The voyage across the sea to North America was more unhealthy and perilous than he himself had imagined. But no one could know in advance what a crossing would be like. Of one thing he was sure, however: since people so often became sick on the sea, they were meant to live on land. Only because God had created water between the continents were they forced to go on the sea at times. It would feel good with solid ground underfoot again.

"Is there nothing you wish, Kristina?"

"Ye-es, Karl Oskar—I would like to—I wish—"

She broke off again, and was silent. He never knew what she wished him to do. The fact was, she had suddenly felt dizzy when her swing almost touched the stable roof, and she had wanted to ask Karl Oskar to help her down from the swing.

2

The second mate unexpectedly came down to the family compartment in the hold. The bedridden emigrants gazed at him; some were even able to gather enough energy from this visit to emerge from their apathy and ask themselves: What errand could the mate have down here? Something must be out of order.

The mate carried a piece of canvas in his hands. What was the canvas to be used for? The emigrants wondered, yet they were fairly indifferent in their wonder. So much they understood, that something was out of order here in their quarters; but they had not the strength to guess what it might be. Something had happened, however, and they were soon to know. It could not be kept a secret.

The first death had occurred on board the ship.

A corpse was to be shrouded in the canvas. The young girl with the throat abscess had died. All the warm porridge which her parents had boiled and applied had been prepared in vain, all the salves from the medicine chest had been of no avail. The captain had been down to look at the girl's throat, and he had said the abscess ought to be lanced. But neither he nor anyone else had dared use the knife. In the end the boil broke, and a few minutes later the girl breathed her last.

It was said that the dead girl was seventeen years old, but she was small of growth, hardly bigger than a twelve-year-old. Now it turned out that the mate had brought a piece of canvas far too large; there was enough to wrap it twice around her body before she was carried away through the main hatch.

A dead person had been lying among the living down here. But now she was gone, and everything was in order again in the hold.

That day the northwest storm spent its force and began to die down. The waves sank and the surface of the sea became smoother; toward evening the weather was almost calm. The lull that came after a great upheaval on the little brig at first seemed strange to the passengers.

Karl Oskar had not mentioned the death in the compartment to Kristina; it had passed her by unnoticed. Now he said: "You'll soon get well when the weather is calm."

"I wonder."

But at the same moment she raised her head from the pillow, and her eyes opened wide. She listened. She could hear something going on on deck; the main hatch was open and she could hear singing from above. "Am I delirious, Karl Oskar, or—"

Did she dream or was she awake? Were they no longer on

board the ship? Had they landed? Was she in church, or in the churchyard? People were singing! If she still was alive, she could hear them singing a hymn.

"Yes—they are singing a psalm up there."

Kristina was listening to a funeral hymn. A funeral was taking place on the afterdeck.

Karl Oskar now told her: the girl with the abscess had died this morning. But it was not from seasickness; she had been ill when they sailed from Karlshamn, she had lain abed ever since she came on board.

Kristina lay silent and listened to the hymn from on deck. It could be heard only faintly down here. Presently she said: "I wonder—"

"What?"

"The dead. Are the dead ones sunk into the sea?"

"Yes. They can't have corpses lying about on the ship."

"I suppose not."

"They lower them. They have to."

"I suppose so. Then the dead sink to the bottom of the sea."

Kristina was lying and staring at the ship's timbers above her, but she saw nothing.

"On the bottom of the sea—one can rest in comfort. Don't you think so, Karl Oskar?"

"Don't think of that! You must only think about getting well."

Karl Oskar wet a rag and tried to remove a few spots from the bedcover. Kristina had always been cleanly and particular, and she must be far gone when she didn't mind her bridal quilt's being soiled with vomit. But she had hardly been interested in anything these last days.

In the bunks around them lay the sick ones, listening to the singing which came down to them through the open hatch. It seemed clearer now, they could distinguish the words—the hymn went slowly and somberly:

"You wicked world, farewell!
        To heaven fares my soul,
        To reach her harbor goal. . . ."

There was one word Karl Oskar particularly noticed, and it seemed as if his wife had marked it too. She turned her face toward him. "I must tell you something: I'll never reach the harbor."

"Kristina!"

"No, Karl Oskar. I'll never put foot on American soil."

"Don't talk such nonsense! Seasickness is not fatal!"

"I have known it the whole time."

"Crazy notions!"

"Ever since I stepped on board the ship I've felt it: I'll never get away from here alive."

"You only imagine it!"

"No. My forebodings never fail."

"Forget it! Get it out of your mind! Kristina, dear—"

He took hold of her hand and patted it. Her hand lay limp and unresponsive in his.

She must know that the seasick always become depressed and downhearted and afraid they won't survive; but as soon as they near land they are perfectly well and full of life again.

"Do you remember, Karl Oskar? I was afraid before we—"

Yes, he remembered. He was sorry to say he did remember: she had been afraid and dubious—he had persuaded her to come. He remembered that he was responsible.

No more singing was heard from on deck. The funeral hymn had been sung to its end. The funeral up there was over, the *Charlotta*'s captain had once more fulfilled his duty as clergyman. There was one human body less on board. And from the bushel of earth which the ship brought from her homeland there were now three shovels less.

"Oh, yes, Kristina," Karl Oskar broke the silence. "We will reach land, you and I—we will reach the harbor in America."

She did not answer. She lay there as before, and looked upward with still eyes; every fiber of her body was still.

And Karl Oskar thought, perhaps he had been too persuasive; perhaps he shouldn't have tried so forcibly to convince her—perhaps he had assumed too great a responsibility.

3

A few days later, in the morning, the second death occurred in the family compartment: Mans Jakob, the old Oland peasant, was found dead in his bunk-pen.

The discovery was made by his wife, who would not believe that he was dead. When she awakened in the morning she shook her husband by the shoulder, as she always used to do. She shook him harder when he didn't respond—the old one wouldn't open his eyes. Finally Fina-Kajsa called Danjel Andreasson, who came to her help. He said that her husband was lying there dead, but Fina-Kajsa refused to believe it. She said he had lain like that many times before in the mornings, and she had had to shake him thoroughly before he awakened; it was caused by his heart, which stopped at times and didn't start as quickly as it ought. Moreover, Mans Jakob had during his whole life been a heavy sleeper—she knew, she had been married to him for more than forty years. Now she was convinced he would awaken if, together, they shook him sufficiently.

But all who looked at Mans Jakob agreed with Danjel: no one could shake life into that body again. Mans Jakob was not to be awakened until Doomsday.

No one could tell what had caused his death, but his fellow passengers guessed it must have been his heart which had missed some of its regular beats and stopped so long that it couldn't get started again. Karl Oskar thought he might have choked to death from his vomit; he had been found lying on his stomach with his face downward, and in this position it must have been difficult for him to get rid of his slime. Perhaps he hadn't got the attention he needed during the night, even though his wife was lying close to him. No one had heard him call for help, but a dying man might be too weak.

The second mate came down again. When the Finn appeared in the hold at unexpected times they now knew his errand. Something was wrong again. The piece of canvas he brought now was not too large; this time it must cover the body of a grown man.

The mate began to remove the dead man from his bunk, but Mans Jakob's wife attempted to stop him: "Wait a little! My man might still awaken!"

The Finn lifted the eyelids of Mans Jakob, and looked carefully into his eyes. "Your man is as dead as he can be. I know what dead people look like."

"Wait a little, be kind! Only an hour."

"You want him to lie here till he begins to stink?"

"Only a little while!"

But he did not heed the entreating old woman; he pulled the corpse from the bunk. Then she let out loud cries, at the same time grabbing hold of one leg of her dead husband, trying to keep the body by her in the bunk. Only after much trouble could the mate break her hold.

Danjel and Inga-Lena attended to Mans Jakob's widow while Karl Oskar helped the Finn with the corpse. After death the old peasant seemed even more black and dirty than he had been in life. The snuff runnels over his cheeks and chin seemed wider than ever. This was not attractive on a living person—it was still more disgusting on a dead one. Karl Oskar felt they should wash the corpse's face before placing the body in the canvas.

"He'll get clean in the sea," said the Finn.

"But that won't be till after the funeral," said Karl Oskar.

He had heard from old people that one ought not to read the funeral service over an unwashed corpse. And Danjel was talking about people's responsibilities when they awoke on the Day of Resurrection; he agreed with Karl Oskar: as Christians, they owed the dead one this last service. His dirty old body had, after all, been the shell for a human soul, created by God. So, as there were no women to give them a hand, the two men helped each other, soaking old scrub rags in sea water, with which they washed the face of Mans Jakob. It was not a thorough cleaning, but at least they were able to remove the black streaks from the face before the corpse was enclosed in its shroud.

Then the mate laid a weight in the canvas, as was his custom. Karl Oskar thought they should have used Mans Jakob's grindstone, which was in the storeroom. This fine grindstone, which he had talked about constantly, which he was so much worried about, which he must get to America—what would happen to it now? Who in America would take care of this grindstone without an owner? Perhaps Mans Jakob would have liked to have the stone with him at the bottom of the sea; there he need not worry over its fate, there it could lie at his side, in safekeeping until the Day of Doom.

The new death in the hold caused some changes in the accommodations for a few passengers. Fina-Kajsa, who one morning had awakened as a widow, must now move to the other side of the sailcloth hanging, among the unmarried women. Two married men, Karl Oskar and another farmer, who until now had slept with the unmarried men, were allowed to move in with their families and occupy the bunk vacated by the old peasant couple.

From the bushel of earth from Sweden three shovelfuls were taken again. And the deathbed of one became the sleeping place of another. Karl Oskar slept from now on in the bunk vacated by Mans Jakob, who himself rested on the bottom of the sea, his face washed, cleaner than he had been in many a day. And the young farmer remembered what he had heard the very first day on board the brig *Charlotta*: "There's more room in the hold the farther out we get."

XIX

AT HOME AND AWAY

1

". . . To the storm he said: Be calm!
To the billow: Lay thee down!
And the billow down she lay
And the roaring storm he died away.
The sun so glorious and dear
Looks down upon the water clear.
Our sails we hoist!
Our Lord we praise,
He heard our prayers' qualm!"

> (Morning hymn sung on the brig *Charlotta's* deck, chosen by homeowner Danjel Andreasson from Ljuder Parish, and sung when the great storm had abated.)

The weather improved, the air was warmer. They had clear days when the sun remained long on deck. And for several days the brig *Charlotta* of Karlshamn enjoyed an even stern wind which gave her good speed.

When the sea had come to rest the disquiet and upheaval in

the passengers' intestines disappeared. When the weather grew calm, calmness also entered into the people. The seasick ones improved little by little; one after another, they returned to the deck. And in the galley, which had been practically deserted during the storm, the women thronged again with their cooking utensils, and the smell of boiling peas and rancid pork again spread over the deck and was diffused by the wind over the sea.

The course of the emigrant vessel was now southwest: the *Charlotta* was sailing into the English Channel.

The land people somewhat wonderingly beheld this water, which was not as they had thought it would be. The English Channel—a channel to them was a broad ditch, dug in order to drain low-lying ground—bogs and swamps. They had hoped they were to sail through a narrow trough; they had harbored a wish to sail a small water, where they had solid ground near on both sides, so they would feel safer than on the open sea. And now they discovered that the English Channel was no ditch. Its water was not moss-brown, its waves came and went as they did on the sea. They discovered that this channel was also a sea.

And they soon learned that this water was an important crossroad of the sea, used by many vessels. Every day they saw other ships—they met them, they were in their company, they passed them, they were overtaken by them; they saw vessels both smaller and bigger than their own, with people from foreign lands on board, vessels flying flags in all colors.

Then one morning they discovered land on the starboard side—a glittering white shore rose before them, like a high, steep bank. It was the coast of England, said the seamen. There were knolls and cliffs of chalk, shining white in the sun. Beyond the shore—farther inland—high towers and steeples rose up; those were forts, castles, and churches. And the emigrants stood there and looked over the bank into the foreign land; they beheld England, a land they sailed by, the soil of which they were never to tread on. This was the first foreign country they had seen so close—when they passed Denmark, land had been a long way off—and the vision was strange to them. But strangest of all was this white wall, this beautiful, high-chested shore which rose up in front of them. It looked like a tremendous whitewashed fireplace, a giant stove wall which the sea's surging waves had been unable to demolish.

They thought, this must be a strong kingdom, with such fortifications.

The white wall was to be their abiding memory of England.

In the Channel the ships thickened, masts from many lands were gathered here; here was the meeting place of the seafaring pines. Here rose masts much taller and thicker than the two from Swedish ground which had been transplanted to the *Charlotta;* but perhaps these foreign masts came from other trees than the family of evergreens.

After one day the white cliffs of England disappeared from their view and sank slowly into the choppy sea astern. And with this the emigrants said another farewell: this stretch of shore was the last they were to see of the Old World. Many days would pass before they saw land again. Now the *big* sea opened its expanse to them, now there remained only the ocean.

And when next they espied a shore, it would rise at the prow, it would be the New World.

2

The emigrant ship met new storms and bad weather, but her passengers were growing accustomed to them as something inescapably belonging to their new existence.

In their early days on board they had willingly talked about Sweden, and bitter, angry words passed, for the most part, as they compared each other's lot at home. But as the days after their departure increased, they spoke ill less often of the land they had left. They had left it, once and for all, and that seemed sufficient. Their homeland lay behind them and it was already far away—already a foreign place. And it seemed wrong to them to speak ill of someone or something that was so far away, and couldn't hear them. Now they did not wish to revile their homeland. They had their relatives there—indeed, the whole country seemed to them a relative. They had left this relative—that was enough; they might never again see what they had left; they had closed their accounts with the kingdom that had borne them—there was no reproach.

But one day they met a ship flying a flag which they recognized: from the stern flew the flag of their homeland. The emigrants stared in amazement, and watched. The time they had been at sea could be measured in weeks only, as yet, but they had already experienced storm and suffered seasickness and endured all the inconveniences of seafarers, and it seemed to them that they had sailed for months. They felt they were immeasurably far out in the world: they had sailed over the unfathomable expanse of sea, their homes seemed to lie in a faraway land behind them. And now, suddenly, that land was close to them—they had encountered it out here on the ocean. Over there, only a few hundred yards away from them, must be people from the same sort of hamlets as their own, people who spoke the same language they did. There might even be someone on that ship whom they knew.

The eyes of the *Charlotta*'s passengers followed the vessel with the known flag waving to them so near. Her course was exactly opposite to their own; she sailed their own route back. Those people sailed home; their own ship sailed away.

Home—they surprised themselves by still thinking of Sweden as their home. Yet none of them had a home left in the land that they had turned their backs on. They had all deserted their old homes—to seek new ones. And yet—Sweden was *home*. It was inexplicable, and they mused over it.

The brig *Charlotta* was loaded with seekers of new homes. Her passengers were people who had left their old homes but as yet had no new ones. The emigrants were a flock of homeless people, roaming the sea. This ship—forty paces long and eight wide—was their refuge on earth.

They were the tramps of the ocean—the ocean was their path, and this little brig was their lodging. And in the evenings before they crept into their bunks they looked out over the sea which expanded round their shelter. The sea darkened at night, and in the darkness rose the roaring, belligerent wave crests, which became downhill and uphill, which became the depths of the valleys and the heights of the mountains around their ship. Then they felt the great depths under them open up, and over them stole the shiver of insecurity: only this fragile little ship, floating like a feather on the water, was their home and protection. Now they must go to sleep in this restless, tossed-about home—down in this ship they must close their eyes. How dared they? How dared they go to sleep down there, and entrust their lives and their belongings to the brittle planks which surrounded them?

The emigrants no longer felt a bond with the earth, they had been thrown out to sea, pulled away from all footholds; they were lost in the world.

A home to these people of the earth meant a peaceful, stable place on the ground, an unmoving room, a house with sturdy walls and closed doors, with secure bolts and locks—a peaceful cottage on land where in the evening they could seek their beds in security and comfort.

Such a home they had left behind. And now they met a ship which sailed in the direction of this home. They stood and looked long after this home-going vessel. It shrank and grew smaller. Soon it was only a gray speck on the horizon. A home-going Swedish ship disappeared in the direction from which they had come.

The emigrants had met a ship sailing *home*. After this they understood and felt still more strongly that they were sailing *away*.

XX

STORIES ON THE AFTERDECK

1

Robert and Elin sat on the leeward side of the afterdeck, close together, their backs against a coil of rope. They were reading a textbook in English which Robert had bought in Karlshamn.

It was a pleasant afternoon on the *Charlotta*; she was sailing in a leisurely way with a moderate quartering wind. The emigrants sat in small groups on deck and whiled away the time; the May sun shone over the Atlantic Ocean, and a continuous penetrating odor of fried rancid pork exuded from the galley, as was its wont this time of day. And two young emigrants sat by themselves and read. *About tongue- and lip-position in the use of the English language.*

Robert's narrow textbook was hardly larger than the Little Catechism. It was designed for the average reader among the peasantry: *Guidance for Immigrants Who Wish to Gather Necessary Knowledge in the English Language in Order to*

Get Along. It was exactly what Robert wanted. He did not wish to become a linguist—at least not at once. And the bookseller in Karlshamn had said that it was written for simple folk. Simplicity and easy comprehension were emphasized, rather than a scholarly approach. But to Robert this *Guidance* was very difficult to understand: after several weeks at sea he had read only three of the simple and easy pages.

Today he began on the fourth page. Today he and Elin read together for the first time. Fortunately, Elin had no need of learning English, as the Holy Ghost was to visit her and all the Akians as soon as they landed in America; they would be able to speak the new language without difficulty at the moment of stepping ashore. But she was curious as she heard Robert use words from the foreign language. Even now she did not wish to seem less learned than he; she must participate. He also was of the opinion that it could hardly hurt her if she learned a little in advance about the difficult pronunciation. When she landed she would then have cleared away a little work for the Holy Ghost, and this could not be a sin.

English was a complicated and tricky language for unlearned people. The most difficult thing of all was that the words were spelled in two entirely different ways: first they were printed as words usually are, then the same words appeared in brackets, spelled entirely differently: "Yes, I am a stranger here. (aj am a strehndjer hihr.) What are you looking for? (hoat ahr joh loking far?) What do you wish? (hoat doh joh oisch?)"—Robert could not understand this arrangement; what use was there in writing and spelling the same word in two ways? It caused only unnecessary time and trouble. It was strange that the Americans, who were considered so clever, couldn't agree on one way of spelling their language. It could hardly have anything to do with the different classes, as all people were equally good in America and no one was above anyone else.

The youth and the girl started with "Conversational Exercises." They sat with their heads very close together, which they must do as they were reading the same book. And they read aloud about the position of the tongue and the lips in the correct use of English: "When English and American people speak, their tongues are usually pulled back in their mouths a great deal farther than is the case when we Swedes speak our mother tongue. The lips are moved less than in Swedish. They are neither rounded nor pursed as much as with us, nor are they opened as much. It is very important that no protruding of the lips takes place, especially in making the difficult ch-sound."

"Do you understand?" he asked.

"Yes, I do. Every word of it," she lied.

"Otherwise I'll show you."

And then he pursed his lips: this she must not do when she spoke English.

"I don't make such an ugly mouth when I speak Swedish!" she said.

"Say the ch-sound!" continued Robert. "Say 'church'!"

"Church," repeated the girl slowly and seriously.

But he thought she pouted her lips too much.

"Pull in your lips! Say it again!"

She repeated the word "church" a few times while his face was close to hers so he might see the movements of her lips. She wanted to protrude them too far, he thought. She said the word half a score times, but he was still not quite satisfied. At last she succeeded: exactly so must the word be pronounced! He gave her other words with the ch-sound, he continued his instructions with the aid of his fingers, and he thought this was a good way to teach English.

While busy with his lesson he suddenly discovered that Elin had a small and sensitive mouth, and that her lips were downy and a little moist from the spray of the ocean.

And then he must teach the girl to keep her tongue far back in her mouth while using the English language. The Holy Ghost might not remember to tell her all the details. Especially when she used the letters *d, e, l,* and *n,* she must keep her tongue as far back as she could; those were the most important letters, used perhaps every day in America.

In order to administer his instruction more efficiently, he now wanted to see how her tongue was shaped. He asked her to stick it out.

The girl obeyed, and the young man carefully scrutinized her extended tongue, which had the light red color of early wild strawberries, and was narrow and pointed like a cat's. He thought she would be able to speak English with it if she had the necessary practice. He let her sit there with her tongue extended toward him so long that she finally became tired and pulled it in. Wasn't he through with his inspection?

He told her that the learning of English required great patience; she must not tire from holding her tongue out such a short while; she might have to endure greater hardships before she knew the new language.

Elin had hardly pulled her little tongue into her mouth again before Ulrika of Vastergohl called: Elin must help her mother with the evening meal. The girl obeyed and left Robert at once. And he sat on alone, annoyed and hurt; no sooner was he with Elin than her mother found something urgent for her to do. Ulrika could easily have prepared the food alone and given her daughter an opportunity to learn English, now that she had such a good teacher.

Fredrik Mattsson, the so-called American, strolled by in his loud-checked jacket. Robert showed him the textbook and asked him to read a piece aloud in English. But the American waved him away: Not today! Some other time. He had read in English books for many years, while in America; he was tired of the English language. He was now taking his afternoon stroll to rest himself. Some other day he would read in the book.

Robert had asked him about North America many times—its government, soil conditions, and climate. But the American only answered that he was not allowed to divulge anything; he had promised the President of the United States not to say a word. The President had become one of his close friends while he was over there, they had caroused together, drunk and played cards through many nights, they were the best of friends. And the President had told him in confidence many of the republic's great secrets—with Fredrik's assurance of secrecy, of course. That was why he couldn't say anything, at least not before the President of America released him from this promise of secrecy. For he, Fredrik Mattsson, was an honest man who stood by his word.

But there were some things in the American's tales which made Robert suspicious.

Now Fredrik went over and sat down among some youths who were sunning themselves on deck, and Robert joined their company. The American told about his various occupations in the United States. For one emigrating there, it was most instructive.

The far-traveled gentleman crossed his legs, pulled out his pipe and filled it; then he looked to the prow, toward the west, as if he wanted to recall his memories of America from that direction, and began.

The second year he spent in America he had taken a position on a ship which sailed the great Mississippi River with a cargo of whores. This river was as broad as all of Sweden, and the whore ship followed the shores; he had charge of the cargo—the women on board. There were more than a hundred of them, and a great sense of method and orderliness was required of the supervisor. Night and day he walked the ship with two loaded pistols in his belt. It was his duty to prevent and shorten all fights on board—between the women themselves as well as between the women and their men customers. If he was unable to stop the participants in any other way he was to shoot them in the legs. He began at the ankles, and if this didn't help he continued higher and higher. But the women he was not allowed to shoot higher than a little below the groin: their calling must not be impaired. The men he could shoot all the way up to the head to subdue them. It was a very responsible position he had held on that river vessel.

The ship sailed from town to town, and they remained a few days in each place while the men came on board and business was conducted. These were the most peaceful days, for the women were not belligerent when they plied their trade.

His work was well paid; his salary included food, clothes, and two women a day—if he wished to use them. Some of the girls were young and beautiful, but others had been at their trade so long that he lost all interest in women when he looked at them. And he never felt really at home in this job on the whore ship on the Mississippi. For if you have to supervise and keep order among one hundred whores, you have little time for rest and serious thinking. There was commotion and noise all through the days and nights. At that time he hadn't enjoyed good health, either, because of a most annoying diarrhea from the hot climate. And he was a serious-minded person, who had need of rest and time to gather his thoughts. The only rest he had the whole week was on Sunday mornings between ten and twelve, when the ship's minister held services and preached to the employees; so as not to disturb their devotion, no one was allowed to fire a pistol then except in extreme necessity.

Otherwise he had had to use his guns almost constantly. He

could do nothing else when the whores bit, scratched, and kicked. They were even inclined to attack him—the job had some undesirable points.

When they had sailed up and down the river a few times he decided to leave his post and go ashore. The captain had given him a fine letter of recommendation—he had this in his sea chest still, if it hadn't been lost during his long voyages over the world. The captain had written of him that he was reliable, and had a sense of order, and a good hand with the whores both during their working hours and in between. He did, indeed, have the best kind of recommendation if he wished to continue in that line of work. But in the long run such occupation would never satisfy a person of his caliber.

The story came to an end. The younger men among those who sat on deck around the American ogled each other. They had not been near a woman since leaving home. In the close quarters in the hold even the married men could hardly get their satisfaction. They might play with their wives, some nights, so quietly that no one heard them. But all those without wives, without anyone to crawl near to, they must pine and suffer. And this description of a whole ship filled with willing women, always ready, tickled the young men's fancy and stimulated secret desires.

Several other men passengers now joined the crowd around the American; a ring of listeners formed, and all sat there, around the man in the checked coat, in inspired silence. The silence could only be interpreted as a wish that the storyteller continue. He looked questioningly at his listeners, as if wishing to know what they thought of his experiences in America. Then he continued.

The Americans had many almost unbelievable institutions. In the United States there were luxurious places where women could seek pleasure with men. There was such a one in the great city of Chicago—a male whorehouse where men attended to women, where the whoring was practiced upside-down, so to speak. It was the same business as on the Mississippi ship—only just the opposite.

One spring in the month of April he and a friend had arrived in Chicago in search of work. In a saloon they had met the manager of this male whorehouse, who was out looking for men. And as both the American and his friend were hard up, they had, after thinking it over, accepted positions; the pay was high, and—of course—they were a little curious about their duties: they had never before heard of a place where one was paid for that which one usually did because one felt like it. They had worked as lumberjacks the whole winter and they needed some change. In the logging cabins they had lived for many months among men only, and some of their fellow workers had completely lost their minds because they were denied women—for this could, in the end, affect the brain; when the seed never is sown it forces its way to the head, where it may cause ugly growths on the skull; a doctor has to open these growths to save a man from insanity. So they were willing to take on any women who came along, after this winter.

Disappointingly enough, they never knew what kind of women they had to take care of, for all who came to this male whorehouse wore masks over their faces. It was mostly women with strong desires, unable to find men in the customary way. There came fine, prominent wives whose wedded husbands were on long journeys and who might not have had any amusement in bed for years; others might have some defect which made them unattractive to men and left them without a chance. But most of them were women who had been widowed while their youthful blood still was warm; they had accustomed themselves so strongly to men that they couldn't get along singly. In this house men were always ready for them, and what the women sought there they always obtained; no one could gainsay this.

In the beginning it had felt strange to lie with masked women. It seemed always to be the same woman, it felt like being married and sticking to one's wife. Of course, there was a great deal of difference in other parts of the body, but he had soon forgotten that. He hadn't looked at the differences; there had been other things to do. At first it had been like a fresh clover field, but this did not last long. Soon it was only a chore which he was employed to perform; soon he didn't care how the women were shaped. At times it happened that a bold woman showed her face, but only a good-looking one would do that. Perhaps they had thought that a beautiful face would make it easier for him, help him in his work, as it were. And this line of reasoning was correct, he thought.

This much he understood, after taking care of a few hundred women: not all of them were beautiful princesses. But he couldn't choose, all must be attended to equally well. The whorehouse manager had issued strong rules about that, and no one was allowed to dodge. Some never got satisfied; they were angry and complained afterwards that they hadn't received their money's worth, not by a long shot. Well, fretful and troublesome women did exist in this world; one couldn't satisfy all.

But soon he and his friend had had enough of their job in the male whorehouse; they tired of it, both of them. They were fed rich and sustaining food in the place, they ate eggs and juicy lamb chops and fat ham and soup at every meal— this was only what the body required in such a job. But even sustaining food was not sufficient in the long run; they grew wan and lost weight and fell off. After a few months their faces were unrecognizable when they looked at themselves in the mirror. Their strength waned; the weakness first attacked their knees, which felt like straws—their legs bent under them when they tried to walk. They were wasting away completely. Their fellow workers who had been longer in the house than they were bare skeletons. They hobbled about the rooms, their bones rattling. No man could remain in the place over three months. Those who stayed longer had never recovered, they had lost their strength of youth for all time, they were ruined for life.

But he and his friend had quit in time—after six weeks' employment they had returned to the forest. In the last analysis he liked it better among the men in the logging cabin than among the women in the house of luxury. But there was a certain satisfaction in this work among the women: he had done good deeds, he had sacrificed himself in an unselfish way. However, neither he nor his friend had been willing to waste their health and strength utterly, not even for a good cause, a sacrifice on the altar of charity, as it were.

For a man has responsibilities toward himself too, concluded Fredrik.

Complete silence ensued in the gathering of menfolk after he had finished his story. The circle of listeners sat and gazed at him. Not one among them could find fitting words to utter, after the story of the male whorehouse in Chicago.

Suddenly a young man let out a roar of laughter. The others looked at him. The laugher stopped short, reddening from embarrassment. The American, too, looked at him with disapproval, with deep scorn, as much as to say: Have you no manners? The man who had laughed met this look of the American, and said not a word, but it could be seen that he felt deeply ashamed. And the teller of the tale wanted him to feel ashamed.

Fredrik rose quickly, nodded, and strutted away.

2

That same day Robert discovered the secret about the American. He happened to mention him to the sailmaker. The old man said that Fredrik Mattsson and he had been born in the same parish—Asarum—in Blekinge. He had known Fredrik since the time he lay in his swaddling clothes. The man had always been a rascal and liar and a ravenous preyer on women. He had managed badly for himself at home: at one and the same time three women were pregnant by him, he owed money to God and everybody, and he had a beating coming from more than one. That was why he was sneaking away to America on the *Charlotta*. But he had never been at sea before he set foot on this ship; he had been a seaman on land only. He had never been to America, he had not even been outside his home parish, Asarum, until now.

Soon Robert discovered that he was practically the last one on board to find out the truth about Fredrik Mattsson: the passengers had called him the American just because he had never been to America.

For a few days Robert felt disappointed in his friend with the loud-checked coat, who had not wished to divulge his secrets about the United States of America. From now on he could not believe what Fredrik told him; one must admit that he did not stick to the truth.

But Robert knew this about himself, also: when he wanted to relate something he had read or experienced, truth alone did not always suffice. He might come to a place in the story, unable to go further, and then he must invent something to be able to continue. Later on he might return to the truth again. And the strange thing with a lie was that it was always there, inside one's head, ready to be used when need be. It was easy and convenient to mix in a lie. Then, afterwards, when he had finished his tale, truth and lie were so intermixed that it was impossible to differentiate—all was truth.

Perhaps this was the case with the American when he described all the various positions he had held in America. That he had never been to that country mattered little, after all. He believed he had been there, and therefore, in reality, he did not lie.

If God had meant people to use truth only, He need not have allowed untruth in the world. Perhaps He had created the lie because He knew people couldn't get along without it.

XXI

IT WAS CALLED SHIP-SICKNESS

1

As the weeks went by most of the emigrants accustomed themselves to the rolling of the ship.

Kristina recuperated from her seasickness; she was up and about and able to eat almost regularly. But she did not feel as well as she used to on land. A certain weakness remained in her limbs, and a weight, as it were, pressed down her whole body—she moved about sluggishly and unwillingly. Something pressed on her chest too, so that her breath became short. Other passengers—men and women—complained about the same feeling; perhaps it was some ailment caused by their long stay on board.

Kristina had also started worrying about her children: they grew pale and their eyes looked yellow. They were no longer lively in their play, and they had lost their appetites; they refused to eat the ship's fare because it was too salty—they complained and wanted fresh milk. And Kristina, too, missed more than anything the sweet milk they used to drink every day. But she understood—they could not bring milch cows with them on the sea. If only she had had a quart a day for her children! They had not tasted one drop of milk for a whole month. The sugar pouch was long ago emptied, her cakes were gone, the honey was eaten, the dried pieces of apple finished. When the children fell and hurt themselves and came to her, crying, or when they wanted to "step off" the ship, then it had been a blessing to have a lump of sugar or a cookie to comfort them with. Now she had nothing to give them when they came and begged.

The weaning of Harald had taken care of itself because her milk dried up after a short time at sea. She had hoped it would remain in her breasts, as she had no other milk for the child. He was otherwise fine for his sixteen months; he had entirely quit creeping about, and had begun to walk upright between the bunks in their crowded quarters. But a ship rolling on the waves, seldom still, was hardly a place for a child to learn to walk. Little Harald had to sit down on his rump many more times than had his brother and sisters at home on the firm floor of their house.

Johan and Lill-Marta were still babbling about "stepping off" the ship and going home. They had not forgotten what they used to eat and drink on land—they wanted to go back and eat cakes and drink milk.

Kristina promised them sweet milk and wheat cookies, as much as they could manage, as soon as they arrived in America. But she soon regretted this promise; now she was beset constantly by the children: When would they arrive in America? Tonight? Or tomorrow morning? They would arrive soon. How far away was soon? It wasn't far, if they were good and kept quiet, said the mother. If they kept quiet the whole day and didn't say one word, would they then reach America by tomorrow?

Lill-Marta was satisfied at times, and kept silent, but never Johan: "Shall we always live on the ship, Mother?"

"No, not after we get there."

"Shall we never live in a house any more?"

"We shall live in a house in America."

"Is it true, Mother?"

"It is true."

"I want to live in a house soon."

"So you shall, if you keep quiet."

"In a house like the one we slept in at home?"

"In such a one."

"Where is that house, Mother?"

"We shall see, when we arrive."

"Is it sure we are to live there?"

"It is sure. Father will build one. Now, keep quiet, boy, otherwise you'll always have to stay on this ship."

At times Kristina thought that maybe it wasn't right to silence the children with promises. What did she know about their new home in North America? Exactly as much as the children! What she knew for sure was that they owned not the smallest patch of ground over there, had not the smallest corner of their own, not the poorest earth but they could call home. Not the most humble shed awaited them, not the most wretched shelter could they move into. When Karl Oskar and she had set up housekeeping last time they had been able to begin in a well-established home where furniture and household gear awaited them. The second time they were to set up housekeeping they must do so in a foreign country, and they must begin from the very ground, with nothing. She dared not think of the settling that awaited them: they had not a single nail for their walls, not a board for flooring, not a shingle for their roof. When they landed in North America, nothing would be ready for them—no table set, no bed made. They had no bench to sit on, nothing on which to rest their heads. This was the only thing she knew. And as she understood it, they were to travel far away into the wilderness to seek their new home. There, she assumed, they must sit on one stone in the woods and eat from another (if they had any food), and they must sleep on a bolster of moss with spruce bows for a covering.

She did not wish to speak with Karl Oskar about this their second setting up of housekeeping; he would only be annoyed by it. He had promised her nothing. What could he promise? But she could think herself, she could imagine how it would be.

They were to begin from the very beginning—as people at home had begun thousands of years ago; they must live with the earth the way the very first tiller and his wife had done.

2.

There had been nineteen children on board the brig *Charlotta* when she left Karlshamn. But two small canvas bundles had been lowered into the ocean from her deck: one one-year-old boy had died with the whooping cough, one five-year-old girl in ship's fever. The seventeen children, surviving now were considered in good health.

Danjel's and Inga-Lena's last-born, little Eva, had been so ill that everyone thought she was going to die. But God let the parents keep their child, she had now gained strength and was completely well. Danjel thought a miracle had taken place, as their daughter had been suffering a much more severe illness than the two who had died.

But the girl was hardly well before the mother sickened. When the seasickness had left Inga-Lena she was often seized by a great dizziness and headache. While she was cooking or attending to heavy chores she would have spells of fainting; then she must go and lie down for a time. Early in the voyage she had suffered from hard bowels—now things had changed and she must run to the roundhouse on the foredeck at all hours of the day and night. This went on week after week, and no one could have loose bowels such a long time without becoming exceedingly weak and worn out. Now there was blood in her stool, too, and this worried her a great deal.

Inga-Lena did not like to complain, but now she confided in Kristina: maybe she wasn't quite well. She had prayed God particularly for help against the bloody stool, which frightened her, but she had as yet received no answer to her prayers. Perhaps she had caught the ship-sickness, or what did Kristina think?

During the whole voyage Kristina had felt sorry for her Uncle Danjel's wife: Inga-Lena never gave herself any rest, but always waited on her husband and children, seeing to it that they had their food regularly and that their clothes were in order. Always she busied herself with something. Inga-Lena was like a ship at sail on the sea, she was in motion every moment. This must not go on, she had become gaunt, worn to the bone. Sometimes she could scarcely walk, she staggered as if every step were her last.

Kristina said that she should go to bed; Danjel must take over her chores.

Inga-Lena looked confounded. "Danjel musn't know! He mustn't know that I am ailing."

"Why not?"

"He has enough troubles of his own, poor man!"

"But he is well."

"No-o." Inga-Lena lowered her voice: "He has sufferings of his own. He must make peace with God."

"Oh. But he could be useful all the same," said Kristina. "He doesn't need to pray every minute."

"He won't suffer worldly things. And now he must make all right for himself with the Lord."

And Inga-Lena spoke almost in a whisper: Kristina must not repeat it to anyone, but her husband had confessed to her that he had committed a great sin, the greatest one of all: he had fallen into the temptation of spiritual vanity by thinking himself free of sin, that he had once and for all been forgiven by Christ, that he could sin no more because he believed in the Saviour. He had held himself righteous, and felt above the law. But then one day God had undressed him, unto his naked soul, and shown him what it looked like; he had been dragged down in seasickness among sinners and the unredeemed. Since then he was much changed.

Danjel had said that he had received a severe box on the ear from the Lord because of his vanity and self-righteousness; now he walked about dazed from that box. He had reproached others because they were doubters; now he asked forgiveness from all of them. He had asked Inga-Lena's forgiveness although he had done nothing but good to her.

Her dear husband had previously held himself better than other sinners, now he considered himself lower. He had told Inga-Lena that there was only one righteous person on the whole ship, and that was Ulrika of Vastergohl. She had gone free of the vermin, and she had escaped seasickness. She was chosen. A hundred times was she guilty of whoredom—yet she was chosen by the Lord.

And for the sake of this one righteous person, for Ulrika's sake, said Danjel, the Lord had buoyed up their ship in the horrible tempest and saved them all from drowning; all of them had the Glad One to thank for their lives.

"That's a lie!" exclaimed Kristina excitedly. "I'll never believe it! That woman isn't a bit holier than the rest of us!"

"Don't repeat what I have said," begged Inga-Lena. "Say nothing to Danjel. And don't tell him I'm ailing. Please, promise me!"

Kristina found she must give this promise. But how much she would have liked to tell the truth to her uncle. Don't you realize your wife is killing herself here at sea? God can never have meant her to give up her health in order for you to escape worldly cares. Doesn't God, on the contrary, require a wedded huusband to be kind to his wife, and assist her when she is sick? And if you have your senses and your eyesight, you must understand that your wife is very ill!

But the strange thing was that she would have been unable to speak reproachfully to her Uncle Danjel. In the presence of this man with the kind eyes one could not use hard words. There was something in his look that calmed one's mind and created reverence. When he bent his knees and prayed, an illumination came over his face—even if he kneeled in vomit on the floor. He sometimes acted foolish, but all hesitated to make fun of him. Kristina could not understand why it was so difficult to reproach him. Perhaps he *was* nearer to God than other mortals—perhaps it was this she was aware of.

The fact remained, however, that his wife was killing herself, without his noticing it. Inga-Lena was like a domesticated animal that follows its master. According to the catechism a wife must be subject to her husband—but did God mean that she was *absolutely obliged and forced to follow him* when he dragged her out to sea?

Kristina was not sure of this.

3

Karl Oskar remained sound and healthy in his body, while at sea, but the prolonged stay in their narrow quarters was depressing to his mind. When he began life anew on another continent he would need an undaunted spirit, and now he was not as he used to be on land. He went about worrying over the future, and this he had never done before. Then, there was a certain something lacking physically: not once during their whole voyage had he been able to satisfy himself with his wife. This was due to bad luck. While Kristina still was well, he had had to sleep with the unmarried men; and when later he had moved to the other side of the sailcloth, she had been ill. As she still remained weak, he could not ask for her.

Ever since his marriage, his satisfaction with his wife had been a habit with him. When he could no longer follow this habit a restlessness and irritation crept into his body, his temper became uneven and his sleep was not restful. There was something missing, and his thoughts were drawn to it—to that missing something. When he could satisfy himself with Kristina he seldom thought of other women—they did not concern him. Now, during his continence, they aroused him so often that he felt annoyed and ashamed. But why must he feel ashamed over this? It was only as it should be: he missed what he couldn't get. It was only natural that a healthy man should enjoy a woman; the situation here on the ship was unnatural.

Nor did Karl Oskar have enough to do at sea. He had time to brood and to wonder. He went about and thought of that which he must be without. The times he and his wife had enjoyed themselves together came back easily to his mind, and this tortured him. It didn't happen to him by intention, he tried to shake off such thoughts; he had other things to think about, now, in the midst of the greatest move in his life. But there he went again, thinking of their bed-pleasure, and again he felt ashamed: what was the matter with him? He should be able to get along without it for a while. This must be something that happened often to many men. Why was it so painful to him? Was his lust stronger than other men's? Here he fought it now, it was his own particular ship-sickness. And he knew for sure—in the long run, he could not survive without a woman.

One night Karl Oskar dreamed that he went in to the unmarried women—to Ulrika of Vastergohl, and used her.

He awakened and felt ashamed of his dream; his thoughts had carried him as far as to the Glad One, the infamous whore, where more than a hundred men had been before! He had been asleep during the act, of course, but it still surprised and shocked him. Though a deed in his sleep, it was nevertheless a shameful one.

He wondered if, while awake, he ever would go in to Ulrika. If he must deny himself and go without long enough, perhaps he might. He wasn't quite sure. He *had* looked at her sometimes, and felt that something about her tempted him. Her body was unusually well preserved, and men were often aroused in her presence. But enough sense surely must remain in his head to keep him away from such a woman. And he began to agree with Kristina: as soon as they landed in America they must separate themselves from the Glad One. Kristina could never make friends with the old whore. If they remained in her company, sooner or later some misfortune was likely to happen.

There was no way of telling how soon he and his wife could live together again as a healthy, happy couple. Kristina complained of new ailments: her limbs and joints ached, she had pains in the small of her back. It was very strange that she, still so young, had joint- and limb-ache, like an old woman. At times she was seized by chills, she said they felt like ice-cold runnels of water over her whole body. This ailment could not be caused by the sea, because she had it both in stormy weather and when it was perfectly calm. She always felt cold—even when she sat on deck in the sun, chills would overtake her. She felt as if all the blood within her had cooled off and could warm her no more. And then there was the pressure in her chest, which interfered with her breathing, and the weakness and fatigue that never left her.

In all her life Kristina had never been sick in bed, except in childbed; but now she was sick.

Her illness was accompanied by "the great laziness," as the old people called it—one of the worst of vices. She did not wish to move, she did not wish to use her arms or legs, to walk or to stand; she didn't want to perform her duties and chores. It was a great effort for her to prepare a meal, it was an effort to undress herself and her children, every morning she had to force herself to arise and wash and dress. More and more of the chores she left for Karl Oskar. She began to feel wretched and useless on this voyage. So lazy she had never been before, so little she had never done in a day. It must be the sea that sucked strength from body and mind of land people.

Kristina had emptied two bottles of medicine which her husband had obtained for her from the captain's medicine chest. But she only felt weaker afterward.

"You bring a wretched wife with you to America, Karl Oskar," she said. "I'm afraid I'll only be a burden to you."

"You'll get well as soon as you are on land," he assured her. "It's just the rotten ship's fare you can't stand."

They received only old salted foods, tainted by the smells of kegs and wooden boxes, tasting of sour barrel bottoms and ancient tubs. They never obtained a drop of milk, never a fresh slice of bread, never a taste of newly churned butter, never a bite of unsalted meat; only food which had been stored away for a long time. Never were they able even to boil a pot of potatoes—potatoes, which more than any other food kept the body in order and gave it its daily and necessary opening. No, Karl Oskar wouldn't be surprised if every person on the ship were to get sick in the end from the fare they received. He, too, felt somewhat loose and limp in his limbs. And nearly everyone he spoke to complained of the same ailment as Kristina, only she was a little worse than the others. But none seemed to improve, they wouldn't until they landed and lived and ate as folk ought to live and eat. Life at sea was destructive and unsound for a human being; this, indeed, he had learned.

Within himself Karl Oskar added: This sea voyage he would never repeat; for the rest of his life he would live on land.

Kristina was convinced that a creeping, treacherous, dangerous disease had taken hold of her—though she kept her knowledge a secret from her husband. This time life itself within her was assailed—and the anxiety she had experienced the first day on the *Charlotta* came over her again: this is not seasickness, this illness attacks life itself. This time you cannot get well; but you were warned, you received a warning from God those last days at home: Do not go out to sea! Stay at home! You do not belong at sea! But you didn't obey, you left. And now you know. That's why you had the premonition, felt it the moment you came into the hold. It's like a grave down here, a musty, horrible grave. Something within you told you it would be *your* grave. One day they will come down with a piece of canvas for you; never, never will you get away from here with life—they will carry you out in a piece of canvas. . . .

Kristina might have heard the name of the sickness which she and several others suffered from down here: the *scurvy*. It was a repulsive name, it seemed like a name for something rotten, fallen apart, contaminated—something already dead.

The evil was also called ship-sickness.

XXII

STORY TOLD AT THE MAIN HATCH

1

The passengers on the *Charlotta* were active people. Their lives had been passed in work; Sundays and weekdays they were accustomed to being occupied. Peasants and their wives always have something to do with their hands. On the ship which now carried them they encountered something new: idleness.

They cleaned their quarters in the hold daily, they prepared food three times a day in the galley, they mended their clothes, mattresses, bolsters, everything that broke, and the mothers attended to their children. But these chores were not sufficient to fill out their time at sea. Almost three-quarters of the day, most of them were inactive—left to themselves without a thing to do. And these toiling people had never learned what to do with spare time.

During their hours of inactivity the emigrants sat listlessly gazing out over the sea. What will we do now? And the endless water, the endless waves that carried their ship, gave them no answer to that question. There was nothing to do but sit and look across the sea. So the days passed, and the days became weeks and months during this long voyage.

The days seemed long and empty. Their lives on the brig *Charlotta* were monotonous. It had never occurred to them that time itself—life, which they had been given to live—would turn into something unpleasant to get rid of, something they must hasten when it passed too slowly. They were driven inward upon themseves, they were dissatisfied with their idleness; they could be alone but never idle. They began to seek each other's company.

When the weather at sea was pleasant they gathered around the main hatch. There they formed a thick cluster of bodies, standing, sitting, lying or half lying, occupying every inch of deck space. Wives might sit on their husbands' knees, children nestled in mothers' or fathers' arms. Then they brought forth whatever might be left in their food baskets from home, and offered each other tidbits: one had a whole loaf of bread left, someone else had saved a smoked, dried quarter of lamb, a third had butter left in his tub, and a fourth proudly displayed a whole, uncut cheese. The bread, lamb, and cheese went the rounds; each one took his knife and carved himself a slice of each part of this trinity, then spread butter over the bread and ate. Sometimes it might happen that a gallon of brannvin was brought out, made in the still at home on the farm, from last year's crop in the barley field.

These were happy moments for the passengers on the *Charlotta*. They regained something of their old home in these gatherings.

Thus while the sea was smooth and the ship rolled moderately, the emigrants sat gathered around the main hatch and helped each other while away the time, so stubbornly slow in passing. Hymns were played on the *psalmodikkon*, and dance tunes on the violin; someone sang a song—well known at home—and someone told a true strange story.

The ocean was broad, the *Charlotta* had contrary winds, and so it was that many stories were told while the emigrants sat around on the deck. One day homeowner Jonas Petter Albrektsson related a strange and unusual happening which had taken place in his home parish in Sweden.

2

It had happened about a hundred years earlier, said Jonas Petter.

Dean Drysell, who for many years had been the pastor in Ljuder Parish, had a stroke in the sacristy one Sunday morning before the service, and died before they had time to carry him out of the church. He was nearly seventy years old, and had had two strokes before the last one. Drysell had been a conscientious, fearless pastor, good to the poor and suffering. He was particularly liked by the women in the parish. He had lived his whole life as a bachelor, but it was known far and wide that he had not led a chaste life. It was said that in his days of strength he had used his favor with women in a way which is forbidden in God's Sixth Commandment. Once in his younger days he had been reprimanded by the bishop, who had heard rumors that the young priest had visited a married woman in her bed. Later, when the bishop came to Ljuder and saw how beautiful the woman was, the minister had received absolution from his whoring-sin.

But now the Ljuder dean had left this earth, on a Sunday, in the midst of fulfilling his duties. The whole week passed—and the dead man was not yet buried! This caused great wonder in the parish, particularly as the death had happened during the dog days of the summer when maggots quickly get into meat, and a corpse soon exudes an evil stench. Eight days was a long time for a corpse to remain above ground at that time of year.

Eight days *more* passed, and Dean Drysell was still not buried! Through the whole parish people began to wonder, and ask what the trouble might be. Why wasn't their departed pastor buried within the usual reasonable time? Some complication must have arisen which was being kept secret. But what could hinder a servant of the Lord from going into the earth and receiving Christian burial?

Pastor Stenbeck from Langasjo, who temporarily held the dean's office, could have answered the question—but no one wished to ask him. On the other hand, many asked Magda, Drysell's maid, who had served her master faithfully for many years, ever since her youth, and who had been closer to him than anyone else. But when the funeral of her master was hinted at, her mouth closed so firmly that a chisel would have been needed to open it. All felt she must know the secret of the delay in the funeral.

Now there was one other person who knew the reason, and he was the carpenter in the church village who had made the coffin for the dead pastor. He had promised Pastor Stenbeck not to say anything, but in a moment of confidence had shared the secret with his wife, who promised to keep it to herself. The wife in her turn confided in two neighbor wives, with the same promise, and in this way the truth was spread over the whole parish within a few days.

For weeks and months nothing else was spoken of in Ljuder Parish than what had taken place with the corpse of Dean

Drysell—that inexplicable sign which after death had appeared on his body.

Magda, the old and faithful maid, had made the discovery in the mangle shed of the parsonage which was used as a corpse-house for the dean. She had gone out to wash her master's body, and had been filled with consternation at her discovery. She had washed the corpses of many men before, but such a sight she had never seen. Her master lay there dead and cold, but his body was ready for a man's action with a woman! Even with men in their best years, the power of that limb disappeared with the arrival of death; and Drysell had been an old man. At the sight of the sign the old woman became weak in her whole body. She was near fainting, and, unable to continue with the washing of the corpse, she left the mangle shed.

She went back the following day, but nothing had changed in the corpse. This time, however, she finished the washing, not mentioning to anyone what she had seen. She had served the dean faithfully while he lived, she wanted to remain equally faithful to him after his death. Nothing must be said that could tarnish his memory.

Magda returned to the corpse-house on the third day, but the amazing sign still remained in her master. That same day the carpenter came with the coffin, and now her discovery could not be kept secret any longer. The carpenter saw the same as she had seen, and he was as disturbed as she. And he agreed with the old maid that their parish pastor could not be buried in this horrible condition. The maid asked his advice: What should she do? The carpenter himself could do nothing; this was not a job for a man of his trade. Against the evil powers that were active here nothing could be done by carpenters' tools—neither hammer nor plane could be used. For he realized at once that the Evil One himself had taken up his abode in the dead corpse's limb—in the very limb with which most of men's sins are committed. By seizing this tool of sin the devil had taken possession of Dean Drysell's remains. Some spiritual man who had his power from God must step in here and save the dead one. The carpenter advised Magda to see the new pastor.

The maid went to Pastor Stenbeck and tried haltingly to explain the situation of her dead master. The minister followed her to the corpse-house. The body was now shrouded, but the faithful servant uncovered it sufficiently so that the pastor could see with his own eyes. He paled at what he saw. He told Magda to cover the corpse, and said: My colleague cannot be buried in this abominable condition. He said nothing more. He did not call by name the power which had seized Drysell, but Magda understood that the carpenter was right.

Dean Drysell's funeral was to take place on Friday—today was Tuesday.

Pastor Stenbeck was a clergyman with powers to exorcise Satan. He had once liberated a farmer in Langasjo, and another time the old wife of the captain in Grimsgol, who had been possessed by the devil for many years. Now he went back to the parsonage and put on his vestments. Armed with the Holy Writ and many pious church books, he returned to the corpse-house and locked the door behind him. He was always alone with Satan when he exorcised him.

The good parson remained in the mangle shed several hours. The following day he returned again: no change had taken place in the body of the dead dean. Pastor Stenbeck locked himself in the shed an hour on each of the two following days, and continued his efforts. But the sign of the devil's presence remained. Stenbeck had failed in his exorcism this time. The funeral must therefore be delayed—a funeral could not be performed with Satan holding on to the mortal remains of his brother in the ministry.

It was the month of sultry dog days, and the deceased dean had now stood above ground for a whole week. Strangely enough, no odor came from the corpse. It seemed as if the power which had taken up its abode in the dead one's limb preserved the body from decay.

Pastor Stenbeck was unable to defeat the old Enemy, he needed help. He saddled his horse and rode to his colleagues in Linneryd and Elmeboda. The ministers of these two parishes were both noted for extraordinary spiritual powers. Stenbeck described to them the calamity which had overtaken their old friend Drysell after his death. Wouldn't they return with him, and assist in forcing Satan to let go his prey?

The ministers in Linneryd and Elmeboda knew of their colleague's weakness for women—those creatures who are so often the ruination of a good man. And they understood that it was because of the dean's sins with women in his youth that the devil had taken possession of him now. They promised to help Pastor Stenbeck.

The following day three ministers in vestments and regalia met in the Ljuder parsonage at the bier of their deceased colleague. They prayed, they sang hymns, they made the sign of the cross, they performed the mass which is used in exorcising the devil. Three living priests prayed for a dead brother. They went on with their mass through half of the night.

The neighboring clergymen remained in Ljuder until the following day, when they went out to the corpse-house to view the results of the exorcism of yesterday. But nothing had changed. Satan still remained in the limb of the dead one, he still retained hold on his prey. By now Dean Drysell had remained above ground for eleven days.

The three ministers took counsel together in great consternation. What was to be done? Spiritual powers did not suffice here. They could not bury their brother and colleague—not commit him to the earth with the Enemy still in his body. Nor could the corpse remain unburied many more days. The secret of the delay had in some way leaked out, all people spoke about it, and this was not an edifying occurrence in a Christian community.

The clergymen spoke of traveling to the bishop in Vaxio, to ask his advice. The bishop was an experienced servant of God, thoroughly familiar with the devices of Satan.

Then old Magda approached Pastor Stenbeck, and asked leave to speak with him alone. She had a confession to make, a terrible secret to divulge. She told the following. When first she came to the employ of Pastor Drysell she had been seventeen. She had come to him a virgin, but after only a few weeks in service her master had enticed her into carnal connection. For a long time she had lived in sin with him. But at last she began to worry about it—she feared for her salvation. And she grew more and more averse to the master who had tempted her and led her astray. She began to hate her seducer. By this hate she had once been led into a cruel deed: she had prayed to God for revenge. She had prayed that her master might receive punishment—that after death he might be delivered to Satan.

Drysell had soon finished his satisfaction in her, and had then turned to another woman. But Magda had remained in his service. She had had nothing more to complain about, he was good to her. She remained year after year; at length she became his faithful old servant; and now, when she no longer lived in sin with him, her peace of mind had returned to her.

After many years she had even forgiven her master his stealing of her maidenhead, and leading her to whoring-sin. Not only had all hate been deleted from her mind, she had become entirely devoted to the man who had led her astray. She served him well, and looked after him in all ways. She had come to depend on him, and he had depended on her. They had both passed the age when men and women seek each other for the sake of bodily lust, but they were in other ways a help and comfort to each other. Magda had learned to know her one-time seducer as a good man, generous, kind, and helpful to the poor and destitute. And she had suffered deeply from the memory that once in her youth she had wanted to condemn this man to eternal suffering and deliverance to Satan. It had been a bloody sin.

And then one Sunday morning the Lord touched the forehead of his servant: Drysell had a stroke in the sacristy and died. And the moment had arrived when Magda made her horrible discovery: the devil had indeed taken up abode in her master's body. With her own eyes she had seen that the Lord had answered the prayer she had uttered in her youth.

Many nights had already passed since her prayer was answered, yet not one wink of sleep had she enjoyed during a single night. She had lain wakeful in agony; the master whom she loved had through her instigation become the possession of Satan.

This was old Magda's confession. And now she wished to make her own attempt to liberate Dean Drysell. She intended to remain through a whole night in the corpse-house, alone with the dead one and the one who had taken possession of him. How she was to save her master, she did not know, but she wished to confess at his bier what she had done.

The pastor advised the maid eagerly: Go and do as you say!

She went to the corpse-house that same evening, and people could see a light burning there throughout the night. What she did to the seducer of her youth no one knew, but they all guessed, and probably guessed aright: she protested to God that she forgave Drysell the evil he had once done her; she assured Him that she no longer hated her master but instead loved him and blessed his memory—she retracted her prayer of hate and substituted for it a prayer of love—she prayed for his soul.

And when Pastor Stenbeck came into the corpse-house the following morning, the body of his deceased colleague was the same as all dead men's bodies. Satan had at last let go his hold of Dean Drysell. What the three learned and experienced ministers, God's servants, had been incapable of doing, this simple, unlearned woman had performed. What three worthy parish pastors had been unable to effect, the poor maid had managed alone; her sincere love had conquered the sinister power in the corpse-house.

Two days later Dean Drysell was at last given Christian burial. All the people in the parish followed him to his resting place, and the joy was great that Satan finally had been driven from his limb. For he had been a good pastor; so said, in particular, the women of the parish, who now thronged about his grave in great numbers.

And this amazing happening, which had taken place a hundred years ago, was now told by an emigrant to emigrants, when, one day in fine weather, they gathered around the main hatch of the brig *Charlotta* as she sailed with her storytellers and her listeners to North America.

XXIII

PEASANTS AT SEA

1

The emigrants—the strayed ones in this world—brought with them a small book, *Almanac for the Year after the Saviour Christs Birth the 1850th*, which they consulted daily. In the empty space between the date and the sign of Taurus, Gemini, Cancer, they marked each passing day with a small cross. They wanted at least to know where they were in the calendar year, even though unable to fathom their whereabouts at sea. On the ship all days were the same, weekdays and holidays. The seamen performed their duties on Sundays and weekdays alike. The emigrants would have become lost in time, as they were in space, without the *Almanac*. The cross marks on the days that had passed gave their lives consistency and meaning. At home on land they had made these crosses only when they took a cow to the bull, so as to know when to expect the calf.

The *Almanac* also predicted the weather: Clear, Cloudy, Occasional Clouds, Rain, Clear and Beautiful Days. Sometimes it was cloudy, or rained, on Clear and Beautiful Days, and many times the sun shone from morning to night on Rainy Days. It also sometimes happened that the weather and the *Almanac* agreed.

The wind was mostly westerly; it was against them. And the wind that hindered them, and delayed their landing, this wind came from the land they were trying to reach. They did not know how to interpret this.

2

The emigrants had now been at sea for five weeks. The year had passed far into May—the month of flowers.

But now the people of the land lived on the sea, which showed no signs of the seasons: from its depths no plants shot forth to tell of spring or autumn, sowing or harvesting. The sea had no verdure, did not blossom. When the cold north wind swept down upon them, and the water turned as gray as the skies themselves, then the sea was like old fields with rotting stubble, and then they might guess at winter. When the sun shone and the sea lay there shimmering as blue and as calm as the small tarns at home, then they could guess it was summer. But the water did not divulge the seasons of the year to the people of the land—not so they could be certain.

During the month of flowers, however, there were days when a balmy air flowed over the deck; then they knew that spring had come on land, and they eagerly inhaled this new wind—perhaps (if it were not westerly) it had blown over their fields and meadows at home. These peasants at sea, sailing from tilled fields in the one continent to an unbroken wilderness in the other, drew the air in through their nostrils, wondering: How far advanced was the spring work at home?

Were the oats sown? Had the potato field been prepared as yet? Had the sheep pens been cleaned? Did the fields reek of dung after the showers? Were the cattle still in their stalls, bellowing and longing, or had they been let loose in the pastures?

The emigrants came from land, and they were traveling to land. To them, the sea was only a passage which they used, a water which they must cross in order to reach land on the other side—they could not understand the sea folk on board who were traveling nowhere, who lived permanently on this ship, who only voyaged back and forth across this sea. The peasants traveled with a definite purpose in mind, the seamen only traveled.

To the peasants the sea was the same everywhere: there was no difference between the water in this ocean and the water in the inland Baltic Sea. The expanse of sea which their eyes beheld was no greater in one place than in another. And what they saw today was the same as they saw yesterday. Had they actually moved?

The wheels of a wagon never roll over the same stone more than once on a journey. But here it seemed as if the same wave lifted the ship on its shoulders day after day. When they traveled on land they passed through varying landscapes—meadows and forests, hills and valleys, brooks and lakes. But on the sea they were constantly surrounded by the same water. They sat and gazed across a desert water-field where nothing interfered with their vision: everything was alike, everything the same. The sea was great and endless as infinity, yet it was also small—it consisted of only *one* landscape, it was one region only. It was always the same landscape, it was the *sea*.

And this monotonous view aroused a longing within them: they wanted to see a patch of green ground soon, if only a tree or a bush—they would be satisfied with a juniper bush, that weed of the forest; anything that grew green would gladden their hearts.

When, now, during "Clear and Beautiful Days," a balmy wind blew into their nostrils, they recognized the spring. But their eyes looked in vain for signs of the season. They sat on the worn and splintery deck of a ship and the month of May failed to bring them armfuls of blossoms. Round and about rose the blue-green crests of the waves—the hills at home would now be covered by the cuckoo's breeches, the butter-cups, the rabbit-foot, the dog-ears, and the bumblebee-blossoms. But the fragrance from these blossoms of spring was not carried to them by the wind.

They were to lose this spring, for they were seekers of new homes. They traveled away, and it was still difficult for them to imagine that *away*, some time in the future, might mean *home*. Yet they felt this must be so.

The passengers on the brig *Charlotta* looked out over an empty, barren water-desert, as formidable and tiresome as the one the children of Israel had passed through when they were seeking the Promised Land. The emigrants were a sailing car-avan: their ship was the rolling camel, carrying them across this unyielding and empty desert known as the Atlantic Ocean.

3

During some "Clear and Beautiful Days" the ship was envel-oped in a thick fog which still further diminished the world of the passengers.

The fog enwrapped the brig *Charlotta* like a thick gray woolen shawl, so that the passengers' range of vision nar-rowed down to a few yards. Now they could see nothing out-side the ship's world; no other world existed. The whole living earth consisted of this old, worn deck. The outside world was only something gray, penetrating, raw, fleeting, impenetrable —it was fog. A sticky, soft wall had been built close to them. They could not see the masts and the sails above them, the wall moved in on deck, it crept into the ship. It increased their irritation to the same degree as it narrowed their space. The downy fog was soft and light, yet it weighed heavily on their minds and caused them to become depressed and short of temper. The world seemed ever more gray and more sad. The emigrants were easily angered now, and quarreled about inconsequentials. As the men talked among themselves all gladness and friendly jesting disappeared, and in the galley the women fought during the preparation of the meals, and used pots and pans as weapons. The people could ill endure them-selves, much less each other.

The gray soft wall enclosed them on all sides, enclosed the whole sea. They sailed through a wall hundreds of miles thick, and it seemed as if they sailed at random. Did their ship move at all? Might not the brig *Charlotta* lie still as an island on the water, tethered to the bottom with invisible chains? They could not see that she was arriving anywhere, she sailed, but sailed nowhere. Their ship lay here in the fog, swaddled in a woolen shawl which hid and wrapped up the whole earth.

And during these days of fog an anxiety began to spread from one to the other among the emigrants: hadn't they sailed astray?

They began to count: six weeks, seven weeks—soon their voyage was in the eighth week. The year had passed into the month of June. How great a distance was still left to America? They had oftentimes asked the seamen, and equally often they had received indecisive answers: almost halfway, about halfway, nearly halfway, a little over halfway. Now they were tired of this halfway, and wanted to pass it. They had been told it would require at the most eight weeks for the crossing to North America, and they ought soon to arrive. But week was still added to week, and the anxiety spread. No one could tell them how far they had sailed, or definitely tell them their location. Perhaps they were lost? Perhaps they had already passed the shores of America? Perhaps they would never arrive?

Could they rely on the captain who charted the course? Could they be sure he would find his way over this water without signs, where no marks were left by those who had sailed before? He might steer in one direction but the winds and currents of the sea drive the ship in another. He might sail by the sun in the daytime and the stars at night, but what could he do when neither sun nor stars were shining? Or when it was misty and foggy, as now? They were afraid that by this time not even the ship's commander knew where they were.

The patience of the passengers was almost at an end from the long sailing, and there were many things they would have liked to ask the captain. But the taciturn little man who was seen on deck only occasionally, spending most of his time in his cabin, encouraged no one to approach him. And there was talk of an answer which he had made to a bold and curious passenger who had asked the question which was in everyone's mind: When do we land in America? The captain had answered: Which day do we arrive in the harbor of New York? That he would willingly say, he was anxious to tell them. Only, first he must have a little information—a little information about the weather. He would like to know what sort of weather they would have in the few weeks ahead, day by day. Would it be cloudy or clear, calm or stormy, would there be good wind or poor, rain or fog? Also, would they be so kind as to tell him from which direction the wind would blow in the near future, day after day? Would it blow from the east or west, from the north or south? When they could furnish him a little information about these things, then he would immediately tell them on what date the brig *Charlotta* would tie up at the pier in the harbor of New York.

It was a chagrined and disappointed interrogator who returned from the *Charlotta*'s captain. After this, none was willing to approach him again with the question. And Captain Lorentz thought that he might perhaps have explained a little about the continuous contrary wind. But why try to instruct these ignorant peasants about the prevailing winds which in these latitudes sweep the North Atlantic? He might as well try to explain the compass to them. Of course, the emigrants suffered, longing for land, but soon enough they would begin their poking in their dunghills again, soon enough they would dig themselves into their holes in the earth. What was their hurry? He could well have forced his speed somewhat, but he was afraid to strain the rigging further. The two full-tackled masts of the *Charlotta* could develop a large spread of sails that, in favorable wind, would give her great speed. The vessel was somewhat overrigged, however, and a moderate breeze was therefore the wind her skipper liked best.

But had all the days of contrary winds been days of favorable winds, then the *Charlotta* would already have landed her passengers in America.

The contrary winds had prolonged the emigrants' voyage so that they had grown suspicious and wondered if they had been misled as to the distance: it must be much farther to North America than they had been told. They did not measure the distance in miles but in the lengthy days which they had spent at sea. And it seemed to them as if they had traversed countless thousands of miles since that second week in April when they had left their place of embarkation. Their homeland was now incalculably remote—and remote, also, was the land where they were to seek their new homes.

The winds and the currents were against them. And the fog. The ocean constantly heaved new hindering waves into the path of the vessel, as if to force them to turn back. They grew bitter in their souls against the sea which delayed their arrival. And many thought: If I could only once more put my foot on firm land, then I would never again entrust myself to the sea.

4

But the sun was still in its place, and one morning it shone again. The west wind—the contrary wind—blew up again and swept over the sea like a giant broom tearing away the thick woolen shawl of the fog, which dissolved and disappeared, leaving behind a blue, cleanswept sea.

The embrace of the fog was loosened, indeed, but now they found themselves in the clutches of the contrary wind. The west wind—the American wind—continued to delay them on their voyage. It was like a greeting from the New World: Don't hurry! You have plenty of time! You'll arrive soon enough! Certain it was that the winds of the sea would not hasten their arrival in the New World.

They had now been sailing for two months. They had passed only a single ship—the one with the Swedish flag —since the English shore had disappeared and they had reached the open sea. During this whole time they had seen no human life beyond the rail of their own ship. It seemed to them as if they alone were traversing this ocean. All other people lived on land—they were vagabonds of the sea, the only human creatures on the ocean, forgotten by the world. And a foreboding burrowed into their souls: perhaps someone still missed them in the land they had left, but no one awaited them in the land ahead.

Then one day, on the afterdeck, it was seen that the brig *Charlotta* had a new passenger. Someone called aloud: Look, a bird! Then many shouted to each other: A bird!

Within a short moment the news had spread throughout the

ship: there was a bird on board! And the emigrants thronged around this new fellow passenger and gaped at him.

It was a tiny bird, hardly bigger than a wagtail. Its head and tail were blue-black, its wings and back were green, its throat and breast white. The bird put up a long pointed beak into the wind, and tripped along on a pair of legs as thin as threads. When he ran about on deck his feet moved so quickly that it seemed as if he used a single leg only, and when he flew his wings fluttered like a yarn winder.

No one among the ship's passengers or crew recognized this bird, no one knew the name of his kind. Some thought he was a wader, because of his pointed beak and quick wingbeats. Others guessed he was some breed of swallow, because his neck and breast were like a swallow's. Others again maintained that the bird was only a fledgling: when he was grown he might turn out to be a seagull, or a stork, or even a sea eagle. But none among them knew much about birds.

His sudden appearance, however, seemed to the emigrants a Bible miracle. They could scarcely remember when last they had seen a bird. Early in the voyage a swarm of seagulls had moved about the rigging of the ship, and daily perched on her masts, but out here on the ocean even these flying companions had vanished. No wings fluttered now above the vessel, and with the gulls, all living things seemed to have deserted the emigrants' ship. But now came this small bird and made himself at home on deck. He came to them a messenger from land—it was a miracle.

How could the tiny flying creature find its way to their lonely little ship? Birds lived on land—in trees or on the ground, in the reeds along the shores, or in the mountain crags. No bird could build his nest on the ocean waves. And it was many hundreds of miles to the nearest land. How had those delicate wings been able to carry the bird this great distance, through darkness and tempest, through rain and storm? From where had the bird come? What was his errand?

It struck the emigrants at once that there was something supernatural about the arrival of the bird; he was not one bird among others. The long loneliness at sea was a fertile breeding ground for thoughts of the supernatural and such strange things as one spoke of in low tones around the hearth in the evenings.

The eyes of the bird gleamed black and deep as riddles

which no one could solve. He made no sound, he never sang. He was completely mute. And his silent beak was still another riddle. They had heard about birds with cut-off tongues, birds which could not sing; was he perhaps such a one?

The new passenger on board became the most cared for among them. All wanted to feed him. The emigrants generously crumbled their bread and ship's biscuits. The bird was treated to so much food that it would have sufficed to burst a thousand stomachs like his. He had the privilege of eating his sufficiency from the hands of human beings, and soon he became choosy, he didn't bother to pick up crumbs from the deck. Unafraid, he wandered about among his feeders. When a wave washed onto deck he fled away on his thread-thin legs —he was so quick that a drop of water never wet his feet. Now and then he went on a flying jaunt beyond the rail, as if he wanted to inspect the sea a moment, but he always returned to deck. The brig *Charlotta* was his home.

A little bird had entered into the world of the people on the emigrant ship, transforming their thoughts and dreams, their very lives. He came with a message from the sprouting ground, from the flowers, from the trees in the forest and the seed in the fields. His wings were green as the newly opened leaves of the birch, his neck was white as from cotton-grass in the marshy bogs. The colors of his feathers came from the earth and that which grew thereon. He came from that part of the globe which God had destined to be home for men and beasts, and because of this he belonged to them. In their loneliness and forsakenness at sea the emigrants were visited by one of their own.

Many days had passed since they last stood on a firm and steady spot. Now the bird reminded them that firm land still existed.

Some among the emigrants had read fairy tales, and they were convinced that this was an enchanted bird. How could he have arrived here, so far out at sea, where no other flying creatures lived, if it were not through magic? Perhaps it was a princess walking here among them on a pair of bird legs. Perhaps it was a king or a prince they fed with their hard ship's biscuits. No one could know for sure. Perhaps the enchantment would end one day, so that he could lay off his feather shroud and put on a golden mantle and a glittering golden crown. Such things had been heard of, they happened rather often. And even if the bird were not a royal person, he was at least of great importance, maybe a duke or a count. Because only people of high station were enchanted into birds; ordinary, simple people became wolves and snakes and similar beasts. Thus the little bird was held in superstitious awe among certain of the passengers, and they felt some fear in his presence. He might do them good, but he could also bring them harm. Still, they wished to be friends with their messenger from the earth, because deep within them they could not help but feel that his arrival was meant as a blessing to them.

The crew men, too, pointed out that the wind had been with them ever since the day the bird first appeared on deck —no one was more careful about his well-being than the seamen, no one took more care that harm should not come to the little creature.

During the days the bird spent his time on deck; at night he found protection behind the sail near the mainmast. The sailmaker had prepared a soft nest for him from sewn-together pieces of wadmal. Each one did his bit to make the bird feel at home on the ship, and every one of his movements was followed by someone's eyes—when he dodged the spray, when he flew along the rail. To the peasants at sea he was a reminder of their mutual home. When they looked at him they were cheered and remembered they were not to remain imprisoned on this ship forever. Another life existed. Tree trunks existed, where birds built their nests, there were fields covered with blossoms, there were forests where the woodcocks flew about in the spring evenings.

Never had a little creature brought so much joy to so many mature human beings as this little bird did on the emigrant ship *Charlotta* during a few days of her voyage to North America. And everyone hoped and wished that the messenger from land would remain with them for the rest of their crossing. But if he were—as many thought—an enchanted king or prince, then he could not be held by anything. This they understood.

And one morning the bird was indeed gone. There was much excitement on board—the whole ship was searched but no sign was seen of the lost one, not a feather, not a dropping, nothing. The puzzling guest had left the ship as mysteriously as he had arrived. If he had died his body would have been found; no, they knew he had deserted them.

Would he ever reach land? The emigrants did not worry about this. They felt that weather and wind and distance had no power over this bird. They were convinced now that he was no real bird.

He had flown away, and he never returned. For many days sorrow reigned on the ship. The people on board had lost a near relative, and they mourned him as one of their own. And they mused and wondered and asked: Why did he not wish to remain with them? Why did he not stay long enough to see the fulfillment of the miracle? He had been a messenger from land; what had he wished to tell them? This they would never know.

Old seamen who had sailed thirty or forty years were serious and said it was an evil omen that the little bird had left. It seemed they might be right: the day after his disappearance another storm broke.

And with the bird gone there was nothing on board to remind the peasants at sea of the green earth.

5

So the *Charlotta* of Karlshamn sailed on—a cargo ship loaded with sundries, an emigrant ship loaded with human beings. She sailed over the boundless Atlantic Ocean through all winds and weathers, through storm and fog, rain and sunshine. But for the most part the wind blew against her, bracing the ship's bow and rigging, hindering her progress. And to the impatient, earth-bound passengers it seemed as if the same billow lifted them up, again and again, the same eternal wave tossing them about.

The emigrants thought of the endless distance they must have traveled since they had left their place of embarkation. Their thoughts went back over the immense water they had sailed for a space of two months, and they were overawed by this sea without end which they were passing over. At home they had never fathomed the immensity of the sea.

And one conviction took still deeper root in their minds:

whatever was in store for them on the new continent, whatever awaited them in the new land they were seeking—a return voyage to their homeland was beyond conception. The move they were now undertaking was to the end of time; never could they sail this eternal distance back again, never again would they cross this endless water.

Theirs was a voyage which people took only once.

XXIV

A LONG NIGHT

1

One night Karl Oskar was awakened by Johan. The child stood at his bunk, pulling at his blanket.

"Father! Wake up!"

"What is it? What do you want?"

"Mother is bleeding!"

"What is Mother doing?"

"She is bleeding—I was to tell you."

Karl Oskar was not far from his wife's sleeping place, and he was at her side in an instant. On the floor beside her bunk stood a quart bottle with a piece of tallow candle in its neck. He lit this, and in the flickering light could see Kristina's chin and throat streaked with blood, her white nightshirt smeared with blood. In her nostrils were stuck two cotton wads, soaked through with blood and looking like a couple of dark-red ripe cherries.

"My God, Kristina! What has happened?"

"I sent Johan—"

"Why didn't you call me before?"

"I thought it would stop."

Her lips were ash-white, her voice weak. She had been about to go to sleep when the bleeding began. At first she had thought she had caught cold, and had blown her nose. Then she had seen that her kerchief was full of blood. She had been lying like this for a long while, she didn't know how long, and the blood was still flowing. She had lain still on her back without a pillow, but it didn't stop. She had put cotton in her nostrils, but the blood ran right through. She didn't know what else might help.

"I'm so tired . . . I can't last this way."

The shining blood streaks on her thin neck made it look as if she had been stuck in the throat. Red cotton wads swam about in a pan by her bed like freshly drawn entrails. It seemed as if a slaughter had taken place in the bunk. Karl Oskar always suffered at seeing blood, and now he felt weak in his legs.

Kristina's eyes were large and glassy. The last few days she had been so weak she had stayed in bed all the time, eating hardly a bite. She did not have the resistance she needed when the hemorrhage began. She lay there stretched out like a dead body, her gray-white complexion the color of a corpse's. Karl Oskar understood what was taking place here: life was running away from his wife.

The number of passengers had decreased by three during this last week. All three were grown people, and all had died in this ship-sickness. It was actually growing roomy in the hold. Inga-Lena too had been very ill, but would not admit it, not wishing to disturb Danjel. And yesterday it was said that she had begun to mend. Tonight no sound was heard from the pen where the Karragarde people stayed—they were sleeping peacefully.

"Are you in pain?" asked Karl Oskar of his wife.

"No. No pain. I'm only tired—so tired."

"It's because of the blood you've lost. We must stop the bleeding."

Kristina moved her head slowly to look at Johan, who was sitting at the foot of her bunk. The red runnels from her nostrils increased from this little movement.

"Lie quiet—please. Still!"

A weak whisper came like a gentle stir of air from her mouth: "If it doesn't slow down I suppose I'll die."

"It must slow down."

"But if there is no help?"

"There must be help somewhere."

Johan listened attentively to his parents and gazed at them with large eyes. He was not old enough to understand everything, but he had a child's intuition. He began to cry: "I don't want Mother to bleed any more. I don't want her to."

"Keep quiet, boy!" said the father. "Lie down and go to sleep!"

Lill-Marta and Harald were sleeping peacefully on the inside of the bunk against the hull. Outside the sea wailed, the waves broke and crashed against the ship. There had been a storm again during the day, and tonight it blew harder than before. A child cried in its sleep, somewhere in its pen. A woman snored noisily. Between the woman's snorings the rolling masses of water could be heard breaking against the side of the ship.

The ship rolled heavily. Kristina lay there and rolled on her bunk, they all rolled—the sick and the healthy.

Someone shouted angrily because a light was lit: could one never sleep in peace? But Karl Oskar was oblivious to sounds, he heard neither the sea outside nor the people around him. He stood bent over his bleeding wife: this flow of blood could not go on for very long. If it didn't stop she would die; if it weren't stopped very soon, he would be a widower before the night was over.

He stood at the side of his fellow worker, his bedmate, his children's mother, and life was ebbing away from her—from her who was the most indispensable human being in the world. Was God going to take her from him—as He took Anna? What must he do? Must he stand by, completely at a loss, wretched and helpless? He must do something. One must always do what one could, use one's senses to the best of one's ability, never believe matters were hopeless. He had never given up, and he could not give up now when Kristina's life was at stake.

At home in the parish there had been many bloodstanchers; here on the ship he knew of none. But perhaps there was one human being here who could help.

"I'm going to call the captain."

"We dare not—" Kristina's voice was hardly audible. "It's the middle of the night."

"The captain must help us. He cannot refuse!"

Their captain had charge of the medicine chest on board, and was supposed to take a doctor's place. He was austere and brusque and the passengers were afraid of him; the seamen too held him in awe. He had never shown feelings of compassion for the sick or dying in the hold. The sick obtained medicines from his chest until they recuperated or died, and when they died he officiated at their funerals and lowered the corpses into the sea. The emigrants thought he was a hard, unfeeling person. But Karl Oskar decided to seek him out. He could not deny help when one of his passengers was in the throes of death.

"Don't go, Karl Oskar," entreated Kristina. "It's no use."

Yes, he knew that Kristina thought it preordained that she was to die here on the ship, that she was never to reach America. But he did not agree. His thought was always that nothing was so definite as to be unchangeable. If one tries, perhaps one can change things. One is forced to try.

"I'll be back at once."

Karl Oskar rushed away. After some trouble he was able to open the hatch, and reached deck, feeling his way in the darkness. The weather was rough tonight. Heavy waves washed over and broke against the deck. He immediately became drenched to his waist. But he hardly noticed it. He must get to the afterdeck. He skidded and fell on the slippery deck planks, he rose and fell again. Tonight the whole ship was in danger, but he did not care: the ship might go down, anything might happen, but they must stanch Kristina's blood.

He held on to ropes and lines and found his way to the hatch on the afterdeck through which a ladder led down to the captain's cabin.

He knocked heavily on the door. Only at his third knocking could he hear a powerful, penetrating voice: "What in hell do you want?"

Karl Oskar opened the door and stepped inside. Captain Lorentz had been asleep, and was now sitting upright in his bunk. He had been sleeping with his trousers on. His gray hair was tousled and stood straight out over his forehead like the horns of a ram. If any man ever looked ready to gore, it was the *Charlotta*'s captain at this moment.

"My wife is bleeding to death. I wanted to ask you to do something for it, Mr. Captain."

Captain Lorentz had thought that some one of the crew was calling him for urgent reasons of duty—for other reasons no one on the ship would dare to disturb him—but nevertheless he had given out an angry grunt. When he now discovered that the trespasser in his cabin in the middle of the night was one of the passengers, his astonishment was so great that he could only glare at the intruder.

"She's bleeding. We can't stanch it—I'm afraid she's giving out!"

The captain yawned, opening his ugly pike-mouth. He needed his sleep more than any other person on the ship. This God-damned weather—because of this weather he had been forced to stay awake more than anyone on board these last days. The damned peasants could take a snooze whenever they pleased, they were not responsible for anything on board. He ought to tell this big-nosed farmer to go to hell. He thought he would—but he didn't.

The man stood there and repeated that his wife was dying. To this the captain couldn't answer that he himself was sleeping. Lost sleep a person might regain, but once he had lost his life it was not easy to get it back.

Lorentz had recognized Karl Oskar by his big nose: the Finn had spoken of him, he was supposed to be one of the more smart-aleck peasants. Hadn't the mate been forced to tell him off?

Yet he might need help if his wife were lying at death's door. She couldn't be too old, the man himself was rather young.

"Has your wife been bleeding long?"

Karl Oskar gave a description of what had happened, and the captain listened.

"Hm, from the scurvy, no doubt. I recognize it."

"You see, she is with child also."

"Hm, that too. Well, it doesn't sound good."

The captain stepped down from his bunk. Then he pulled on boots and a slicker. Karl Oskar followed his movements with a grateful look.

"We'll see if we can't stanch the blood."

Lorentz searched for his *Medical Adviser for Seafarers*. He found it among the papers on his table and opened it:

"Bleeding from mouth or nose can in some cases be so strong and last so long that it becomes dangerous.

"Treatment: If the bleeding becomes strong enough to weaken the sick person, one may attempt to stanch the blood flow by bringing the patient out into fresh and cool air, then make packs from sea water and place over forehead, nose, back of the neck, and if this does not help, also around the sexual organs. In very severe cases one may bind a towel around each of the four limbs, above the elbows and the knees, so as to stop the blood in these parts.

"If there is suspicion of scurvy . . ."

It had been a long time since the *Charlotta*'s captain had last stanched blood—he had had to refreshen his knowledge. From a chest he pulled out some clean rough linen towels which he threw over his arm. Then he lit a small hand lantern and followed the young farmer up the ladder.

While crossing the deck Karl Oskar nearly fell down twice as the *Charlotta* dove into the waves; both times the captain grabbed hold of his shoulder and steadied him. "Hell of a choppy sea tonight."

The captain himself followed the movements of the ship as if his feet had been nailed down with seven-inch spikes to the planks of the deck.

Kristina lay with closed eyes as they approached her bunk. "Here comes the captain—"

Slowly she opened her eyes.

Captain Lorentz took one look at her face, then at the pan with the blood, and he thought to himself: This has gone too far; anyone who has lost such a pool of blood must also lose life. This woman had suffered from scurvy for a long time, that he could see.

And now the end was near. He felt sorry for the bleeding woman; she was still in her youth, no doubt she had been good-looking in her healthy days. Her husband would need her to get along in North America. And a pity about the three brats, too, lying there curled up together in the family pen; the lot of the motherless was doubly hard in life. And this woman was supposed to have another child inside her— they were regular rabbits, these peasants, dropping offspring like that. This whole emigration to North America was caused by crowded conditions, the result of constant spawning and multiplying in their cottages and bed-pens.

How much better it would have been for this poor young couple had they not attempted to cross the ocean. Then the wife's young life might have been spared, the youthful husband would not have needed to become a widower, the three children motherless.

The captain looked from the wife to the husband: poor devil!

To Karl Oskar the face of the captain was as hard as if carved from a piece of wood. He thought: that man can never have any sympathy for other creatures.

"We will try to stanch."

Lorentz was, after all, going to do what he could. He sent Karl Oskar after a bucket of fresh sea water, soaked his towels, and laid them as cold packs around the head of the sick woman. He had still a few towels left which he did not soak; he tied these around Kristina's limbs, near elbows and knees. He tied the knots as hard as he could; she groaned faintly, and he knew it hurt, but they must be tight if what blood was still left in these limbs was to remain.

When a patient bled so profusely a cold pack should be laid around the sexual organs as well. But Lorentz omitted this: the women of the peasantry had a deep-rooted shame for that part of the body, and Kristina might have become frightened and tried to defend herself if he had as much as uncovered her stomach. When he touched her body her eyes opened wide and full of fear, as if he were trying to kill her. He was sure that no man other than her husband had ever laid hands on or come near this young farm woman.

What he could do here was soon done—no doctor in the world could do more. Before he left he gave Karl Oskar his instructions: Kristina must remain absolutely still in this position on her back, and the wet towels about her head must be changed every hour so as to keep them cool.

It sounded brusque and final, it was an order from the commander of the ship. Karl Oskar would have liked to know how to manage in keeping his wife's body still in the bunk with the heavy rolling of the seas.

Captain Lorentz returned to his cabin. Now there would be no more sleep for him tonight. If this storm kept on increasing they must reef down to the very rigging. A skipper could never take his rest when he needed it, only when he could get it. But first he must sit for a moment and squeeze his girl on the ale-stoup, his most pleasant occupation while resting. Her muscles were hard, hard as stone, and she did not warm the hands of a man, but she was always there, always to be relied on. The girls with the soft flesh, the fickle ones, had belonged to his younger years; the girl on the stoup was a woman for a seaman's old age.

The young peasant and his dying wife lingered yet for a moment in the mind of the *Charlotta*'s captain. He wondered if the loss would break the man. But most of these greedy, earth-hungry peasants hardly cared about the human being in their wives: when they mourned them they mourned mostly their loss of labor. And the farmer with the big nose would soon find comfort and another female beast of burden in America. He seemed a capable man, and capable men went without women less than others. It was the men with strong natures who did most of the things in this world. What a pity this fellow was a peasant—had he been born near the coast, instead of inland, he would no doubt have made a very able seaman.

Now they were nearing the end of their voyage—the seventh for the *Charlotta* as emigrant ship. It had been a pleasant voyage with moderate storms. The mortality on board had also been moderate: seven deaths among seventy-eight passengers; there had been more among fewer on other crossings. Apparently the eighth death was to take place; for the eighth time this voyage he must fulfill the duties of minister.

It was indeed true—people were the most unhealthy cargo a vessel possibly could carry: ". . . a great deal of attention was then required from the captain . . ." Who knew this better than the captain on the brig *Charlotta*?

Happy those captains who carried other cargo across the seas! They might sometimes get a wink of sleep, even on a stormy night.

2

Karl Oskar had changed the cold pack once; but the bleeding from Kristina's nose was continuing as before.

Johan had at last gone to sleep. He lay across the bunk, over his mother's legs. Lill-Marta was dreaming and talking in her sleep about a cake which someone wanted to take away from her. From the neighboring bunks came groans and puffs. The woman who had already snored for hours snored still louder. And outside, against the side of the ship, the Atlantic Ocean heaved as it had heaved during all tempests since the day of creation. Kristina lay there and rocked on her bunk, as she had rocked many nights and days. The ship rolled, and Karl Oskar grabbed hold of the bunk planks now and then so as not to fall off the stool on which he was sitting.

Now and again he lit his piece of taper and looked at his wife. She lay mostly with her eyes closed, but at times they would open and then he tried to gain her recognition. But she was away from her eyes, he could not find her there. He sat by her but she was not with him. Another woman snored. Some people snored, while others lay at death's door. And from the pen of the Karragarde people an even, monotonous mumble was occasionally heard. It was prayer; Danjel was praying. He must, then, be awake now. Inga-Lena lay very sick, but she denied her illness and insisted she was well—who could fathom these Akians?

Another hour passed. When Karl Oskar again changed the cold pack, he thought he could notice that the flow of blood had stopped a little.

The watch was changing on deck, it was four o'clock, the dogwatch was over, the early-morning watch was going on. Karl Oskar continued his vigil, he was watching over Kristina, he had stood all the watches this night.

A heavy thunder was heard from above—a sound of splintering timbers, as if a wave had broken something on deck. Kristina awakened and opened her eyes. Karl Oskar looked into them and found his wife: she was awake and clear in her mind. From her mouth came a weak breath—he bent down to hear what she was saying: "Karl Oskar—"

"Yes?"

"I only wanted to ask—be kind to the children."

"Of course I will."

"You'll look after the little ones, won't you?"

"You may be sure of it."

"That's good to hear. You'll have to be father and mother, both."

"Don't think of that now, Kristina."

"No. We shan't mention it again."

"Is there anything you wish?"

"No. Not a thing."

From the pocket of his jacket Karl Oskar took out a few lumps of sugar, wrapped in a piece of old paper—they were from home, he had saved them a long time.

"Will you have a piece of sugar in your mouth?"

"No."

The sugar lumps had been in his pocket for weeks. They were no longer white; he blew off the dust to clean them. "I've saved these for you."

"You are kind, Karl Oskar—but—I can't chew."

"Isn't there anything I can give you?"

"No."

He took a firm hold of Kristina's hand on the quilt; it felt even colder than the sea water which had cooled her head.

Now it came over him, that which he always tried to evade, that which he never wished to feel or admit: he had persuaded her to follow him, he had taken wife and children with him on this voyage across the sea; he it was who had forced their emigration—someone had had to take the responsibility; I shall take it! That was what he had said—and now was the day of reckoning, now he must shoulder the responsibility. If he had known what it would be like—if he had known—if he had known the price. Now it came over him, overpoweringly it rushed forth. *Regret.*

Karl Oskar regretted what he had done.

"Kristina!"

"Ye-es."

"I want to ask you—ask your forgiveness."

"What must I forgive?"

"That I wanted to go—"

"I too wanted it."

"But I forced my will through."

"You didn't mean anything wrong with it."

"You know what I meant, Kristina."

"You wanted to improve things for us—for all of us."

"Yes. One might mean well—yet spoil it all—spoil it for all of us—"

"Don't regret it, Karl Oskar. You can't help it."

"I'm to blame most."

"You have only struggled for us. You mustn't be sad."

"You will forgive me, Kristina?"

"I have nothing to forgive you. Remember I said so."

"That is good to hear."

"I like you, Karl Oskar, always have. We are the best of friends."

"Yes. The best of friends—that's what we are!"

Thus Karl Oskar and Kristina spoke to each other as those people do who may have no more chance to speak to each other in this world.

Kristina was in her swing again. She closed her weak eyes. "I wish to sleep a little longer."

"Sleep! You need it."

"Only a short while."

"Of course you will sleep—only you must not—not—not—"

His tongue froze in his throat, he could utter no more words, he was unable to finish: *only you must not die and leave me!*

"I wish to rest now, quietly," it came from his wife. "I'm so tired."

"Yes, rest now. I'll change the packing."

"Let me down now!" she said. "Let me down from the swing, Karl Oskar! It's no fun any more."

Then he understood she was delirous.

3

The taper had burned out. He sat in the dark and listened to Kristina's breathing. Of course you will sleep! You may sleep as long as you wish—the rest of the night—the whole day tomorrow—many days. Day after day you may sleep—only, you must wake up again, you must promise to awaken—you must not die.

Be father and mother both, she had said. Shall I arrive alone—alone with the three little ones? And the fourth one? The fourth she takes with her—it follows her. The other three follow me—the other three—who no longer have a mother—no! They still have father and mother—I can hear her breathing. She is only asleep. But if she shouldn't—if it so should happen, then I can blame only myself. I myself have caused all this. I said: Someone must take the responsibility, I take the responsibility. She has been against it the whole time, she was against it from the very beginning. But I persuaded her. She came with me but I think she regretted it the whole time. But she said nothing. I was the one who insisted, I and no one else decided. And now she could blame me, but instead she says: I have nothing to forgive you; we are the best of friends. And I am causing her to lose her life—and she says—I like you—

This is your payment for being so stubborn and insistent. Now you feel what it's like! You wanted to push your will through—and now, see what has happened! If you had listened to her, if you had listened to your wife, and your parents and other people—those who wished to put a stop to it—then you would not have to sit here tonight, fumbling with a burnt-out taper, wondering if she is dead or alive. Do I look at my wife Kristina? Or at a corpse? Then I would not be sitting here, rocking back and forth, in this rolling ship—in this tempest tonight. Then I would never have set foot on this devil's ship, never been on this damned ocean—damned for time and eternity! That's what it is, if it takes her. If that damned Finn comes down with his canvas—comes up to this bunk—right here—and takes her—and says, as he usually does: We must—yes, now we must—If he comes—if HE comes—and I must blame myself. Stubborn and obstinate—the big-nosed are always stubborn. It's your big nose, Karl Oskar.

You didn't mean it wrongly—you didn't want to harm us—you mustn't feel downhearted—don't be sad! But if that Finn comes—at early dawn, he usually comes in the mornings—and tries to touch her—to find out—It must not be morning—not yet—not for a long while yet. It's better the night should last, better than that morning should come—morning, and a Finn, with a piece of canvas in his hand. You have yourself to blame. . . .

Thus Karl Oskar Nilsson stood watch at the bedside of his sick wife—the longest night watch of his life.

And with daylight and full morning he heard a child's voice—his little son Johan crawled up on his knee and took hold of his trousers and said: "Father—Mother isn't bleeding any more."

4

Night had passed and calm weather had come with morning. The ocean had lowered its rough, roaring storm-voice—no more waves were heard against the side of the ship, and the rolling was negligible. In fact the rolling was all but gone when the emigrants began to crawl out of their bunks and waken to a new day in their old quarters in the hold.

Johan had crept down from his mother's bunk. "Mother has stopped bleeding!"

Kristina lay quietly on her back as before, her eyes gleamed open and bit in the meager daylight which came in through the main hatch. Her lips moved slowly: "Karl Oskar. Are you here?"

"Yes."

"I believe—I think I've slept."

"Yes. You've been sleeping a long time."

"I don't feel so tired any more."

"That's good."

"I think—I think—"

But that was all. She was too weak to say anything more. Karl Oskar noticed that the blood no longer ran from her nostrils; the flow of blood had stopped—perhaps many hours ago. He had not been able to see in the dark, and he had been afraid of striking a light, he might have awakened her. But the blood was stanched. There was at least one blood-stancher on board the ship—the captain himself. One must always do what one could, things might change if one tried.

While raptures of joy went through Karl Oskar, a man approached him and touched his shoulder, timidly and clumsily. It was Danjel Andreasson. He was pale and his eyes were red from the night wake—they seemed strangely glazed and distant when he looked at Karl Oskar and then at Kristina. His voice, too, was foreign and distant, as if he were speaking from another world: "She is dead."

"No! She lives!" said Karl Oskar. "I think she will survive now!"

"She died just now," said Danjel.

"But can't you see for yourself—"

"You must believe me, Karl Oskar, she died a moment ago. She had never told me how ill she was."

"Don't you see she is alive?"

"She is dead—you can see for yourself, if you doubt me."

"Am I asleep? What are you talking about?"

Karl Oskar looked in consternation at Danjel.

Beside him stood a man in deep sorrow. Danjel did not speak of Kristina, he spoke of his own wife: Inga-Lena had died without admitting to her husband that she was ill.

Another man than Karl Oskar had become a widower this morning.

XXV

ANOTHER THREE SHOVELFULS OF EARTH FROM SWEDEN

1

Captain Lorentz sat in his cabin and mused over a piece of paper with a few lines written on it: "Wife Inga-Lena Andersdotter from Karragarde in Ljuder Parish, Konga County, born October 4, 1809; joined in marriage with homeowner Danjel Andreasson, June 23, 1833. . . ."

Name, sex, and age—that was all he required, all he needed to know to conduct the funeral. This was now the eighth funeral. But there was something about the information which did not check. Nothing checked, as he thought further about it. He had seen the woman's bleeding body, he had tied her arms and legs. She had been a young woman, barely thirty, but now it seemed that the dead one was forty years old. And he had been told that she left behind four children, all on board with their parents. Yet he remembered definitely having seen only three small ones in the bunk of the dying woman.

Apparently another death had occurred than the one he had expected.

Once more on this voyage must he stand on deck and from the prayerbook choose suitable prayers and thought-worthy hymns, "as well as some sentence from Holy Writ," as it was prescribed in "How to Bury a Corpse on Board."

"Teach us all to remember that we must die and thereby gain understanding. . . ."

This potent prayer could have two meanings: either that we gain understanding and use our lives well before we die—or, the meaning which no doubt had been in the mind of the author, that we gain understanding to prepare ourselves for death. But the person who used his intelligence well would not concern himself in life with constant preparation for death. There could be no meaning in thus wasting one's few allotted days. Man must live in comfort and good cheer as long as life lasted—soon enough death comes with joy to no one.

And the thought of his own death—probable within the next few years—occupied the captain of the *Charlotta* for some fleeting moments. While still young, his death-day had often been in his mind; but the older he grew, the less often did he think of it. Some wisdom he had gained with the years. At sixty he was still sailing the seas in fairly good health. Nearly all the comrades of his youth had been taken by the sea, and their bodies had become part of the water that had surged about their ships. Some had sailed five years, others ten, still others thirty. He himself had already been allowed forty-six. Why? Nothing could be more foolish than to brood over this question. He might just as well ask why the wind was southerly today and northerly yesterday, and not the opposite. Once one knew there was no answer to the question, one ceased to ask. Only a simpleton would query the inexplicable.

It might be difficult to die, but it was rather common. All people must die, people had done so throughout time, and he too must face up to it when his time came. Since he couldn't escape it, he might as well pretend that he would live forever. For all eternity he would sail the seas, his ship would rot down but the master remain. By thinking death nonexistent, he could best use his life.

How had the wife Inga-Lena Andersdotter used her life—the forty years that had been given to her? A funeral officiant on a crowded emigrant ship could seldom know anything about those over whom he read his prayers. His passengers had been removed from their parish registers on leaving home, and had not yet been recorded elsewhere. They were registered nowhere—the emigrants on his ship were homeless, they had no plot in a churchyard. Only the sea opened its depths to them. The sea had room for all of them.

These peasants often feared death at sea, because of the final resting place—they wanted to be put in consecrated ground, and the ocean was not consecrated. But they were caught in deep superstition: this water where so many good seamen had found their graves ought to be a good enough resting place for the wretched land-rats.

Perhaps the wife Inga-Lena Andersdotter had died, too, in fear of the unconsecrated burial place of the ocean. Her forty years she had lived on solid ground, bending over the earth in her potato furrows and barley fields, poking in pens and manure piles, tramping between byre and barn. Yet she would find rest in the sea, in the most extended churchyard in the world, where nothing marked the graves. She would not be registered anywhere—she was an emigrant who had failed to reach her distination, a wanderer in the world.

But this peasant woman had still left her mark after her on earth: she had borne four new citizens for the North American republic.

With his stiff fingers, wasted and gray from the salt of the sea, Captain Lorentz picked up his pen to add a few lines on the small paper: "Died June 17, 1850, on board the brig *Charlotta* of Karlshamn, on voyage to New York. Certified, Christian Lorentz, Master."

2

It was a calm and beautiful June morning on the Atlantic Ocean. The emigrant vessel sailed with a feeble southerly breeze. The sun mirrored itself in the water, its rays reflected like burning flames. This morning at sea the emigrants had their first feeling of summer.

A group of passengers were gathered on the *Charlotta*'s afterdeck. The people stood in a semicircle around an improvised bier: a few planks had been laid upon two low sawhorses, and on these was placed an oblong bundle wrapped in canvas. The emigrants had dönned their Sunday best—the men, gray or black wadmal jackets; the older women wore silk kerchiefs. Those of the crew who were free mingled with the passengers.

The men stood bareheaded, the women's covered heads were bowed. All faces reflected the gravity of the moment. They were an immobile, solidified group of people, gathered around the bundle on the improvised bier. A human body was wrapped in the white canvas; the bier leaned toward the water, the feet touching the rail.

The *Charlotta*'s flag was lowered to half-mast. The captain emerged from his cabin and issued a quick order: the mainsail was braced, reducing the slow speed of the ship to almost nothing, hardly enough for steering. The brig *Charlotta*'s voyage was delayed for the sake of a human corpse on the afterdeck this beautiful summer morning.

The captain had exchanged his oilskins for a black redingote; on his bare head his thick gray hair now lay smoothly combed. He went to the head of the bier, then looked for a moment into the rigging as if to see how his ship carried her sails. Under his arm he held a prayerbook. As he opened it the emigrants folded their hands and their faces took on—if possible—a still more serious mien.

Captain Lorentz turned a few pages in his prayerbook, turned them back again, made a jerky, impatient movement with his shoulders when he was unable immediately to locate the place: he must remember to turn the page at "How to Bury a Corpse." And what was the number of the hymn they were to sing?

While he was looking for the prayer he happened to notice the man standing beside him: a small peasant with a bushy brown beard. He remembered that man well. The first day out he had stumbled on him praying on deck. Now the little man held a baby in his arms; beside him stood three other children. Together they were four children and a father.

Lorentz quickly turned his eyes away from this group and looked about him on the deck. There was something he needed—there, at his feet, it stood, the wooden bushel measure half filled with earth. In it was stuck a small shovel, resembling a winnowing scoop.

He found the page in the prayerbook and began to read. His voice was clear and resonant, trained during many years at sea to rise above the roar of the waves and the storms:

"O Lord God! Thou Who for the sake of sin lettest people

die and return to earth again, teach us to remember that we must die, and thereby gain understanding. . . ."

Now all the people present held their hands folded, in reverence they bent their heads and listened to the words of the prayerbook. The ocean's water played softly against the side of the ship, a breath of air lifted a few tufts of hair on the captain's uncovered head. With the last words someone was heard sobbing, but the sound was quickly drowned in the captain's powerful voice.

The seagulls had returned, and they swarmed this morning in large flocks through the rigging. Life was again visible on the sea.

The funeral officiant took up a hymn. It began haltingly, and he had to sing half of the first stanza alone. But gradually the people joined in—slowly as the rolling of the ship the singing proceeded:

> "You wicked world, farewell!
> To heaven fares my soul,
> To reach her harbor goal . . ."

When the last notes of the hymn had rung out over the sea, the captain bent down and from the bushel at his feet picked up the little scoop. Three times he filled it with the earth his ship carried with her from the homeland, three times he emptied it over the dead body in front of him. With a soft thud the soil fell on the canvas. But heavy and terrifying fell the captain's words over the bent heads of the people: "Dust thou art, to dust thou shalt return. Jesus Christ shall awaken thee on the Day of Judgment! Let us pray."

Heavy was the truth, but the prayer was a mild comfort. Someone cried out at the words "Day of Judgment." It was not a cry of hope, it sounded rather like a bird's eerie and hopeless cry. It might be a sea bird calling, and some of the people turned their eyes toward the rigging—it might be a gull disturbing the solemnity of the funeral. But the cry did not come from a hungry seagull—it came from a child.

On the canvas-covered bundle there still remained the sprinkling of earth, three unshapely little mounds with a few pinches of mold in each, three ugly gray-black spots on the clean white cloth. But before the captain had finished reading the ritual, the lighter particles of earth separated from the

mounds and trickled down the side. With the bier leaning
toward the rail, toward the water beyond, some earth ran
slowly across the rail, into the sea.

This was soil that had traveled a long way. It came from
the land where the feet of the dead one had tramped the
earth during her forty years, where she had struggled with her
potato baskets and her barley sheaves, where she had carried
milk pails and water buckets, where she—in concern for the
food of her dear ones—had locked the larder every evening,
where she had lived out her summers and her winters, all her
autumns and springs—all except this single spring, when she
had followed her mate out on the sea. It was a little earth
from Sweden, a little of the three shovelfuls which accompany the words about creation, destruction, and the resurrection, which now trickled into the sea as if anxious to reach it
before the human body which had just been consigned to its
watery grave.

But no one noticed the movement on the canvas. As the
grains of earth separated and rolled on their way the group
now sang the second and last hymn of the ritual:

> "Let my body then be hidden
> In a humble, nameless tomb;
> When at last I shall be bidden
> To forsake that narrow room,
> Jesus knows where they are sleeping
> Who were given in His keeping. . . ."

The sun shone down on a peaceful sea which had calmed
this morning and now lay quiet before the song about a patient and resigned human soul who sought his sleep with God
until the end of time. Still a little more earth trickled down
the canvas toward the water.

Captain Lorentz was ready to give his crew men the sign:
Lower away.

At that moment someone stirred behind him—the little
brown-bearded man with the baby on his arm stepped up to
the captain. He looked at the ship's commander beseechingly,
hesitatingly. Lorentz stepped aside, leaving his place at the
head of the bier to the surviving husband.

Danjel Andreasson wanted to say something. His voice was
not strong, he had never issued orders, he had no command-

er's voice. And few were the words he had to say to his mate in the canvas: "The Lord said unto you as He said to Moses: 'You shall not get into that land.' You, my dear wife, were not allowed to see the new land—yet you reached the harbor before us.

"When I wanted to move over there, then you spoke to me and said: 'Say not to me that I should separate from you; where you go, there will I go, where you die there will I die and be buried.' "

Only those closest to Danjel Andreasson could hear his voice, his words were uttered in such low tones.

He took a step back from the bier, a long, hesitating step. Then the captain gave the sign—two seamen stepped forward and the oblong bundle glided into the sea. Almost as it disappeared over the rail a vague splash was heard from the side of the ship. It sounded as if some of the sea's creatures had moved in play on the surface, or perhaps it was a little billow breaking.

The ship's flag was raised and lowered—three times this was repeated.

Meanwhile the emigrants began to disperse. Soon the bare rough bier stood alone. But two crew men came and took it to pieces, carried away the planks and moved away the sawhorses, while the mainsail was spread to its full capacity, and the brig *Charlotta* sailed on—with one passenger less.

It was a radiant morning on the Atlantic Ocean. The sun had risen still higher and the beams glittered in the clear water where a moment before the ship had left part of her cargo from the hold. It was almost as if a fire glowed below the surface, a flame burned down there.

XXVI

SAILING TOWARD MIDSUMMER

1

Robert and Elin stood leaning against the rail and watched the porpoises play alongside the ship. The fat round fishes looked like suckling pigs, and they tumbled about in the water as a mill wheel turns in its channel. These were the largest fishes the youth and girl had ever seen. But Robert had no fishing gear handy. His fishpoles, lines, and hooks were in the America chest, put away in the storeroom below the main hold at the embarkation in Karlshamn—Robert had not seen it since.

The eternal westerly wind was blowing; because they had contrary winds the porpoises moved faster than the ship. They swam and jumped and played around the bow as if mocking the tardy vessel: Here we are! Where are you? How far have you come? What kind of old pork barrel are you, splashing about like that?

Elin pointed at the water where the porpoises played: right there the water was green, she had seen similar spots before on their voyage—how did it happen that the sea water was green in some places? Had some ship spilled green paint there? Robert thought a bit before he answered: perhaps God at the Creation had intended to make the sea water green, perhaps He had at first made a few sample lakes of that color and later changed His mind and created all waters blue. Then afterward He might have thrown the green lakes into the sea here and there, just so as to make some use of them.

There was always something to observe at sea. Robert did not agree with the other passengers, he did not think the sea was a desolate landscape, depressing to watch day after day. In storm the sea was a hilly landscape, each knoll mobile and rolling about. In sunshine and calm weather the sea lay there outstretched like a blue and golden cloth of silk or satin which he would have liked to stroke with his hand. The sea in moonlight at night was made up of broad, light paths, for the angels of heaven to walk on. A hill or a knoll on land always remained in the same spot, and looked exactly the same each time one passed by it. But the sea was never the same.

During a few nights early in the voyage Robert had thought he was going to die at sea. While the first storm raged he had lain in his bunk, his forehead moistened by the cold and sticky sweat of death-fear. This experience he had not liked. To be enjoyable, an adventure must not involve fear for life. But he had grown accustomed to the sea, and now he felt ashamed when he thought of his fear during that first storm. Now he could go to bed in the evenings without fear of drowning during the night.

And as they approached the end of the long-drawn-out voyage he had even begun to like the sea. Soon he must part from it. It was said they might expect to see land almost any day now. Every day passengers gathered in the prow and looked for America, as if thinking that that land was such a small speck they might pass it by if they didn't keep a lookout for it. Those among them who possessed almanacs, and marked the passing days by crosses, said that it would be Midsummer in a few days. Perhaps they would reach the shores of America for the Midsummer holidays.

"Shall we read in the language book?" asked Elin.

"If you wish, let's."

She was now as eager as he to learn English words. He suspected he no longer relied on the Holy Ghost to give her power to use the new language immediately on landing. And he had several times reminded her that the descending of the Holy Ghost upon the apostles on the first Whitsuntide had taken place long before the discovery of America, long before the English language was invented. Therefore no one knew for sure if it could be taught in the same manner as the languages of the Greeks, the Elamites, the Syrians, and the Copts, which the apostles learned in one day—and this a holy day to boot.

In the textbook Robert and Elin had now reached the chapter about "Seeking Employment." It was an important chapter; the very first day when they arrived in America they both must earn their own living, and anyone who must earn his living must also know how to find employment.

Robert had finally decided that they must pronounce the English words as they were spelled in the first sentences and disregard the spelling within the parentheses which only confused and complicated the language for them.

Could you tell me where to get work?—What can you do?

Here the work-seeker must answer that he was a carpenter, a tailor, a cobbler, a harness maker, a tanner, a spinner, a weaver, a mason, a waiter, or whatever occupation he pursued. But Robert had skipped all this, he was not concerned about what a harness maker was called in English as he couldn't make harnesses anyway. He himself stuck to one single sentence: *I am used to farm work.*

He was a farmhand. The only work he had done was farm work, the only chores he had performed were those of the farmer. And he had long struggled with this sentence, but he knew it now—he repeated the words slowly and tried to pronounce them carefully as they were spelled.

I am used to farm work. He wished already the very first day to astonish the Americans by being able to tell them what he could do, and he wished to say it correctly in their own language. He wished to inspire respect from the very first day.

At home in Ljuder Elin had only worked as nursemaid, but now that she had passed sixteen she hoped to find a position in America more worthy of a grown woman. She read the chapter in the textbook entitled "Doing Ordinary Household Chores." It dealt with every hour of a maid's workday in America, and Robert urged her emphatically to learn this chapter well before she landed: having done so she would inspire respect.

I am the new servant girl. You must get up at six o'clock in the morning. Make fire and put water to boil. Get the broom and sweep the dining room. Clear off the table. Wash your hands before you handle food.

When Elin had gone so far she looked at her hands, which were clean and white, with a fragrance of soap. It was early in the morning and she had just washed them.

"In America they must think all maids have dirty hands," she said.

"The Americans hate all kinds of dirt," said Robert. "Everything is cleaner in the New World than in the Old. That's why you'll fit in well there."

"Do you really believe it's true that a maid need not get up before six in the morning?"

About that, Robert dared not offer anything definite. There was the chance that she might accuse him of having told her something untrue. He answered cautiously: "Perhaps she isn't allowed to sleep so late in all places. But I've heard that farmhands can sleep till five o'clock."

Where Elin had served as nursemaid she had always been awakened by her mistress at four o'clock or half past. She liked to sleep late in the morning, and now she was a little disappointed in Robert's answer. He had once said that all women in America were waited on, and if this were true, then it was only right that they be allowed to sleep later than the men.

The deck rolled slowly under the youth and the girl, the

changing world of the sea surrounded them, the same eternal billows lifted them and carried them to a New World where they must find their way. And they sat there close together and with inexperienced, obstinate tongues tried to learn a new language—seriously and persistently they struggled through the English sentences, reading the words aloud as they were spelled.

I am used to farm work. I am the new servant girl.

In these two sentences the youthful emigrants must let the Americans know what kind of people they were, and they must pronounce them correctly, inspiring respect. This was of great importance for their future.

2

The brig *Charlotta* of Karlshamn was sailing toward Midsummer.

The eagle on her prow still looked incessantly toward the west, his eyes washed clean and clear by the spray. And the two tall masts—fir trees from the forests of the ship's homeland—bowed gracefully as the vessel glided down the billowy vales, rose proudly again as she encountered the crests of the waves. So they bowed while they carried the sails across all the sea, always rising to their full height again, proudly, defiantly. They had bent a little in hard gusts of wind, they had been pressed down by the storms, but they had always come back up again. They were slim and slender pine spires, in appearance so delicate at the top that they could be broken with the fingers—but these the ship's pinions had endured the tempests of all seasons on the sea. They were pines from a little land far away, they came from the same stony meadows and moors as the people on this ship—they were related to these voyagers, they were tough and indomitable as the people they helped carry across the sea.

And soon they will have conquered the ocean once more. The *Charlotta* now met other vessels daily, sailing ships and iron steamers, she was passing vessels, she was overtaken by vessels, she kept company with vessels. The swarm of sea birds was thickening in her rigging. In the water—up till now uncontaminated in its clear blueness—slime and flotsam began to appear, various discarded objects sailed about on the surface. All signs indicated that land was near. And soon the ship would no longer sail on the sea, she would enter a broad river mouth.

The sun was high in the heavens and bathed the deck in warmth. Sick passengers were carried up from the hold and lay the whole day through in the beneficial sunshine. Slowly mending, they felt they were enjoying a warmer sun than the one that shone on them at home. It was high-summer weather, Midsummer weather.

Kristina had improved slowly after her bleeding during the night of the storm. But as yet she was too weak to stand. Karl Oskar carried her out of the dark and stuffy quarters up on deck every day when the sun was out, and each day her sensation of returning strength increased. It worried her that she was lying here so useless; she could not help them now when they had so much to do: they were getting themselves in order for their landing.

The passengers had begun their great cleaning up and were busy preparing themselves for the landing. There was washing and scouring and scrubbing in the hold, garments were washed and rinsed and hung to dry. Clothing of all kinds, Sunday best and underwear and bedclothing, must be cleaned, mended, patched and brushed. This was not work for menfolk, but Karl Oskar must do it now, and he found it a tedious task. Many things had been ruined on the long voyage— worn out, torn, rotted, drenched with vomit. Mattresses and bolsters and garments were in shreds—these he could only throw into the sea. And nearly everything smelled musty and evil—like the quarters where they had spent more than two months. He gathered, sorted, and discarded a large pile.

"There should be a rag-and-bone man on the ship. He would have a thriving business!"

Now he, like the other passengers, must throw his rags into the sea. And he mused that little by little a whole mountain of ragged discarded belongings of emigrants must have accumulated near the shores of America, if each new arrival threw overboard as much as this.

Kristina thought that he threw away too much. Some of the things in his pile could have been cleaned and mended, could well have had more use. But Karl Oskar felt it a relief to get rid of the stinking rags, reminders of his anxiety during the storms and the plague of seasickness—he wanted to free himself of these witnesses to the troubles of the crossing. The sight of them would only torment him on land when they were to begin anew.

"I don't want to feel ashamed among the Americans," he said. "If they were to see these rags, they would wonder what kind of people we are."

Karl Oskar admitted no debt to the homeland where all his struggle had repaid him so little, but he did not wish to shame Sweden in the eyes of America: he wished to show that it was a land with a cleanly, upright peasantry, that those who came from there were decent and orderly, even if they brought nothing more than their poverty in their knapsacks. He wanted to be neat in his dress, and appear sensible and experienced as he passed through the portals of the New World.

He discarded the *old* with the rags that he heaved overboard—now the *new* was to begin.

Of their bedding, Karl Oskar saved only one piece: their blue bridal cover which Kristina herself had sewn. It too was spotted, and several holes gaped in it. Tears came to Kristina's eyes as she now beheld it in full daylight, and saw how badly it had fared. But maybe she could wash it, remove the disgusting spots, mend the holes—once they had landed and her health and strength had returned. Her bridal quilt was dearer to her than any other possession they brought with them from home. It had been part of her setting-up-of-home in Sweden, she had made her bridal bed with it, Karl Oskar and she had slept under it for six years—during their whole lives as husband and wife. She could now hope that they might rest together under it once more, and use it for many years. Surely they would never be happy and prosperous unless the bridal cover was part of their new settling in America.

During their preparations for the landing Karl Oskar showed himself so handy and efficient with the chores of womenfolk that Kristina could not help but admire him. It seemed he could do almost anything he wanted—if he only wanted to. His old disposition had now returned, and he was more cheerful with each day. Midsummer was imminent, he said, he must have on his holiday disposition.

The closer they came to land, the more Karl Oskar became himself.

3

One morning at daybreak Robert was awakened by Arvid, who excitedly shook him by the shoulder. "They see America!"

Still half asleep Robert jumped into his trousers, still half asleep he emerged through the main hatch onto deck where he continued to button himself up. Many passengers had already gathered up here, mostly menfolk, but also a few early risers among the women. They all stood there silently in grave expectation: they saw North America.

As yet there was not much for the eyes to behold. They sailed up the mouth of a broad river, a broad bay of the sea. It was not yet full daylight, and a mist hung over the land: America was still sleeping this morning, had not yet shed her blanket of night. Land rose over the stern and on the prow and on either side of the ship, but in the mist of dawn it appeared fragmentary, visible in places, hidden in others. As yet no one could discern if this land was barren or fertile, rich or poor, beautiful or ugly. But they had reached the shores of America, and this knowledge sufficed them.

Their speed up the bay was good—now, during the last stage of this long voyage, the wind was with them, and their sails were full as women's skirts in a breeze. Innumerable ships filled the passage, sailing ships, sloops, steamers, vessels of all sizes and kinds. The brig *Charlotta* had long traveled alone on the ocean, now she was in great company.

Little by little the land threw off its morning shroud. Slowly the naked shores arose. And soon a populated stretch of land jutted out in the path of their ship, like a large peninsula. Here the clearing mist gradually uncovered a multitude of clustered roofs, long rows of houses could be seen, and high above the roofs stretched spires and steeples, exactly like the church steeples at home. Before them lay a town, greater than any they had ever seen before. When full daylight broke through, they could see their harbor: New York.

Robert and Arvid stood in the prow, as immobile as people can stand on a moving deck. Next to them stood the second mate, the Finn, who had taken part in every one of the *Char-*

lotta's voyages to North America. He told them that the land they saw was only a large island. It was originally called *Manna-Hata*, which was an Indian word—the name of a favorable god among the Indians, he had heard. The god had lived on this pretty island of *Manna-Hata* for thousands of years, until it once was flooded by the river and he had been forced to move. Now it was mostly people who lived here, but the Finn had never been to any church while in port so he was not sure which god—if any—lived on *Manna-Hata* nowadays.

The *Charlotta* steered toward a shore which seemed to them made up of fortifications and piers. But above these rose also a large, round, yellow-gray building with a tremendous round tower. Robert wondered what this could be.

"That's called Castle Garden. It's a *kastell*."

Robert did not know what a *kastell* was, he had never heard the word before, but he didn't wish to ask. Instead, Arvid asked the mate.

"A *kastell* is the same as a prison," said the Finn.

Robert looked at him with wide-open eyes. That yellow-gray house with the large round tower was a prison? There were then imprisoned people in the house called Castle Garden. He had not imagined that the first house he saw in America would be a prison, a house where people were locked up when they lost their freedom. And he said that he had hardly expected to find any prisons in the United States of North America, where all evil and criminal people were exterminated.

The mate then explained that Castle Garden was no longer used as a prison. There were no prisoners there any more—it was instead a hell of a good place, a saloon. He knew, he had been there himself. The fare was good, and the ale of first quality. One could eat there to one's satisfaction, and get good and drunk too. On Sundays the saloon was crowded, people sitting on each other's knees while they ate and drank. Castle Garden was indeed a damned good saloon, a place where one was free to do as one pleased, use one's knife in a brawl and all other kinds of entertainment.

Then it was really as Robert had thought it would be: the prisons in America were actually not prisons with prisoners, as was the case in Sweden, but rather fine inns with guests who there could enjoy and entertain themselves as best they pleased. No doubt about it, America was a land with a kind government.

4

Only a short time elapsed before all of the *Charlotta*'s passengers were gathered on deck. Those unable to crawl up by themselves were carried: America was visible, and all wanted to see. They saw houses, churches, embankments, piers, streets and roads, people and carriages. But the eyes of the emigrants missed something—they looked in vain for something which the shores of America as yet had not shown. Their eyes had been searching for it during the whole passage up the bay—at last they found it, on the outjutting tongue of land over the prow: behind the big house with the round tower the morning mist was lifting, uncovering a grove of trees—large leaf-trees with thick foliage, and grass on the ground around the strees. The shore they had left at Karlshamn had been a dark shore—here a light shore greeted them. Bushes and trees grew there, leaves and green boughs, herbs and grass: at last they could see the green earth.

The long-drawn-out voyage with all its storms, sufferings, ills and troubles—the confinement on the ship during endless days—all this had gnawed hard on the emigrants' lives and spirits. Scurvy and ship's fever had lowered their resistance. From the monotonous life on board they had grown depressed and downhearted, and many had ceased to care what life and fate would bring them. But now this new vision unfolded before them, a bit of living ground near them—and they knew they had safely crossed the sea, and were here with the earth lying before their eyes again.

They stood crowded together on deck like a herd of cattle —shackled in the narrow stalls of the byre during a whole long winter, and at last stretching their necks and turning toward the door when it began to smell of spring and fresh grass and meadows: soon they would be let out, soon their imprisonment would end. And in this moment a new energy and ambition seized the emigrants. They felt cheered, encouraged, born anew, as if a fresh spirit were blown into their breasts.

The scurvy-sick feel now that they will recover. The weakened ones come to life again, a new strength enters them. Fresh power comes to the tired ones, initiative returns to the depressed, boldness to the timid. The spirit of indifference flies away from their minds, as the mist and fog this morning had lifted from the earth.

It was *land-frenzy* that overtook the passengers on the *Charlotta*. The life at sea had undermined their bodies and souls. The land-frenzy was bringing them new strength. They had again seen the green earth. As seekers of new homes they had come sailing from the earth—now they were back on the earth, and felt life returning.

5

The little Swedish vessel had anchored at the pier. The gangplank was lowered, and the passengers had begun to disembark. A burning-hot summer day met them in the new land.

The family from Korpamoen had gathered in a group, waiting their turn. On one arm Karl Oskar held his youngest son, with the other he held his wife around the waist. Kristina wanted to walk down the gangplank on her own legs. Many passengers had come on deck for the first time in a long while today, and some were so weak that they must be carried ashore. But Kristina told Karl Oskar she did not wish it said that she had been unable to walk onto land in America on her own legs. It would not be a good omen if she were carried ashore. Her limbs were weak, however, and she leaned heavily on her husband. Robert looked after Johan and Lill-Marta, and stood there holding one child with each hand. The children were not yet quite awake, and were troublesome and complaining, frightened by all the noise and jostle at the landing. Little Harald wanted to get down from his father's arms. He, too, wanted to walk on his own legs.

The children were pale and agunt, and the flesh hung loosely on their limbs, but they would soon improve with fresh food on land. A fourth child was still slumbering in its unconsciousness within the protection of the mother. This unborn life would be the first one from among the *Charlotta*'s passengers to gain citizenship in the North American republic.

Of the sixteen people who had emigrated from Ljuder Parish and gathered at Akerby Junction a bleak morning in early April, fifteen had arrived at the threshold of a new continent. One was missing. Of the seventy-eight people who had embarked at Karlshamn, seventy had arrived. The *Charlotta* had given up eight of her passengers to the ocean.

But Karl Oskar Nilsson had his whole family around him, and he himself stood there, healthy and sound and filled with deep satisfaction that they had all traveled safely over the sea.

He did not worry about the journey over land, where all lay firm under his feet. For the landing he had polished his splendid high boots, tried on for the first time the last evening in their old home. With the fat from a large pork rind he had greased the leather until it was shining black. His boots were of the best leather, made from oak-tanned ox-hide. He was well shod—they knew how to make fine boots at home. In this footgear he was well prepared. If the roads of America were poor, he would get through with these boots on his feet.

Otherwise, he, along with his fellow passengers, was poorly equipped. When their ship at long last landed, the emigrants were shabby and worn in faces and clothing. They must now go ashore in the same garments they had worn during the long voyage, and these did not resemble the clothing one wears to festivals. Men and women alike looked like molting hens. And when they had gathered together their possessions —chests, bundles, baskets, and boxes thrown together in a pile on deck—then the ship looked like a large high-loaded gypsy wagon. When they had driven to the harbor town of Karlshamn, Jonas Petter had likened the emigrants from Ljuder to a pack of gypsies. At their disembarkation this comparison was even more appropriate than then.

But however shabby and weak they seemed, however wretched and poor they were—North America admitted them.

It was time to go over the gangplank. The pier was high and their small ship was low—the gangplank became a steep uphill. But Kristina used all her strength, and walked onto land by herself. And little Harald was let down from Karl Oskar's arms at last, and walked on the plank at his father's side. Even the youngest in the Korpamoen family walked on his own legs into America.

But at the very first steps on solid ground Karl Oskar

stopped still: his head swam—he felt dizzy. The ground under him rolled exactly as the deck had done. Giddiness made him stumble a bit. Never once at sea had he felt this way. Now when he stood on firm land dizziness overtook him and his legs were wobbly. He could not understand it. Perhaps he had forgotten how to walk on solid ground, perhaps he must begin anew, as he must with his whole life. But in this unknown new land, which he now entered, he must stand firmly on his legs. That much he knew.

It was on Midsummer Eve, in the year 1850, that the brig *Charlotta* of Karlshamn tied up at the pier in New York, after ten weeks' sailing from her home port. Precarious, insecure, and unstable were the first steps of the immigrants on American soil.

The Emigrants is the first volume in a planned trilogy.
Monterey, California, August 1949

V.M.

FREE
Fawcett Books Listing

There is Romance, Mystery, Suspense, and Adventure waiting for you inside the Fawcett Books Order Form. And it's yours to browse through and use to get all the books you've been wanting . . . but possibly couldn't find in your bookstore.

This easy-to-use order form is divided into categories and contains over 1500 titles by your favorite authors.

So don't delay—take advantage of this special opportunity to increase your reading pleasure.

Just send us your name and address and 35¢ (to help defray postage and handling costs).